WHISPER OF PASSION

He laughed softly at her. "You don't have to whisper in here, my dear. There's no one to overhear you."

Dionne silently prayed for the right response. She pressed her lips close to his ear. "But when I whisper, it sounds so much more intimate."

He pulled her close to him. "Perhaps you have a point there," he said, nuzzling his lips against the column of her throat.

Dionne gasped.

"What's wrong?" he asked sharply.

"Nothing is wrong, nothing at all," she murmured. Then slowly, but unwaveringly, she raised her lips to meet his.

Christopher's breath quickened as he tasted her eagerness. Hot desire raced through his veins, sparked by the wild abandon he sensed in her. He could think of nothing beyond the fact that he was a man and she was a woman.

Dionne moaned softly beneath the demanding pressure of his lips, shivering as Christopher loosened the ties of her gown and began to slip it from her shoulders. She knew she should push him away, regain her shattered senses before it was too late. . . . But it was already too late. . . .

JEAN HAUGHT
ISLAND TEMPTRESS

ZEBRA BOOKS
KENSINGTON PUBLISHING CORP.

To my husband, Jim, thanks for all your help with this one. You are one in a million! Also to my dear, dear friends, Helen and Ed Baker. You may be gone, but you are not forgotten!

Chapter One

Island of Martinique, 1852

"Wait for me here, Nigel," Dionne said to her driver as he helped her down from the carriage. She straightened her dress and smoothed errant tendrils of her light brown hair back into place. "I want to browse through the marketplace today at my leisure."

"Oui, Mademoiselle Martin."

She started to turn away, but at the sight of disappointment sweeping over Nigel's face, she stopped and pressed a coin into his hand. "Just in case you get thirsty you may buy a tankard of rum punch, but only one," she cautioned. "You know how Monsieur Debierne feels about you drinking when you accompany me or Celeste."

A wide grin broke across Nigel's dark face as he accepted the coin. *"Oui,* Mademoiselle Martin, only one, and only then if thirst overcomes me," he added sincerely.

Nigel always enjoyed the days he drove Monsieur Debierne's young housekeeper to market. They were much more pleasant than when he had to drive the daughter on her endless rounds. The Mademoiselle Martin was always considerate, while Andre Debierne's daughter never gave a second thought about

7

leaving him to wait, at times, all day long in the sweltering heat without benefit of food or drink. And to actually accompany the Mademoiselle Celeste through the marketplace was even worse than having to wait, because she would load him with her purchases, then leave him to stand, heavily burdened with the numerous packages, while she haggled over prices or visited with her empty-headed friends. Mademoiselle Martin, on the other hand, seldom asked him to accompany her while she did her shopping. Instead, she would give him a coin for a tankard of rum punch and hire street urchins to bring her packages to the carriage. Also, this young woman always had a pleasant smile on her face, while Mademoiselle Celeste usually wore a tolerant scowl, one that showed a hint of contempt for anyone whom she considered beneath her social class. Still, Mademoiselle Celeste came from the loins of Monsieur Debierne, and that fact alone was worth his loyalty, but not his affection. He doubted if he would ever be able to give her that.

Dionne bit her bottom lip to prevent Nigel from seeing the smile that threatened. She knew the moment she disappeared into the teeming marketplace of Fort-de-France, Nigel would head straight for the nearest tavern, suddenly overcome with a terrible thirst. There, he would dawdle over one tankard of cheap rum generously laced with sugar syrup and lime peel, then make a beeline for the carriage when he figured it was time for her to return. But what did it hurt? Absolutely nothing. He was one of the most loyal servants the Debierne household had, and furthermore, she had often overheard the other planters say that Nigel was the best and most trustworthy driver on the island. Many had tried to hire him away from them but he had always refused. He had been with Andre for years, and

8

even long before slavery was abolished, in 1848, Andre had freed him, along with all of his other slaves. In return, Nigel and the servants who remained after the official abolition gave Andre and his entire household their loyalty and devotion. But there seemed to be an even deeper bond between the former slave and master. She doubted if there were anything Nigel would not do for Andre Debierne.

But then, even though Andre was small in stature, he was such a warm, generous person, his very being commanding respect and affection. The moment Dionne and her mother had arrived at his home fourteen years ago, she had adored the man and, in childlike fashion, had insisted upon calling him Uncle Andre. And even though her mother was only a very distant relative and had been hired to be his house-keeper and governess to his four-year-old daughter, he had not minded her familiarity and, in fact, had encouraged her to address him by that name.

Oh, but what a fright that dear man had given them all when he had suffered that crippling stroke ten years earlier. For days he lay close to death, but gradually, in answer to so many prayers, his health had returned and now he was almost as active as he had been before he was confined to his wheelchair. It was difficult to think of him as being crippled.

Dionne stopped suddenly, pensive shadows darkening her hazel eyes. Why were her thoughts wandering in such a strange direction? One simply did not dwell on why he loved a certain person. Love was an emotion that should be given freely and without question, or not given at all. Shrugging off her uncomfortable feelings, Dionne went on along her way but without the enthusiasm she usually had on market day.

Having plenty of time to shop for the spices the cook needed back at the plantation and for the material she

9

needed for the new gown she wanted to make for the Summer Carnival, Dionne meandered through the marketplace, stopping occasionally at the stalls, booths, and shops in the market square to inspect bolts of beautiful material or racks of pretty lace and ribbons.

Dionne greeted most of the individuals and merchants by name and was greeted fondly in return. But then, it was no wonder she was so well thought of by them. The young woman was always polite and courteous, not like so many of the other Europeans and fair-skinned patrons who wrinkled their noses and haggled over prices as though their lifestyle depended on obtaining merchandise at a cheaper price. What they did not know was that people like the young mademoiselle received the best bargains in the marketplace.

After finally making her way around half the square, Dionne found an empty chair at one of the sidewalk cafes. She decided to treat herself to a fresh fruit tart and a steaming cup of chicory coffee. Leaning back in the chair, she closed her eyes, hoping to recapture her earlier cheerful feelings, and allowed the pungent odors of the marketplace to assail her senses. Surprisingly, the smell was not unpleasant.

The scents of freshly cut flowers, bananas, pineapples, mangos, coffee, cinnamon, nutmeg, chicory, vanilla, tobacco, and fish all combined with the happy, bustling chatter of the square to produce a rather euphoric effect. It was difficult for her to imagine that in only a matter of a few hours the marketplace would empty and become almost devoid of human life until late that afternoon when the summer heat had abated. Then the bustling streets would come alive once again.

She breathed deeply and smiled. Coming to market was the most favorite of her duties. Not that she was expected to perform the menial chores of house-keeping, although she did help at times. Instead, her main responsibilities were to see that the servants performed their tasks, to plan the daily menus, and to do the shopping—everything her mother had done before her untimely death five years earlier.

Dionne recalled how doubtful Uncle Andre had been that she could assume the burden of so many responsibilities, being so young, only seventeen at the time. But he had not taken into account the fact that her mother had been an excellent teacher, having taught her daughter all that she knew. Of course, nothing could take the place of experience, but Uncle Andre, bless his kind heart, had shown a vast amount of patience, and within a few months the household again ran smoothly and had continued to do so throughout the last five years.

Dionne's pleasant feelings were again replaced with an uneasiness as she continued to think about her uncle. She sat straight up in her chair. Perhaps the situation concerning her uncle was what was bothering her so much. Without a doubt he was deeply troubled about something. Worry lines had creased his brow for weeks now, but he had refused to discuss his problems with anyone, not even her, which was highly unusual, since they often shared confidences. At first, she'd thought he had heard the ugly gossip racing around the island about Celeste and that scoundrel, Louis Fairmount. But, knowing her uncle, he would have simply put a stop to it by refusing to let Celeste see the man, even if it meant locking the girl in her room. And from the rumors she had heard, that is exactly what Uncle Andre would have to do to end Celeste's outrageous affair with the blackguard. However, since he worshipped his daughter and would do anything within reason to protect her, she strongly doubted if he had

11

heard the gossip. His worries had to stem from something else, but what on earth could it be?

Dionne was so lost in her thoughts that she did not see the man hurrying across the cafe floor as she rose from the table and opened her parasol. The man, looking behind him, apparently did not see her either. He accidentally bumped into her and sent her sprawling to the hard-packed dirt floor.

In a midst of disarrayed ruffles, lace, petticoats, and the badly bent parasol, Dionne found herself being helped to her feet by two strong arms. Her lips settled into a thin line when she decided the arms remained around her waist just a little bit longer than necessary. She glared at him with burning, reproachful eyes, which then widened in surprise, tinged with a tiny flicker of fear. The towering giant of a man holding her was horrendously ugly. Red straggly hair stuck out all over his face and head, and a black patch covered one eye.

She shouted at him, more out of fear than from anger, *"S'il vous plait enlever vos mains tout de suite!"*

His expression was that of puzzlement. "'Tis sorry I be, ma'am. I don't understand French very well . . . especially if it be spoken with a rapid tongue."

"I said, please take your hands off me!" Dionne muttered in perfect English.

The man dropped his hands as though they had been burned by hot coals. "Sorry, ma'am, and I be sorry for runnin' into ye like I did." He offered a feeble grin. "Guess I wasn't lookin' where I was goin'. Did I hurt ye?"

He started to brush the dirt from her dress, but from the expression that suddenly swept across her face, he decided it was not the right thing to do.

Now that Dionne realized this man was not a monster about to devour her, she felt a little sheepish over having been frightened by his appearance. "No, monsieur, I think my pride suffered more than I did." She brushed at the dirt on her dress, then dabbed at the spot that the dregs from her coffee cup left when they spilled on her.

"Did I ruin ye dress?"

"No, monsieur." She attempted a smile. "A little soap and water and it will be as good as new." She felt relieved that the crowd that had gathered had now dispersed.

"Barney, what seems to be the trouble?" a deep, masculine voice asked from behind Dionne.

An obvious expression of relief swept over his rugged features. "Ah, Cap'n Chris! I be glad to see ye, mon!" Then, he grinned sheepishly. "A wee scamp grabbed me coin pouch. I chased 'im, I did, and ran into this pretty lass and sent her sprawlin' o'er the floor."

"Are ye injured, mademoiselle?"

"No, I am fine. . . ." Dionne's voice caught in her throat as she turned around and saw the other man. Bold blue eyes stared into her startled ones and a faint, almost mocking smile appeared on his lips. His eyes were set in a handsome face bronzed by the sun. Although his black hair appeared to have been recently combed, it was still unruly but not unattractively so. She noted that his long sideburns were neatly trimmed, thus accentuating the leanly fleshed cheekbones and firm masculine jaw. His nose was well formed and slightly aquiline, and beneath it were wide, generous lips. Her eyes narrowed slightly at his arrogant stance. The concern of his words somehow did not quite match the haughty manner that emanated from him. Rarely did she form first impressions about anyone, but this man was an exception. She disliked him instantly and it immediately showed in the expression on her face.

The man apparently noticed the tightening of her features, and the rich timbre of his voice held a challenge. "I will be happy to pay for any damages."

Dionne squared her shoulders under his piercing gaze. "I assure you, monsieur, there are no damages."

He offered his arm. "Then allow me to escort you to your carriage and carry any packages you might have."

Dionne's brow wrinkled with her contemptuous thoughts. She had met men like him before, so cocky and arrogant that they believed women had been put on this earth for the sole purpose of swooning at their feet. Her voice was cool and distant. "That is not necessary, monsieur; I have no packages. Also, I am not ready to leave yet; I still have several items to purchase."

The man was not about to be thwarted. "Then I will accompany you—just on the slim chance that you might later have a fainting spell." He turned to the other man, who had been momentarily forgotten. "Barney, please return to the ship and tell the men to start to unload it."

Whirling toward him, Dionne gasped, "You are a seaman?"

"Aye, since I was a wee lad."

"B—but you are not supposed to be here!"

Confused, Barney squinted his one eye. "I not be sure I follow ye, lass."

"This part of the island has been placed off limits to seamen."

With an angry glint in his eyes, the other man asked, "Why? By whose orders?"

Dionne nervously wet her lips before replying, "It is not a written law, but one of mutual consent between the planters and the ships' captains. The seamen are usually so unruly and have caused considerable trouble

14

in the past. . . ."

The handsome man tossed his head angrily and clamped his hands on the side of his hips. "It so happens that I am the captain of the *Blue Diamond*, and I have consented to no such agreement! If I and my men are not welcome on this island, then my goods are not either!" He had pride in his crew and it made him furious that they were forced to suffer the consequences of others.

Dionne bristled under his anger. "That, monsieur, is between you and the officials. If the majority of the seamen did not behave like barbarians, they would be most welcome here."

He sneered with contempt, "Barbarians? That's what you think we are?" With cold deliberation he raked his eyes over her, noting the expensive cut of her dress, the ivory pallor of her complexion, and her superior attitude. He decided rather quickly that it was women like her who had complained. "I guess a woman such as you would not know the difference between a barbarian and a real man."

Dionne stiffened into a rigid stance. Forcing her voice to sound syrupy sweet, she said, "Oh, but monsieur, I am positive I know the difference." With an arrogant wave of her hand, she gestured at Barney. "Monsieur Barney has behaved like the perfect gentleman, while you, his captain, fit the description of a barbarian extremely well."

Ignoring the sudden clenching of the captain's hands and the way his face mottled with rage, Dionne tossed her head, gave an irritable tug at the damaged parasol, and haughtily walked away, extremely aware that the barbaric captain's angry glare burned two perfectly round holes in her back.

Nigel, standing in front of the tavern, sipping slowly

at the tankard of rum, sputtered when he saw Dionne hurrying toward the carriage. Shoving the tankard into the hands of one of his friends, he rushed toward her. "Mademoiselle Dionne, is something the matter?" It was plain to see that she was very upset.

"N—no. Just take me home, Nigel. A—and please, drive as fast as you can."

This is the best book I have ever read! I almost cried to death!

Signed

TO Softharted

Chapter Two

After reaching the plantation, Dionne, still seething with anger, barely waited for the carriage to come to a stop before she jumped down and raced for the house. She slammed the front door behind her and ran to her room.

Shaking with rage and an emotion she did not readily recognize, she yanked the gloves from her hands and removed her bonnet. Not only had that horrid man spoiled her shopping day, but she had left the marketplace in such a hurry that she had not taken the time to look for the perfect piece of material to make her new gown for the Summer Carnival. Next to Mardi Gras, the Summer Carnival was the largest social event of the year, and now, unless she threw her schedule here at Desirade to the winds and returned to the marketplace tomorrow, she would not have a new gown to wear. There simply would not be enough time to make one if she waited to purchase the material on the next market day, because the Carnival was only two weeks away. And she certainly did not have the money to buy a ready-made gown. They were far too expensive.

Dionne pressed trembling fingers to her throbbing temples. There was more at stake than just having a new gown to wear. If Celeste had not made such a malicious remark several days ago, she might not have planned to go at all. Lately it seemed as though the girl delighted in hurting her feelings. There was absolutely no need for Celeste's ugly remark about her appearance being an embarrassment to the Debierne family. She was always well groomed, and while her clothes were not always in the latest fashion, Dionne knew she always looked presentable. She had decided then that there were two possible reasons for Celeste's behaving so viciously. Celeste was either too embarrassed for her to accompany them to social events because of her position as their housekeeper, or she was still angry and used the occasion to spite Dionne for refusing to wear her hand-me-downs.

Dionne shuddered at the memory. She supposed the animosity had all started when she had casually mentioned that she had to take in a few tucks in the waistlines of the gowns Celeste had given her. But it had been an innocent comment, not meant viciously at all. Afterwards, though, it seemed as if Celeste took a perverse delight in making ugly remarks about how matronly she looked or how she never seemed to do justice to the pretty gowns. Once she even had the audacity to demand that Dionne model one of the gowns at a tea party she gave, pointing out to her friends that the proper clothing could make all the difference in the world to a person's appearance, that the right gown could even make a servant look presentable. There had been no graceful way for Dionne to refuse, but from that day on, she never wore any of Celeste's cast-off clothing.

How a sweet-dispositioned man like her Uncle Andre could have fathered a sharp-tongued, selfish offspring like Celeste she would never know. But Celeste had not always been like that. When Dionne and her mother had first arrived at Desirade, Celeste had been only a child, sweet and loving. For years they had been the best of friends, even though Dionne was older. But then, when Celeste began to mature into a young woman, a rift gradually formed between them. Celeste became extremely aware of the fact that she was the daughter of one of the island's most wealthy planters and that Dionne was only the daughter of one of their servants, and later, a servant herself. Once she had even overheard Celeste arguing with her father, objecting to the way he allowed a servant to attend social functions with them. He staunchly overrode her objections and sent her to her room for punishment. After that, Celeste's hostility was clearly evident, as long as her father was not around. In Andre's presence she was as sweet and charming as she could possibly be.

At times, Dionne had actually considered leaving Desirade and even Martinique altogether. But she really had no place to go and was too afraid of the outside world to strike out on her own. Her mother's family, who lived in Natchez, Mississippi, were wealthy in their own right, but they had disowned their daughter when she had come to Martinique. Besides, when it came right down to making a final decision, she could not bring herself to leave Uncle Andre. He was her only family, the father she never had, and the only person in the entire world that she loved.

Men and marriage? No, they did not seem to be in her future. She had faced that realization several years ago. In her opinion there were only two categories of men on the island: the upper-class society who would never give a second look at a woman who was not their social equal and the merchants, small planters, and bankers, the majority of whom already had wives. There were a few exceptions like Monsieur Hermann Sarte, who had tried to court her, but the mere thought of becoming his wife was unthinkable. Not only was he unattractive, being fat and bald, but his stinginess and cruelty were common knowledge. If he or a man like him were her only chance at marriage, she would gladly remain a spinster.

Dionne was pulled from her reverie by a sudden rap at her door. She glanced at her clock and frowned. Where had the time gone? And who on earth could that be? During the extreme heat of the day everyone retired to their rooms until the afternoon breezes began to stir.

"Yes? Who is it?"

"It's me, Lucy," the cook said softly. "Monsieur Debierne wants to see you in his study."

Suddenly alarmed, Dionne quickly opened the door. "Is he all right? Did he complain of feeling ill?"

"He is fine . . . I think." She twisted her broad face into a thoughtful grimace. "Leastways he didn't 'pear to be sick. But the Monsieur sure has got a bee under his bonnet. I ain't never seen him so worked up."

Dionne did not stop to listen to Lucy's incessant chatter. The doctor had warned them years ago not to allow Andre to become too upset, and if something had happened for him to deem it necessary to interrupt the household's siesta, it must be extremely serious.

Pausing at the study door to regain her composure, Dionne smoothed first her hair then her skirts. Then she took a deep breath before opening the door. He sat in his wheelchair, his back to the door, staring out through the open French portals at the garden. "Uncle Andre? Has something happened? Are you ill?"

He slowly turned his chair around. His shoulders were slumped, his brow was creased with obvious worry, and his eyes held such sadness that Dionne felt a sharp pain go through her own heart. She realized then just how much he had recently aged. She felt her eyes fill with tears but quickly blinked them away. It would not serve any purpose for him to see her cry.

"No, Dionne, I am not ill . . . unless being deeply troubled could be called an illness." He stared at her, then gave a wry chuckle. "Don't look so worried. My heart beats strong, perhaps . . . too strong. I suppose that is little wonder because I believe I have two hearts now!" He pointed to his chest and gestured emphatically with his hands. His voice rose loudly, "The one that used to be here has been broken into two parts!"

"Uncle Andre, please don't excite yourself so much!" Dionne cried, hurrying to his side. "You know what the doctor has said. . . ."

Andre waved his hands impatiently. "If I listened to everything that idiot said, I would still be confined to my bed, or worse, six feet beneath the ground." He pointed toward his legs. "Just because these are useless does not make my mind stop thinking or my heart stop caring! . . ."

"Uncle Andre, please!"

Andre stopped his ranting once he saw Dionne's worry and the threat of tears in her eyes. He drew a deep, shuddering breath. "All right, child," he murmured in a calm voice. "I cannot reach a reasonable solution concerning this problem while raving like a madman. Pour us each a glass of sherry. There is something I want to discuss with you."

Dionne quickly filled two glasses, then deliberately chose a chair right across from his desk. She had never seen him this upset before and wanted to be within arm's reach if anything happened to him.

Andre took a small sip of his sherry, placed the glass on his desk, then calmly asked, "Have you heard any rumors about Celeste and Louis Fairmount?"

"Rumors about Celeste?" she parroted in a small voice as she pulled her gaze from his. "I—I am not sure I know what you mean."

"Damnation!" he thundered, striking the desk with

21

his fist. "I merely asked you a question that can be answered with a simple yes or no! Have you heard any rumors?"

Startled, Dionne jumped at his display of anger. She could not lie to Andre, but neither could she repeat idle gossip that could possibly hurt him. If his question had referred to anyone or anything other than Celeste, she would not hesitate for a moment to tell him. But how could she repeat the ugly rumors about his beloved daughter?

Andre spread his fingers wide apart and studied them momentarily, then he stared intently at Dionne. When he finally spoke, his voice was soft and gentle. "Your loyalty to my daughter is admirable, especially since, at times, she is less than kind toward you. However, I did not call you in here to seek information. Unfortunately, I already have knowledge of her disgraceful affair with him."

Dionne's cheeks colored at his misunderstanding her silence. She had not held her tongue to protect that foolish girl; instead, it was because of her affection and loyalty to him that she had remained silent. "But, Uncle Andre, you have never listened to gossip before. Why should you now? You know as well as I do rumors hold only a fraction of the truth."

"Yes, normally I would agree with you, but not this time . . . not this time." He drew a deep, ragged breath. "I have taken steps to end her liaison with him by arranging a suitable marriage for her."

Andre had spoken so softly that at first Dionne thought he was merely testing the idea. Then she realized he actually meant it; that he had already made the arrangement. Biting her lower lip, she stared at the floor.

"You disapprove?"

"I—it's not for me to say, Uncle Andre."

"I agree, it is my decision to make, but I do value your opinion just as I valued your mother's. Raising a motherless child—especially a girl—has not been easy, and I doubt if I could have done it without your mother's help. But now . . . I wish I had listened to her more . . . not allowed Celeste so much freedom. Maybe I would not be faced with making this decision now." His misery was so apparent it looked as if it were a physical pain. He sighed wearily. "I have already told Celeste. Needless to say, she is extremely upset and has fled to her room and locked the door."

Dionne raised worry-filled eyes to meet his. "Why do you tell me this, Uncle Andre? You, of all people, should know how I feel about arranged marriages. I'm sure you recall how unhappy Mother was and how she and I suffered at the hands of the husband her family arranged for her." Dionne tightly closed her eyes, remembering the terrible beatings she and her mother had received from that cruel and merciless man. And it was so ironic that Celeste was apparently following the same precarious path.

The past swam uneasily before Dionne's eyes. Her own mother had fallen in love with a man who did not meet her family's approval. She had refused to marry Falkner Martin, the man her family had chosen for her, instead running away with the man she loved. But he had been killed before they could be married. Her mother was brought back home in shame and in disgrace. When the family discovered she was carrying a child, they approached Falkner, who agreed to marry her and give her bastard child a name. And Dionne was that bastard child. Seldom did a day pass that she and her mother were not taunted by ugly, vicious names. Later, as she got older, the taunts turned into beatings. Of course, her mother tried to protect her, which only made Falkner turn his wrath on both of them. The

23

following seven years were a nightmarish hell. Then, mercifully for them, he died, and her mother escaped her manipulating family by coming to the island of Martinique. And now, with Andre's revelation, the almost-forgotten painful memories were as sharp as though they had occurred only yesterday.

Andre's voice cut through Dionne's painful memories. "Of course I know the story of Mary Ann's past. That is one reason why this was such a difficult decision to make. However, I am confident the man I selected for Celeste is nothing like Falkner Martin . . . just as Louis Fairmount is nothing like the man your mother loved. Mary Ann's unhappy past lay heavily on my mind when I first learned of Monsieur Fairmount. I did not want it to cloud my judgment, because I do want my daughter to be happy."

Dionne could not hold her tongue any longer. Regardless of her personal feelings about Celeste, she had to come to the girl's defense. "How can she be happy if you force her to give up the man she loves? After all, they are only rumors. How can you make such an important decision based on gossip?"

"That's just it, Dionne, it isn't merely idle gossip." He took a deep, ragged breath. "I began hearing the rumors about Celeste and Louis months ago. Since he never asked permission to call on Celeste, I made it a point to meet him. I suppose I wanted to decide for myself what kind of man he was. Needless to say, there was something about him I did not like. It was nothing I could put my finger on, and at first I thought it was probably because he was seeing my little girl without seeking my approval." Andre gave a humorless chuckle. "I doubt if there are many fathers who sincerely believe any man is good enough for their daughter. I realize now it was a terrible mistake, but I decided, for the time being, not to interfere. Then I began hearing things about Monsieur Fairmount—things I could no longer ignore. I had him thoroughly investigated—very discreetly, of course—and this is the report I received." He showed Dionne a thick stack of papers. "Monsieur Fairmount is a gambler, a blackguard, an unscrupulous man who stops at nothing to obtain what he wants. The report also suggests that he is a blackmailer. It seems there are several prestigious families in and around New Orleans who have had the misfortune of knowing him. He apparently delights in seducing young women, then when their reputations are on the brink of ruin, he approaches their father and agrees to remove himself from their lives if he is paid a healthy sum. There are, however, two instances when the young woman's father refused."

"Oh, Uncle Andre, I had no idea Louis Fairmount was so—so . . . evil!" Dionne gasped.

Andre shook his head in agreement. "Apparently no one did either. Unfortunately, I am not finished with this sordid tale. Both times the young lady in question disappeared. One was later found working in a brothel, and the other was found floating in a bayou with her throat slit. Charges were brought against Monsieur Fairmount concerning the murdered girl, but nothing could be proved so they were dropped for lack of evidence. The report suggests he had something on the judge who tried the case, but that could not be proved either. So, you see why I feel an arranged marriage is the lesser of the two evils."

Dionne shuddered inwardly at the thought of what could have happened to Celeste if her father had not stepped in. "Yes," she said slowly. "I do see why and I fully understand, but I am confused. Why have you

25

told me all of this? I know you have taken me into your confidence in the past, but this is such a personal matter."

"Because I require your help, your cooperation. And not only that, I am sure you realize I need your silence. If Monsieur Fairmount somehow discovered the existence of this report, I fear the consequences."

Leaning forward, Dionne said, "It goes without saying, my lips are sealed. How can I help?"

"By staying as close to Celeste as possible. It is of the utmost importance that she does not see Louis Fairmount again. As I said earlier, I have discussed this with her—not Louis's reputation, of course, but her upcoming marriage to Christopher Phillips. She has reluctantly agreed to become his wife. However, I am not sure Monsieur Phillips would agree to this marriage if he thought she was in love with another man."

"Do you know this man well?"

"No, I have never met him, but I do know his father and grandfather, Edward and William Phillips. They own a shipping line located in New Orleans. It is my understanding that the young man is quite active in the family business."

Dionne's foreboding was like a steel weight upon her shoulders. She sensed impending disaster. "Will the marriage take place here or in New Orleans?"

He shook his head. "The actual plans have not been discussed yet. I would prefer for them to be married in New Orleans so that Celeste is away from the island and out of Monsieur Fairmount's evil clutches, but I cannot appear too eager. The final arrangements will be made tonight. The Phillipses arrived in Fort-de-France last night and I have invited the gentlemen to dinner. Will you see to it that something special is prepared?"

"Yes, of course, but you said, *gentlemen.* Do you expect more than one guest?"

"I suppose I did not make myself clear. Christopher's father and grandfather will be here too." Andre removed his watch from his pocket and peered at it intently. "If you will excuse me now, I have other matters to attend to."

Dionne stood, walked around the desk, and placed a gentle kiss on his forehead. "Do not worry, Uncle Andre," she said with an assurance she did not really feel. "Everything will be fine, and within a few months, this will all be an unpleasant memory."

He patted her hand absently. "I hope so, child, I sincerely hope so."

Later, after the sun was well past its zenith and a cooling breeze wafted over the land from the ocean, Dionne went to the garden to cut flowers for the dinner table. As she strolled among the heady fragrances her thoughts wandered. The day's events had been incredible. So much had changed since dawn. For the first time in months, perhaps even years, she felt compassion for Celeste. After instructing Lucy and her helper on what to prepare for dinner, she had gone up to Celeste's room, but the girl had staunchly refused to see her. In a strange way, Dionne was glad. What could she say to her? She doubted if there were any words that could comfort Celeste now, even if the girl would listen.

Dionne's thoughts turned to the man who would marry Celeste. What sort of man would he be? Try as she might, she could not imagine him to be anything other than a tiny, bespectacled man with thin, wispy hair sitting at a desk in some cramped, dusty office. Just the kind of man Celeste abhorred and snickered at behind a gloved hand. Dionne sighed heavily. The saints would have to protect them all if that type would indeed be her husband.

So preoccupied with her thoughts was Dionne that she did not hear the stones covering the paths crunch beneath stalking footsteps. Then, suddenly, she stiffened. Just as she started to turn, arms as strong as steel grabbed her from behind and spun her around. Before she could even scream a protest, lips pressed firmly against hers with a ruthlessness she did not know existed. She beat her fists against his broad chest. Then the lips softened and the man's tongue invaded her mouth, seeking, exploring, plundering its sweet depths. Dionne continued to struggle but to no avail. He was much too strong for her to resist. She could feel her head reel and her knees start to give way. The realization that she was about to faint and be completely at this fiend's mercy was terrifying.

When the man realized she was about to faint, he minutely relaxed his hold on her. Then, instant recognition flashed in both their eyes.

"You!" they chorused in unison.

The man dropped his arms in surprise, thus allowing Dionne to fall to the ground.

Giving an outraged cry of consternation, Dionne raised herself on her elbows. Intense rage flared in her as she glared at the man she had met earlier at the marketplace. The man she had disliked immediately. "What are you doing here?" she sputtered indignantly. "And how dare you attack me that way! If I were a man . . . why, I—I would challenge you to a duel!"

The man took a couple of quick steps backward. He stopped and shook his head. "Damn! If this doesn't beat all! This is exactly what I deserve for agreeing to this harebrained idea." Then, his legs splayed in a powerful stance, he placed his hands on his hips, threw back his head, and laughed. His boisterous, mocking laughter filled the garden.

"Go ahead and laugh, you—you . . . blackguard! I fail to see what is so humorous!"

"Oh, but mademoiselle, you don't know what I know." He made a low, sweeping bow. Then, with a mocking grin still playing havoc with his lips, he pretended to contemplate the future. "If nothing else, we should have a fiery union. After all, we have so much in common . . . *intense dislike!*" he added crisply, offering her his hand.

"What do you mean, we have something in common?"

"Why, Mademoiselle Debierne, I am your betrothed."

Dionne's mouth fell open in surprise. He had her confused with Celeste. "Y—you mean . . . y—you are C—Christopher Phillips?"

He clicked his heels in an obvious gesture of mockery. "Yes, mademoiselle, or do you prefer to address me by my other name?"

"O—other name?" Her mind refused to function properly. This entire scenario would end as soon as she told him her real identity.

"Oh, how quickly we forget, mademoiselle." He laughed again, but the humor did not reach his eyes. "The lady and the barbarian. What a delightful couple we will make. Do you not agree?"

For the first time since their confrontation, a tiny flicker of wry amusement swept over Dionne. Although it was difficult for her to understand her dislike for this man, it gave her a great feeling of satisfaction that she momentarily held the upper hand. Her eyes narrowed slightly as her thoughts raced quickly ahead. It would certainly take the wind out of this captain's sails if she allowed him to continue thinking that she was indeed Celeste Debierne. She could imagine the expression on his arrogant face when he discovered her true identity, and that thought alone forced her to bite her bottom lip to stifle a grin. But the urge to deceive him quickly disappeared as she realized he would have to be told the truth—and he would have to be told the truth this very moment. As ill-tempered as he was, there was no telling how angry the deception would make him, and his upcoming marriage to Celeste was far more important than her desire to make him feel like a fool.

She spoke with remote dignity. "I believe a mistake has been made, monsieur."

Christopher's brows arched mischievously and an insolent grin flitted across his mouth. "A mistake? What do you mean, a mistake?" His sigh of disappointment was highly exaggerated. "You disappoint me, mademoiselle. I had no idea that one little kiss would frighten you so much. Could it be that you are having second thoughts about our . . . shall we say, arrangement?"

Dionne squared her shoulders defiantly, her eyes smoldered with sarcasm. "You give yourself too much credit, Monsieur Phillips. You and your kiss did not frighten me. And, as for having second thoughts, the mistake I spoke of . . ."

"Then you must have liked my kiss," Christopher chuckled knowingly.

"Don't be ridiculous! If you would only listen . . ."

Christopher had never taunted a woman in this manner before, but after her snobbish behavior earlier in the marketplace, he figured she deserved every moment of it. Interrupting again, he breathed an exaggerated sigh of relief. "For a moment there you had me worried. No woman, and I mean *no woman,*" he repeated, placing special emphasis on the words, "has ever complained about my kisses before." He took a threatening step toward her. "I think you must want another one. And this time, relax. I don't bite."

Dionne's eyes widened as she took a step backward. Her heart hammered wildly against her chest. This man was even more contemptible than she had first thought. "If you . . . touch me again . . . so help me, I'll scream!"

Christopher arched his brows and made a whistling sound between his pursed lips. "Scream? No, mademoiselle, I doubt if that is necessary."

Dionne tried to regain her shattered composure. "If you will only stop your arrogant rambling for a moment . . ."

He touched his chest in a condescending gesture. His voice was taunting and sarcastic. "Arrogant? You think I am arrogant? Why, you have no idea how much that hurts me."

Although Christopher pretended to enjoy this bantering exchange of teasing sarcasm, deep down inside, he meant it. Now that he had actually come face to face with the woman who was to become his wife, the enormity of the situation settled heavily on his consciousness. He immediately regretted going along with his family's wishes for him to marry. Why he had ever agreed to this arranged marriage he would never know. Perhaps if they had liked each other it could have been tolerable, but this woman was a shrew! He stared hard at Dionne. He decided that while she could not be considered beautiful, she was attractive—that is, until she opened her mouth and began uttering those barbed words. He felt doomed. His first instinct was to spin on his heel, go back to his ship, and set sail, getting as far away from Martinique as possible and never returning. But that would bring disgrace to his family's name. Once a Phillips gave his word to an agreement, he was honor-bound to see it through. Then a slow grin tugged at Christopher's mouth. If she called off their wedding, his family's honor would be saved. It would be easier for his family to face the embarrassment of a broken engagement than for him to be forced to live the rest of his life with this shrewish creature. His eyes narrowed slightly. Now, if only he could antagonize her just a little bit more. . . .

He chortled, "I see now why your father was forced to search outside the island for your husband. That certainly doesn't speak well of your disposition, mademoiselle."

"I don't understand how you have the audacity to say that I have a bad disposition!" Dionne sputtered angrily.

"I do," Christopher said after a contemptuous chuckle. "Since apparently all of the eligible bachelors on Martinique have refused your hand, your father had to arrange your marriage with a perfect stranger. And now, after meeting you, I can certainly see why."

Dionne's eyes narrowed considerably. The cynicism of his remark grated on her, and for a brief moment she felt a searing stab of pity for Celeste. Folding her arms together, she angrily tossed her heavy mane of hair and began tapping her foot against the ground. "Monsieur Phillips, undoubtedly you are the most rude, arrogant man I have ever had the misfortune to meet. Apparently it never crossed your mind that the same questions could be asked about you, since you have agreed to this arranged marriage. Fortunately for me there has been a mistake made—a deliciously wonderful mistake. It so happens that I would not marry you if you were the last man on this earth! And, furthermore, I have never felt so sorry in all my life than I do right now for—"

Frowning, Christopher grumbled, "I had no idea it

would make you so happy." It was perplexing that she sounded so cheerful, which was completely confusing. He wanted to make her so angry that she would break their engagement, but she certainly did not have to sound so pleased about it. Women! He would never be able to figure out these whimsical creatures.

Her voice came syrupy sweet. "No, not happy. Instead, I believe the word for it would be relieved. You see, I am not Celeste Debierne—thank God!" she added under her breath.

Christopher was momentarily at a loss for words. Then his astonishment turned into raw fury. He abruptly grasped Dionne by her shoulders. "You're not— Then who in the hell are you? Why did you lead me to believe you were Celeste?" His eyes darkened with rage.

Dionne wrenched herself from his grasp. She took great delight in watching his ever-changing expression as she haughtily explained, "My name is Dionne Martin. It so happens that I am in the Debierne family's employ and have been for many years. And you are mistaken, monsieur. If you will recall, I did not lead you to believe I was Celeste. The moment I realized you had mistaken me for her, I tried to tell you that a mistake had been made. . . . But no, you were so intent on behaving like an insufferable boor, you wouldn't listen to a word I said. So, don't blame me for your own rash behavior!"

"Then . . . where is she?"

Dionne replied with a haughty toss of her head, "The last I heard she was in her room, suffering from a terrible headache. But if the girl had any sense at all, she would remain there until you left the island."

Relief had instantly swept over Christopher when he realized he would not be forced to spend the rest of his life with this woman. And with that relief his good sense of humor returned. "You behave awfully high and mighty for a mere servant girl."

Dionne placed her hands akimbo and glared at him. "And that, sir, is a pious remark coming from a man who is probably nothing but a pirate! Besides, I am not a mere servant girl. It so happens that I am Monsieur Debierne's housekeeper." She sniffed self-righteously. "There is a big difference, but then, after speaking to you for the past few minutes, I realize you are too ignorant to know what the difference is!"

Christopher ignored her barbed remark. He had never been the sort of man who looked down on anyone, regardless of his wealth or social standing, but he refused to let her know it. Forcing what he hoped to be a snobbish expression on his face, he snorted, "A servant is a servant, regardless of his title. It puzzles me, though. From what my father and grandfather have told me about Andre Debierne, I would have never thought he'd allow his servants—regardless of their status in the household," he added sarcastically, "—to be so rude to an invited guest. Perhaps he should be made aware of what goes on around here behind his back."

Panic gripped Dionne. She gasped, "Oh, no! You cannot do that! You must not!"

With a lift of his brow, he uttered coldly, "And why not? Afraid you would lose your position?"

Dionne swallowed the hard lump that had suddenly formed in her throat. Andre had enough to worry about without having to listen to unfounded complaints from this man. God forbid that she would have to apologize to this snobbish boor, especially when she felt as though she had done nothing wrong. But if an apology would help to soothe his ruffled feelings, then she would have to swallow her pride. When she was

34

able to speak, her voice had a pleading tone to it. "My position here at Desirade has nothing to do with it, monsieur. You see, I am quite fond of Monsieur Debierne, and he is in ill health. His . . . heart is . . . not strong. I have always done everything within my power to prevent him from becoming upset unnecessarily. I think . . . a complaint about me from his . . . daughter's betrothed . . . would upset him greatly."

Dionne pulled her gaze from his intense blue eyes. She stared at the ground and bit on her bottom lip before she could find the courage to offer the apology she did not feel she owed. Raising her eyes, she said humbly, "I am sorry. I was wrong in bandying words with you. I should have told you my correct identity immediately. I promise, nothing like this will ever happen again."

This time, it was Christopher who pulled his gaze from hers. In that brief moment when their eyes met, he saw many things: anger, hurt, and defiance. But most of all, he saw something he had never expected to see: loyalty, and a burning love for Andre Debierne; and that surprised him. It was not the sort of love that shone from a woman's eyes when she gazed tenderly at her mate. Instead, it was the kind of love that Christopher knew was reflected in his own eyes when he looked at his father or grandfather. He immediately felt ashamed of himself. When he spoke, his words held none of his previous sarcasm. "An apology is not necessary, Mademoiselle Martin. I was certainly out of line. If there is any blame then it should be placed on my—"

Color stained Dionne's cheeks as she interrupted, "Please, monsieur, I believe enough has been said." She smoothed her skirts, and not wanting him to hear how upset she was, Dionne forced what she hoped to be a proper but expressionless tone to her voice. "I suppose

35

Monsieur Debierne is expecting you. If you will follow me, I'll show you to his study."

Christopher silently agreed. Enough had been said. But one startling realization had come from this encounter. He was about to marry a woman he did not know, a woman he did not love, and with those dark, chilling thoughts, a cold feeling crept up his spine.

Chapter Three

It took all of the strength and dignity Dionne could muster to walk passively in front of Christopher Phillips as she led him inside the house to Andre's study. Inwardly, she seethed with anger, and combined with the loss of pride over the apology she had been forced to give him, a sour taste had been left in her mouth. It was a humiliating feeling she would not easily forget.

Dionne rapped lightly on the door and felt a deep sensation of relief when Andre answered immediately. She opened the double doors. "Excuse me for interrupting you, sir, but your guest has arrived."

Andre looked up from the stack of papers he had been examining. "My guest?"

"Yes, sir. May I present Christopher Phillips," she said, and gestured toward him with a sweep of her hand.

Christopher stepped around Dionne and strode quickly across the study, stopping when he reached the desk. He extended his hand and grasped Andre's in a hardy shake, speaking to him in a mixture of French and English. *"Bonjour,* Monsieur Debierne. I have heard a lot about you, sir." He added sincerely,

"Needless to say, I regret that it has taken so long for us to meet."

A broad smile spread quickly across Andre's face as he shoved the papers aside with his free hand. "Christopher Phillips! It is my pleasure to meet you, young man. But I wasn't expecting you until later this afternoon." He peered anxiously around him. "Did your father and grandfather come with you?"

"No, sir. They are still in Fort-de-France. They had some unexpected business to attend to, so I decided to ride on out to Desirade. I've heard so much about you, I decided I couldn't wait until tonight." He allowed his gaze to linger on the man sitting behind the desk. "I was led to believe you were in ill health, but I must say, you look remarkably well." He deliberately turned so that Dionne could see the sudden smirk that lifted the corners of his mouth. Christopher had never intended to say anything about his and Dionne's argument, but the fact that she had used Andre's health as a reason for his silence grated on him.

Dionne saw the look he threw at her and immediately sensed that he thought her earlier concern for Andre had been nothing but a farce to prevent him from voicing a complaint about her behavior. She colored fiercely and blood began to pound in her temples. Without knowing why, she found it impossible to move. It suddenly felt as though her feet were rooted to the floor.

"Oh, I can't recall when I've ever felt better!" Andre replied with a smile, missing the unspoken exchange that passed between the two. He pushed his chair back from the desk, revealing for the first time that he was sitting in a wheelchair. He propelled himself across the floor to where several chairs had been arranged to accommodate his bulky chair and still allow his guests

38

to sit comfortably while they spoke.

A sensation akin to amusement swept over Dionne when she saw Christopher's look of surprise upon seeing Andre's wheelchair.

"Do you need any assistance, sir?" Christopher asked in a rush, once his moment of being startled had passed. He felt Dionne's eyes on his back and knew if he turned he would see them gloating. He deliberately kept his back presented to her.

"Oh, no. I can handle this blasted contraption just fine. I've gotten used to it over the years. Please, be seated." Noting the young man's surprise, Andre bluntly added, "I see you weren't aware that I am confined to a wheelchair. I find it strange that your father or grandfather did not tell you about my condition."

"No, sir, no one said a word to me about you being in a wheelchair," Christopher admitted hesitantly as he sat down and, feeling slightly ill-at-ease, stretched his long legs before him.

"Does it bother you?"

"No, sir. Not in the least," Christopher stated matter-of-factly.

"Good!" Andre gave with a wave of his hand. "The apoplexy affected my legs, not my mind."

"I can certainly see that, sir, and I imagine that is why neither my father nor grandfather mentioned it." Christopher chuckled and said, "If you don't mind me saying so, it's not just the fact that you are in a wheelchair that surprises me. I was under the impression that you were cut from a very old French cloth, and to be perfectly frank about it, I didn't expect you to speak such good English." He chuckled again. "My grandmother insisted that I bone up on my French so that when we met, as she put it, I would be able to hold an intelligent conversation with you and with my future wife."

Andre laughed aloud. "Oh, I am definitely French, but for the most part, English is the prevalent language spoken in this house. And, the fact is, Celeste speaks the language better than I do, but to be honest, I doubt if that will help when it comes to having an intelligent conversation with her." Seeing Christopher's brows raise questioningly at his statement, Andre leaned forward so as to take him into his confidence. "Don't misunderstand. My daughter is an extremely intelligent woman, beautiful, and charming. But unless you are interested in what Adrianne is wearing to the next party or what Rose wore to the afternoon tea or what new fabric Camile has ordered, I'm afraid you will be quite bored."

Christopher threw his head back and laughed heartily. "Your point is well taken, sir. In other words, Celeste is a typical female."

"Exactly!" Andre joined Christopher in his laughter, as though they had shared a private joke.

Turning her oval face toward the two men, Dionne stared at them with openmouthed amazement. How could this charming, easygoing, friendly man be the same one who had treated her so atrociously only a few minutes before? It was as if he were two entirely different people. Her hazel-colored eyes narrowed thoughtfully. His manner reminded her of a chameleon, changing instantly in the blink of an eye.

Andre glanced at Dionne, who still stood motionless in the doorway. "Dionne, please pour us a glass of brandy, then go upstairs and see if Celeste is feeling better. If she is, tell her that Christopher is here. I'm sure she is eager to meet him."

Dionne knew his simple request held a double

meaning. It wasn't so much that he wanted Celeste informed of Christopher's presence so that she could come downstairs and meet him. Instead, he wanted her to know that Christopher was here in the house so that she would do nothing to jeopardize their future relationship by continuing to throw her tantrum. Dionne also realized he was counting on her to help keep Celeste under control. Without saying a word, she moved quietly to the liquor cabinet. Her squared shoulders and steady expression did not betray the turmoil she felt as she filled the brandy glasses. Inside, her emotions were raging. She cast a sidelong look at Christopher, still amazed at how quickly he had changed. How he could sit there so calmly and nonchalantly was well beyond the depths of her imagination. His easy, self-confident manner was a far cry from the maniacal beast that had accosted her only minutes earlier.

"Will there be anything else, sir?" she asked, setting the brandy decanter and glasses on the table between them in easy reach if they wanted a refill.

"Yes, bring me my pipe from the desk and also that box of cigars. Brandy isn't worth a damn without a good cigar," he said to Christopher. "There is something about cigars and brandy that should be declared a crime to enjoy one without the other. Do you agree?"

"Wholeheartedly!" Christopher replied as he removed a cigar from the box that Dionne offered and deeply breathed the rich aroma. He removed another one and handed it to Andre, but the older man declined.

"No . . . thank you," he sighed wistfully. "As much as I would like one now, that dim-witted doctor of mine insists that I only have one a day—and I prefer to have it after dinner. But go ahead; don't let me stop you."

Satisfied that Andre had all he needed to entertain his guest, Dionne discreetly left the study, closing the doors softly behind her. It was only then that she realized her hands were trembling as they never had before. Taking a minute to compose herself, Dionne drew a deep breath, smoothed back her hair, then slowly crossed the foyer to the winding staircase. She deliberately forced all thoughts of her earlier encounter with that horrible man from her mind. It would be difficult enough to convince Celeste to come down-stairs and behave herself without having to cope with the memory of his daring kiss and outrageous behavior.

Dionne stopped in front of Celeste's bedroom door and placed her ear next to the intricately scrolled panel. Upon hearing soft, sobbing sounds, she rapped lightly. "Celeste, it's Dionne. Please let me in."

"Go away!" the muffled voice cried.

"No, I am not going away," Dionne stated firmly. "I will remain here until you open the door—even if it takes a week." She waited a few moments more, but when she did not hear any movements, she called again, "Celeste, please, your father asked me to come up here and speak to you. He—he has a surprise for you."

Dionne waited patiently for Celeste to make up her mind. She knew the girl well. Celeste seldom resisted anything that had to do with a surprise. She breathed a sigh of relief when she finally heard footsteps padding slowly across the floor, a click of the door latch, and the door being opened hesitantly. Pity for Celeste filled Dionne when she saw her tearstained face and red, swollen eyes. But even in her torment, the girl was still beautiful.

"A . . . surprise?" Celeste asked, hiccuping a sob.

"Yes, and I believe you will find it to be a pleasant one." Dionne did not like the taste the lie left in her mouth, but under the circumstances, she felt she had no choice. She considered Celeste's meeting with Christopher Phillips to be anything other than pleasant. But at least he was reasonably attractive, probably just the sort of man Celeste would be attracted to if she did not have such strong feelings for Louis Fairmount. "Christopher Phillips is downstairs and he appears anxious to meet you."

"Well, I certainly do not want to meet him! I never want to meet him . . . not as long as I live! Father told you what he is doing to me, didn't he?" Celeste accused when she saw Dionne's pitying expression.

"If you are referring to the arranged marriage . . . yes, he did." Her words, though quiet and softly spoken, had an ominous quality.

Celeste spat angrily, "And I suppose he sent you up here to try and convince me that I should forget all about Louis and marry that little emasculated clerk he picked out for me!" She then turned, flung herself across the bed, and began sobbing raggedly. She did not have the slightest idea that Dionne's speculations about the man had been the same as hers, nor did she know the description of her betrothed was the exact opposite of what she expected.

Dionne quickly shut the door so that the sounds would not carry throughout the house. She stood over Celeste, not knowing what to say or do. There were no appropriate words to soothe a broken heart, but if for no one else but Andre, she had to try. Sitting down on the bed beside where Celeste lay, she began talking to her in a kind, gentle voice, "Celeste, you have to stop

43

crying. Tears are not the answer to anything. The only thing that will help you is to face this situation head-on."

Celeste turned her head and stared at Dionne, pain lying naked in her eyes. "But . . . I don't want to! I want to marry Louis. I love him . . . not that other man. Why, he is a perfect stranger!" A sob tore from her throat. "I never knew Father could be this cruel! And Dionne, he told such lies about Louis! Louis would never do the terrible things Father said! He never would! He couldn't!

Gently taking Celeste's hand in hers, Dionne began speaking in what she hoped to be a soothing tone, "Celeste, your father has your best interests at heart."

"No, he doesn't! If he did, he would not force me to marry a man I did not love!" Celeste bolted upright in the bed. "I know what I will do! I will pack a small bag and run away. I'll go to Louis . . . we'll be married . . . and there will be nothing my father can do about it!" She then pressed her hand over her face. "Oh, no! I cannot do that! Louis isn't even here on Martinique right now. He had to go over to Union Island on business and won't return until next week. But I will leave Desirade when he comes back!" she swore adamantly.

Alarm spread through Dionne as she grasped Celeste by her shoulders. She could only hope that Celeste felt enough love for her father to realize what the consequences would be if she resorted to such rash actions. "No! You can't do that to your father! You will not do that to him! You know that his heart is not strong, and if you did something like that . . . why, it would kill him!"

Celeste glanced sharply up at Dionne. Her green eyes

flickered at what she knew to be the truth. When she spoke again, her words, although laced with anger, were unconvincing. "No . . . he wouldn't . . . die. He just uses his heart condition as an excuse to get his way around here! To make me do what he wants . . . instead of what I want to do!"

"Now, Celeste," Dionne chided gently, "you know that is not true."

"Then why is he forcing me to marry a man I do not love?"

"Because he loves you and has your best interests at heart." Dionne stared at her hands knotted together in her lap. A pang of wistfulness stabbed at her. At long last she and Celeste were sitting together, talking. It was almost as if they shared their old friendship, the bond that had been long ago forgotten. It was a pleasant feeling—or would have been if the situation with Celeste were not so serious. Suddenly clearing her throat, Dionne asked, "Did your father tell you why he opposed your seeing Louis Fairmount?"

"Yes, and I suppose he told you all about that silly report he received on Louis," she spat hatefully.

"I do not know that he told me all about it, but yes, he did mention it," Dionne reluctantly admitted.

Celeste's misery was so painful that she grasped Dionne's hand, momentarily forgetting the animosity she had felt toward her for so long. "But, Dionne, if only you knew Louis, you would know that report was nothing but a fabrication, something someone made up for spite or out of jealousy. . . . Or it could possibly be something that my father invented to prevent me from marrying him!"

"Look at me, Celeste," Dionne demanded, anger smoldering in her gold-flecked eyes. "And please be honest. Think about your entire life, all that your

45

father has done for you." Dionne waited a moment, then continued, "Now can you honestly say that you believe your father does not love you?"

"No."

"Then any actions your father has taken are for your own good. He would not invent a report about Louis just to keep the two of you apart. He would never do that; he's not that sort of man." Dionne could see that she was beginning to get through to Celeste, that the girl was listening to what she actually had to say.

"Perhaps I was wrong in accusing Father," she said softly. "But what if someone else started those lies about him? Louis is so handsome and charming, it could very well be that another woman wanted him for herself, and when he spurned her, she told lies about him! That is possible, you know," she added pointedly.

"Yes, I suppose it is." Dionne had a feeling deep down inside that Celeste's wishful thinking was anything but the truth of the matter, but how could she convince her otherwise? Suddenly, she had an idea, one that just might prove to be successful.

"Celeste," Dionne began slowly, "do you mind if I offer a suggestion? And it could possibly prove what you just said about Louis is the truth." She wisely phrased it that way so Celeste would not think she was interfering. Knowing Celeste as she did, that would be the wrong thing to do.

She looked at her hopefully. "No, I don't mind—especially if there is a chance it will help Father change his mind about Louis."

"Before I make my suggestion, first tell me . . . has Louis ever actually proposed to you?"

"N—no . . . not yet. But I know he would—that is, if Father had not meddled in my life!"

Dionne took a deep breath. "What do you think about pretending to go along with your father's request? And by the way, you could at least give Christopher Phillips a chance. Who knows? You may even find him attractive. I met the man a few minutes ago . . ."

"Go along with it? Pretend that I am anxious to marry a stranger? A man I don't even know? No! Never . . ."

"No, now wait a minute, hear me out," Dionne rushed to say. "Perhaps my saying to go along with his request was the wrong way to put it, because I believe your father would become suspicious if you had a sudden change of heart. However, if you were civil to the man Uncle Andre selected for you and if you attended a few social functions with him, when Louis returns from Union Island, he would surely hear about it." She eyed Celeste warily. "I am sure you are well aware that your father intends to keep a close eye on you, that he will not allow you through the gates of Desirade unless you are well chaperoned. And, if Louis is innocent of those charges in that report and if he truly loves you, then I'll wager that he will stand up to your father and demand your hand in marriage. However, if the charges against him are true . . ."

"But they're not! They couldn't be!"

"But if they are," Dionne persisted, "and you ran away with him, then your life would be ruined and your father would die from a broken heart. I have no sure way of knowing, but I would imagine if you remain stubborn and refuse to even meet Christopher Phillips, you will not leave Desirade unless you are his wife. And then . . . there is still yet another possibility. . . ."

Celeste squirmed uneasily. "And what is that?"

"If you refuse to meet Monsieur Phillips, there is

always the possibility that he would break the engagement and return to his home without you."

"And what would be wrong with that?" Celeste asked eagerly, a devious light shining from her eyes.

Dionne sighed deeply. "Your father believes that report. If I were to hazard a guess, if all else failed, he would probably send you away so that you would never see Louis again. Perhaps to France to live with distant relatives."

Celeste slumped back against her pillows as if all the wind had been knocked from her lungs.

Dionne slowly rose to her feet. "Well? What is your answer?" she pressed. "What do you want me to tell your father?"

Celeste nervously chewed on her bottom lip as she thought about all the possibilities Dionne had mentioned. Finally, she squared her shoulders and said, "All right. Tell Father I will be down. But . . . not right now. I will join them for dinner." She sniffed and wiped her eyes. "I must look a fright. I have to have time to make myself presentable."

Dionne nodded and turned away slowly. Nothing else remained to be said. But once outside of Celeste's bedroom, she breathed a deep sigh of relief and sagged wearily against the wall. For a while there, all of her old feelings of affection for Celeste had returned and her conscience now played havoc with her. She felt guilty over having deceived Celeste that way. But no, Dionne reasoned to herself, her suggestions had not been deliberate deceptions. Every word she had spoken had been the truth. It was not her fault Celeste refused to believe the reports against Louis. But then, she recalled the old saying that love was blind, and she supposed in Celeste's own way, she loved Louis. Bearing that in mind, it was little wonder Celeste did not believe Louis

48

was capable of doing those terrible things. But for now, that was all immaterial. At least she had been able to convince Celeste not to try and run away. That was a step in the right direction. She could only hope Andre would understand why she'd had to make such vague promises to his daughter.

Chapter Four

Not one to shirk her duties and wanting to keep her mind occupied, Dionne made her way down the stairs and across the foyer toward the kitchen so that she could check on dinner preparations. But as she approached the study, she could not help but notice the doors were standing wide open. Pausing, she was suddenly undecided over what to do. There was no doubt in her mind that Andre would be anxious to know if she had been able to talk some sense into Celeste, but with Christopher Phillips in there it would be next to impossible to get the older man alone. If she asked to speak to him in private, in all likelihood Christopher would probably think she wanted to tell him what had happened between them earlier. Then there would be no telling what Christopher would say or do. She would not put it past him for a minute to resort to lies. But still, Andre had to be made aware of Celeste's decision and the part Dionne had played in it.

Then, Dionne's brow drew into a worried frown. She could not help but wonder if she were hesitant to go in because of her dread of making Christopher suspicious. Or was it the fact that she did not care to see him again? If it were anyone else, Dionne knew she would simply march in there and tell Andre that a matter of importance had come up and she needed to see him.

She pressed trembling fingers to her temples. You have to stop this, Dionne! You have to stop behaving like a frightened schoolgirl! But deep down inside, she was vaguely aware of another feeling about Christopher, one that she was not yet ready to acknowledge.

Taking a deep breath and pushing all of those worrisome thoughts from her head, she marched staunchly into the study. . . . Excuse me, please, I—" Seeing Andre sitting back at his desk, her eyes quickly swept the room. "W—where . . . where is Monsieur Phillips?"

Andre surveyed her judiciously before speaking. "Christopher will be back in an hour or two. He went to his ship for his personal belongings. He was going to stay on board, but I insisted that he and his father and grandfather come out and stay with us for as long as they are here."

Dionne blanched at the thought of having that man beneath the roof for an indefinite period of time. It would be next to impossible to avoid him without appearing rude. Not that she cared what he thought about her, but Andre would be sure to notice it.

With a rapid wave of his hand, Andre motioned for Dionne to step forward. "Well? Did Celeste talk to you? Or better still, were you able to talk to her?"

Dionne assumed the chair on which she usually sat. "I think so. At least she has agreed to meet Monsieur Phillips. But she will not come down until dinner. And quite frankly, I think that is a wise idea because she has been crying and her eyes are red and swollen."

"H—has she reconciled herself to the fact that Louis is out of her life for good?"

Finding it impossible to look at the hope shining in his eyes, Dionne pulled her gaze from his. "No, far from it. In fact, I am afraid I gave her false encouragement."

52

"How?" he asked worriedly.

Dionne quickly related their entire conversation. Upon finishing, she added, "It goes without saying I do feel guilty for leading her to think there still might be a chance for her and Louis." Noting the thoughtful expression on Andre's face, she asked, "You are not angry at me, are you? Honestly, Uncle Andre, I didn't know what else to tell her!"

Andre's brow narrowed as he thought about what Dionne had told him. Finally, he said, "No, I'm not angry at you. Quite the contrary. I believe you bought us some precious time." He reached out and patted her hand, then squeezed it gently. "I don't know what we would do without you, Dionne. You are so much like your mother, never thinking about yourself; instead, always placing everyone else's interests first." His voice took on an infinitely compassionate tone. "I know how difficult Celeste has made it for you at times, and I suppose that is why I am doubly grateful for your help. Few people would forget the snide remarks Celeste has directed toward you so many times in the past."

Dionne lowered her head, not from the praise but from the shame that suddenly washed over her. She picked at a piece of imaginary lint on her dress. If Andre only knew how she really felt about Celeste, he would not be so quick to praise her. Not that she disliked the girl; she didn't, not really, but Dionne detested how Celeste had caused her father so much unnecessary worry. Being spoiled was one thing, but being deliberately cruel was something altogether different.

Dionne took a deep breath. It was time for honesty. "U—uncle Andre, you give me too much credit."

"I don't think so."

"Please, hear me out. W—what I did was more out of affection for you. I abhor the way she treats you, the

53

way she makes you worry. At times, I would like to turn her over my knee!" Dionne added adamantly.

To Dionne's surprise, rather than a stern admonishment, Andre laughed boisterously. "Yes, at times so would I. But," he chided gently, "you place too much blame on her. I am the one who is responsible for spoiling her so much, so I should shoulder the blame. There is one other thing you should keep in mind. It is a human fault to judge others when one has no experience. I suggest you remember this conversation a few years from now, when you are married and have children of your own. It is easy to make mistakes. No one knows until the shoe is on the other foot what lengths he or she will go to to protect his children and to give in to their wants and needs, and sometimes what they merely think they need."

The protests to deny that she would ever find herself in that situation died on her lips when she saw the kind expression on Andre's face. To deliberately disagree with him over something that would probably never happen would, in effect, place her in the same company as Celeste. It was best to let the subject drop. "Perhaps you are right, Uncle Andre."

He smiled benignly, as if dealing with a temperamental child. "I see you are not thoroughly convinced, but time will tell, Dionne, time will tell." He suddenly pushed his chair away from the desk. "Enough of that. Tell me, what you think of Christopher?"

"W—what do you mean?" The abruptness of his question took her by surprise.

"Why, your opinion of him."

Dionne began to stammer, "Why . . . I . . . to be honest . . . I . . ." She swallowed hard and tried to think of something that would not be a lie. "I doubt if I have ever met anyone like him."

Andre beamed. "Neither have I." He had no idea

their statements meant the exact opposite. "My hopes are high that once Celeste meets Christopher she will forget all about that pompous fool."

Dionne's eyes shifted uneasily. Yes, pompous fool. That description fit Christopher Phillips perfectly.

"There's no doubt in my mind," Andre continued without pause, "Christopher is just the man to do it."

Wanting no part of this conversation, Dionne stood. "If you will excuse me, I have duties I have to see to." She forced a smile. "After all, we are having three extra people for dinner."

"Yes, of course." He called to Dionne just as she was about to leave the study. "You are planning to dine with us tonight, aren't you?"

Dionne nervously wet her lips. "N—no. I thought it would be best if I had dinner in the kitchen with Lucy."

"Nonsense! I want you at the table. You are a part of our family, and besides, there is always the possibility that Celeste will change her mind. If that happens, I will need your presence to help smooth things over."

"As you wish, Uncle Andre," Dionne said softly, hoping her expression did not betray the distress she felt at his request.

Christopher walked alongside Andre's wheelchair as they made their way to the dining room. He deliberately shortened his naturally long strides. His well-groomed appearance was incongruous with his sun-tanned skin and the way his dark curly hair seemed to become more unruly with each step he took. He was well aware of the fact that his hair seemed to have a mind of its own. Regardless of how carefully he brushed and combed it, the many years of manning a quarterdeck and having his hair assaulted by the crisp sea breezes prevented it from remaining well-groomed for any length of time.

Upon reaching the dining room, Andre quickly looked to see if Celeste had come downstairs yet and was disappointed to see that she had not. Then a smile tugged at his lips as he realized she intended to make a grand entrance—or at least that is what he hoped she had in mind to do. He glanced at the elaborately prepared dining table, beaming his approval at Dionne who stood quietly beside the serving table. Then he glanced sharply back at Dionne and frowned. She had pulled her long brown hair into a severe bun, and while her gown was neat and definitely presentable, the starkness of its design did nothing to enhance her pretty features. It was as though she had deliberately tried to look matronly and ten years older, and if so, she had certainly succeeded.

Dionne felt her chest swell with pride at Andre's unspoken praise. The table did look nice. It was adorned with a delicate lace cloth, their best silver, the finest Chinese porcelain money could buy, fragile crystal wine goblets and water glasses, three centerpieces of freshly cut flowers, and four elegant silver candelabra. She was satisfied that at least the Phillipses would not think this arranged marriage Andre proposed was because of dire financial straits.

"Miss Martin! How nice to see you again." Christopher's mouth curved into a taunting smile as his eyes took note of her stark appearance.

Dionne suddenly wished she had chosen a more attractive gown. If for nothing else but to show him that her status here was more than just ordinary hired help. Deliberately avoiding Christopher's mocking perusal, she looked to see if his father and grandfather followed him.

Addressing her question to Andre, she asked, "Excuse me, sir, I thought there would be two other guests for dinner?" Her thoughts quickly raced. If the other men were not present, it would ruin her seating arrangement. She had strategically placed the table settings so that she would be seated on the same side of the table as Christopher, with his father between them. She did not want to have to sit by or across from him.

Andre's face darkened with disappointment. "I'm sorry, I should have told you earlier. Christopher's father and grandfather were detained in Fort-de-France on business and will not be here tonight." He took his place at the table. "Has Celeste been told that dinner is ready?"

"Yes, sir. She will be here in a few minutes."

Andre nodded, swallowing his worry that she would not appear. "Christopher, will you please see Miss Martin to her chair?"

Christopher acknowledged his request with a slight nod. "It will be my pleasure." He stared momentarily at Dionne with amusement still shining from his eyes, then started around to the far side of the table where she stood.

Suddenly uncomfortable beneath his disconcerting stare, Dionne stammered, "Th—this is your p—place, sir," indicating the chair she now stood behind. She had intended for Christopher to sit at Andre's left so that he could see Celeste when she made her entrance. It was much to her chagrin that Christopher pulled out the chair that was directly across from his chair. "Oh, no, this one is for Celeste," she protested.

"If you don't mind, I would rather she sit beside me," he said, smiling, ignoring the smoldering look Dionne threw at him.

Dionne had no recourse but to accept the chair.

Noting the stiffening of Dionne's shoulders, Christopher deliberately allowed his hands to graze her slender waist. But it was to his surprise that a tingling sensation

57

ran the length of his arms when he touched her.

Andre, impatiently waiting for his daughter to appear, directed his conversation at Christopher after he sat down. "Did Edward or William happen to mention what time they will arrive tomorrow?" He shook his head. "It's too bad their business took longer than they anticipated. I had hoped we would all be able to enjoy a pleasant evening together."

Christopher squirmed uncomfortably. "Sir, I have a confession to make. I lied to you."

Dionne lowered her lashes and bit back the smile that threatened. So, he was an admitted liar along with his many other faults. His revelation certainly did not surprise her.

Andre looked at him curiously. "Oh?"

"My father and grandfather were not detained in Fort-de-France on business. They remained there by choice."

Andre calmly digested that bit of information. "Have I offended them in some way?"

"Oh, no, sir," Christopher was quick to reply. "The truth is, they did not want to overwhelm your daughter. They felt it might make her feel she was under too much scrutiny if too many Phillipses were present tonight. But I do bring a peace offering from my father." He reached into his pocket and removed a beautiful string of pearls. Holding the pearls entwined in his fingers, he asked, "Do you think she will like them?"

"Why not ask me, Monsieur Phillips?" Celeste questioned from the doorway. She smiled when all eyes flew in her direction. She was beautiful and she knew it. Her emerald gown enhanced her milk-white complexion, the green lights of her hazel eyes, and the russet shine of her gleaming dark hair. She had carefully interwoven a delicate string of pearls into one long braid, then coiled it around the crown of her head. The bodice of her gown was trimmed with fragile lace and the neckline plunged just enough to hint at the beauty that lay beneath it.

For just an instant, Christopher's eyes widened in surprise as he glanced at Dionne then back to Celeste. Even with Dionne's abject attempts to deliberately make herself unattractive, the resemblance between the two was startling. If he did not know better, he would have sworn the women were identical twins except for the obvious few years' difference in their ages. But from what he understood, they were not even related. His eyes flickered toward Andre and a ghost of a smile appeared on his lips. He could not help but wonder if the man had had more starch in him during his younger years than he had given him credit for. But then, he had heard of several occasions where a man had found a place in his home for a bastard child—if indeed this was the case.

Quickly regaining his composure, Christopher hurried across the room to where Celeste stood waiting. Inclining his head, he took her hand in his and brushed his lips across it, then offered her his arm. "Had I known you were so beautiful, I would not have waited so patiently."

Dionne raised her hand and rested her forehead on it in order to conceal the sarcastic roll of her eyes. Good Lord, she thought scornfully, I cannot believe it. He's actually fawning over her like a . . . a mongrel in heat! This is certainly a different face than he presented to me a little while ago. But then, I should have expected as much. Not only is he a barbarian, but a flirting scoundrel as well!

Celeste tittered and coquettishly fluttered her small hand fan. "Are you attempting to flatter me, Monsieur Phillips?"

"Please, do not be so formal. Call me Christopher."

"As you wish . . . Christopher." She had deliberately lowered her voice to a throaty tone so that his name would sound sensual and seductive.

"As for my attempt at flattery, my grandmother always stressed that I should give credit where credit is due." He flashed a wide, brilliant smile. "If the truth sounded like flattery, then I suppose I am guilty."

Dionne suppressed a contemptuous snort while keeping her eyes riveted to the table. Oh, you silver-tongued devil, she thought to herself. And you, Celeste, I never knew a broken heart could heal so quickly. For just a brief instant, her sympathy went out to Louis Fairmount. She wondered if he would ever know how quickly he had been replaced and forgotten.

Suddenly, a knot formed and tightened in the pit of Dionne's stomach. She brought her eyes up, allowing her gaze to follow Celeste and Christopher as they became acquainted. For one brief moment, an intense longing swept over her. She desperately wished that a man would look at her just once in her lifetime in the same adoring way Christopher looked at Celeste. It suddenly seemed unfair that one person could have so much and another person could have so little. So many people said she and Celeste bore an uncanny resemblance. Yet, Celeste was so beautiful and she was so plain. They had the same slender build, but it seemed as though Celeste's figure was femininely soft, shapely, and almost voluptuous, while her own shape was much like a slender reed. Their eyes were both hazel in color, but Celeste's at times appeared to have green and gold lights shining from them, while hers were neither brown nor green. And their hair. One would think that brown hair was ordinary, as Dionne felt hers was. But Celeste's hair, especially the way it was arranged tonight, resembled a russet crown.

Why did it always seem people who had everything never appreciated it? Celeste had a father who adored her, a lovely home, beautiful clothes, and two men—even though both were scoundrels, vying for her hand. And her attitude was that she could care less. Oh, it was all so unfair! Dionne could feel the color drain from her face as she realized what had just happened. For the first time in her life, she had been jealous of Celeste. Then, realization swept over her that it was not jealousy she felt; instead, it was a longing, a wishfulness for something she could never have.

Later that night, Christopher sat on the private balcony attached to his guest room, unable to sleep. He reclined in a chair, his hands laced together behind his head and his feet propped on the wrought-iron railing, his mind meticulously studying the events of the day.

His disagreement at the marketplace with Andre's housekeeper had been a sore beginning. Her manner had been so snobbish and self-righteous that it had infuriated him almost beyond reason. But now, he had to admit a mistake had been made. He had jumped to the wrong conclusion. It was not Dionne Martin who objected to the sailors patronizing the local shops; instead, from what he gathered during the evening's conversations, the blame belonged to the matriarchs of Martinique society. As for that episode in the garden, he knew he ought to feel ashamed. Looking back on it now, he was the one who had made a fool out of himself, but his male pride had demanded he take it all out on her. She had tried to tell him her real identity, but he had refused to listen. He had never before deliberately been so rude to anyone like that. Christopher did not know why, but he felt she could possibly be an ally in the future. Perhaps a small gift would be in order; it might soothe her injured feelings.

The only thing that had gone right was his meeting Andre. He liked that old man. But, for the life of him, he could not figure out why he had such a worried look about him.

Then Christopher's thoughts settled on Celeste. He did not see the irony in the fact that she filled his thoughts last. Lighting a cheroot, he inhaled deeply and watched as the smoke formed a foglike cloud between him and the faint glow of the waning moon.

The enormity of it all settled heavily over him. Celeste was everything he had expected her to be. But, somehow, he found it difficult to think of her as his future wife. In his opinion, she was a spoiled, tittering female—just the kind of woman he had always avoided getting seriously involved with. Women like that were fine for an affair or for a romantic fling, but not for marriage. Just the thought of spending the rest of his life with an empty-headed woman was unsettling. The coming years stretched out in his mind until it felt as though his head were about to explode. Could he live with a woman like that? Could he share her bed and have faith that she could produce sons he would be proud of? Could he face years of her senseless prattle and coquettish ways?

Christopher suddenly felt cold. It was as if the blood in his veins had turned into ice water. He had to stifle the desire to make a mad dash for his ship and never return to this island. But he quickly pushed those feelings aside, realizing he could never do anything like that. His father and grandfather had given their word, and their word of honor was much more important than any reluctant feelings he had.

He sighed heavily and squared his shoulders. He would have to give their marriage a try, and later, if he found it unbearable, he could always return to the sea.

The sea was his first love anyway. Also, if he later decided he needed a more substantial relationship with a woman, that could be arranged too. But for now, he would have to take it one step at a time.

At that moment, he caught a glimpse of movement from the courtyard. Frowning, he rose quietly to get a better look. From the dress the woman wore, he realized it was Dionne walking in the garden. Then suddenly, without warning, a deep sense of sadness drifted over him as he saw her drop her head onto her hands and the soft sounds of weeping assailed his hearing. Something tugged at his heart, making it lurch painfully. Soon the few clouds that caressed the sky scudded across the face of the waning moon and all was dark. From somewhere in the distance came the mourning cry of a bird, then all was silent.

Chapter Five

Deep in sleep, Dionne smiled at her pleasant dream. She felt a euphoric sensation—warmth, happiness, a void where unpleasantness did not exist. Realizing she was not alone in her dream, she felt protected, loved, wanted. A man was with her. He held her tightly in his arms. Then a frown drifted across her brow as the swirling fog seemed to dissipate and in its place appeared a soft, glowing light.

The man's hoarse whisper broke the gentle silence. "Do you have to leave me now?"

"Yes, but I don't want to go." She rested her head against his masculine chest. She did not think it strange that his face remained a mystery.

Strong arms wrapped around her slender waist and held her tightly. "Stay with me, my love," his deep voice murmured huskily. "Your lips taste like heady wine and my thirst is not yet quenched." He moved away slightly, and his eyes devoured and caressed each of her features. "Oh, how I marvel at your beauty, the sooty length of your lashes, the upturned tilt of your nose, the blush of your cheeks, the sensual pulse at your throat. Stay with me, Dionne," the soothing voice urged. "Stay with me and together we will walk toward Paradise."

"B—but . . . who are you? Where is Paradise? I am happy here! I have always been happy here . . . that is, until you came. Now . . . I don't know. I am so confused."

The man's form became a tall silhouette standing in front of a brilliant burst of light. His voice was mesmerizing, "Stay with me."

"But . . . who are you?" Dionne pleaded, strongly aware the man was drifting further and further away. The light had become so bright she had to shield her eyes from the halo glare.

His voice echoed, "You know who I am."

Suddenly disturbed by a shaft of early sunlight streaming through her bedroom window, Dionne scowled sleepily at the offending brightness. She squeezed her eyes tightly shut and turned over, hoping to be able to go back to sleep so that she could recapture the pleasant but disturbing dream she had been having.

But the longer she lay there, the harder the bed became, until she could have sworn the mattress had been filled with pebbles instead of soft cotton. Raising herself up on one arm, she pounded the pillow in hopes of making it more comfortable, but within a matter of moments it too began to feel as though it had been carved from stone. Finally, filled with total aggravation, she sat up on the side of her bed, shoved the mosquito netting aside, then yawned and stretched languidly.

What a strange dream, she thought as she slowly shook her head. It seemed so real . . . and it was almost as if I knew the man.

Then a feeling of foreboding washed over her. The dream was forgotten as she remembered all that had happened the previous day. Regardless of Celeste appearing to accept her upcoming marriage to Christopher Phillips, there would still be trouble. Of that, she was sure.

66

Standing, she padded across the floor and looked out the window. Usually, mornings were her favorite time of day. She had always felt that with morning came a fresh start, a new beginning, a chance to complete anything that had been left undone from the day before. But not this day. Never had she felt such a fierce turmoil burning through her, and suspecting what lay ahead of her and the entire Debierne household for the next few weeks, she had an overwhelming feeling that the confusion had just begun.

Dionne pressed her fingertips to her temples. Perhaps it was fortunate that she had arisen early. With more people in the house, she would have extra duties to perform. There was every possibility that Christopher's father and grandfather would arrive in time for breakfast. Would Lucy be prepared? Yes, the cook always seemed to be prepared for any emergency that might arise. What about their rooms? No, thank goodness they had been made ready yesterday.

She threw up her hands in protest. What am I doing? Dionne mentally chided herself. Here I am, working myself into a bundle of nerves and I've not even dressed or had my morning coffee. I've never been able to think clearly until I've had my coffee.

After hastily but carefully attending to the regime of her morning toilette, Dionne stood at her closet trying to decide which one of her dresses she should wear. It had to be nice, one that she would not normally wear around the house if guests were not present. She had no idea how Andre would present her to his old friends—whether as the housekeeper or, as he sometimes did, as a member of the family. Regardless, she could not look like a street urchin. Bearing all of that in mind, she finally chose a lilac-colored dress with white cuffs and collar, trimmed with plum-colored piping and lace.

Giving the cheval glass one last quick glance before she went downstairs, Dionne grimaced with annoyance. Her hair looked terrible. She had styled it into a chignon, a very practical and durable coiffure, but curly tendrils of new growth had loosened from the bun, producing an overall frumpy effect. It would never do. Grasping the hairbrush, Dionne hurriedly ran it through her hair, but the more she brushed, the more it curled. Finally, in exasperation, she rummaged in the top bureau drawer and found several ribbons that matched the color of her dress.

Giving one last glance at the mirror, she ran her fingers through her hair and said aloud, "I guess I will just have to braid it and allow it to hang down my back." She shuddered at the thought. "I have no choice—even if it does make me look like I am twelve instead of twenty-two!" She stared at the hairbrush and then back at the mirror, smiling triumphantly. "Since it is impossible to know when William and Edward Phillips will arrive, I think I had better braid it while I have my coffee. I may not get another chance until much later if I don't."

After making that decision, she grabbed the hairbrush and ribbons, and with long gleaming hair flying behind her, she hurried from her room and down the spiral stairs.

"Good morning, Lucy," she said with forced cheerfulness as she entered the kitchen and filled a cup with steaming hot coffee. "Is anyone else up yet?"

"And good mornin' to you, missy," the cook greeted Dionne amicably, still riveting her attention on the huge mound of sourdough she was kneading. "No, it appears we're the only ones up this morning. That is 'cept Nigel and Francis. Nigel is tidying the monsieur's study and I sent Francis down to the smokehouse for a side of bacon and a shank of ham." She wiped a fine bead of perspiration from her forehead with the back of her hand. "As for me, I'm just gettin' fixin's ready for breakfast so it'll only take a little while to cook when the rest decide to rise and shine." She peered curiously at Dionne. "Do you think Miss Celeste will be up 'fore noon, or perchance you think she might decide to show her face early since her intended husband is here?"

"How do you know about Christopher?" Dionne asked, surprised.

Lucy grinned broadly, her white teeth gleaming against the darkness of her skin. "Why, Miss Dionne, you ought to know better than to ask a question like that! You know the walls of this old house have ears." She turned her attention back to the sourdough and muttered under her breath, "Lord, yes, does it ever have ears!"

Dionne chuckled. That was true. Rarely did anything happen here at Desirade without the entire household staff knowing about it. And by evening, the entire plantation would also know Celeste was about to be married.

"I don't know if she will get up early or not. It would not hurt to be prepared though." Dionne glanced at the cameo watch she always wore on a ribbon around her neck. She noted that it would be at least thirty minutes before Andre would arise. "Do you need help with anything in here?"

"Lands no, child," Lucy chuckled. "Even if I did, I wouldn't dare ask you for it until you've had another cup of coffee." She wrinkled her nose. "I don't know how you can drink that nasty stuff. Coffee by itself is bad enough, but the way you and the monsieur like it . . ." She shook her head questioningly. "Phew, it's more than half chicory."

Dionne laughed aloud as she filled a small silver pot. "Maybe it isn't the coffee so much; maybe it is all the sugar we get to use." Teasingly, she wiggled her brows as she licked the sugar spoon after adding several heaping spoonfuls to the coffee.

"I reckon so. I reckon you have to have somethin' to disguise the taste!"

Laughing, Dionne picked up the tray. "I am going to the garden to have my coffee. If you need me, send Nigel or Francis."

Lucy tapped her foot impatiently. "Now, missy, this kitchen has been my domain for more years than you've been born. I can manage just fine!"

Impulsively, Dionne leaned forward and affectionately kissed the woman on her cheek. "I know, Lucy. But I only wanted you to know that I will help if you need me."

Lucy shooed her with a dish towel. "Scat, child, 'fore I change my mind. And if you don't mind my saying," she called after Dionne as she went out the door, "you ought to do something about your hair. Why, it's standing up all over your head!"

"Don't worry, I intend to braid it while I'm having my coffee," Dionne replied over her shoulder.

Hurrying through the courtyard, Dionne made her way to her most favorite place, a small gazebo located on the far side of the garden. It sat at ground level, its thatched roof proving to be beneficial against the blazing tropical sun. The two-foot-high lattice work enclosure was covered with fragrant rose bushes. If any breeze blew, the gazebo's simple design allowed it to drift gently through.

She entered the gazebo and sat on a soft padded bench that ran the entire length around the lattice work. Placing the coffee tray beside her, she filled her cup, took a sip, then leaned back for a moment to enjoy the solitude.

Instead of the peaceful feeling the surroundings usually brought, the events of the previous day lingered around the edges of her mind until, finally, she had to pay attention to them. With a shiver of vivid recollection, the image of Christopher's face loomed in her memory. Suddenly, her hand began to tremble as she raised the cup to her lips. Christopher's face! Was he the man in her dream? How could that be? She disliked him intensely. Why on earth would she dream of him, especially in such a sensual way?

Still deep in thought, Dionne brought the massive length of her hair over her shoulder and separated it into three equal portions, then began braiding the long tresses. She was unaware of anyone else's presence until she felt soft lips press against the back of her neck.

Completely startled, she whirled around. Her eyes widened in surprise, then narrowed into anger when she realized Christopher had been standing behind her. He was the guilty culprit who had kissed her.

"You!" she shrieked.

Christopher rolled his eyes and groaned. Then he began to chuckle. Not necessarily with amusement, but rather ironically. "I know you're not going to believe this," he finally said.

Outraged, she sputtered, "Believe what?"

He shrugged sheepishly. "I thought you were Celeste."

Folding her arms together, Dionne scoffed, "Oh, you—you have your nerve! Do you honestly expect me to believe that ridiculous story again?"

Quickly, he bounded into the gazebo and stood in front of Dionne, his legs splayed into a powerful stance. He grasped her arms and peered deeply into her eyes. "I hope you do believe me, because it is the truth."

Struggling free, she faced him, so furious she could

71

hardly speak. "You certainly have your nerve!"

Christopher's slight embarrassment was quickly turning into annoyance, not so much at her but at himself. He shifted uneasily. "Look, surely you know how much you and Celeste resemble each other."

She replied icily, "It has been mentioned to me before, but I don't agree."

Christopher stated stubbornly, "I don't care if you agree or not, but what I said is a fact. Just as it is a fact that I mistook you for her."

"Do you make it a habit to go around molesting innocent women?" she demanded to know.

Clearly agitated, Christopher threaded his fingers through his hair. "No, ma'am, I don't," he drawled sarcastically. "It so happens, I haven't had to molest a woman for years now!"

Although she spoke quietly, her voice held a tone of cold contempt. "You undoubtedly must think I am an imbecile if you expect me to believe that nonsense! Almost every time we've met, you have attacked me!"

Christopher glowered at her, then his temper seemed to instantly abate. "Look, the simple fact of the matter is I awoke early this morning, and believing everyone was still asleep, I came downstairs, and since there were a few things I wanted to think about, I came out to the courtyard. Then . . . when I saw you sitting here, I decided this would be the perfect opportunity to get further acquainted." Seeing the still-doubtful expression in Dionne's eyes, he swallowed hard. "Honestly, I thought you were Celeste."

"Why, I . . ." Dionne's voice broke when she saw the light of sincerity shining from his eyes. Suddenly flustered, she stiffened, momentarily abashed. Finding the crisp blue of Christopher's eyes disturbing, Dionne pulled her gaze from his. Her mind raced furiously over

72

the excuse he had given. Finally she drew a deep breath and said, "All right, just for the sake of a doubt, let's say you did mistake me for Celeste, I still maintain your behavior was atrocious. A gentleman simply does not . . . pounce on a lady from behind and kiss her!"

In spite of the seriousness of the situation, Christopher found Dionne's indignation slightly amusing but terribly straitlaced. Folding his arms together, he raised his brows in a mocking perusal. "Then I certainly would appreciate it if you explained how it is supposed to be done." He grinned mischievously. "Better still, perhaps you could show me." For the life of him, Christopher did not know why he suddenly pulled her into his arms and smothered her lips against his with demanding mastery.

Caught completely off guard, Dionne could only momentarily stand there. His hands held her in a viselike grip. His lips at first were brutal, then they became softly tantalizing, eager but not aggressive, challenging yet surprisingly gentle. Her senses reeled. Blood pounded through her veins, straight from her heart, and her knees began to tremble. She could feel herself melting against his hard masculine body. Then a voice from somewhere deep inside demanded she return to her senses. She wrenched from his embrace and struggled for a breath, for it felt as though all air had disappeared from her lungs.

"H—how dare you!"

Christopher felt wounded to the core at the frightened look she gave him. He could not understand his actions much less explain them, but he felt he had to try. "Miss Martin . . . Dionne, I'm—I'm sorry."

"Sorry?" she mouthed in anguish. She frantically looked for a way to make a hasty retreat. Christopher stepped in front of her, blocking her path. She then tried to dodge past him on his other side, but he caught her wrists and refused to let go.

"Let me go!"

"Not until we get a few things settled."

"There is nothing to settle!" Dionne knew she had to escape him. But she also knew she had to escape from her own ragged emotions, the emotions he had stirred by his embrace and sweet but passionate kiss.

"Yes, there is!"

Dionne forced contempt into her voice. "You have your nerve, Christopher Phillips! You mean to say you honestly expect me to agree to stay here so that you can . . . molest me again!"

"I'm not going to hurt you, Miss Martin. But I cannot let you go, not while you are so upset. You have to hear me out, you have to."

"No, I don't!"

"Yes, you do, I'm not going to let you go until you calm down and listen to reason." The fear he saw in her eyes made him feel terribly ashamed. His voice grew husky. "I will tell you this once and only once. *I apologize.* And so help me God, I think you are the first woman I have ever apologized to in my life. I meant what I said a while ago. I did mistake you for Celeste. But when you said what you did about 'pouncing on a lady from behind,' you looked so serious and strait-laced . . . well, I only meant to tease you. For the life of me, I don't know why I kissed you. I suppose I could invent a cock-and-bull story about your beauty and charm completely mesmerizing me and that I lost all of my senses, but we both know I would be lying. And that is one thing you will discover I do not do—at least when it comes to something like this." With those words, he released her, turned, and was gone.

Dionne could only stand there, staring open-mouthed at his retreating form. A strange feeling swept over her as she realized she had seen a side of Christopher Phillips that few people had ever seen. Dionne knew she should still be angry, furious beyond reason, but try as she might, she could conjure nothing but a feeling of sad regret, a longing, a feeling that she had lost something that was never hers to lose.

Dion
smoothl
only of
handyma
care of th
handmaide
had guests,
wife and two

as a wide, pleased smile stretched across his f...
clasped each man's hand in a hardy shake. "H...
years has it been now?" He waved his o...
"It does not matter. The point is it...
long!" William grasped his old fri...
agree wholeheartedly! We'...
not happen again, but...
related, I suppose t...
that!" "How is yo...
she remai...
The...
cep...
...eer's
...m to help.

All mornin...   worker's children had
stationed hims   front porch with strict orders
to immediately let them know when a carriage
appeared at the end of the long drive leading toward
the house.

Ever mindful of his responsibility, Boomer ran
inside the house and shouted, "Carriage be comin'!
Carriage be comin'!" He jumped up and down
excitedly.

Dionne and Francis hurried into the foyer. Francis
took his place at the door, and Dionne sent Boomer
scampering back to the kitchen to receive his reward—
a huge piece of sugar cake.

Andre, hearing the commotion, came out of his
study and propelled his chair toward the front door. He
was very anxious to see his old friends. "William!
Edward! Come in, come in!" his voice boomed loudly

ce. He
ow many
uestion aside.
has been far too

nd by his shoulder. "I
have to make sure it does
then, since we are soon to be
here is not much of a chance of

ur beautiful wife?" Andre asked. "Does
in good health?"

nan beamed. "She is as lovely as ever, and ex-
for having to use a cane occasionally, she is as
healthy as the day we married forty-seven years ago.
Jeannine sends her regrets that she could not accompany us. Although she never said it, I'm sure it broke
her heart to think she would have to miss her grandson's wedding."

Edward looked casually around and spoke up, "By
the way, where is that son of mine? I thought he would
be here to meet us."

Clearly puzzled, Andre said, "Why, I don't know. He
left Desirade early this morning. I merely assumed that
he went to Fort-de-France to drag the two of you out
here."

William and Edward exchanged glances. "No, we
haven't seen him, not since yesterday," Edward said,
then he shrugged his shoulders. "It's not important. I'm
sure he will return shortly. He might have forgotten
something on board ship."

Dionne stood across the foyer, politely waiting until
the men had exchanged their greetings. My, what
handsome gentlemen, she thought. It was difficult to
believe that William Phillips, the patriarch of the

family, was nearing seventy years of age. Even though he had silver-colored hair and a few lines in his face, the only other clue to his advanced age was his slightly stooped shoulders. Her eyes then studied Edward, Christopher's father. His black hair was threaded with silver strands and the laugh lines around his mouth and eyes revealed what she considered to be a good-natured disposition. It was easy to see where Christopher got his towering height; she guessed that his father stood well over six feet tall. And she figured William had been that tall too at one time—that is, until age had stooped his bones. It was clearly evident that William, Edward, and Christopher bore a strong family resemblance.

Andre began leading the way to his study. "Let's go in here and have a glass of brandy, or if you prefer, a pot of coffee. There are quite a few things I want to get caught up on. After we visit for a while, I will introduce you to my daughter, Celeste." He glanced around. "Dionne, we will serve the brandy ourselves, but please bring us a pot of coffee, then go tell Celeste to come to my study in about an hour."

Dionne curtsied. *"Oui,* monsieur."

Andre admonished gently, "Speak English, child. We want to make these gentlemen feel at home."

"Yes, sir."

William laughed and said, not reproachfully but as a statement of fact, "That is one of the problems of Englishmen living in a city that is predominantly French. Most people think we speak and understand the language well."

Edward threw back his head and laughed heartily. "Even though the Phillipses came to America in the early 1700's, my father still refers to us as Englishmen."

"Now, son, I disagree. We are Americans and proud

79

of that fact, but a man should never forget his heritage."

Upon entering Celeste's bedroom, Dionne looked around in dismay. Celeste was still fast asleep and her room looked as though a disaster had struck. Clothing had been strewn everywhere. She marched angrily across the room and threw open the heavy drapes that prevented the bright sunlight from streaming through.

Celeste sat up and squinted one eye sleepily. "What are you doing? Close the drapes!"

Ignoring her, Dionne then stomped saucily to the tiny room adjacent to Celeste's and threw open the door. Her mouth settled into a thin line upon seeing Nettie sitting on a rocking chair doing needlework. "What are you doing sitting in here when Celeste's room looks like a pigsty?"

"B—but . . . but, mademoiselle . . ." the girl stammered, her eyes wide with fright. While Mademoiselle Celeste was hard to please and almost always spoke to her in a snappish voice, the housekeeper seldom raised her voice to anyone, much less to her. She scrambled to her feet. "The mademoiselle gave me strict orders not to disturb her this mornin' until I heard her movin' about." Tears threatened in her eyes.

Dionne instantly regretted scolding Nettie. She was terrified of Celeste, and rightly so, the way Celeste screamed and yelled at her constantly. Naturally she would do as she had been told. Dionne's tone softened, "Well, all right. You can clean her room later. Right now, I want you to prepare her bath."

Celeste sat up on the side of her bed, yawned sleepily, then scratched very unladylike. "You have your nerve! Barging into my room at the crack of dawn . . ."

"Crack of dawn my foot! It so happens to be eleven

o'clock, and your father wants you downstairs in his study within the hour. Christopher's family is here and they are anxious to meet you."

With that, Celeste scrambled to her feet. "They're here? Already?"

"Yes, they are."

Celeste yawned again, attempting to feign her excitement. "I didn't know it was so late. After you left the dinner table so abruptly last night, we retired into the parlor."

Dionne stiffened. It was true. She had left rather hurriedly, but it had been sickening the way Celeste and Christopher were fawning over each other.

Celeste's voice droned on, "They played two boring games of chess before Father became sleepy. Then, Christopher and I went for a walk in the garden . . . where we became rather well acquainted," she added smugly.

Now I see, Dionne thought. If in truth he did mistake me for Celeste this morning, it is no wonder he felt so free with his kisses.

"Tell me, what do you think of Christopher?" Celeste asked as she plopped back down on the bed and sighed.

"What do you mean?"

"Do you think he's handsome?"

Seeing in her mind the crystal clarity of his blue eyes, Dionne felt her knees begin to tremble. Finding that extremely upsetting, she shrugged and remarked offhandedly, "Oh, I suppose he could be considered attractive."

"I would say he is definitely handsome!" Celeste rose, strolled casually to her mirror, and peered at her eyes. "Shadows! My God! I have shadows under my eyes!" She sniffed. "Probably from all that crying yesterday. When I have my nap this afternoon, I shall have to place cucumbers on them."

Dionne began to place the strewn clothing on hangers, deliberately presenting her back to Celeste to prevent her from seeing the expression on her face. She could not believe how Celeste was behaving. What had happened to her deep love for Louis Fairmount? It took all of her willpower to keep from making a sarcastic remark.

Celeste moved to her closet, studied the gowns for a moment, then removed a beautiful yellow organdy one. "I think this would be perfect for today . . . then tonight, I shall wear my lavender silk. Oh, it is so difficult to choose, since I hardly have anything decent to wear. I simply must have some new gowns! If only I had known what Father planned to do, I would have been prepared."

Dionne raised her brows questioningly. There were already so many gowns in the closet that there was hardly enough room to hang all of them.

"A moment ago you only mentioned Christopher's family. Is he waiting in the study too?" Celeste asked curiously.

"I don't think so. I overheard something about him going into Fort-de-France this morning. Did he not mention anything about it to you?"

"No, he didn't," Celeste replied crossly.

Not wanting Celeste to slip into a bad mood, Dionne forced a smile and said, "I must say, you are taking all of this remarkably well. I am sure your father will be so proud of you."

Celeste reclined onto her chaise lounge and dramatically pressed her hand to her brow. "One does what one has to do." Then she flung her arm to her side and tears brimmed in her eyes. "Oh, damnation, Dionne, there's no need to pretend around you. I do love Louis! I swear I do! But . . . I also have to reconcile myself to the fact that there is every possibility I will have to marry

Christopher." She closed her eyes and shuddered visibly. "Thank God he is not only wealthy, but handsome and charming as well. Last night I realized something very important. I know I am . . . shall we say, spoiled. I am also accustomed to luxury." She sighed heavily. "I am going to be completely honest with you, Dionne. There are too many ifs involved for me to follow my own heart. I may be spoiled and perhaps even selfish, but I do love my father. I love him too much to go against his wishes—even if it means giving up the man I love."

Dionne let out a visible sigh of relief. "I'm happy you feel that way, Celeste."

Celeste continued to speak, but it seemed to be directed more toward herself than to Dionne. "But if he was in good health, I might reconsider." Then she slumped dejectedly. "Who am I trying to fool? I forgot. I said that I would be completely honest—and I will. If Father was in good health and if I went against his wishes, in all likelihood he would disinherit me. I have no idea if you know it or not, but Louis is not a wealthy man, and even though I love him, I doubt if my love is strong enough for me to accept his poverty. However, if Father's suspicions prove to be false, I am sure he will make a place for Louis here at Desirade, and then one day, we shall inherit it all. . . . If that happens, I will have the man I love and the wealth I cannot live without." She laughed wryly. "So, in the meantime, I have to think with my head instead of my heart, even if it means pretending something for Christopher I do not feel. Of course, all of this is much easier to accept now that I know he is not a gnomish little man." She shuddered. "You cannot imagine my relief when I entered the dining room last night and saw him."

It was difficult for Dionne to contain her astonishment. This was one face of Celeste's she had never seen.

While her motives and declarations were far from admirable, at least they were honest, and for Celeste, that was certainly a step in the right direction.

"Oh, Dionne," Celeste cried as she suddenly rushed over to Dionne and hugged her. "Please don't think badly of me! I know you must think I am a terrible person at times, but I don't know how to stop being the way I am!"

"Now, hush, Celeste," Dionne crooned softly, her own eyes growing misty. "Your eyes will be all red and swollen again, and we certainly cannot have that." She urged the sobbing girl to look at her. "I don't think badly of you, honest I don't. I think you have been placed in a precarious set of circumstances and you are handling it extremely well." She removed a handkerchief from her pocket and dabbed at Celeste's eyes. "I mean this with all of my heart. I wish you nothing but happiness for the rest of your life—whether it be with Christopher or with Louis."

Celeste took the handkerchief and wiped her eyes and blew her nose. "Thank you, Dionne. Thank you so much! It helps for me to know that someone understands how I feel and why I have to pretend to be happy about my upcoming marriage to Christopher."

"Speaking of marriage, you had better hurry and get dressed. Christopher's father and grandfather want to meet you." She tried to look stern. "In less than an hour I expect you to come downstairs with a pretty smile on your face and looking absolutely ravishing!"

Walking slowly down the stairs, Dionne's brows knotted as she stopped and listened carefully. Laughter and shrieks of joy were coming from the front porch. Immediately curious, she hurried across the foyer and opened the door. Christopher was sitting on the front steps laughing, and almost all of the plantation workers' children were swarming around him.

"Children, children, please!" She clapped her hands together, then motioned for them to leave. "You know you are not supposed to annoy any of Monsieur Debierne's guests! Now, go on. Shoo!"

"But . . . missy!" several of them cried in unison. "We're not—"

Dionne forced her voice to be firm. "Now, you heard what I said." She tried unsuccessfully to ignore their disappointed faces.

Christopher caught two of the children by their hands when they sadly turned to walk away. "Wait a minute, children." He looked at Dionne. "They are not annoying me. In fact, I enjoy them and it is my fault they've clustered around me. If there are any scoldings due, I'm afraid I have to be first in line and Barney has to stand right behind me." He gestured toward his first mate, who was carrying goods to each workers' cabin. "That's Barney over there. I'm sure you remember him. He is the man who introduced us at the marketplace," he added slowly, wondering whether it was a good idea to bring up the events of the previous day.

Dionne would have recognized the man anywhere. "Yes, I remember him quite well. He is the sort of man who makes a lasting impression."

"We brought a few gifts back from Fort-de-France and somehow"—Christopher shrugged innocently—"three large bags of candy got mixed up with them."

Smiling, Dionne said, "Purely by accident . . . I'm sure."

He glanced down and winked at Boomer, who was standing right beside him, then turned his attention back to Dionne and said very solemnly, "Of course it was an accident. I have no idea how that candy got into the baskets."

85

Dionne peered at the open carriage in the driveway. With a quick glance she could see eight straw baskets completely filled with goods. "What is all of this?" She gave a wide sweep of her hand.

"Why, gifts, of course. I have something for everyone here at Desirade. And, naturally, that also includes the field workers."

Wondrously, Dionne shook her head. "Why did you bring gifts? I'm sure it was not necessary, Mr. Phillips."

Christopher chuckled. "So it's Mister, now, huh? That sounds so stiff and formal. What happened to Monsieur? I sort of liked the way you said it."

Uncle Andre instructed all of us to speak English . . . and you are avoiding my question."

"If you're not going to call me Monsieur, why not call me Captain?"

"As you wish . . . Captain. Now, back to my question. Why did you bring gifts? Are you by chance trying to buy friends? If so, my guess is you've been extremely successful." She nodded toward the children, all busy licking their peppermint sticks.

Christopher folded his arms and splayed his legs arrogantly. A teasing smile flirted with his mouth. "Oh, I'm not in the habit of buying friends. But I thought the gifts would be a good idea just in case someone decided to tell them that Miss Celeste was about to marry a barbarian." He stared intently, curious as to what her reaction would be.

Dionne boldly met his eyes and purred innocently, "Why, Captain, who in the world would give them an idea like that?"

His lips widened into a gleaming smile. This woman's opinion of him should not have made any difference, one way or the other. But judging from what she had just said, apparently the bitter animosity between them had eased, and that made him feel good.

Why? He did not know. She was just a household member of his future wife's home, and once he and Celeste married, their paths would rarely cross. He was just about to speak when Barney joined them.

"Good day to ye, ma'am," he said, removing his recently purchased wide straw hat and bowing low.

"And how are you?" she asked pleasantly. Dionne had not heard a Scottish dialect very often, and she found his manner of speech delightful.

"I be fine, thank ye, except for the heat." He fanned himself with his hat. "Last I recall heat like this, we were caught in the doldrums. Remember that, Cap'n Chris? I doubt if we sailed over forty leagues during two entire weeks. But when she finally blew, she blew hale and hardy."

"She?" Dionne asked.

"Aye, ma'am, the wind."

Christopher was quick to say, "I doubt if Miss Martin is interested in the hazards we face while at sea."

Dionne's voice held a challenge, but it echoed her amusement, "Oh, no, I find the sea very interesting. But, Captain, whatever happened to Mademoiselle? I particularly liked the way that word sounded."

Raising his brows, Christopher grinned and said, "Touché, Miss Martin. Shall we call it a draw?"

"Agreed, Captain Phillips, a draw it shall be." She turned her attention back to Barney. "I have no idea what your plans or commitments might be. However, if you like, you are more than welcome to join us for the noon luncheon." When they entertained it was a standing agreement for Lucy to prepare extra food for the guests' drivers and any servants they might have brought along.

Suddenly ill-at-ease, Barney cleared his throat. It seemed to him the invitation had been sincere, but after what had happened between the wee lass and the captain yesterday, she could possibly be trying to prove a point. Surely she didn't mean she wanted him to go inside the house and sup with them.

He finally found his voice, "I thank ye kindly, ma'am, but I still have these presents to pass out."

"The workers have waited this long; another hour or two will not hurt," Dionne argued. Then she fell silent, fully realizing, after what had happened the previous day, how her invitation must have sounded. She became strongly aware of Barney's discomfort and a slight stiffening of Christopher's shoulders.

"But, ma'am"—he adjusted his eye patch and looked to his captain for help—"it be too hot to eat right now."

Christopher had been watching Dionne, studying her closely to see if this were just her way of getting a piece of revenge, a way to pay him back for some of the things he had said and done. He could not be sure, but since there was a chance, he was not about to let Barney be made a scapegoat. He interrupted their conversation, not rudely but in an easy manner, "Barney, why don't you go sit under that shade tree over there, then after you cool off a bit, I'm sure Miss Martin can arrange to have a tray sent out to you." He glanced toward Dionne. "I am sure that is all right with you."

She detected a sudden condescension in his attitude, but she was relieved that he had been gracefully able to extract the foot she had placed in her mouth. "Oh, yes, it is perfectly fine with me."

Barney breathed a visible sigh of relief. "Now that I think about it, I could stand to have a bite to eat . . . but like the Cap'n said, under the tree where it is cool," he hastened to add.

Suddenly, it was Dionne who felt ill-at-ease under Christopher's thoughtful scrutiny. A flicker of apprehension coursed through her. Her first instinct was to flee inside the house, but that could in effect prove Christopher's suspicions if he had any. Be calm, Dionne, she told herself. Just be calm and act as though nothing out of the ordinary has happened.

Nonchalantly, she removed her cameo watch and glanced at the time. "Lunch should be served in thirty minutes." Then she thought miserably, Oh, why did I have to be so eager to prepare the dining table? That would have given me the perfect excuse to leave.

Christopher reached out and took the delicate timepiece in his hand. "This is pretty. I don't think I have ever seen one quite like it before."

Dionne's breath caught in her throat. Slowly, she raised her eyes to meet his and saw in them the same reaction caused by his touch. Her heart beat raggedly beneath her breast and her skin tingled as though she had been standing next to where lightning had struck. Christopher dropped the cameo as if it had burned him.

"Why, thank you," she finally murmured. "It belonged to my mother. It's my most cherished possession. I only remove it when I—" Suddenly embarrassed, her words faltered. She had intended to say she never removed it except to take a bath, but that would have sounded far too personal. Instead, she finally managed to stammer, "I—I seldom remove it." Frantically looking around for a way to extricate herself from this awkward situation, Dionne spied the gifts in the carriage. "What do you have here?" she asked, in what she hoped to be a normal voice as she hurriedly walked toward the carriage.

Christopher was also relieved that the awkward moment had passed. "Oh, many things." He offered an explanation as he fell in step with Dionne. "Naturally, I know that slavery has been abolished here, but I also realize each of the plantations have workers and most do not pay their workers well."

Dionne stiffened. "Although I know very little about the actual running of Desirade, I am sure the monsieur is extremely fair. He is not a cruel man, and it is my understanding that even before slavery was abolished he treated his people very well."

"After meeting Andre, I'm sure he did and still does. But please be fair to me. Having never met the man, it was something I couldn't know. Before I left New Orleans, I asked a friend of mine, who owns a plantation, what the workers could use the most and he offered several suggestions." He began removing items from the baskets. "I brought pots, cast-iron skillets, and material for the workers, and a few personal items for the household staff."

Her heart lurched. That is all he thinks I am, she thought. Just a member of the household staff, only a single step away from being a slave. Stop it, Dionne! Stop it! What difference does it make what he thinks about you? You care nothing about this man! Why, after all, he is Celeste's betrothed!

Christopher glanced at her and grinned sheepishly. He removed a small bundle from one of the baskets. "I even have something for you."

"Oh?" Dionne mouthed painfully as she accepted the package.

He then removed a ribbon from his pocket and dangled it in front of her eyes. "Before I went into Fort-de-France this morning, I went back out to the gazebo and found this. I decided, if you were in the habit of losing them, you could possibly be running in short supply."

Dionne opened the package and, to her surprise, found a multitude of variously colored hair ribbons. "Why . . . they . . . are beautiful. Th—thank you, Mr. Phillips."

"You are very welcome." He was pleased that she found them attractive.

Dionne swallowed hard. She could not stand here a moment longer. This man stirred too many emotions within her. Emotions she had no business feeling. She had forgotten her place, her station in life, and this man could never be a part of it. Oh, how she wished his wedding were tomorrow. Then he would be gone and she would never have to see him again.

"Please," she mumbled, "you will have to excuse me. I am sure Lucy could use some help in the kitchen." She turned and walked away with stiff dignity, well aware that Christopher's eyes followed her retreating form.

Chapter Seven

Dionne sat at her bedroom window, staring up into the sky as the stars slowly faded from sight and the sun began to peek lazily over the distant horizon. She longed to go out to the gazebo and try to sort through all of the troublesome thoughts that seemed to pound continuously through her mind. But the gazebo was no longer her sanctuary; it had been invaded by a predator. There would be no safety there until Christopher Phillips had left the island.

The Phillipses had been at Desirade for four days—four days fraught with tension and frustration. Until Celeste and Christopher were married, Dionne knew she would not be able to feel a moment's peace. Even though Dionne had had several conversations with Celeste and felt fairly confident she would not do anything foolish, there was always the possibility the girl would try to go to Louis or at least attempt to get a message to him.

Then there was the situation with Christopher. Since the day he had given her the hair ribbons, she had tried to avoid him with a polite determination but had not been completely successful. She had certain duties to perform and with those duties some personal contact had been unavoidable. Still, she thought about him often and that evoked too many uncomfortable emotions, emotions she did not understand, emotions she dared not allow herself to feel. There was an odd animal magnetism about the man that attracted yet frightened her.

Perhaps if he had not been so unpredictable everything would have been easier to place in its proper perspective. One moment he was jolly, laughing, and the most pleasant man she had ever seen. Then, instantly, his mood would change and he would become moody, sullen, and almost unbearably arrogant, just as he was the day she had first met him. And just last night, when no one else was looking, she had observed him watching Celeste, and the darkest, most foul expression had slipped across his face, making him look almost sinister.

Dionne mused aloud. "Why would he look at her that way? It was almost as if he hated her. No, perhaps hate is too strong a word. Resentful? Yes, that is it. He resents her. But why? Unless there is a woman in New Orleans whom he loves and he was somehow forced to agree to this arranged marriage. And I wonder why he would agree to an arranged marriage? Oh, I realize there have been arranged marriages since the beginning of time, but usually, they are arranged when the people involved are mere children, sometimes even at birth, and then it is done to cement family ties. Since that is completely illogical, especially with what I know about the reason why Uncle Andre arranged the marriage for Celeste, the only other possible solution is that Christopher agreed to the marriage because he needs the Debierne fortune."

Her shoulders slumped dejectedly. That was ridiculous. She recalled how Celeste and Andre had accompanied the Phillipses to the docks to see the *Blue Diamond* and *Emerald Tempest* in the harbor at Fort-de-France, how boastful Celeste had been over the magnificent ships, and how Andre had even appeared to be thoroughly impressed. And from what she had overheard, the ships were only two in a fleet of ten. No, it was highly unlikely that Christopher was after the Debierne fortune. Unless they had kept any financial difficulties well concealed, the Phillipses appeared to be far more wealthy than Andre.

Dionne could not let it alone. Her thoughts continued to wander. If Christopher did not need to cement family ties and if he did not need the Debierne fortune, then why would he agree to marry Celeste, a woman he did not know and probably did not love, when in all likelihood he could have had any woman he wanted? Celeste was definitely a beautiful woman, but when Christopher had agreed to marry her, he did not know that. Since money and family were out of the question, what other possibilities could there be?

"Perhaps I should voice my doubts to Uncle Andre?" She quickly discarded that idea. "No," she mused thoughtfully. "He has enough to worry about with Celeste. He does not need me to invent obstacles."

Hearing the huge clock softly chime the hour, Dionne looked at her watch with surprise. Where has the time gone? she wondered. At least one hour had passed, one more hour applied to the many that remained before the frustration would end. But how much longer will that be? How much longer would Christopher and his family be here? There had been no mention of wedding plans.

Taking a deep breath, Dionne pushed all thoughts of Christopher and Celeste from her mind and began her morning toilette.

Andre waited until everyone had finished their dessert before he made his announcement. "Celeste,

95

Christopher"—he glanced at William and Edward—"I have something to say to all of you. There has been a development in Desirade's business that requires my attention. Although it is not immediately pressing, it will have to be attended to before long. I only mention my business matters because it concerns all of us. I believe the time has come for us to discuss the wedding plans."

For just one brief moment the smiling facade Celeste had been presenting slipped, and dread took its place. Then, just as quickly, her face became a mask of acquiescence. "Father, could we not discuss this matter in a more civilized place than the dinner table?"

He nodded. "Perhaps you are right. May I suggest we all retire to my study?"

Christopher's expression was completely unreadable except for a minute darkening of his eyes.

Andre picked up a small bell and rang it. Immediately Dionne came into the dining room. After Christopher's first night at Desirade, she had been having her meals in the kitchen with the other servants.

Andre said pleasantly, "Celeste, please show our guests into the study. I shall be there shortly, but first I have a few instructions to give Dionne."

He waited until they had gone before motioning for Dionne to step closer. "We are about to discuss plans for the wedding. I want you to bring refreshments into the study, then I want you to remain there with us. Just blend into the background so that you will know what the plans are. I think it will be easier this way than for me to tell you later what happened and all that was discussed." Doubt flickered in his eyes. "I know Celeste seems to be taking all of this quite well, but I have a nagging voice in the back of my mind trying to tell me that everything is proceeding too smoothly. Raising his brows, he sighed deeply. "Do not be alarmed by anything I say in there. My plans are to invent a few problems—nothing major, but serious enough to necessitate our hasty departure from this island. I am afraid Christopher will hear rumors, and after getting to know him, I am more afraid now than ever he would not be willing to marry a woman with a blemished—" His words quickly broke off when Celeste returned to the dining room.

"Father, are you coming?"

"Yes, child, I do wish you would give me a hand with this blasted chair, though. It doesn't seem to be rolling as well as it should."

Celeste glanced at Dionne. "Will you please bring some refreshments into the study?"

"Oh, I've already told her to do that." He smiled at his daughter and smacked his hands together. "Let's go, child. They're waiting for us."

As they entered the study, the Phillipses all stood up until Celeste had sat down. William moved to stand beside her. He removed a black jewel box from his pocket and said in a proud voice, "I want everyone to know that the union between these two young people meets with my approval. And this, my dear, is a token of my feelings." He raised the lid to reveal an elegant diamond and emerald necklace.

"Oooh!" Celeste gasped. With trembling hands she removed the necklace from the box. It had been fashioned from a pendant design, one fabulous emerald surrounded by at least twenty sparkling diamonds. "Why . . . it is beautiful!" she gasped breathlessly. "How can I ever thank you?"

He chuckled and fondly patted her hand. "It is just a mere token of the affection I feel for you, my dear." He glanced at Christopher. "Come here, lad, and fasten this around your future wife's lovely neck. I'm sure you can handle the intricate clasp better than I can."

For a brief moment, Christopher just sat there. His eyes narrowed and his back became ramrod straight. A muscle flicked in his jaw, then a tight smile appeared on his mouth. Finally he rose, placed the necklace around her neck, then brushed his lips lightly across her cheek.

Andre noted Christopher's apparent reluctance. A worrisome thought crossed his mind that he might have waited too long to call this meeting.

At that moment Dionne entered the room, carrying a coffee and sweetmeat-ladened tray. After she made available cigars and brandy, she took a chair close to the door, where hopefully she would be inconspicuous yet still able to hear all that was said.

Clearing his throat, Andre began, "Gentlemen, Celeste, I will be as brief as possible. I received word today that my presence is required in New Orleans. While I do not have to go, it would be to my advantage if I did. Which brings us to the situation at hand . . . this impending marriage. Christopher, Celeste, I am sure the two of you would like to have more time to become better acquainted, but since this business opportunity is too good to refuse, I will have to leave Martinique as soon as I possibly can. Therefore, I propose that the ceremony take place as soon as possible." He paused for a moment to draw a deep breath. "To be more precise, tomorrow or the next day is what I have in mind."

Celeste gasped. That would never do! She could not marry Christopher until Louis had a chance to return. Even though Christopher was extremely wealthy, she loved Louis, and if there was any chance at all that the reports were untrue, she had to grasp for it. Her life with Louis would not be as luxurious as with Christopher, but they would still be able to live in the same manner to which she had been accustomed. But it would be impossible if she were already married to another man. Somehow, some way, she would have to think of a way to stall them.

"B—but . . . but . . . that is impossible!" she stammered.

"Why?" Andre asked.

Rubbing her arms in a worried fashion, she began pacing the floor. Christopher's eyes rested heavily on her. "Why . . . it is impossible to prepare for a wedding with only a day's notice! I will need a wedding gown, there are guests to invite, food to prepare. . . ."

"I was thinking of having just a simple ceremony."

Celeste knelt by his chair, her anguish sincere. "Father, please, I do not want to sound defiant. . . . I have accepted your wishes. And . . . I am sure Christopher will understand when I say that at first I was upset when you told me about this arranged marriage. I think any woman would have been. But I have found him to be kind, gentle, and yes"—she blushed coquettishly—"even attractive. And I believe we will be happy together, but please, please do not deprive me of the dream I have had all of my life."

Christopher spoke up, "Sir, I have a problem with a hasty wedding myself. It appears you have forgotten what I told you the first day we met."

Andre gazed at him intently. "Yes, I suppose I have. Perhaps you should refresh my memory."

"Remember I told you I have a load of cargo to pick up in Brazil."

"Oh, yes, now I recall your mentioning it."

"Considering the nature of the cargo, I have to depart by the end of next week. I would not want to leave a new bride behind and I could not take her with me. I deal with natives down there, and shall we simply say it would not be a suitable place to take a woman."

Edward said, "Son, I have a possible solution to that problem." He glanced hastily at Celeste and smiled. "I

99

do understand your objections and only offer this suggestion as a possible alternative." He turned his attention back to his son. "I could pick up the cargo for you."

Christopher shook his head. "No, that wouldn't be fair to my crew, since they share a portion of my ship's profits."

"I suppose I could sail the *Blue Diamond.*"

"I appreciate the offer, Father, but she's my ship—and I am her captain."

Celeste let out a sigh of relief and showed her gratitude by flashing Christopher a brilliant smile.

William had been listening carefully. "Andre, how long do you think it will take to wrap up your business?"

"Two or three months at the least."

Edward rubbed his chin thoughtfully. "I am sure Andre would not want to leave Celeste behind for that long. I know if I had the responsibility of raising a daughter by myself, I wouldn't." He shook his head. "Looks to me like there is no other possible choice but to set the date for about six months from now."

Andre's shoulders slumped and disappointment swept across his face. "I suppose you will all think I am nothing but a foolish old man, but I had hoped for an earlier wedding. I am reasonably sure that William feels the same as I do. Neither of us is getting any younger . . . and I hope to see a grandchild before I leave this earth."

William snorted good-naturedly and looked at his grandson affectionately. "I would like to see a child of Christopher's myself!"

"Wait a minute!" Andre declared excitedly. This was proceeding exactly as he had hoped. "I have an idea and I believe it is a damned good one!"

"Father!" Celeste scolded. "Watch your language!"

"Well, it is a good idea," he sheepishly repeated. "Christopher can go ahead and set sail to that heathen coast of Brazil, and we can go with William and Edward when they return to New Orleans. The wedding could take place there, and you could have time to plan the beautiful wedding you've always wanted. Then when Christopher returns from Brazil, the two of you can be married!" Smugly, and with a triumphant gleam in his eyes, he leaned against the back of his chair and folded his arms as if daring anyone to find fault with his suggestion.

Celeste chewed thoughtfully on her bottom lip. "B—but all of my friends are here. They will miss my wedding."

Andre leaned forward and said, with quiet emphasis, "Daughter, this is a give-and-take world. Think of it this way: Your home will be in New Orleans with Christopher. You will make new friends there. Why, I am sure Jeannine, Christopher's grandmother, will introduce you to all of the right people. And it might even be that your wedding is the social event of the year." Andre knew his daughter well, and if anything would make her agree, that idea would.

Celeste quickly but carefully pondered his suggestion. All she needed was a little more than a week. That way, she would know one way or the other with whom her future would lie. "Well . . . if you promise we can stay here until after the Summer Festival. That way, I can say good-bye to all of my friends."

Andre realized this was the best he could do. He did not want to appear unreasonable. "It meets with my approval, as long as you gentlemen agree."

"I have no objections."

"Neither do I. In fact, it sounds very agreeable."

All eyes flew to Christopher when he stood and spoke in a quiet but firm voice. "It so happens I don't agree—*yet."* He took Celeste by her arm, urging her to stand and join him. "Gentlemen, I am afraid I will have to beg your indulgence for a few minutes. There is something I have to discuss with Celeste in private." He asked politely, "My dear, will you walk with me in the garden?"

"W—why, yes, Christopher, of course." Celeste was stunned, not knowing what to expect. "Father, gentlemen, w—will you please excuse us?"

The men, having no other recourse, nodded in agreement.

Once outside, Christopher turned to Celeste. "Now, my dear, we have to face the moment of truth."

Celeste tittered and fluttered her fan. "Christopher . . . my, you sound so serious."

"I am serious," he said with a chuckle. "For a moment in there I felt like a fat rat surrounded by three hungry cats. And, I might add, I didn't relish the feeling."

She agreed. "They did seem rather eager, but I am sure they have our best interests at heart."

"Oh, I'm sure they do, too, but we are the ones who will have to live our lives—not your father, or mine, or my grandfather." His mellow baritone was edged with concern. "I think you ought to know that I have had doubts about this arranged marriage. And I also think we have to get a few things straightened out before we go any farther."

Celeste stared up at him and, with honest sincerity reflecting from her eyes, asked, "Do you think I haven't had any doubts?"

"I'm sure you have. That is one of the reasons why I asked you to come out here. I have to know, without any undue influence from your father or from mine, if you have any objections to marrying me."

"Why do you want to know?" Suddenly she was

nervous and apprehensive. She felt threatened. Her hands moved quickly to the necklace that felt so good around her neck.

His voice was resigned, "Because I could not, in good conscience, marry a woman who cared for another man."

Biting her lip, she looked away. "W—what makes you think I care for someone else?"

"Let's not play games with each other, Celeste." There was a bitter edge of cynicism in his tone. "I have heard rumors in Fort-de-France, rumors about you and another man. I want to know if there is any truth to them."

A cry of warning screamed through her mind. She knew her entire future hinged on the next few moments. Christopher had given her the golden opportunity to tell him about Louis. All it would take was one word and she would be free to marry the man she loved. But what if Louis was a scoundrel as her father claimed? What would happen to her then? Regardless of her love for Louis, her pride would never allow her to marry him if he were only interested in her father's wealth. And, if she told Christopher the truth now, he would not want to marry her. What position would that leave her in? What would be her chances of capturing a suitable husband in the future if two men had scorned her in the past? If only she could think of a way to stall Christopher until she could find out about Louis!

"Am I to assume, from your silence, that you do care for another man?" he asked coldly.

Celeste's mind worked at a furious pace. She had to think of a reasonable explanation—and quickly. Suddenly, she had a devious but inspiring thought. She clamped her hand across her mouth and pretended to stifle sobs.

"Celeste? Are you all right?"

"Yes . . . I . . . no! No, I am not all right!" She dropped her head onto her hands and sobbed. "How could she do this to me, Christopher? How could she betray me? How could she betray my father?"

Puzzled, Christopher's brow wrinkled into a frown. "What do you mean, *she?* What are you talking about?"

"Why . . . Dionne, of course. I am referring to her."

At the mention of Dionne's name, Christopher felt a knot form in the pit of his stomach. Slowly, he asked, "What does your housekeeper have to do with it?"

Celeste had to stall for a few minutes. She desperately needed time to formulate this incredible idea. "Please . . . I need to sit down. The shock of all of this has made me feel faint."

"All right, the gazebo is right over there." He took her arm and escorted her to the tiny garden house.

Celeste took a deep, shuddering breath and began slowly. "I have to admit your question caught me by surprise. I never thought it had gone this far." She demurely slipped her hand into Christopher's.

Christopher chuckled wryly. "In all honesty, Celeste, you have lost me. I merely mentioned that I have heard rumors in town, rumors about you and another man. I only wanted to know if you cared for him. Then all of a sudden I am faced with a mountain of silence, then babblings about your housekeeper and how she has betrayed you and your father. I wish you would explain this to me."

Celeste deliberately made her speech faltering, "Of course you need an . . . explanation . . . and I will try, although it will . . . be difficult. First of all, there is absolutely no truth to the rumors about me and another man. But tell me, who is the man . . . this time?"

"This time?"

It was all Celeste could do to keep from cackling with glee. Her hastily thought of plan was working perfectly. "Yes. Unfortunately, it has happened before." Feeling laughter threatening, she deliberately turned her gaze from his.

Christopher was stunned. He could not explain his feelings, but suddenly it was as if he did not want to hear what Celeste had to say. He gave an anxious cough. "The name I've heard linked with yours is Louis Fairmount."

"Oh, no, not him!" She wrinkled her nose and wrung her hands together. "I never dreamed Dionne would deliberately try to destroy my reputation!"

Some compelling force drove Christopher to demand answers, even though each time Celeste spoke, a strange sensation of pain stabbed through him. "Will you please tell me what you are talking about!"

"I will try—although it is difficult for me to understand, too." She drew a ragged breath. "You see . . . several months ago, I discovered that Dionne has been pretending to be me."

"She what?" he mouthed incredulously.

Celeste nodded. "Yes, as incredible as it sounds, she has. And from what I have gathered since then, her masquerade has been quite successful."

Christopher shifted uneasily. "Why don't you start at the beginning? Maybe it would be less confusing." It was not that Christopher could not understand; instead, he had the vague sensation of not wanting to understand.

She sighed and gave a resigned shrug. "I have really tried to be tolerant about Dionne, but I am afraid this time she has gone too far. You see, Dionne has always been jealous of me. She is jealous of my clothing, my jewels, but most of all, I suppose she has been even more jealous of the relationship I share with my father. From what I've overheard through the years, her mother had to marry a man just to give Dionne a name. It is nothing I know for sure, but I suspect her mother deceived that man and tried to pass her bastard child off as his own. When that failed, naturally the man resented Dionne, and I think . . . he even mistreated her. Then when her father—or rather, stepfather—died," she added pointedly, "Dionne's mother secured a position with my father. Dionne immediately began to think of my father as her own. I'm sure you have heard her refer to him as Uncle Andre?"

"Yes, yes, I believe I have," Christopher admitted reluctantly.

"Which is completely ridiculous, because we are not even related." She paused for effect, but a warning voice whispered in her head for her not to act overly dramatic. "As the years passed, she wormed her way further into Father's heart. Then, when her mother died, how she convinced him to allow her to remain on as housekeeper I will never know, but she did."

Christopher's voice came strangled, "Are you trying to say she loves your father?"

"Yes, she loves him." Then it dawned on Celeste what he meant. She rushed to say, "Oh, no, not that way. It isn't a romantic love; it is the kind of love a daughter would have for her father. I really think—at times—she imagines she is me. And what makes the problem even worse is our uncanny resemblance. Why, I've even caught her wearing some of my gowns and jewelry!"

Christopher knew all too well about their resemblance. "What does your father have to say about all of this?"

"He does not know." She placed her elbow on the back of the bench and rested her forehead against her

106

hand. "I have purposely kept the truth from him. I'm sure you are aware he has a weak heart, and I will be the first to admit that he is very fond of her. I am afraid if he discovered what she has been doing, it could—it could . . . be too much for him. I've tried to ignore her deceptions in the past, but I doubt if I can any longer." Celeste was so caught up in the role she now played that tears filled her eyes.

"Let me make sure that I understand you correctly. Are you saying these rumors about you and Louis Fairmount are the results of her pretending to be you?"

"Yes," she whispered, "that is exactly what I am saying. I have been extremely foolish for not putting a stop to it—because it has happened once before. A few months ago we had a party and invited a son of one of Father's business associates. We had quite a few other guests and I did not spend much time with . . . that young gentleman—I would prefer not to mention his name. But a few days later i was visiting with a friend of mine and she wanted to know all about my romance with . . . that young man. Why, I had no idea what she was talking about! But, finally, I began to put two and two together, and after contacting some other friends, I discovered Dionne had actually been pretending to be me! Naturally, I confronted her about it, and she promised it would never happen again!" Celeste threw her hands up in the air with disgust. "But now she's still pretending to be me while seeing that—that . . . scoundrel, and my reputation is ruined!"

Remembering how Louis had always boasted that it made him feel so manly to comfort her, she leaned her head against Christopher's shoulder. "Dionne has betrayed me again!"

Christopher gently smoothed his hand over her wealth of dark hair. "I suppose you know your father has to be told about all of this."

She gasped, "Oh, no! I can't! And . . . Christopher, please, you have to promise not to tell him either!"

"But that woman is damaging your reputation!" he argued.

"I know," she whimpered miserably. "But, considering my reluctance over telling him about the little things, like borrowing my jewels and my gowns"—she closed her eyes and shook her head, pretending to imagine the worst possible consequences—"I shudder to think what it would do to him."

"Well, I suppose you have a point, but I don't like the idea of her getting away with this!"

"Neither do I, but thank God there is a solution in sight."

"Oh? How is that?"

"After the Summer Festival, everyone will know about our engagement and that I have left for New Orleans. . . . Then she can no longer pretend to be me."

Christopher was so upset over what Celeste had just told him that he did not take the opportunity to declare his own personal doubts, his personal reluctance about their upcoming marriage. In the space of a few short days he had grown extremely fond of Andre, and it infuriated him that anyone would take advantage of the man. "Maybe so, but we can't go off to New Orleans and leave him in the clutches of that woman! Why, there's no telling what she would do!"

Sudden panic filled Celeste. Perhaps she had been too convincing. "Now, wait a moment. Let's remain calm," she urged. "Let's think this problem out rationally."

Christopher raised his brows and chuckled, but it was without humor. "I'll have to admit, you are more calm about this than I would be."

"Maybe so, but the point is I cannot tell my father. The news could possibly kill him," her voice faded to a hushed stillness. Then, when she finally spoke again, it was with confidence. "Christopher, I have to ask you to trust me in this matter. I know Dionne—probably as much as anyone could know someone else. I also know that she loves my father dearly. I can honestly say I believe she would never do anything to deliberately or intentionally hurt him. I am sure she never stopped to realize the consequences of her actions."

"It's not just that, Celeste. There is a question that keeps going through my mind. She may not ever do anything to hurt him, but what about you? People like that have no conscience. If we are in New Orleans, there's nothing to prevent her from working on Andre—and she could possibly end up with Desirade. This sort of thing has happened before."

"I know, but my father is not a foolish man. He would never let that happen. I am confident she would never be able to persuade him to leave her his fortune, although I do think he should remember her in his will." Celeste continued to choose her words carefully. "I am sure once we leave the island, Dionne may even be able to obtain gifts from my father. But what can a few gowns or a few pieces of jewelry hurt? Absolutely nothing. My father is extremely fond of her, and even if she does wheedle a gift here and there, it will make him feel good, too, because he is a kind and generous man. And we can visit every now and then to see how he is doing." She turned to him solemnly. "I want you to give me your word that you will remain silent about this. And I promise, later, if we discover she is taking unfair advantage of him, I will pursue the matter then—even if I have to tell him the truth." She looked at him with soft amber eyes. "Please say you agree. For me?" she added pleadingly.

Christopher stared at her with astonishment. He could not believe what he had just heard. When he had first met Celeste he had figured her to be so much like many of the other women he had known—selfish and self-centered. But there were very few women who would have been so understanding in a serious matter such as this. What other woman would have so readily agreed to allow a person like Dionne to reap rewards such as gifts of jewels and beautiful gowns for her despicable deeds? He admitted to himself that he had been terribly wrong about Celeste. Perhaps marriage to her wouldn't be so bad after all. At least the marriage would begin with admiration and respect.

He spoke in a tone filled with awe but with a reservation, "All right, Celeste. We will try it your way. I only hope this decision does not come back to haunt us."

Celeste squealed with joy as she threw her arms around him. "Oh, thank you, Christopher! Thank you!" Then she blushed and lowered her lashes demurely. "Oh, I beg your pardon. You must think I am terribly forward."

Christopher laughed and said, just before his lips met hers, "No, I don't think you are forward at all."

Chapter Eight

Celeste anxiously paced from the foyer to her father's study, out and through the huge parlor and dining room, then she began the trek all over again. Every so often she would go to the front door, peer expectantly down the long drive, sigh with disappointment, then continue with her anxious pacing.

The days had flown by so quickly it was hard to believe the Summer Festival was now at hand. In the past they had always gone into Fort-de-France a week early so that she could attend the many social functions that were mere stepping stones leading to the great celebration on Festival night. Alas, but not this year. Oh, they had attended a few parades and had even given a small party here at Desirade, inviting her closest friends, but she had always been under the watchful eye of her father.

The entire household was in such an uproar over preparations for their journey to New Orleans that it had been impossible for them to take part in all the festivities. At least that was the feeble excuse her father had given her. But Celeste was no fool; she knew the real reason they had stayed so close to home: Her father had been afraid she would find a way to see Louis.

Celeste thought she had been most convincing in her

111

pretense of accepting Christopher and their marriage. Maybe she had, at first. But now her father knew differently. He had quite skillfully intercepted the messages she had tried to send to Louis through her personal maid, Nettie. However, that did not really surprise her. After all, he had taken such drastic measures just to keep her and Louis apart.

Celeste chuckled smugly to herself. Her father was none the wiser of her alternate plan, a plan hastily but brilliantly conceived after two of her messages to Louis had been intercepted. How she had ever thought of such an ingenious scheme so quickly she would never know.

Now, if only that package from her seamstress arrived in time, her plan would at least have a chance to work. But it would have to arrive soon, because she and Christopher would be leaving for Fort-de-France within the hour. Judging from his protective behavior over the past week, her father would have never allowed her to leave so early without a good reason, and what better reason was there than a personal invitation from Christopher?

She had carefully dropped hints so subtly that Christopher had unknowingly believed it was his own idea to invite her for a tour of his ship, the *Blue Diamond*. Then, later that day, he would escort her to a friend's house so that she could dress for the Festival. It had been imperative that Dionne not see her gown before tonight, and that would have been impossible if Christopher had not invited her to visit the *Blue Diamond* first. Apparently her father had seen no harm in allowing her to go on ahead without him, as long as Christopher was with her. And he was right. She could never take the chance of rousing Christopher's suspicions by slipping away from him—at least

112

not today—but tonight would be a different story altogether.

Christopher came down the spiral staircase. When he saw Celeste, his face brightened with a smile. "You look lovely this morning. I see that you are anxious to go. I've made arrangements for us to have lunch on the ship. I thought you would like that."

Her spirits sagged momentarily as she realized they would leave before the package arrived. Then, she summoned the courage to manage a happy smile. "Oh, yes! Lunch on the ship will be nice. And, Christopher, I am so excited I could hardly sleep last night. But I'm not sure which excites me more—visiting your ship, or the thought of the Festival finally arriving." She allowed her smile to slowly disappear. "I have to admit, I will miss attending the Festival next year."

"Who knows?" Christopher shrugged but not indifferently. "It may be that we can come for a visit about this time next year. That is, if you have recovered from our Mardi Gras."

She frowned. "But that is early in the spring."

"I know," he said laughingly. "But you have never celebrated Mardi Gras in New Orleans."

Not to be bested, she raised her brows and replied, "And you have never been to our Summer Festival."

He glanced at the huge grandfather clock. "No, and I may not if we don't get a move on. Are you ready?"

"Yes, except for my things."

She called for her servant. "Nettie, go find Francis and have him take my costume to the carriage. Be sure and don't forget anything. My shoes, my jewelry case, my parasol, my—"

"No, ma'am, we won't forget nothin' at all!" Nettie

113

replied solemnly.

"And be sure and put on a clean starched apron. We cannot have Rose's maid looking nicer than you, can we?" Celeste smiled when she thought about the note she had tucked into her dainty handbag. As soon as they reached Rose's house, she would slip it to Nettie, then the girl would have plenty of time to deliver it to Louis while she and Christopher were on his ship. It would work perfectly. It had to. It simply had to!

"Oh, no, ma'am, Irma won't look any finer than me!" She sashayed proudly. "I even made me a new dress out of the goods Mr. Christopher brought for me. Irma will turn green with envy when she sees me!" She giggled, then hurried to find Francis.

Amused, Celeste laughed. "Oh, my, it is simply amazing how much rivalry exists between Nettie and my friend's servants. Each one of the silly girls tries so hard to outdo the other."

Christopher chuckled to himself. Apparently, Celeste did not realize there was no difference between the servants and the women they served.

"Christopher, I have to see Dionne for a moment. Will you please be a darling and see to it that my hatbox is not crushed by my trunk. Francis is so scatterbrained at times his every movement has to be watched."

At the mention of Dionne's name, Christopher's lips settled into a thin white line. After what Celeste had told him that night in the garden, he could barely tolerate the devious bitch. Many times he had been sorely tempted to tell Andre what she had been doing. If it had not been for the fact that Andre's health was not good and that he had given his word to Celeste, he would have. He did not take it kindly that a woman such as she had placed Celeste's reputation in jeopardy.

"Don't worry, I'll see that everything is placed in the carriage very carefully," he reassured her.

Celeste knocked on Dionne's bedroom door and only had to wait a moment before it was opened. She swept through the doorway without waiting for Dionne to ask her in.

Dionne's expression revealed her surprise. "What are you still doing here? I figured you and Mr. Phillips would have left by now." She had been careful to formally refer to Christopher over the past few days; anything else would have been too forward. Just thinking of Christopher made her frown. He had been behaving so strange lately. So cold, so distant, it was almost as if he could not stand the sight of her. That in itself had not been too distressing. . . . No, that was not true, his behavior had upset her. But it was imperative they remain distant, especially after realizing she could become too emotionally involved with him. And that would have been a futile, if not impossible, situation.

"No, not yet. I have been waiting for something to arrive, something very important."

Skeptically, Dionne raised her brows. Knowing Celeste and how anxious she appeared to be about visiting Christopher's ship, it had to be something extremely special. "Important? How so?"

"It's a gift for you!" Celeste said excitedly. She placed her hands behind her back, crossing her fingers in the hopes that it would arrive in time.

"A gift? For me?" Dionne could not believe her ears. Then a cynical inner voice cut through her thoughts. She'd had a few surprises from Celeste before and they had not been too pleasant.

"Yes, a gift to show my appreciation for all that

115

you've done for me lately." She had chosen her words carefully so that Dionne would have no idea of their double meaning. She had decided, a few days ago, that Dionne had been taken into her father's complete confidence and that he must have told her everything. Her eyes narrowed slightly as she remembered all the private conversations she'd had with Dionne who, in turn, must have run to her father immediately, because he had been able to thwart each attempt she had made to get a message to Louis. Dionne's actions had, in part, been the inspiration behind her present scheme. However, even if she were somehow found out, she would still be able to make Dionne the scapegoat.

Dionne's eyebrows rose in amazement. Perhaps all of this had indeed brought them closer. "Why, it's not necessary to give me a gift. I'm only glad I was able to help."

"Oh, but I disagree; it is necessary. I don't know what I would have done without you. And I simply must ask you to give me your word that you will wear my gift to the Festival tonight."

"Wear it to the Festival? But . . . what is it?"

Celeste giggled mischievously. "I cannot tell you."

"You can't or won't?"

"Let's just say I don't want to spoil it for you. And I guarantee you will be surprised—pleasantly surprised," she added smugly.

Dionne hated to agree to something without knowing what it was. "B—but you don't even know what gown I plan to wear. It could clash."

"I am positive it won't. I honestly believe you will like it as much as I do." She clasped her hands together. "I will even go one step further: If you find my gift the least bit offensive or too garish, then you do not have to wear it. Agreed?"

"Well . . . I suppose so." Dionne did not know what

116

else to say. Once Celeste made up her mind about something, it was next to impossible to change it.

"Good!" Celeste started to leave.

"Wait a minute," Dionne said, laughing. "Do you really intend to not tell me anything else about the surprise?" Her curiosity had been aroused.

"No! I will only say that I know you will love it." Celeste was confident with that statement. Dionne would have to be a fool not to like the heavenly creation coming from her own personal seamstress. And a fool was one thing Dionne was not—at least not yet.

Completely stunned but wracked with curiosity, Dionne could only watch helplessly as Celeste hurried from her room.

A few minutes later, Celeste met Christopher on the front steps. She opened her parasol and walked toward the carriage. A satisfied smile appeared briefly on her lips when she looked down the driveway and saw her seamstress's carriage approaching at a rapid pace.

Dionne sat at her small desk, her chin resting on her hand as she thought about the purpose behind Celeste's visit. She was so deep in her thoughts that she jumped when a knock came at her door.

Aha! She had to come back to tell me more, Dionne thought, hurrying to open the door.

It was to her great surprise that Francis stood there with his arms heavily ladened with packages. Simone DuPree, Celeste's seamstress, pushed her way inside.

"Put the packages here." She pointed to the winged-back chair. "And please be careful! That is not a stalk of bananas you are tossing around!" She flashed Dionne a wide smile and placed her hands akimbo. "Now, as for you, mademoiselle, remove your clothing

117

so I can see what I have to work with."

Dionne stared at her with openmouthed astonishment. "You want me to what?"

Madame DuPree waved her arms impatiently, her many bracelets jingling noisily. "Hurry, hurry, we do not have long. I may have to make alterations."

Dionne finally found her voice. "Alterations on what?"

"Why, your beautiful new gown, of course! What else would Simone DuPree alter?"

"B—but . . . but . . . I didn't . . . order a . . . new gown!" Her eyes widened. "Is this Celeste's surprise?"

"*Oui*, mademoiselle! And such a beautiful one. I have worked day and night to complete it in time. But I am not a magician. Since I was not able to measure you, I might have to take a few tucks here and there."

"How did you know my size?" Dionne asked, thoroughly confused.

"Mademoiselle Celeste sent an old gown of yours. I measured from it."

"Oh, I see." So that is what had happened to her mint-colored dress. She had searched high and low for it.

Dionne gasped when Madame DuPree removed the garment from its delicate wrappings. It was the most beautiful gown she had ever seen. It was made of silvery lace sewn with tiny sparkling beads and shimmering stones that looked almost like diamonds, and lined with a smoke-colored material. Madame DuPree then handed her a delicate matching-colored chemise made from the softest batiste she had ever touched. She could only stand wordlessly as the seamstress then began removing voluminous folds of petticoats, a pair of slippers that perfectly matched the dress, a silk shawl and, lastly, a black mask trimmed with silver lace, which would only cover her eyes.

118

Finally, when Dionne was able to speak, she murmured, "Oh, no, I cannot accept this. . . . It is much too expensive."

Madame DuPree gasped with horror. "But you must accept it! It has been made especially for you." She gestured wildly. "I have worked my fingers to the bone in order to complete it in time. I have gone without sleep . . . I have gone without food . . . I have . . . I have . . ." Her shoulders slumped wearily. "You have to accept it, you simply have to! It is a gift from Mademoiselle Celeste."

Dionne ran her hand over the gown, relishing the feel of the elegant material. Now she knew why Celeste had insisted she would not find her gift offensive. Then she smiled, realizing that a gift as expensive as this must have been with her father's permission.

Madame DuPree handed Dionne a note. "Mademoiselle Celeste told me to give this to you also."

Dionne broke the seal on the paper and read:

My dear friend,
Please accept the gift as a token of my affection for you. Wear it with my deepest wishes that the right man will find you irresistible. I remain in your debt forever,
Celeste.

Dionne dabbed at the tears that had suddenly appeared in her eyes. She looked at Madame DuPree and smiled. "Oh, yes, yes, I will accept the gift and I will wear it proudly!"

Chapter Nine

Dionne settled back against the carriage seat, knowing the ride to Fort-de-France would be long and tedious. Always before, the Phillipses had traveled the coast road where the dry slopes plunged into the quiet leeward sea, but today, of all days, they had requested to be taken over the winding woodland route in order to see more of Martinique. She could not help but feel disappointed and, yes, even slightly irritated. What was it about men that prevented them from being eager to attend parties? She looked down at her beautiful gown and smoothed her hands over it. How could the men know of her desire to hurry? How could they know that, for the first time in her life, she felt like a princess and was anxious to attend the ball?

Dionne, in love with the printed word, had read everything in Andre's library, giving particular attention to the fables and fairy tales he had purchased especially for his daughter.

She smiled to herself. Cinderella! That is who I feel like. Then she pressed a gloved hand over her mouth to prevent her laughing aloud as the entire story came to mind. She visualized the great pumpkin from which the coach had been made. She stole a peek at the Phillipses and at Andre, and tried to imagine them as mice. Bubbling laughter erupted at the thought of Celeste being her fairy godmother. In the past, she would have thought Celeste was the least likely person to fit that particular description. Then her thoughts grew somber. Who would Prince Charming be? Christopher's face loomed in her mind's eye, but finding that thought disturbing, she quickly discarded it.

She closed her eyes, trying to recapture her festive mood as the rich forest scents invaded her senses.

Great tree ferns sparkled from a recent rain shower as sudden sweeps of the sun burst through the heavy foliage. Birds squawked and brightly colored wings took sudden flight as man and beast invaded their sanctuary. Bamboo, a foot thick, swayed, gently curving and forever climbing. Vines dropped straight to earth from orchid-ladened limbs of tall trees. The jungle smelled of life and death, of fresh sweetness and decay.

Andre's mellow voice broke into her thoughts as he spoke to his friends.

"I see a great change taking place here on the island. As you might know, the French colonists gradually took Martinique over from the European buccaneers, who used the island to plunder selected European shipping. Although we were invaders, too, I like to think we were much more civilized even if we did make this land prosper by the use of slavery. Man cannot prosper long when another man is enslaved. Which, Edward, William, brings to mind your own homeland. The United States is a great, powerful nation. I cannot help but wonder, though, how long it will take for the issue of slavery to rip it apart."

Both men nodded their agreement, and Edward spoke, "I don't know, Andre. My guess is that I will see it in my lifetime."

Andre nodded. "Some of the other planters were not as fortunate as I. When slavery was abolished here, ninety percent of my people stayed on. But not so with other plantations. Most of the African population now is more mulatto than pure black." He shrugged. "And most mulattoes do not care for land work any more because it smacks of slavery. The other plantations could not exist if it were not for laborers from India who work the land on contract, with the promise of being able to stay on later as free men. Perhaps that will be the same solution for the States when pressure is applied to free your slaves."

William shook his head slowly. "Maybe so. At least it is a possibility, and something free men in the South should consider before the end of slavery is pushed upon them. I think you should know, though, there are many men in the southern regions who do not abide with slavery. My family, for one, certainly doesn't."

Dionne had heard the same sort of discussion many times in the past. She became completely lost in her thoughts as the men's voices droned on and on. Finally, she sensed excitement in their mood as they crested a small hill.

"Look"—Andre pointed—"there is Fort-de-France. From this vantage point you can see why they say she lies with her head in the hills and her feet in the sea."

Dionne came to attention, her heart beginning to beat rapidly as excitement coursed through her veins like molten lava.

William remarked casually, "It is amazing how this area has grown. When I first started sailing these waters, Fort-de-France was only a military garrison, but now I feel there is a strong probability she will overtake St. Pierre as the largest city."

"You know why this is so, do you not?" Andre asked.

"No, I am not sure."

"Before slavery was abolished, many of the people settled close to the Fort for protection. They felt there

was a strong possibility of the mulattoes revolting. . . ."
Andre glanced at Dionne and chuckled. "Gentlemen, I am afraid we have bored the young lady. All of this talk of slavery, land, and the problems we face, when I am sure the young lady wants to hear tales of music, laughter, and of the joyous time that awaits us all." He beamed with pride. "And can one blame her? Dionne, my dear, you are beautiful, and if my useless old legs worked, I would ask for the first dance tonight." He squinted one eye thoughtfully and grinned. "No, maybe not the first dance but definitely the second. The first should always be reserved for a special young man."

She blushed and demurely lowered her lashes. "Now, monsieur, you know there is no one special in my life."

Her reaction seemed to amuse him. "Perhaps not now, but the night has just begun. If I ask tomorrow, I doubt if you can give me the same reply." Andre leaned forward and touched Nigel's shoulder. "Best get a move on, Nigel. There are three carriages behind us and I think they are growing impatient. Oh, and before I forget, be sure and come to the square as soon as you have taken care of the horses. These gentlemen may not want to push me around all night."

Nigel grinned. "Yes, sir." He did not have to be reminded to take care of the monsieur. He gladly did it without any urging at all.

Loud blaring music and costumed people wearing masks greeted the carriages that entered the city. The custom was that if anyone of quality was caught without a mask, he was placed in jail or in the stocks and remained there until some generous soul paid the exorbitant fine. Therefore, Dionne, the Phillipses, and Andre hastened to put on their masks. Nigel stopped the carriage, assisted Dionne, then removed

Andre's chair from the specially designed rack on the back of the carriage before bodily lifting him and gently placing him in it.

The marketplace had been strung with multicolored lanterns, and a huge bandstand had been erected in the center of the square. Many cloth-covered tables lined the walls and on them sat huge bowls filled with rum and fruit punch, casks of ale, and bottles of whiskey and wine. Sugar cakes, pies, cookies, candies, and iced delicacies were plentiful, as were tables loaded with roasted beef, ham, fish, and shrimp. It was clearly a sight to behold.

Andre glanced around at all the noise and confusion, then he peered at his pocket watch. "Celeste and Christopher are supposed to meet us at the bandstand at seven o'clock, which is thirty minutes from now. Dionne, you do recall the conversation we had earlier?" He referred to the fact that he wanted her to help keep an eye on Celeste and to report to him or Nigel immediately if she saw Louis.

"Oh, yes, sir, I remember," she reassured him, relieved that Nigel was aware that a problem existed, although he had not been taken into Andre's confidence as she had been.

"Then be off now and enjoy yourself." He looked at his friends. "Gentlemen, the carriage ride has caused a great thirst. Shall we find some liquid refreshments?"

Edward laughed boisterously. "Andre, my friend, you are a man after my own heart." He stepped behind him and grasped the handles on the chair. "I am so thirsty, I will gladly push."

Pretending impatience, he hammered on the arm of his chair. "Then what are you waiting for? Let's go! Nigel, you will find us at the bar."

*   *   *

125

Dionne began to wander aimlessly through the streets, stopping occasionally to admire the jugglers, dancers, and magicians who performed for themselves as much as for anyone else.

Seeing people clustered in a tightly packed group, she stood on her tiptoes to try and catch a glimpse. Laughter soon engulfed everyone as an organ-grinder's monkey scampered up a man's leg and finally came to rest on the top of his head. The monkey's eyes widened, then he began jumping up and down and screeching, which sent the man scurrying and screaming at the top of his lungs. The organ-grinder rescued his pet, and his huge belly shook as he laughed when the monkey hurried to each person, shaking his cup. It was a festive mood and every single person had been caught up in it. The crowd slowly melted away and Dionne gradually made her way back to the center of the marketplace.

As the sun sank further in the west, shadows began to fall and lamplighters hastened to light the lanterns. The flickering lights cast an eerie glow on the square, making some of the masked people appear almost grotesque.

Dionne saw Andre and the other two gentlemen at the bandstand, but when Andre removed his watch then slowly shook his head, she knew there had been no sign of Christopher and Celeste. Acknowledging his concern with a slight nod of her head, she turned to search for them.

As she approached the tables on the far side of the marketplace, she came to a sudden stop and gaped with astonishment as she looked at a mirrored image of herself. It was Celeste, dressed exactly like her except she wore a white mask instead of a black one. Judging from the masculine physique of the man standing beside her, he was undoubtedly Christopher.

Her legs trembled and she suddenly doubted if they

126

would carry her weight. A hard knot formed in the pit of her stomach as she realized Celeste's beautiful gift had not been given out of kindness and affection; instead, it must have been given as part of some devious scheme. Regardless of how Celeste had seemed to change, no woman in her right mind would want another woman to dress exactly like her. But what could the scheme be? Then she knew. Somehow, Celeste planned to switch identities. Her eyes narrowed thoughtfully as she walked slowly toward them. She would have to remain on guard.

"Celeste? Mr. Phillips? We have been searching for you."

Celeste gasped, "Why, Dionne! I saw you and I . . . didn't know for certain . . ." She glanced up at Christopher and smiled nervously. "Please excuse us for a moment, Christopher." She grasped Dionne by the arm and hurried her away so that Christopher could not overhear them.

"Our gowns are just alike, Celeste. Why?" Dionne asked stiffly.

The girl shrugged. "Why? I have no idea. I told that stupid Simone DuPree I wanted her to make a nice gown for you . . . but I had no idea it would be like mine! And it is even the same color! Just wait until I see her; I will give her a piece of my mind!"

Celeste sounded so sincere but Dionne knew she was lying. "Have you seen Louis yet?" she asked bluntly.

Celeste blinked her eyes and pure innocence flickered through them. "Of course not. I have put that man completely out of my heart and mind." She gestured toward Christopher, who stood glowering at them. "And to be perfectly honest, a woman would have to be out of her mind to choose a man like Louis over someone as handsome as Christopher. No, my feelings for him have been forgotten." She gave Dionne a gentle

127

shove. "I see Christopher is growing impatient. You go on ahead and tell Father you found us. We will be along in just a moment."

When Celeste reached Christopher's side, he rasped hoarsely, "Why in the hell is that bitch wearing the same dress as you?"

"Now, Christopher," she chided gently, "watch your language. I do believe you have had too much wine to drink."

His eyes glinted coldly. "My dear, a rose by any other name is still a rose, just the same as a bitch is a bitch! Again, why is she wearing the same dress as you?"

Celeste lowered her voice, hoping to be purposefully mysterious. "I do not know. I instructed my seamstress to make a pretty gown for her . . . I mean, after all, we Debiernes do have our reputation to uphold and I could not have her wearing something that would embarrass me. But I had no idea it would look like mine. In fact, I selected a pattern and material very different than mine."

"Did she know about the gown?" He nodded his head, indicating Dionne.

"Why, of course. How else could the seamstress fit her?"

"Did she see your gown beforehand?"

"Naturally. It was so pretty, I had to show someone."

His features tightened. "Do you think it is possible that when she saw your gown, she deliberately gave the seamstress instructions to make her one like yours?"

"I have no idea, Christopher, no idea at all." She forced a bright smile and placed her hand in his. "We will just have to wait and see what happens."

A few minutes later they all stood at the bandstand. Edward and Andre immediately noticed the identical gowns, and Celeste offered the same excuse to them as she had to Dionne and Christopher. But from Andre's reluctant acceptance, it was evident that he doubted her as much as Dionne had.

Later, Andre was able to get Dionne alone, and again he stressed the importance of watching Celeste closely. His fears ran much deeper than they had before and for different reasons. Now that it was common knowledge Celeste was about to be married, he was afraid Louis would try to spirit her away. He kept remembering the terrible fate of those other two young women and was afraid the man would stop at nothing if he felt a large sum of money was at stake.

As the evening progressed, Dionne became more and more uncomfortable, especially when several of Celeste's friends found her in the noisy, jostling crowd. Suddenly, under the smirking stares of the other women, Dionne became extremely self-conscious of the way she was dressed. Feeling as though she were their main point of ridicule, she slowly moved away from them, finding a secluded place a distance from the mainstream of the Festival but where she could still keep a watchful eye out for Celeste.

It appeared that Celeste was having the time of her life as each of her friend's beaus whisked her out on the dance floor. The annoyance on Christopher's face gradually turned into a dark mask of jealous anger as Celeste went from one man's arms and into another. Dionne noticed he rarely moved away from a table that was well supplied with whiskey and rum. She also noted he was getting extremely unsteady on his feet.

Suddenly, she lost sight of Celeste and she began to peer anxiously into the boisterous crowd. Then, before she could make her way to Nigel to warn him, strong hands grabbed her from behind and pulled her into the dark shadows.

Struggling to free herself, Dionne's eyes widened in fright when she whirled around and gazed into the face of Louis Fairmount. Every word in Andre's report about how mean and wicked Louis was screamed through her brain.

"Wait a moment, Louis. Allow me to speak to her," Celeste said as she seemed to appear out of nowhere.

"All right, but hurry up," he growled, releasing his hold on Dionne and glancing cautiously from side to side. "We don't have all night."

Dionne grabbed Celeste's arm. "Hurry, Celeste, run!"

Celeste yanked her back. "No, Dionne, don't be a fool!" she hissed. Lowering her voice into a mere whisper, she said, "Louis insists upon talking to me." She wet her lips nervously, afraid he would somehow overhear. "He threatened to go to Christopher and tell all sorts of lies if I do not go with him for a while. You have to rejoin the party and keep Christopher occupied for an hour or so. It is vital to my future that his suspicions are not raised."

"But—but . . . you cannot be safe with that man! Your father is afraid he will do you bodily harm!"

"Hush, you fool, he is not going to hurt me—that is, if I do as he says. But if Christopher finds out about my affair with him, why there is no telling what he will do! And if he breaks our engagement, the shock and disgrace will break my father's heart. Now go on, please!" She gave Dionne a fierce shove then, all in the same movement, pulled her back and began yanking at her own mask. "Change masks with me. As much as Christopher has had to drink, he will never know the difference, especially if you get him out of the bright lights. Suggest that you go for a walk, anything, just keep him occupied for an hour or two and I promise to be back by then." Celeste pressed her mask into

130

Dionne's hand, turned, and quickly disappeared into the night.

Dionne knew she had no other choice than to do as Celeste demanded. With trembling hands, she fitted the mask into place and tied the ribbons. She felt like a fool. This was what Celeste had planned all along and she had stupidly allowed herself to be completely duped. But how would she ever be able to fool Christopher? In all likelihood he would know immediately that she was not Celeste. Unless . . . she did as Celeste suggested and managed to get him away from the lights. And her voice. How could she talk to him? While they bore a striking resemblance, their voices were not the least bit similar. He would recognize the difference immediately.

She glanced up to see Christopher making his way through the crowd toward her. Oh, dear Lord! she thought. What am I going to do now?"

Chapter Ten

Dionne was paralyzed with fear. From the taut set of Christopher's jaw and from the manner in which he shouldered his way through the crowd, she knew he was furious. A feeling of helplessness raced through her, then it turned to raw anger. If she could have gotten her hands on Celeste, she would have throttled her. Then Dionne took a deep, shuddering breath. Perhaps anger was what she needed the most. Perhaps it would help sustain her through the ordeal ahead. Squaring her shoulders and bravely raising her chin, she waited, dreading the moment when she would meet Christopher as Celeste, ever fearful that he would instantly recognize her and her true identity.

His mouth took on an unpleasant twist as he clamped his hand tightly around her arm. "How could you stand there and allow that bitch to leave with that man?" he shouted, reeling drunkenly on his feet.

Sheer black fear swept through Dionne. Oh, my God, she thought. He knows about Louis and Celeste! What am I going to do now?

"How can you allow her to ruin your good name? Why didn't you stop her?" His lips settled into a thin white line. His liquor-muddled mind made his anger even worse, and he began to back her against a storefront wall. "And not only that, it is worse than we

133

first thought. I know that man—or rather I know of him. He's been in New Orleans before and from what I've heard, he is nothing but venomous scum." He smacked his fist into an open palm. "I thought that name sounded familiar, but I never connected it until I saw his face!"

Numbly, Dionne dropped her eyes and shook her head. It was over. Christopher had found out about Celeste's affair with Louis. When she finally found her voice, she mumbled sorrowfully, "I could not stop her. I tried, oh, how I tried, but she would not listen to reason."

Grimly, Christopher continued, "This also answers any questions we might have had about the coincidence of your gowns being the same. The little bitch must have planned it down to the last detail. I'll swear, Celeste, if it were not for your father's ill health, I would go to him in a minute and tell him what that woman is not only doing to you, but doing to the entire Debierne family as well!"

Dionne glanced up at him in surprise. Celeste! He actually called me Celeste! Then, when it dawned on her what he had just said, her relief quickly turned into confusion. She hesitated, blinking with bewilderment as her mind raced furiously. If he thinks . . . I am her, then . . . he must think Celeste is me. But why is he referring to me in such a derogatory manner? Other than the few misunderstandings we had when we first met, I've never done anything out of the way in his presence. To my knowledge, I have always behaved like a lady should behave.

Suddenly, her body stiffened as the pieces began to fall into place: the accusations he had just made, all of the dark glowering looks he had thrown her way, the barely civil tone in which he had spoken to her over the past days, and the supposed confusion involving the two identical gowns. What had Celeste done? Told him that she had been posing as her? The girl must have. There was no other possible explanation for his accusations and the way he had been behaving.

Then, an even more terrifying realization washed over her. What would Christopher do if he discovered the entire truth? More than likely every sordid detail would be revealed and the scandal would in all probability kill Andre. It now went much further than Andre's desire to see his daughter safely married. It reeked of deliberate betrayal, lies, and deceit. If Celeste was the only person involved, Dionne knew she would suffer no remorse in exposing her for the cheating, despicable person she was, but Andre had to be considered. However unpleasant she found this terrible situation, she would have to do everything within her power to make it succeed. Dionne was so upset she found it almost impossible to breathe. It felt as if an iron band had closed around her throat. She was trapped—trapped in a hopeless situation from which there was no escape.

Christopher pressed closer, bracing himself with an upraised arm against the wall while his other hand held her jaw in a viselike grip. "How can you stand there so calmly when she's ruining your reputation?"

The pain in her jaw was excruciating. Christopher was so angry he did not realize his own strength. Her nails dug into his hand as she tried to pry it loose. "Stop it, please, you're hurting me," she muttered under his powerful grip.

The expression on his face instantly changed from anger to regret. He quickly dropped his hand and ran it raggedly through his hair. "I—I'm sorry. I—I don't think I've ever hurt a woman before. I guess I've had too much to drink . . . and I guess . . . I lost control of my temper. It didn't help matters any when I saw you

135

dancing with all of those other men," he accused. "I have never liked for any man to put his hands on something that belongs to me! Then when that . . . bitch took off with that—that snake . . . in the grass, I guess I saw red."

Knowing she had to get his mind on other things, Dionne somehow made her brain function. She placed her fingertips across his lips and tried to make her voice sound like Celeste's. "Hush, I know you did not mean to hurt me. And let's not let . . . D—Dionne and that man ruin our evening together any more than they already have. If we sounded an alarm now, think of the scandal it would cause." Dionne had no idea she was repeating what Celeste had said earlier.

"Well," he drawled slowly, "I suppose you are right, but as I said before, I damn sure don't like it."

"I don't either, but there is nothing else we can do right now." She tried not to think about what would happen the following day if Christopher faced her with his accusations.

He forced a smile. "No, I guess not."

Dionne thought her heart would stop beating when his eyes fastened with puzzlement on the ribbon that held her pendant watch around her neck. She swallowed hard. If Christopher remembered the watch, the game would be over.

Dionne knew she had to get him to a place where it was darker and where she could hold their conversation to a minimum. Thinking quickly, she wrapped her arms around his neck and pressed her lips close to his ear. "Let's forget about everything that has happened tonight. I don't want to go back to the party—not for a while yet. I would rather be alone with you." Her mind desperately raced. Being devious was not one of her better qualities. "Why don't you . . . go get a bottle of wine and a couple of glasses, then tell Father we are . . . going for a walk so he will not worry. I'll wait for you here, but please hurry." It was clearly evident he'd had too much to drink, but she reasoned that another bottle of wine would help to insure the success of this terrible scheme.

His eyes boldly raked her, his breath quickened. "I think that is the best idea you have had all night!"

"Then go! Hurry!" she whispered urgently.

"All right, but first I need a kiss." A slow, arrogant grin lifted the corners of his mouth.

Swallowing hard, Dionne tightly closed her eyes and puckered her lips.

Christopher swayed on his feet then began to chuckle devilishly. He squinted one eye and leered at her. "After what happened on board the *Blue Diamond* today, I believe we can do better than that." With those words, he lowered his mouth to hers and caressed her lips with his tongue.

The jolt of having his lips pressed so intimately against hers sent shivers of fear rippling down her spine. Her eyes widened with dismay. Exactly what had happened on board that ship? With Christopher thinking she was Celeste, what demands would he place on her? What would she do if he wanted more than she was willing to give? Wait a minute, Dionne, calm down, she told herself frantically. Do not panic. Take one step at a time. You can worry about that later. Right now, the most important thing is to keep him convinced that you are Celeste. Remember, not only do you have to act like her, but you have to think like her as well.

After he had kissed her, she forced a smile. "Now, please, go get the wine—and hurry."

Dionne breathed a silent prayer of relief when he turned without arguing and began making his way back through the crowd. She had never liked to be around people who were greatly inebriated, but this particular time she was thankful Christopher had had too much to drink. She knew if he'd had a clear head, he would have realized immediately that she was not Celeste. Worry wrinkled her brow and tears of frustration filled her eyes. How would she ever be able to pull this off? One wrong word, one wrong gesture, and it would all be over. Damn Celeste for getting her into this predicament!

Knowing it would only take Christopher a few minutes, Dionne quickly untied the ribbon holding her watch and placed it inside her reticule. Her neck felt naked without it, but she could not take the chance of discovery by continuing to wear it. She felt fortunate that Christopher's suspicions had not been aroused when he had seen the ribbon earlier. Again, a sense of helplessness washed over her. Just one tiny slip as simple as him noticing a ribbon around her neck could ruin everything.

As Dionne caught sight of Christopher weaving his way toward her, holding two bottles of wine and two glasses high above his head, she took a deep breath to try and steady her nerves, then she forced a smile to her lips.

"I decided one bottle of wine might not be enough for me and my lady," he said, bowing low and almost losing his balance by doing so. Regaining his balance, he switched the wine and both glasses into one hand and wrapped the other arm around her tiny waist. "Now, my sweet, where do you suggest we go so that we can be alone?" He wiggled his brows devilishly. "Back to the ship?"

"No," she mumbled, being careful not to speak too clearly. "Let's just walk around until we can find a quiet place." They could not walk too long. She could not take the chance that the fresh air would clear his mind.

138

"What about your friend's house?" he asked suddenly. "It's not far from here."

"M—my . . . friend?"

"Yes, you know, where you got ready for the Festival."

"But . . . they will not be at home. The only ones there will be servants, and they gossip too much."

His voice was a husky whisper against her ear, "I wasn't thinking of the house. Today, when I put the horse and carriage up, I noticed the stable had just been cleaned and there was a huge stack of sweet-smelling hay. And besides, it is only a block or two away."

Dionne forced a coquettish laugh. "Then what are we waiting for?"

With her heart in her throat, Dionne stood in the shadows and watched as Christopher sneaked into the stable to see if it was clear. He was back in a few minutes.

"Not only is the stable deserted, but there is an empty, unused stall as well. I took the liberty of spreading hay around so that we would have a comfortable place to sit. Besides, we cannot have you getting your pretty dress dirty, can we?"

Taking Dionne by the hand, he quickly led her inside the stable, struck a sulphur match for light, and showed her the stall he had prepared. "Now, isn't this nice and cozy?" he asked, pulling her down into the hay with him. He then ripped off his mask and carelessly tossed it aside. "I've been wanting to do that all night. I would never make a good bandit, not if it meant I had to wear a mask. I find them much too uncomfortable."

She gave a sharp cry of consternation, "But . . . you shouldn't have thrown it away. When we return to the Festival, they will either place you in jail or in the stocks if you are seen without it." The fleeting thought crossed her mind that that would be the best place for him until Celeste returned. If only she had thought of it sooner, she would not be snuggled into the hay with him now.

"You would pay my fine, would you not?" he asked as he slipped her mask from her head.

Dionne rescued her mask just as he was about to toss it away. She cringed, feeling naked without it.

His arm tightened around her. Chuckling, he asked again, "Would you pay my fine?"

"Oh, yes, of course I would," she murmured softly, grateful that only a few faint shafts of lights were able to pierce the darkness of the stable.

He threw his head back and laughed. "You don't have to whisper in here, my dear. There's no one to overhear you."

Dionne rolled her eyes and mouthed a silent plea for the right response. She pressed her lips close to his ear. "But when I whisper, it sounds so much more intimate."

Laughing, he wrapped his arms around her and pulled her close to him. "Perhaps you have a point there," he said, nuzzling his lips against the column of her slender throat.

Her eyes widened with fright. She realized, from the tone of his voice, that he was beginning to get sober. That would never do. She had to keep him intoxicated. Shying away from him, she stammered, "I—I'm thirsty. I would like to have a glass of wine."

He struck another match, handed it to her to hold, then removed a corkscrew from his vest pocket and brandished it proudly. "See, no one can ever say that Christopher Phillips has been caught unprepared." After opening the bottle, he filled the glasses and handed one to her. "Allow me to propose a toast." In the flickering light he caressed her with his eyes. "To the most beautiful woman in all the world."

His voice, so deep and sensual, sent a ripple of awareness through her. The sensation was so strong Dionne had to fight a battle of personal restraint. After she had first met him and her initial dislike of this man had passed, she had found him to be very personable. Moody at times, stubborn, even arrogant, but she somehow had the feeling that it was nothing but a false facade, a front he presented to most people so that they would not see the real Christopher. If their circumstances in life had been different, she could have had deeper feelings for him than mere friendship. And now, thanks to Celeste, even that was destroyed. She thought it was ironic that she was alone with him, his mood was sensual, his manner so kind, gentle, and charming, and it was all for naught. Suddenly, she felt like a thief, stealing words and embraces that were meant for another woman.

"What's the matter? Did I say something wrong?" Christopher asked when he felt her body tense.

Ever mindful that she had to think and act like Celeste, Dionne fought for control of her voice, "N— nothing is wrong. It's j—just . . . everything is moving so quickly. My life has changed so drastically in such a short period of time . . . it leaves me feeling limp."

Christopher chuckled easily. "That isn't the effect I hoped to have on you." He touched his glass to hers once more and murmured gently, "To our future. May it be fruitful and full of happiness."

The moment he made reference to their future, sobering thoughts filled his head: thoughts of remorse, thoughts of regret over losing his carefree bachelor life. Celeste had just said that her life had drastically changed, but his life had been altered as well. He could pretend forever but it would not change how he felt

141

deep down inside. Thankfully, Celeste was not as shallow as he had first thought, but she was not the woman he would have chosen. It was unfortunate he had never met a woman he wanted to marry. And now, there was nothing he could do about it. Whether he liked the idea of marrying her or not, his word of honor had been given, and a man without honor was not a man at all.

Christopher gazed at Celeste and decided it could have been much worse. His future bride could have been cold and unfeeling. What had almost happened on board ship was proof enough they would have a passionate union. Just a few minutes more and their emotions would have gotten completely out of hand; they would have been past the point of no return. And for that, the credit had to be given to Celeste. If she had not regained her senses at the last minute, she would have never been able to truthfully wear the traditional virginal white to their wedding.

He pushed all of those worrisome thoughts from his mind and turned his attention back to her. "More wine?" he asked, hoping she would say yes. He hated to drink alone and he was just about to lose the warm glow he had felt earlier.

"Yes, but let me pour it." Dionne realized he was quickly becoming sober, and she also knew something had to be done about it. After filling his glass to the brim, she added a mere drop to hers then drank it quickly. "Mmmm, this is delicious." She pretended to refill her glass again.

"Whoa, wait a minute," Christopher said, then he quickly drank his glass of wine and held it out for her to refill. "Don't be so greedy. Save some for me."

Dionne willingly obliged. Then she led him into light conversation, making sure he did most of the talking while continuing to ply him with wine.

Before long, that bottle had been emptied and the second uncorked, only this time Christopher held onto the bottle, filling their glasses at will.

Although Dionne knew she had to remain on guard, the effects of the heady brew made her relax and gradually the tension seemed to ease from her body. Not once did she protest when Christopher offered her more wine. Then, when her speech began to slur and run together, instead of being alarmed, she felt rather pleased, thinking it was a clever way to further disguise her voice.

Feeling giddy and light-headed, she snuggled deeper into the crook of Christopher's arm, savoring the way it felt around her, marveling over how wonderful his hard, muscular body felt next to hers. A numb but tingling sensation enshrouded her. It was a sensation that one part of her mind screamed against in protest, yet another part of her demanded that she yield to this strange but mesmerizing feeling. She found herself toying with the thick mat of hair on his chest and enjoying it immensely. She gradually felt her moral reservations slipping away. It was as if someone else had taken possession of her body and soul. She blinked, trying to clear the fog that had somehow filled her head, but try as she might, her eyes would not focus properly.

Deep inside the reaches of her imagination, the demon liquor raised its ugly head and began coaxing Dionne, enticing her with thoughts that would have never otherwise entered her mind.

The demon slowly lifted himself from an acrid smoking abyss and spoke in a smooth, lulling voice. *Look at Christopher, Dionne. See how handsome he is? See how attractive? See how masculine and manly? Do not shake your head at me. You know you are attracted to him. You found the man exciting the first moment you met him. You may be able to lie to yourself but you cannot lie to me—I know everything. I know how many nights you have lain in your bed thinking about him, not consciously, but the thoughts of him have been slowly eating away at you, gnawing relentlessly. And now you have the opportunity of a lifetime. For the first time in your life, you are being held by a real man. How does it feel? Oh? What is this I hear? You say you like it! Good! You had better enjoy it while you can, because you'll never be held this way again.*

The demon leaned forward and mockingly wagged its gnarled finger at her. *You are a spinster, Dionne, twenty-two years old, an old maid, and you are doomed to a life of loneliness. I suppose you're pretty enough, but how long will it be until your face begins to wrinkle, your hair becomes streaked with gray, and your shoulders stooped with age? That time will come before you realize it. With what will you fill your spinster's bed? Memories or longings? Memories of this one night when you reached out and became a complete, fulfilled woman? Or longings because you once had this chance, this one opportunity, and you chose to remain an empty shell? The choice is yours, Dionne. The choice is yours . . . the choice is yours. . . .*

Trembling violently, Dionne began making tiny gasping sounds from deep within her throat. The dream, vision, or whatever it was caused her to feel a gamut of perplexing emotions. She found it difficult to draw a breath.

Concerned, Christopher tossed aside the bottle of wine and gathered her gently into his arms. "Celeste, what's wrong?" He smoothed her hair back from her eyes.

She looked at him in the dim light and her heart lurched wildly, then she froze as her senses leapt to life.

144

Something deep inside told her that the demon was right, that this was her one chance to achieve full womanhood. She remembered the kiss Christopher had given her earlier, and suddenly there was an overpowering need to be kissed by him again. "Nothing is wrong, nothing at all," she murmured. Then slowly but unwaveringly she raised her lips to meet his.

Christopher felt his breath quicken as he tasted the eagerness of her mouth. Suddenly, hot desire for her raced through his veins. It had been instantaneous, sparked by the wild abandonment he sensed in her. He had been too long without a woman. His passion had been pushed to the limit earlier that day on the ship and now his body demanded to be satisfied. Christopher knew he would know no peace until the fire in his loins had been cooled. The fact that Celeste was his bride to be never entered his mind. Instead, his only primal thought was that she was a woman and he was a man.

Dionne moaned softly beneath the demanding pressure of his lips, the ravaging insistence of his tongue inside her mouth. A strange half-frightening, half-thrilling shiver seemed to engulf her as Christopher loosened the ties holding her gown together and slipped it from her shoulders. She knew she should make an effort to push him away, to regain her shattered senses, to stop before it was too late, but the sane voice deep inside her consciousness was silent the moment his tongue flicked at her breast, and a delicious tingling sensation began spreading throughout her entire body.

One tiny crack appeared in the door of Paradise, and Dionne's soul vowed that the door would be opened completely so that she could feast on the forbidden fruit that lay inside the portals, the fruit that had been beyond her grasp until this moment.

Christopher's mouth traveled to the slender column

of her neck, then made the full circle to her cheek, ear, eyes, lips, and back down to the erratic pulse beating in the center of her throat. He murmured gentle words of love before his lips closed over the tiny rigid bud of her other breast that eagerly awaited him. He felt her hands thread through his unruly mane of hair and that excited him greatly.

Now consumed with a frenzied passion, Christopher tugged at his clothing and gave assistance when she needed help with hers. Then it was flesh against flesh and body against body as his desire reached the pinnacle of heights.

Dionne was like a woman possessed. She had not shown any inhibitions or virginal innocence; instead, she was driven like a wanton temptress, driven beyond the reaches of sanity as she grasped for the fiery flames of rapturous desire.

Even though Dionne could feel each sensation, it was as if she had stepped outside of her body and watched from afar. Stabbing white hot pain streaked through her, and the sharp painful cry that came from her breast mingled with the triumphant sound Christopher made when he realized he was the first to know this priceless treasure.

Then Dionne plummeted back into her body and the pain was excruciating. She moaned and tried to writhe from his impaling manhood, but the more she resisted, the more excited his rhythmical thrusts became. Finally, she realized her movements were encouraging him. Dionne forced herself to lie completely still in hopes that he would soon be finished and that her torment would then ease.

Christopher, being an experienced lover, realized he had proceeded too quickly, that her virginal body needed time to grow accustomed to this first invasion. His lips sought hers again, his tongue exploring the sweetness, twisting, twirling, seeking. Then, partially withdrawing, his lips found her breast, his teeth nibbling and teasing until he felt the tautness gradually ease from her beautiful body.

Every sound was magnified. Dionne heard the erratic sound of her heartbeat as it sent blood rushing like a wild, untamed river through each and every vein. She heard his heartbeat and his breath hot and heavy in her ear. Even the primitive, rhythmic sounds the hay made as he thrust gently into her grew in intensity. Slowly, the pain ebbed from her body as though it had been washed away by cleansing water, and in its place remained a soft, warm glow that spread throughout with each ragged breath she took. Without warning, she could feel herself opening, welcoming this invasion, caressing it with all her being.

Christopher also sensed her acceptance of him. He began making longer but gentle thrusts. The soft moaning sounds she made were no longer from pain but from pleasure. Her hands no longer pushed at him; instead, they wound around and caressed his back. He could feel his muscles strain and stir beneath her hands as he began to plunge into her faster and faster with a passionate, all-consuming fury.

Trembling all over, Dionne's head spun dizzily as she felt her loins start to churn tumultuously, like a rumbling cloud building to an exploding crescendo, blinding her, shattering her to the very depths of her soul.

Almost simultaneously, Christopher plummeted into her fiercely for one last time as his body erupted with the fruit of his passion.

Beneath him, Dionne lay weak and exhausted, physically and emotionally drained as sanity slowly trekked its way through her mind.

Oh, my God! her conscience screamed in protest.

What have I done? Tears of regret began to flow effortlessly from her eyes.

Christopher murmured tender words and gently kissed her tears. "It's all right, my sweet," he soothed. "It's all right. We got carried away. It's just something that happens. I think none the less of you. We'll be married soon and no one will ever know, no one but us." He continued to croon soft, endearing words as he gently stroked her hair, her shoulders, and her softly rounded hips. Then his words came slower, farther apart, as he drifted into a satisfied sleep.

Agony tore through Dionne, agony such as she had never known before. His words, so soft and gentle, had not been comforting. They had been spoken to someone else, someone else who was too selfish to know what she had and was too foolish to want. Dionne felt cheated and abused, and not by Christopher; perhaps she could direct her anger at him later, but not now, perhaps not ever. It was with a painful reality that Dionne knew she had lost something very precious. Not just her virginity, but a man she could never have, a man she could never lay claim to. It was a devastating, shattering feeling.

Waiting until Christopher was fast asleep, Dionne rose and repaired her clothing as best she could, then slowly made her way back to the Festival.

Celeste was furious. She had been searching for Dionne and Christopher for what seemed like hours and they were nowhere to be seen. Then she saw Dionne in the shadows, sitting slumped over a table, her forehead resting on her hand. Celeste's eyes widened with rage as she flounced toward her.

"Where on earth have you been?" she demanded to know, her hands placed akimbo and her foot tapping angrily against the hard, packed ground.

Feeling sick at heart, Dionne raised her eyes and stared at Celeste through a red haze of tears. "Leave me alone," she muttered. "Just leave me alone."

"I will not! Do you have any idea the trouble you've caused? Father has been worried half out of his mind! My God, I asked you to keep Christopher occupied for an hour or two, and you're gone half the night." She glanced around. "By the way, where is Christopher?" Her eyes widened with surprise, then with rage as she noticed a few pieces of hay clinging to Dionne's hair. "You bitch! You little twit! What have you done? Tumbled in the hay with him?" She was livid with rage.

Dionne clenched her hands into tight fists. Gritting her teeth, she mumbled angrily, "Will you please shut your mouth? Just shut up and leave me alone!"

Unaccustomed to being spoken to in that manner, Celeste gasped as her curt voice lashed out at Dionne, "I will not! And how dare you speak to me that way! And how dare you tumble with the man I am about to marry! And you had better answer me! Where is Christopher?"

Dionne was not about to go into any of the details with her, not tonight, not ever if she could help it. Finally, she said, "Christopher has passed out in a stable."

"Passed out?" She folded her arms together and sneered, "My God, don't tell me your little tumble exhausted him that much!"

Her hazel eyes clawed Celeste like talons. "I suggest you keep your dirty thoughts to yourself! Besides, you have your nerve after your . . . sordid affair with that . . . Louis Fairmount!" Dionne retorted angrily.

Tossing her head defiantly, Celeste sneered, "What I do with Louis Fairmount is no one's business but my own. But what Christopher does with the first trollop that comes along is most definitely my business!"

Suddenly, Dionne did not want to argue; she just wanted to be left alone. Sighing wearily, she said, her tongue stumbling over the lie, "N—nothing happened between me and Christopher. You ordered me to keep him occupied, remember? What better way than with wine? I suppose I had too much to drink, too." She whispered raggedly, "I—I just want to go h—home."

Celeste was not entirely convinced. But not to be bested, she muttered threateningly, "If you talk to me like that again, I'll see to it that you don't have a home to go to! I'll see that you leave Desirade and never step foot on that land again!" She tugged at Dionne's arm. "Now get up and straighten your dress and get that damned hay out of your hair. Father can't see you looking like that. Better still, go on to the carriage and I'll think of some excuse to tell him." She gave Dionne a shove, took a deep breath, smoothed her gown, then made her way through the disappearing crowd to where her father was waiting.

Chapter Eleven

Celeste stood over Dionne as she lay sleeping, her hands planted firmly on her hips. A cruel expression twisted her normally pretty face. "Well, now, isn't this a pretty sight!" she sneered.

Dionne awoke and glanced groggily about. For a moment, she saw Christopher staring mockingly at her. Then, upon blinking her eyes and trying to focus them, she realized it was Celeste. "What . . . are you doing in here? I didn't hear you knock."

"For your information, I didn't knock. I didn't feel as though I had to! After all, this is my home."

"Yes, but it is my room," Dionne said pointedly. She was not in a mood to talk to anyone right now, much less Celeste. She had too many other problems on her mind.

Ignoring her, Celeste continued sarcastically, "I must say, I don't know how you can lie in bed and sleep, especially after what you have done! Why, if it were me, my conscience would not allow me to get a moment's rest." Celeste was not finished with her. She gestured wildly. "You act as if you have no shame at all! After that terrible thing you did, how can you even look me in the face?"

Alarmed, Dionne sat upright in her bed, her thick dark hair tumbling in disarray about her shoulders.

From Celeste's thinly veiled innuendos, she must know what had happened between her and Christopher! How could she have found out so quickly? She moaned softly. Would there be no end to her shame?

"Well, tell me, aren't you ashamed of yourself?" Celeste ranted angrily.

Dionne turned heavy, troubled eyes toward Celeste, and without warning tears gathered in them. Oh, yes, I have shame, she thought sadly. Shame such as I have never had before. A tortured frown appeared on her brow as she leaned forward to pensively rest her chin upon her knees.

After they had arrived at Desirade last night, she had gone straight to her room and attempted to wash the unclean feeling from her body. After scrubbing for what seemed like hours, she realized it was all for nothing. Soap and water would never cleanse her memory, it would never cleanse the stain left on her soul. Finally, she had gone to bed and tried to sort through all of her confusion, but answers to her many tortured questions refused to come. Dawn had streamed through the windows before she had been able to fall into a restless sleep.

And now, hopes she'd had that things would seem better today quickly disappeared. She doubted if it would ever be any better. Her behavior in the stable last night was almost impossible to believe. How could she have gone so eagerly into Christopher's arms without any hesitation, any reluctance whatsoever? While she was definitely attracted to him, how could she confuse attraction with love? She had always considered herself to be a decent woman, but how could a decent woman allow a man to make love to her if she was not married to him? How could she have so carelessly tossed aside all of her moral decency, self-respect, and innocence? And how could she have responded to him so wantonly? What was so awful was that she could not even claim Christopher had taken advantage of her. That fact was terribly devastating to her pride and sense of decency. It was a sobering thought that it had been her fault as much as his—if not more so.

Suddenly, determined not to allow Celeste to see how badly her conscience bothered her, Dionne swallowed her tears and stared defiantly at the sullen girl. "You, of all people, have no right to talk to me about being ashamed. I want you to get out of my room right now, and I want you to leave me alone!" she muttered bitterly.

Celeste stomped across the room and plopped onto a chair, her eyes flashing with outrage. She stubbornly folded her arms and glared at Dionne. "From the impertinent tone of your voice, I think you have forgotten a few things, Miss High and Mighty Dionne Martin! Apparently you have forgotten that I am mistress of this house and you are nothing but a servant! I will enter or leave any room in this house when and if I choose!" She wagged a finger threateningly. "And I strongly suggest you remember that!"

Wearily, Dionne rose, slipped a robe over her shoulders, tied the belt around her waist, then sat down on the foot of the bed. Celeste had come into her room obviously looking for a confrontation. If that was what she wanted, that was what she would get. There was no avoiding it. But, if she only had suspicions about what had happened between her and Christopher, Dionne quickly decided to admit to nothing unless she was forced to.

Sighing heavily, she said, "All right, Celeste, I will concede the fact that you are the mistress here and I am nothing but a servant. I'm quite sure you did not come in here just to remind me of that. Why don't you tell me what you have on your mind?"

153

Her laugh was scornful and taunting. "A very smart move on your part, Dionne. Unfortunately, it will not work. I refuse to be put on the defensive—especially after what I discovered this morning."

Dionne could not allow Celeste to see how apprehensive her visit made her feel. "Why don't you tell me what you discovered this morning, then we'll both know what you are talking about."

Celeste's unamused laughter did nothing to melt the icy shards that laced her voice. "I'll have to admit, I reluctantly admire the way you are able to sit there and act as though nothing at all has happened. But, it so happens that I had the strangest visit this morning."

Dionne pulled her gaze from Celeste and riveted her eyes to the floor. She could hear the roar of blood as it rushed through her head. She sensed impending doom.

"I see you are not the least bit surprised over that tidbit of news. Would it surprise you to learn that my visitor was Christopher?"

A faint thread of hysteria edged Dionne's voice as she said, "I—I thought Christopher was already a guest here. How could he pay you a visit?"

Celeste pretended to study her fingernails with great detail, then she raised her eyes and stared maliciously at Dionne. "It seems that Christopher did not spend the night here at Desirade; instead, the poor dear had too much to drink and had to sleep in a stable."

"I—I told you that last night. And if I remember correctly, I also told you we had too much to drink." If Celeste knew anything for certain, why didn't she just get it over with and quit toying with her like a cat does to a mouse before devouring it?

Celeste angrily slammed her fist against the top of the table that stood beside the chair. "Yes, and you also said nothing happened! However, Christopher had a much different story to tell this morning!"

Dionne's head jerked up sharply.

Celeste's nostrils flared with fury and her voice rang with malevolence. "I'm sure you can imagine my dismay when he called me out to the privacy of the gazebo and pleaded for my forgiveness!" Although that was not entirely how it happened, Celeste was not about to let Dionne know differently. "It seems he was so—o—o regretful over his having made love to me last night." She rolled her eyes. "I shudder to think what would have happened if I had not kept my wits about me."

Those words sent Dionne's head reeling. Oh, God, no! Please, let me be hearing this wrong!

"Why, Dionne," Celeste tittered cruelly, "you actually seem surprised. Don't tell me you really thought no one would ever find out that you seduced my betrothed? Why, that was totally naive of you! But I am curious. How did you expect to get away with it? Surely you must have realized he would say something to me!"

Nervously, Dionne wet her lips. "You have to listen to me. It didn't happen that way. It wasn't something that was planned. It . . . just happened."

"Like hell it wasn't planned! You've had your eyes set on him since the moment he arrived. You are not fooling me. I know exactly what went on in that stable!"

Dionne realized it was useless to argue the point. Celeste would believe what she wanted to believe.

Celeste gestured melodramatically. "Nevertheless, I'm sure you would have been thoroughly impressed with the act I put on for Christopher—especially after the way you have pretended to be so innocent this morning. Naturally, I cried such sorrowful tears over my lost virginity. And of course Christopher immediately offered to make an honest woman out of me, but I so graciously refused." Her voice turned hard and callous, "After all, I think it would be extremely unfair if I was cheated out of an elegant wedding in New Orleans just because you could not resist spreading your legs for him!" She leaned forward. "Tell me something, Dionne, and be completely honest. How long have you been wanting him? How long have you been waiting and planning for the right opportunity to present itself so that you could seduce the man I am going to marry?"

"That's enough, Celeste!" Dionne shouted, leaping to her feet. Rubbing her arms, she began to pace the floor. "It wasn't that way at all. What happened between us was not deliberate. It's bad enough that it happened, but to sit here and listen to those horrible accusations is something else entirely!" She stopped pacing and stared somberly at her. "I accept the blame for what happened between me and Christopher. Even though we both had too much to drink, it . . . was my fault."

"Well, that is certainly gracious of you, but is it supposed to make me feel better?"

"I don't know how it is supposed to make you feel. In a strange way, I guess I can understand your anger. But on the other hand, if you had not tried to deceive him, if you had not been intent upon seeing Louis Fairmount, playing both ends against the middle, then last night would have never happened!"

"How dare you try to blame your scandalous behavior on me!" Celeste snapped indignantly.

Dionne stared at her in astonishment. So this was how it was going to be. Even between themselves, Celeste intended to claim total innocence. Well, she could fight just as unfairly. "By the way," she said slowly, "since you still apparently intend to marry Christopher, am I to understand that your father's suspicions were correct, that Louis is nothing but a scoundrel?" Dionne knew she was being spiteful, but at that moment she did not care. Celeste had been too eager with her cruel taunts.

Celeste stiffened visibly. "What Louis is or is not is no concern of yours."

"I doubt if I would admit the truth, either," she muttered contemptuously.

Celeste had too much pride to let Dionne's remark go unchallenged. "I don't owe you an explanation, but it so happens that Louis loves me too much to stand in my way of happiness. He told me that the charges against him were false but he had no way to prove it, and if I married him my father would disinherit me completely . . . and that it would be impossible for him to provide the sort of life I am accustomed to. If there were any way I could retain my wealth and still marry him, I would at a minute's notice." She sighed miserably. "But, unfortunately, that is not possible, so I am forced to marry Christopher." She thrust her jaw forward defiantly. "Just because I am marrying him does not mean I don't love Louis. I'll always love him."

"How can you cheat Christopher that way?" Dionne asked, completely amazed that Celeste could act so flippant about it. Didn't the girl realize her happiness was at stake?

"I'm not cheating him any more than he is cheating me!" Celeste was quick to argue. "I'm not a fool. I know he doesn't love me, but diamonds, jewels, an elegant home, can compensate very handsomely in place of love. Oh, I am sure, as time passes, we will grow fond of each other. . . . After all, he is a handsome man and I am a beautiful woman. And I am also confident that we will share a happy life together. That is, if we are not reminded of too many unpleasant memories." Squaring her shoulders, she looked at her smugly. "Speaking of unpleasant memories, I think you will be one."

Dionne shrugged in mock resignation. "Perhaps so, but unpleasant memories can work both ways, Celeste. I don't want to ever again be reminded about last night. I think it is fortunate that you and Christopher will be making your home in New Orleans."

Celeste's eyes glittered with malice. "Oh, you are quite correct, Dionne. Christopher and I will live in New Orleans. However, I am sure we will return to Martinique occasionally to visit my father. That is why I think it would be best for all concerned if you left Desirade. In fact, I don't care if I ever see you again, so perhaps it would even be better if you left Martinique entirely."

"What?" Dionne was not sure if she had heard Celeste correctly.

"You heard me," she muttered cruelly. "I believe I made myself extremely clear."

Dionne was aghast. "You must have lost your mind. I do not want to leave Desirade, and I certainly do not want to leave Martinique. This is my home, it is the only home I have ever had." Just the thought of never seeing Andre and all the others was heartbreaking. And Christopher . . . No, no, she never wanted to see him again. Why had his memory invaded her thoughts at this precise time? In part, he was the reason behind all of this trouble.

"That is where you are wrong," Celeste sneered contemptuously. "Desirade happens to be my home, and you only live here. It is your place of employment, nothing more."

Dionne looked about frantically. "If you think I am going to leave just because you have a silly whim . . ."

Celeste folded her arms and smiled smugly. "Oh, I wouldn't call it a whim if I were you; I would refer to it as a firm decision."

"And what if I refuse to leave?"

"I doubt that you will."

"Don't be so sure of yourself."

Celeste smiled, her victory was so sweet. "But I am sure of myself."

"What makes you think . . ."

"Because if you don't leave, I will go to my father and tell him that I caught you trying to seduce my future husband."

"You wouldn't dare! You know how ill your father is!"

"Wouldn't I?" she asked with a malicious gleam.

A warning ran through Dionne. Maybe Celeste unconsciously wanted her father to find out. If something serious happened to him, then she would inherit Desirade and all that would go with it. No, no, she pushed that horrible thought from her mind. Even Celeste was not that conniving.

"He would not believe you." Dionne's face became more ashen with each word she spoke.

"Be realistic, Dionne. You are nothing but a servant here, and I am his flesh and blood daughter. When everything is all said and done, who do you think he will believe?"

Dionne slumped onto the bed and dropped her head into her hands. She did not doubt for a minute that Celeste would not carry through with her threats. Regardless of how fond Andre was of her, he would have no choice but to believe his daughter. That is, if he survived the shock. Dionne snorted bitterly. Who was she trying to fool? She would never allow Celeste's ugly accusations to reach Andre. She loved the man too dearly to be responsible for what would probably happen.

She raised her eyes and looked at Celeste through a

haze of tears. "All right, since you give me no other choice, I'll leave. But please answer a few questions for me. Why do you take such delight in destroying my life? What have I ever done to you?"

Celeste strutted her victory triumphantly. "The answer to both questions is really very simple. I hate you. I've hated you for years now and you were too stupid to realize it."

"But I've never done anything to deserve your hatred. For such a long time we were closer than sisters."

"That is precisely the problem. Oh, I will admit that for a while everything was so nice between us. Then you began to push yourself just a little too much. You sidled up to my father, and for a while there, I was actually afraid he loved you more than he did me." She grimaced from the memory. "I never got so sick of anything in all of my life as when he would hold you up to me as a shining example. 'Why can't you be more like Dionne? Ladies do not remove their shoes, Celeste. Why, look at Dionne; she is the perfect little lady.'" Celeste laughed bitterly. "Don't you think it was just a little ironic that my father insisted I behave like the bastard child of his serving wench!" She ignored Dionne's painful gasp. "I hope that satisfies your curiosity!"

She turned to leave but paused at the door. "Before you start to pack, I suggest you think of a convincing story to tell my father. And please make it a good one; I don't want him to become suspicious or unduly upset. If something were to happen to him, it would rest solely on your conscience. And, just in case you are able to think of some way to get out of all of this, I want you to inform me before you have your little chat with him. I want to be present. Oh, and by the way, if you think that Christopher can somehow come to your rescue, think again. He is already gone. He will set sail for Brazil within the hour." Smiling smugly, Celeste closed the door firmly behind her.

For a moment, Dionne could only stare numbly at the door. How could Celeste do this to her? How could anyone be so cruel and selfish? How could Celeste pretend to play God and change her life so drastically? Just the thought of never seeing Andre or Desirade again was heartbreaking. Her misery was so acute that it was actually a searing physical pain.

An even more terrifying realization swept over her. What she and Christopher had done was wrong. Was having her life ripped apart her punishment for committing that terrible sin? Tears began to fill her eyes, then she flung herself across the bed and cried deep, rasping sobs.

"Celeste, are you sure this is what you want me to do? Please . . . isn't there some other way?" Dionne asked sorrowfully. Even if it meant pleading with Celeste, she would. "I'll do anything, just . . ."

"That's right. You will do anything!" she hissed, grabbing Dionne by her arm. "You are going to go in there and tell my father you are leaving! And you are going to do it right now!"

"But . . ."

"Oh, shut up! Stop being a crybaby. You should have thought about the consequences before you tumbled in the hay with Christopher." She shoved Dionne, her face a dark mask of cruelty. "And just one final warning: You had better make your story good. If you raise Father's suspicions, so help me God I will completely destroy you!"

Clenching her hands into fists, Dionne's nails bit painfully into the palms of her hands. Never had she

161

hated anyone so much in all her life. Then she realized that hate was such an ugly thing. After all, look at what it had done to Celeste. She took a deep breath and made a silent vow to never let hate destroy or turn her into a cruel, vicious woman the way it had Celeste.

Nevertheless, defeat rested heavily on Dionne's shoulders as she and Celeste entered Andre's study.

"Good afternoon, my pets," Andre greeted warmly, presenting his cheek for Celeste's customary kiss. He glanced at Dionne then looked again, this time scrutinizing her carefully. Her eyes were red and swollen, and her face was gaunt and pale. She looked like death warmed over. "Dionne, you look terrible!" He attempted to laugh. "I realize that is not what a young lady enjoys hearing, but . . ."

"Oh, that is all right, Uncle Andre. I had a little"— she threw Celeste a withering glare—" too much wine to drink last night. Then, too, y—you see, I wasn't able to sleep very well." Wringing her hands together, she sat down. "Uncle Andre, I have been thinking about something . . . for a good while now, something that I find extremely difficult, but nevertheless I feel it is something I have to do."

Andre raised his brows and leaned forward. "What is it, my dear? I have never seen you so upset."

Frantically, Dionne looked to Celeste as if for a silent plea for help. Celeste quickly hurried to Dionne and placed her hand on her shoulder. Even though it seemed to be a thoughtful, caring gesture, Dionne knew it was a well-concealed threat.

"Father, I believe Dionne finds this a little difficult, and understandably so, because it is a major decision. Although she has spoken to me about her intentions, she has not mentioned her actual plans."

Andre gestured helplessly. "Now I am even more

162

confused. I suggest one of you tell me what is going on."

"Dionne has decided to leave Desirade, and not only that, but Martinique as well."

This revelation took Andre by complete surprise. His mouth gaping, he stared at Dionne. "Is this true?"

Unable to find her voice, Dionne could only nod mutely.

"I . . . never knew you were . . . unhappy here."

"Oh, I haven't been . . . it's just that . . . " Her mouth worked frantically but no words would come.

A glimmer of light dawned in Andre's eyes. "Don't tell me you have found a young man?"

Dionne felt the pressure of Celeste's hand as the girl began to squeeze. "N—no, there's no young man."

"Then tell me, child, tell me why you want to leave. If it is something you really want to do and if it is in your best interests, I will not stand in your way."

Dionne took a deep, shuddering breath then swallowed hard. Squaring her shoulders, she raised her chin and looked directly into Andre's eyes. She knew she would have to find the courage to be thoroughly convincing, even though what she was proposing was quite impossible. "I have decided I want to meet my mother's family. I realize my mother had hard feelings toward them, and maybe even rightly so. But perhaps the years have mellowed their feelings." Dionne rushed on, "This is not an overnight decision. It is something I have been thinking about for a long time. Since you and Celeste will not be here for several months, the house will be closed and I will not be needed. It seems to me that this is the perfect opportunity. And I would really like to meet my family. I do hope you understand."

Andre's face was troubled. "Yes, I do understand

163

your feelings, child, but this is a big step for you to take. I don't want to dash your hopes, but you may not be welcomed there or you may not like them once you meet them. It seems to me that you are making a big decision without considering all of the consequences."

Celeste felt Dionne had invented a marvelous excuse. Her mind raced for a way to lend help. "Father, Dionne, if you do not mind my interrupting, I believe I have an excellent suggestion."

"I don't mind, and I'm sure Dionne doesn't, either."

"As Dionne said, since Desirade will be closed for several months, this would be the perfect opportunity for her to visit her mother's family. But it would not have to be carved in stone that she had to stay with them. If she found it to be uncomfortable there, she could always return."

"That is certainly true," he conceded. He reached out and grasped Dionne's hand. "You know that you will always have a home here if you want it."

Celeste continued eagerly, "It would not have to be anything definite, at least for right now. That decision could always be made later."

Dionne stood up quickly. She knew she had to leave Andre's study before she burst into tears. Forcing what she hoped to be a cheery tone in her voice, she said, "Now that everything is settled, I guess I should start packing. S—since I have been saving a good portion of my salary, I can manage quite well, but I will probably need assistance in making arrangements for passage. . . ."

"Oh, but that is not necessary," he said with a wave of his hand. "Since we are leaving tomorrow, you can accompany us. I will speak to Edward, but I'm sure there will be quarters available."

Celeste was quick to inject her feelings. "B—but, Father, maybe she would rather go by herself."

Dionne going with them was something she had not counted on.

"Nonsense! I see no reason for her to strike out alone when she can travel with us. Why, there is no telling what could happen to her if she did." He shook his head adamantly. "No, I won't hear of it. My decision is final. Dionne, you are to go with us and that is final."

Dionne looked first at Andre then to Celeste. Seeing Celeste slightly nod in agreement, Dionne forced a feeble smile. "Well, since that is all settled, I guess I had better start packing."

Chapter Twelve

Dionne stood at the ship's railing, pensively reflecting upon the events that had led up to her being on the *Emerald Tempest*. She had gone over them again and again in her mind, and as always, it left her feeling limp and drained. Never had she been more miserable. The memories and shame she felt concerning Christopher were numbing, but the pain she felt over having to leave Andre and Desirade was completely devastating.

Before they had left Desirade, she and Celeste had had another confrontation, and some of her suspicions had been proven true. Celeste had actually had the nerve to taunt her with the complete truth—that she'd had an affair with Louis and the fact of her lost virginity had been a dire problem for her. She had worried about how she would ever be able to explain it to her husband on their wedding night. Celeste had smugly thanked Dionne for solving that dilemma. After all, now Christopher would never have to know that he had gotten goods soiled by another man.

Dionne realized Celeste did not care that she and Christopher had actually made love. It had just been a good excuse to force her to leave Desirade. Celeste was so jealous and hated her so much that if it had not been this, another reason would have been found just as easily.

Not only did Dionne feel anger and resentment, she felt bitterness as well. She had sacrificed her entire future for nothing. If only Andre had not asked her to help. If only she had realized what lengths Celeste would go to destroy her, things could have been different. While in all probability she would have still been forced to leave Desirade, at least she would not have lost her virginity and a portion of her heart to a man she would never see again, to a man who did not even know she existed.

Trying to push those torturous thoughts from her mind, she turned her eyes toward the heavens and watched as the red dawn broke across the distant sky.

The cabin boy hurried toward the beautiful young woman who stood alone at the ship's rail. He knew for a fact that she was the friendliest, nicest lady he had ever seen, to say nothing about her being comely. Why, her hair was the prettiest color, all sparkling and shining, and her features were such that a man could gaze upon them for hours at a time and never grow weary. If only she didn't have such a sad expression in her eyes. He often wondered why such a fine-looking lady seemed to be so unhappy. Ever since she and the others had come on board at Martinique, he had noticed it. Maybe she was leaving her gentleman behind on the island. Perhaps that was what made her so sad. Whatever it was, it was something powerfully strong. 'Course, it could have had something to do with that woman who seldom left her cabin. Good God above, she was constantly harping at everybody. If he'd had to stay in the same cabin with someone like her, maybe he'd be sad and unhappy too. Even though that woman had stayed holed up in the cabin most of the time, he'd certainly caught the brunt of her meanness; in fact, most everybody on the ship had at one time or another.

She was just the opposite of this fine lady—whining, foul-tempered, barking orders, sniveling, constantly complaining, that is, when she was able to get her head out of the retching bucket long enough to fuss. He grinned to himself, doubting if he had ever seen anybody so seasick before. Scuttlebutt had it that the onerous woman was the daughter of the man in the wheelchair, and that she and Cap'n Chris were bound for the altar as soon as he returned from Brazil. Lord, he pitied any man who hitched up with her. 'Course, he'd met Cap'n Chris a few times himself, and he was just the sort of man who would plant his foot in the middle of her backside. He only wished he could be there to see it.

Awkwardly, he cleared his throat and shuffled his feet. "Beg pardon, ma'am, don't mean to intrude, but I have a message from the captain."

Dionne turned to face him, immediately noticing how a dark blush covered his face and ears. She gave a friendly smile, hoping to put him at ease. "Good morning, young man, and you are not intruding. You say you have a message from the captain?" Her eyes followed the lad's to the quarterdeck where Captain Edward Phillips stood.

"Yes, ma'am, an important message," he said, trying not to stare at her. His embarrassment stained his face an even darker shade of red. "Cap'n Phillips wants to know if you'd like to join him for coffee and biscuits. He told me to tell you that if you accept his invitation, just to nod your head at him, then I was to go tell the cook to bring the coffee and biscuits out here on the deck and he would join you."

Dionne thought about the foul odor that permeated the small cabin below. Regardless of how often she and Nettie had cleaned it, the stench of Celeste's seasickness

169

had been impossible to completely remove. Since they all had been instructed to stay below as much as possible when the majority of the crew was up and about, the thought of having to return to that dark hole instead of remaining out in the clean fresh air was enough to make Dionne instantly decide to accept his invitation.

When she gracefully nodded, the boy scampered off to the galley and the captain joined her.

"Good morning, Miss Martin. I've noticed these past few mornings how much you seem to enjoy the fresh sea air. Most women don't. Have you sailed much before?"

Dionne waited until the cook served their coffee and biscuits before replying, "No, this is only my second sea voyage. And, sir, if you do not mind my saying so, you seem so different on board the *Emerald Tempest* than when you were at Desirade." She smiled. "If you will forgive the pun: While you were there you seemed like a fish out of water."

The captain laughed boisterously. "I heartily agree, ma'am, I heartily agree." He leaned forward. "Is Miss Debierne better this morning? I doubt if I have ever seen anyone as sick as she has been."

Dionne had to bite her bottom lip to prevent a grin from spreading across her face. "No, she is still sick. I doubt if she will feel better before we reach land."

He shook his head. "That is too bad. I had hoped to be able to spend some time with her, to get a little better acquainted. We never had much of a chance to visit while we were at Desirade."

Dionne did not care to discuss Desirade or anything that had happened while the captain and his family were there. It was much too painful. Wishing to change the subject, she glanced uneasily at the red sky. "Tell me, Captain Phillips, are we in for a blow?"

The captain, taking a sip of coffee, sputtered, "Where have you heard an expression like that? I thought you said you were unfamiliar with sailing."

"I am unfamiliar with sailing, but one does not live on an island with the Atlantic Ocean on one side and the Caribbean Sea on the other without learning something about storms." She wet one finger and held it high. "I've read many of the mariners' sayings:

> 'When the wind moves against the sun,
> Trust her not for back she'll run.'"

"And do you think the wind is moving wrong?" he asked.

"Considering the sailors' poem, it is. And there are also others."

"What are they?" he asked, his eyes remaining expressionless.

"Oh, only a couple more come to mind:

> 'Red sky at morning,
> Sailor take warning.
> Red sky at night,
> Sailors delight.'

"But the saying that concerns me the most is this one," she said, glancing anxiously again at the sky:

> 'Mackerel skies and mare's tails,
> Make tall ships carry short sails.'"

The captain suddenly turned his interest to his coffee. "A beautiful young woman should not worry about things such as sailors' old folklore. They are merely superstitions, that's all."

"Now, Captain Phillips, you are the last person in

the world I thought would be condescending. You know as well as I that sailors set great store by their sayings because they are usually correct."

He chuckled, slightly embarrassed over having been caught in a fib. "Yes, they do. And forgive me for trying to make light of your worries. I did not want to alarm you needlessly." He chose not to tell her that he and his crew had sensed the approaching storm earlier the previous day.

"You haven't alarmed me," she quickly reassured him, "but the sky has." She worriedly rubbed her arm and again peered at the red clouds. "I have a strange feeling when the storm hits, it will be a bad one, and I suppose there is nothing much we can do about it. We have been at sea for eight days now. That means we are into the Gulf of Mexico and probably well away from any land mass, so we cannot make a run for shelter. We will have to ride the storm out when it hits."

Chuckling still, the captain rubbed the back of his neck. "Miss Martin, for a woman who has never sailed, you certainly know a lot about the sea. If you were a man, I might consider offering you the position of second mate."

From the tone of his voice, she realized he had not been sarcastic; instead, he had paid her a compliment. "Thank you, Captain Phillips. I will admit that my knowledge comes from books and a few bits of conversations I have overheard through the years."

Draining his cup, he said, "Let me assure you, Miss Martin, the *Emerald Tempest* is a fine seaworthy ship. True, she has age to her, but we have always come safely through even the fiercest of storms, and I have no doubt that we will ride many more to safety. I feel it is needless to caution you to remain below when the storm hits." He shook his head and sighed apprehensively. "However, to be completely honest, it is not the storm I fear."

"Oh?"

"No, ma'am," he stated adamantly. "Miss Debierne has been so ill and foul-tempered, I fear she will think we conjured up the storm just to make her feel worse."

Dionne clamped her hand over her mouth to stifle her laughter. "Why, Captain Phillips, shame on you!"

He shook his head, his features grim. "It's true. I realize you owe your loyalty to the Debiernes, but that woman has a tongue sharper than a barb. I only hope this is a side of her my son never sees. God forbid if he does." He swallowed hard and added hastily, "Of course, I realize this voyage has been most difficult on her, and more than likely her foul-temper stems entirely from her being seasick."

When Dionne offered no comment on that remark, he indicated he had duties to perform. "It has been my pleasure, Miss Martin. Perhaps we can do it again before we reach New Orleans."

"Perhaps so, Captain Phillips. Not only have I enjoyed our breakfast, but the company as well." She glanced about her. "Do you mind if I remain here for a while longer?"

"No, just stay out of the way of the crew, and if the wind picks up, please go below then. I would hate to have to try and fish you out of an angry sea."

"So would I, Captain," she said sincerely. "So would I." Then her eyes turned anxiously back toward the darkening sky.

In the northwestern corner of the Caribbean basin, there is an area of trapped, shallow warm water and saturated tropical air. It is hemmed in on the eastern side by the island chain of the Greater Antilles, trapped to the west by the huge sweep of the Yucatán peninsula,

173

and held tightly to the south by Panama and the great land mass of South America.

To the south and east of this devil's spawning ground, a partial vacuum had been formed and the surrounding surface air tried to move in and fill it. But it had been forced into a counterclockwise track around the center by the mysterious forces of the earth's rotation. Compelled to travel the long route, the velocity of the air mass accelerated ferociously, and the entire system had become more unstable, more dangerous by the hour, forever perpetuating itself by creating greater wind velocities and steeper pressure gradients.

The center of the storm opened like a flower, the calm eye extending upwards in a vertical tunnel with smooth walls of solid cloud rising to the summit of the dome. The entire mass began to move faster, spinning and roaring upon itself, devouring everything in its path as the she-devil launched itself across the Caribbean Islands, past Cuba, and onward, picking up speed when the devil's spawn reached the deep waters of the Gulf of Mexico.

The wind chopped the Gulf Stream into quick, confused seas. It did not blow steadily, but flogged the *Emerald Tempest* with squally gusts and rain of startling suddenness. The night was utterly black. There were no stars, no source of light whatsoever, and the ship lurched and heeled in the patternless sea.

"Barometer's rising sharply, Cap'n," the first mate called suddenly.

"Yes, the trough has reached us," Edward said grimly. "It's about to overtake us now."

As he spoke the darkness lifted. The heavens seemed to burn like a bed of hot glowing coals, and the sea shone with a sullen, ruddy luminosity.

All of the men on the quarterdeck, along with the entire crew of the *Emerald Tempest*, lifted their faces with the same awed expression as devout worshipers on Judgment Day, but instead of eagerness, they looked fearfully up at the strange glowing skies.

A low cloud raced above them, a cloud that glowed with that terrible ominous flare. Slowly, the light faded and changed, turning a sickly greenish hue, much like the shine on putrid meat.

Edward's face blanched and he said slowly, "My God, it is the Devil's beacon." He wanted to rationalize it, to break the superstitious mood that gripped the entire crew. He knew it was merely the rays of the sun on the western horizon, catching the cloud peaks of the storm and reflecting downward through the weak cloud cover of the trough, but somehow he could not find the right words to deny that phenomenon that was part of the mariner's lore, the malignant beacon that leads a doomed ship to its disastrous fate.

The strange glowing light faded slowly, leaving the night even darker and more foreboding than it had before.

"Oh, my God!" Celeste screamed as a thundering wave heeled the ship precariously to one side. She desperately clawed at the railing that ran along the edge of her bunk. "I'm going to die! We're all going to die!"

"For God's sake, will you please shut up! The storm is bad enough without us having to listen to your senseless whining!" Dionne shouted over the shuddering sound the ship made as she finally righted herself.

The tiny six-by-eight-foot cabin was pitch dark, but the women's fear permeated the tiny space, making them feel as though they had been entombed alive in some dark, dank cavern. They had been imprisoned there for what seemed like hours.

Nettie had long ago become a mindless creature, driven beyond the bounds of sanity. She now sat in the corner, curled into a tiny fetal ball, her hands clamped tightly around her head as if hoping that would somehow protect her if the raging sea came crashing in on them.

Celeste clawed her way to Dionne and clutched frantically at her dress. "I've got to get out of here! I've got to get out of here. I'll be trapped alive! This wretched cabin will be my tomb!"

When seawater began coming in from underneath the cabin door, Celeste screamed, then scrambled frantically toward the door.

A tiny insane voice deep inside Dionne's head told her to let her go, but another voice, the part of her that had retained a glimmer of sanity, said that she had enough on her conscience without adding more guilt. She made a desperate lunge to drag her back inside. "Stop it, Celeste! You cannot go out there!" Somehow, she sensed the water had come from a wave that had washed down the corridor, and they were not in danger of sinking—yet. "The waves are too high! You'll be washed overboard! The captain knows what he is doing. He ordered us to stay in here and this is where we will stay until he says differently!"

Celeste was too terrified to think rationally. She began hitting Dionne savagely about her face. "You're trying to kill me! You're doing this deliberately!" she screamed.

Realizing she could not hold her much longer, Dionne doubled up a fist and smacked Celeste soundly in her jaw. Astonished, Celeste could only stare openmouthed at the dim shadow Dionne's figure made in the darkness. Whimpering pitifully, she crawled along the floor until she found her bunk, climbed into it, and resumed her desperate hold as the raging sea tossed the ship about.

Suddenly, the door burst open and Nigel, carrying Andre in his arms, rushed inside. "Is everybody all right in here?" he asked, setting Andre down as gently as possible.

"Other than being frightened half out of our wits, all of us are all right—at least for now," Dionne said, trying to force a calmness she did not feel into her shaking voice. "How are you and Uncle Andre faring?"

Worriedly, Nigel shook his head. "I be fine, but I'm not sure about the Monsieur. The last bad wave that hit tossed him out of the bunk 'fore I could catch him. Banged his head real hard on the floor. I thought it best that we come in here with you women folk . . . jest in case . . ." The whites of his eyes widened when another wave sent the ship reeling.

When Dionne could hold herself steady, she knelt over Andre to see what she could do for him. He moaned softly, and for that she felt a great burden lift from her shoulders. At least he was alive. That in itself was a small miracle considering how weak his heart was. Then she blinked, startled at the bright starlight that suddenly streamed through the porthole. She could not understand what was happening. She thought her hearing had gone, for suddenly the terrible tumult of the wind was muted, fading away.

Celeste came off her bunk quickly. Tears of joy mixed with her hysterical laughter. "We're saved! We're saved! Thank God!" Then, the realization that they were in the eye of the hurricane washed over her and her features blanched. Martinique had been caught in the path of too many fierce storms. She, along with the others, knew what lay ahead. The second part of the storm always seemed to be more fierce, stronger, more

177

destructive than the tempest that had just passed.

A knock sounded at the door and the captain entered quickly. He looked terrible. He was visibly haggard, weary, and his eyes were blood red from all of the stinging wind and salt spray. His glance immediately took in the hysterical condition of Celeste and her maid, and the fact that Andre and Nigel were now in the women's quarters. He also noted that Dionne was apparently calm, but that did not surprise him. "Is everyone all right down here?"

Dionne tried to speak rationally. Even though her entire body was shaking, her voice sounded steady. "I am not sure about the Monsieur. He was thrown from his bunk and suffered an injury to his head."

The captain frowned. "Nigel, try to make him as comfortable as possible. Miss Martin, will you please step out into the corridor with me?"

Dionne readily complied.

"Miss Martin, I must ask you to be brave, and please do not get hysterical on me. There's not time for me to try and comfort a hysterical female."

She drew a deep breath and looked up at him with worried eyes. "I promise to remain calm."

"Good. I will be frank and as brief as possible. The calm will last no more than twenty minutes. And when the storm hits again . . . it will be much worse than before. The *Emerald Tempest* is a stout ship, but this is also a devil storm. I've never seen one so fierce." He took a ragged breath. "There is a strong possibility that we will lose the ship. If that happens, God help us all. When the storm hits again, I want you and the other women to remove all clothing except for your undergarments. If worse comes to worse, the sodden weight of your gowns and petticoats will drag you down." He pressed a sheath knife into her hand. "You have to promise me that you will remain in your

178

cabin . . . unless the ship starts to break up—God forbid if that happens—get topside as quickly as possible. My men are lashing crates to the mast. Use the knife and cut them loose, then bind yourself to the crates. Then, if you have any prayers, say them. And please, pass all of these instructions on to the others . . . and try to keep them calm. Tell them we are doing everything within our power to stay afloat."

Dionne placed a hand on his arm as he turned to leave. "Captain, what about you and your men? What will you do? Even with us being down here, the force of the waves is tossing us about effortlessly. How will you and your men ever be able to hold on?"

He reached out and gently stroked her cheek, as if her caring about the fate of others moved him greatly. "Do not worry about us, my dear. We will do as others have in the past and as, I am sure, others will do in the future. Before, when we have had the misfortune of being caught in a savage storm, in our despair, I have always strapped myself to the wheel, and the crew tied themselves to the main mast." He managed a brave smile. "But don't worry. I have not lost a man yet, and I don't intend to lose one now!"

Tears filled Dionne's eyes as the captain turned and made his way down the corridor. "May God go with you, Captain, and may God be with us all," she murmured.

When the *Emerald Tempest* began to break apart, Dionne knew; they all knew. It sounded as if the gates of hell had been thrown open and the ship, seeing her condemnation, issued echoing screams of protest. She fought hard, every timber, every plank resisting the wind and raging sea, but her back had been broken and she was only minutes away from her doom.

179

"Everybody, we have to leave!" Dionne shouted above the shriek of the wind and the shuddering death moans of the ship.

"But we'll drown!" Celeste screamed. She had finally realized the force of the wind and waves, and she was terrified to go topside. She wanted to remain below.

"The ship is breaking apart. If we stay here, we'll all be trapped and the ship will carry us down with her. Up there, we may have a chance—at least more of a chance than if we stay here!" Dionne felt that either way they were lost, but she did not wish for her body to remain entombed in the ship throughout eternity. She would rather be free. Free for her soul to roam with the currents; free for her soul to reach the place where sea met sky and together they blended into infinity.

"Nigel, can you carry the Monsieur?" She looked at Andre's ashen face with worry. He had not yet regained consciousness. Then, with a shuddering calm, she realized he was fortunate. At least he would never know their horrifying fate.

"Yes, ma'am," Nigel said solemnly. "Me and him have been together 'most all our lives. It wouldn't be fittin' to separate us now."

"Celeste, you'll have to help me with Nettie. I cannot carry her by myself!"

Celeste was wild-eyed in her frantic state. "I can't! I can't! I have to get out of here!" In her frenzy, her strength had greatly increased, and she roughly shoved Dionne aside and made a mad dash for the door. A wall of water swept her from her feet and washed her backward, but again she scrambled past the others and clawed her way down the corridor, which was rapidly filling with water that came from the bottom of the ship instead of waves washing aboard.

Dionne forced Nigel to take the knife. "Here, take this to cut a rope. Try to secure yourself and Andre to a crate or something; it will be your only chance. I'll come behind you with Nettie. And if possible, stick the knife into a board where I can find it when we reach topside."

"What about Mademoiselle Celeste?"

"If we can find her, we'll help. If not, she'll have to fend for herself." It was not a conscious thought, but Dionne figured Celeste was as able-bodied as any of them. Since in her fright she had thought only of herself, then she could take care of herself.

Nigel lifted Andre into his arms, and staggering from the force of the water and the weight of the man he loved, he made his way slowly topside.

The task of getting Nettie out of the cabin was more difficult than Dionne had thought it would be. She had to drag, carry, push, and shove. Once she was even tempted to leave her behind, but the memory of her own fears of being trapped below spurred her onwards, until finally they reached the deck.

For one brief moment Dionne allowed herself to gaze in horror at the ship. Her mouth opened in a scream but the screeching wind stole it from her as she looked at the place where the main mast had been, the mast where the crew had lashed themselves. Instead of the mast, there was an open, gaping hole. At the wheel was another horror just as great. The broken leather strap was whipped crazily by the wind, and a single bloody hand gripped the wheel in the throes of death.

"God go with you, missy!" Nigel shouted just before he shoved a huge timber holding Andre over the side. But, instead of lashing himself to a timber, he held onto the rope holding his friend.

Dionne's eyes widened when she saw a monstrous wave crashing over the bow and down upon them. She made a desperate lunge for Nettie, trying to hold her while still clutching onto something stable as the killer

181

wave tore at them. It was as if the water had suddenly grown long, menacing tentacles and was a ravenous beast as it pulled and tugged, trying to claim more victims. Dionne could feel Nettie slowly slipping away, and try as she might, she could not hold on to her. After that wave had subsided, another wave was upon her and another and another, until finally her hold loosened, and she could feel herself being swept into the merciless sea.

Churning water closed over her head, and Dionne could feel herself being forced down and down. Her lungs screamed in agony. For one brief moment, Dionne thought how easy it would be just to open her mouth and allow the sea to claim her completely. But her instinct for survival was greater. She began to claw her way to the roaring surface, and at the precise moment when her lungs could no longer tolerate the lack of air, she burst through the surface and drew a huge gasping breath.

Once again she was forced back down, and once again she clawed her way back to life. How many times this happened she did not know, but there was a realization that her strength was quickly fading and that she would not be able to elude death's grip much longer. It was at that moment of abject hopelessness that Dionne felt something of substance within her grasp. Reaching desperately for it, she found several large pieces of timber that had been lashed together by heavy rope. Later, she would realize that before the storm had reached its fury, someone had prepared a raft. She clung to it tenaciously, knowing if she was to survive, this was her only chance. When the raft fell into a trough, she weakly crawled on it, lacing her arms through and around the rope.

Dionne heard a loud crackling roar. Raising her head, she saw the *Emerald Tempest* one last time.

Tattered pieces of sail clung to the remaining masts like spiderwebs hanging on trees. The storm had torn a huge gaping hole in her bow. It was opened, as if it were a great yawning mouth, and the *Emerald Tempest* gave one final agonizing scream before plunging into the depths of the sea.

Wind, rain, and waves lashed at Dionne and her precarious raft, but still she held on. It seemed as though the raft were more buoyant than a larger structure. It rode high on the crest of each wave, until gradually the sea began to subside as the storm passed in its fury.

The instinct for survival had given Dionne colossal strength, but as the storm gradually abated, half drowned she raised her head, and the fact that she had survived pierced her mind. Drawing a deep, ragged breath, she slumped forward and fell into the throes of unconsciousness.

Somewhere, miles and miles away, another half-drowned figure, caught in the gulf stream, clung precariously to life aboard a huge buoyant crate. She, too, was determined to live, determined to survive.

Chapter Thirteen

Dionne's mind became unclear and muddled as she and her tiny raft drifted upon the unrelenting sea. Seconds slowly dragged by and turned into minutes, the minutes into hours, and the hours into days, until she finally lost all track of time. She only knew there were periods of darkness and light.

There was a oneness about the sea and the sky that made it difficult for her to understand where one stopped and the other began. The storm had been the beginning of her hellish nightmare and the aftermath was nothing but a continuation of the same yet different kind of terror.

At times, she would have gladly bartered her soul to the devil for one drop of water or one tiny morsel of food. Then, at other times, whether it was during periods of lucidness or insanity she did not know, Dionne would raise a clenched fist toward the heavens and vow that she would not be beaten, that the sea would not win this ferocious battle of wills.

Her flesh became raw and blistered, bathed by the spray of salty sea water and scorched by the relentless burning sun. Her lips cracked, her throat became parched. Dionne knew she had lost the great battle when a gray fog settled over her raft and death hovered right above her; she heard its slow silent hissing and saw its great eyeless face. But there was elation in her defeat because somewhere in the tortured chambers of her mind, she knew she had won a victorious battle over the Devil. She had cheated him of his prey. She had not been cast into the pits of hell; instead, her soul soared into the lofty heights of heaven, for soft white clouds billowed overhead and kind, gentle hands touched her, bathed her face, and gave her cool sweet water to drink. During one vivid moment of lucidity, she opened her eyes and smiled into the faces of the crew that had been lost at sea.

When Dionne was conscious of opening her eyes again, she had difficulty in focusing them. She felt the overwhelming desire to touch something of substance but found she was too weak to move. Her mouth opened but no words would come. Terrified, she struggled to raise her head but that, too, seemed impossible. Her mind worked frantically. She did not know if she were alive or dead, or caught in some fearful world in between. Then, again when she felt gentle hands upon her brow and heard a soft, crooning voice, she knew she was safe. Closing her eyes, she drifted into a deep, restful sleep.

"Good evening," a distant voice said softly. "It is time for you to wake up." Although the voice was gentle, there was a firmness about it, like a mother calling to a stubborn child. "The doctor has said you have been asleep long enough. Now wake up."

Dionne tentatively blinked her eyes as if testing her ability to do so. Then they fluttered open and she held her breath, wondering what her first sight would be.

It looked to be an ordinary room. For just a brief moment, disappointment flickered through her. She had expected to see soft fluffy clouds and pearly gates.

186

"A—am . . . I in heaven?"

"Lands no, child," the gentle voice could not hide its amusement. "Although I must say, I am relieved to know that that was your first inclination. Now, I want you to remain calm. You showed signs of regaining consciousness a short time ago and I have already sent for my doctor. You have been extremely ill and it is imperative that you lie still and not become unduly upset."

Turning her head to one side, Dionne blinked, then slowly a woman came into view. At first glance it was easy to tell that the woman was much older than her voice implied. Shining silver hair framed her ageless beauty, the lines around her wide, generous mouth revealed that she smiled often, and her eyes were the gentlest blue she had ever seen. Dionne recognized her immediately.

"I've seen you before—or at least I think I have. But I thought you were an angel," Dionne murmured wondrously.

The woman chuckled easily. "Well, thank you for saying so, but I am very much alive—and you are, too."

The bedroom door opened and a large man carrying a small black bag entered.

The woman stood and anxiously went to greet him. "Andrew, thank goodness you could come immediately. I sent for you the moment I suspected she was regaining consciousness."

"Did she say anything about? . . ."

"No." She lowered her eyes apprehensively. "She just woke up a few minutes ago, and . . . I was afraid to try and go into any detail with her until you arrived. I did not know how upsetting my questions would be."

"I agree. I think it is best you waited for me to talk to her first." The doctor stepped close to Dionne's bedside. "Good evening, young lady. I see that you

187

have finally decided to join us. I am Dr. Blackmon, and this is Jeannine Phillips. You are in her home."

Dionne gasped and reached for the woman's hand. "Madame Phillips? Why, you must be Christopher's grandmother. But . . . how did I get here?" Her eyes widened with painful memories. "The ship . . . there was a terrible storm! Oh, my God!" Covering her face with her hands, she began to cry hysterically.

Jeannine gathered Dionne into her arms and gingerly rocked back and forth until her tears finally abated. Then, gently, the woman held her at arm's length and looked at her with sad, troubled eyes. "Child, were you on the *Emerald Tempest*?" The girl had babbled incoherently during the weeks she had been here about the *Emerald Tempest*, and while they still clung to a small shred of hope, they all feared the worst.

Closing her eyes, Dionne nodded and said, in a small tortured voice, "Yes, we all were."

"Tell me, do you know what happened to the . . . others?" She glanced anxiously at the doctor, then back to Dionne. She wet her lips nervously. "Do you know if there were any other survivors?"

Dionne tried to swallow but tears had closed her throat. In her mind's eye she could see the ship's deck, Andre and Nigel as they went over the side, the gaping hole where the mast once stood, and the wheel with the broken leather strap and the . . . Dionne screamed, shattering the silence. "No, no!" she cried hysterically. "One minute they were there on the ship, then the next minute they were . . . gone! The wind . . . the waves . . . then the water . . . it devoured the ship!"

Jeannine slumped back into the chair, her face reflecting every year she had lived. Her eyes were dark and haunted, as if she had come face to face with reality and found the sight too painful to bear.

The doctor knelt down on one knee and gave his strict attention to the woman he had known for so long. "Jeannine, I am so sorry."

"I knew all along they were lost, that they would never return. But I guess there was one part of me, deep down inside, that refused to give up hope." She took a long, shuddering breath. "At least I have the consolation that they died at sea. I think I prefer it this way, but I only wish I had a second chance to tell them both good-bye . . . just one last time." She rose slowly to her feet, leaning heavily on her cane. "I am very tired. I think I should go to my room and lie down for a while." She glanced at Dionne, who was still crying. "Andrew, will you please see to the young lady. . . . And tell her that I shall visit with her later, perhaps tomorrow."

"Jeannine, would you like something to help you sleep?" Andrew was worried about her. She had been clinging to this last shred of hope for so long, and now she had to face the stark, painful reality that her son and husband would never again return.

Shaking her head, she whispered softly, "Oh, no, I do not want anything. I am fine. Really I am. I just want to lie down for a while and be alone with my memories. And I have to think of Christopher. Strange as it may sound, I have to be strong for him when he comes home."

"Christopher is a grown man, Jeannine. He will be fine. It is you that I am worried about," Dr. Blackmon said as he lightly took her hand.

"That is precisely the point, Andrew. Christopher is a grown man. While I have lost a husband and a son, he has lost his father and grandfather, two people whom he worshiped more than life itself. I am a woman and I am permitted to cry and wail to my heart's content, but Christopher is a man and society demands that he keep all of his feelings locked up inside." She took a deep breath. "No, I am the one who will have to be strong. I cannot allow myself to grieve too much until he returns. I can show my grief then. By his being able to comfort me, he will also comfort himself." Turning, she walked slowly to the door and silently left the room.

The doctor turned his attention back to the girl. Her hysterical tears had subsided but she still sobbed quietly. He sprinkled a small amount of white powder into a glass, lifted her head, and urged her to drink it, telling her that it would make her sleep.

"No, no, please . . . I have to know what happened," she moaned softly. "How did I get here?"

"First, drink the medicine, and I will tell you what I know. And don't be alarmed, you will not go to sleep immediately. It will take a few minutes before the drug takes effect." He waited until she had swallowed the medicine before continuing, "You will have to bear in mind that we will never know all the details. I can only tell you our speculations and what the captain of the other ship told us."

"Other ship?"

"Yes, the *Storm Tide*. They were the ones who fished you out of the sea. And, using the captain's own words, you were more dead than alive. He said he figured you had been on that raft for at least three days, maybe more."

"But . . . the storm was so fierce . . . how did I survive . . . how did they survive? How could anyone survive that terrible . . . terrible . . ."

"From what the captain told me, they were close enough to land to be able to run to safety. Usually, a captain waits until there is no danger of a storm doubling back, but they had a load of perishable cargo and had set sail as soon as the storm had passed. Which, I might add, was very fortunate for you. If you had been on that raft for one more day, I am afraid you would never have made it. The captain said they had seen signs of debris and knew that a ship had either been lost or was foundering. He posted a lookout to watch for possible survivors. When they took you on board, they continued to watch for survivors." He sadly shook his head. "But there were none. However, we had hoped you might tell us that there were other rafts . . . and that you had become separated. We thought maybe, just maybe, others had been picked up by other ships."

With obvious dismay, Dionne rubbed her forehead. "I would like to give you and Madame Phillips encouragement, but from what I can remember, I am sure it would be false hope. The storm and the actual sinking of the ship are so vivid in my mind, but everything else seems so distant, so hazy."

The doctor nodded. "Yes, I suppose it does. I have always believed when one is faced with extreme danger or shock, the mind will sometimes retreat within itself in order to survive. And, to be blunt, you have been out for so long we were beginning to worry if you would ever come to your senses." He peered closely at her. "I feel it is a miracle you can remember anything at all."

Dionne sadly shook her head and her bottom lip began to quiver. The tragic expression in her eyes spoke of her misery. "I think . . . that was one miracle . . . I would rather have done without. I wish I could forget," she added solemnly.

"Perhaps in time you will." He closed his bag and prepared to leave.

"Dr. Blackmon, wait, please do not go yet. How long . . . how long have I been here?"

"Six weeks."

"Six weeks!" she repeated numbly.

"Yes, that is why we were so concerned about you." He gently patted her hand. "And now, Miss Debierne, you need your sleep. If my speculations are correct, you have someone other than yourself to think about. Now, go to sleep and try to get some rest."

A hazy glow had already started to slip over her when the doctor left the room. She wanted to call him back. She wanted to tell him he was wrong, that her name was Martin—Dionne Martin—not Debierne, but he was already gone. Just before the drowsiness overtook her, she remembered him saying something else, something that should have been very important, but for the life of her she could not recall what he had said.

"My, you look so much better today," Jeannine said with forced cheerfulness as she sat down beside Dionne's bed.

"Thank you, Madame Phillips," she said shyly. Dionne felt the woman was just being kind by saying how nice she looked. She had seen her reflection in the mirror early that morning when a maid gave her a bed bath and brushed her hair, and she thought she looked dreadful. All of those hours on the raft under the hot, blistering sun had played havoc with her usually fair complexion. While she had never been overly vain about her appearance, sun-darkened skin was something she had always gone to great lengths to avoid. But she did feel much better, and that in itself was something to be thankful for.

Peering at her luncheon tray, Jeannine frowned. "But you really should try to eat more. The cook said you hardly touched your breakfast, and now you've scarcely touched your lunch. You cannot regain your strength by eating like a bird."

"I ate as much as I could, honest."

"Yes, I suppose you did. Considering how long it has

been since you have been able to eat solid food, I guess we should not force you to eat more than you want. But I have to insist that you drink all of your orange juice. It is good for you."

Dionne's face clouded with uneasiness. "Madame Phillips, I am so confused. Yesterday the doctor called me Miss Debierne. But that is not my name. . . ."

Tears instantly filled the older woman's eyes and she pressed a trembling hand against her cheek in dismay. "Oh, no, child! We hoped you had not suffered a memory loss, but it seems as though you have . . . and so much is at stake!"

Dionne began breathing rapidly. "But I haven't lost my memory—at least I don't think I have! And, I swear, my name is not Debierne!"

Jeannine quickly took the girl's hand in hers. "Please, do not become alarmed. The doctor said it was possible that you might suffer from a loss of memory and that we would have to be patient." Gently, she brushed Dionne's hair from her forehead. "I cannot count the times you called Christopher's name in your anguish. And, aside from the fact that you and your maid were the only female passengers on board the *Emerald Tempest*, my husband sent me a letter describing you." She adamantly shook her head. "No, there's no doubt in my mind. You are Celeste Debierne."

"He wrote you a letter? But when?"

"Immediately after meeting you, then he wrote another letter before you left Martinique." Seeing Dionne's obvious confusion, she explained further, "He knew I was concerned over the fact that a marriage had been arranged for our grandson, and I suppose he wanted to reassure me that you were everything we hoped you would be."

The words were on Dionne's lips to deny everything,

to explain exactly who she was, when the woman began to sob. "Madame Phillips . . . please don't cry."

Jeannine dabbed at her eyes with her handkerchief. "I'm sorry, I seldom lose control this way. It is just so . . . what you said was so upsetting. . . ." Then she shrugged. "You have no idea how important it is to me—and to Christopher—that you do remember your identity, because I have a rather startling proposal to make to you."

"I don't think I understand." She bit her lip, her throat feeling raw from unuttered protests.

"Bear with me for a moment, child, then you will. You see, I had a visit earlier this morning from Christopher's cousin, a man by the name of Nicholas Dumont. Accompanying him was his shyster lawyer, a man who has no scruples, no morals whatsoever, and I might add that he and Nicholas are two of a kind. They had in their possession a copy of my husband's will. Actually, it was not the original will—our attorney has that—but they had in their possession a stipulation that has been passed down from generation to generation." Noting the doubtful, confused expression on Dionne's face, she sighed heavily. "I realize I am not making much sense, but please, just hear me out, then hopefully you will understand. You see, my husband came from an extremely wealthy family. I believe the expression commonly used is 'old money.' Years ago, before the Phillipses ever left England—I am referring to my husband's grandfather when he was a young man—Peter Phillips had two sons: one son wanted to dedicate his life to the priesthood, and the other . . . well, to put it delicately, he preferred relationships with men over women. Peter was so afraid the Phillips name would end with him, he forced his son to leave the priesthood in order to marry and produce an heir. Without going into all of the legal details, it was

194

stipulated in his will, and in the wills following his, that if the last male member of the Phillips family was not married by the time he reached his thirtieth birthday, then the fortune would revert to the next male member of the family, however distant, as long as he agreed to change his last name to Phillips and there was a direct blood line."

Fear knotted up inside Dionne as she watched the woman with impotent fascination.

"Although I knew about the stipulation in the will, I have been so worried over William and Edward's fate, I had forgotten about it. Unfortunately, Nicholas did not. He has been hovering around this house like a vulture, just waiting—I think, hoping—for proof that William and Edward were lost. Before I was even dressed this morning, he arrived, smacking his greedy lips with a petition in hand to change his name and making demands that the will be executed immediately." Worriedly, she shook her head. "Naturally I sent for my attorney, but after he looked over their documents, he said Nicholas had a legal claim."

Dionne's mind worked frantically. "Well . . . can't you stall them? Can it not wait until Christopher returns? Surely he is due any day now?"

"Those were the very same questions I asked our attorney. And, yes, Nicholas could be stalled if it were not for one major problem. You see, today is Christopher's birthday. And even if he arrived tomorrow, it would be too late." She closed her eyes, tears falling silently down her ashen cheeks. "Perhaps it would not bother me so much if Nicholas were a decent man. But he is a rogue, a scoundrel. His parents died last year and left him a considerable amount of money, but he has already squandered it on women and gambling." She slammed the base of her cane against the floor. "Who am I trying to fool? It would not matter if Nicholas Dumont were a saint. I would still fight to see that Christopher gets what is rightfully his. Do not misunderstand. I have been provided for. This house is mine and I have enough money to see me through the rest of my years. But Christopher has worked so hard to build this shipping line into what it is today. He has poured his heart and soul into it. Since he has lost his father and grandfather, I shudder to think what it will do to him if he loses the shipping line too."

"Madame Phillips, why are you telling me all of this?" Dionne asked softly.

The woman smiled smugly. "Because you, my dear, can prevent this from happening."

"How?" Suddenly, Dionne had a wild impulse to flee. She had the most horrible feeling she would not want to hear what Christopher's grandmother was about to propose.

"By marrying Christopher's proxy."

"I . . . don't know what you mean." Dionne eyed her warily.

"A proxy marriage is when the bride or groom cannot be present and someone else stands up for him or her. I asked my attorney about it, and it is quite legal and binding." Eyes unwavering, she returned Dionne's gaze.

"But—but wouldn't Christopher have to agree to something like this?"

"In a sense of the word, he already has. You see, my husband, my son, or my grandson never sailed on a voyage without leaving behind their power of attorney. This gives me the right to sign their names to any legal document."

Dionne stifled a sob. She had to put an end to this. She could not continue to give Madame Phillips hope—hope that would soon turn into bitter despair.

Jeannine mistakenly took Dionne's silence for

196

reluctance. "My dear, I hate to bring any undue influence on you. I know how much store a young lady places in a proper wedding, but you really should think of the child as well."

Dionne felt as though someone had hit her soundly in the chest, knocking every ounce of breath from her lungs. A child? Did the woman actually say a child?

Jeannine gripped Dionne's hand and squeezed it. "Now, don't worry. I am not about to condemn you. If I did that, I would have to condemn Christopher as well, because it does take two to make a baby. I know how young love is. Although it is definitely not proper, emotions get out of control and . . ." She struggled to find the right words. "You should consider the baby. Christopher may return tomorrow, but he may not be back until next week or next month or, heaven forbid, three months from now. Dr. Blackmon said you were about two months along. While the gossips' tongues will not be silenced, at least a seven-month baby can be explained to the child when he is old enough to count on his fingers the date of his parents' anniversary and the date of his birth." She lifted her head defiantly. "However, I will be completely honest with you. The child's welfare is not my greatest worry right now, but the loss of my grandson's rightful inheritance is."

Completely stunned, Dionne had only heard half of what the woman had said. The word *baby* seeped like icy fingers into her brain. She gazed at Jeannine in despair. Her voice was horror-stricken: "A baby? I am actually going to have a baby?"

Jeannine gasped and remorse swept her features. "You mean . . . the doctor did not tell you?"

"No, he told me nothing about a child."

"Oh, child, I am so sorry!" Her apology was sincere. "I thought he told you last night. And I guess I failed to realize—to remember—that you have no idea what has

197

happened over the past few weeks. Other than you and Christopher being ... intimate, being unconscious like you were, you would certainly have no cause to suspect you were pregnant."

Suddenly feeling very weak, Dionne collapsed against her pillows. She felt as though her thoughts had been dredged from a place beyond logic and reason. A baby! Dear God, what was she going to do now? Tears began to fill her eyes.

Jeannine squared her shoulders, drawing from within herself the strength and courage that made her the grand woman she was. There was an air of defiance in her tone, as well as subtle kindness, "Child, I do not want to sound harsh, but crying will not solve anything. The only thing that will solve our problems is for you to do as I have suggested. And I have to have an answer immediately."

Dionne placed her hands over her face. She rued the day she had ever met Christopher Phillips. From the moment he had entered her life, he had brought nothing but pain and heartbreak. And now, an innocent little child would have to bear the shame of their sins. Unpleasant memories raced through her mind: memories of being called a bastard; memories of being the object of cruel children's taunts and their parents' even more cruel rejection. Would her child suffer the same fate? After all the lies Celeste had told Christopher, he would never believe the child belonged to him, and that left her in the position that she and she alone would have to be responsible for her unborn child.

With all of this in mind, Dionne began to seriously consider Madame Phillips's proposal. What if she did agree to marry Christopher by proxy? Maybe that would be the perfect solution, not only for him but for her as well. That would give her baby a legal name—its rightful name—and Christopher's fortune would not end up in the hands of someone else. Then, later, when he found a woman he really wanted to marry, their marriage could be dissolved, and they would both be able to go on with their lives.

She closed her eyes and the mental image of him holding another woman in his arms the way he had held her was painful. Still, she would have to be realistic. . . . He could never love her. But if she saved his fortune, perhaps she could eventually win his gratitude. That was a poor consolation, but it seemed better than nothing.

That left the problem of her identity. She wondered if Madame Phillips would agree to the marriage if she knew her real identity. As adamant as the woman was about preventing the blackguard cousin from inheriting her grandson's rightful inheritance, perhaps she would; then again, maybe she would not. If her child was to have a legal name, it was a chance she could not take.

Taking a deep breath, Dionne squared her shoulders and looked directly into Madame Phillips's eyes. "If I understood correctly, the marriage has to take place today."

"Yes, it does."

"Considering my lack of strength, would it be suitable for the ceremony to be held in here?"

Jeannine found it difficult to contain her glee. "I see no harm in that whatsoever!"

"How soon can the arrangements be made?"

Smiling, she slammed the tip of her cane against the floor. "Just as soon as I can send for the judge and my attorney. It will only be a civil ceremony. Later, you and Christopher can get married in the church, but for now, this will be quite legal and binding." She started to rise, then she sank back onto the chair. A satisfied gleam shone in her eyes. "Would you object if I sent for Nicholas and his attorney? If they attended your wedding?"

For a moment Dionne thought about how unscrupulous the men were, and she could not help but smile. "I think they would make excellent witnesses."

Jeannine chuckled. "Young lady, you are a person after my own heart. I see that we will get along famously."

Dionne turned her face aside, fearing what her expression would reveal. She could not help but wonder if the woman's opinion of her would remain the same after she learned the truth. Somehow, she did not think so.

Chapter Fourteen

The light breeze was tropical as it mingled with the salty sea air until it felt like damp silk against Christopher's skin. As it had numerous times in the past, a feeling of awe swept over him when the *Blue Diamond* came at last to the mouth of the Mississippi. He noted with satisfaction that the river was as it had always been—a long brown ribbon of water running and intermingling with the deep blue waters of the Gulf.

In the river's open mouth, a hundred tiny islands had been scattered. Turning and curving among them, the *Blue Diamond* began to move upstream. The ship quickly glided past bayous and creeks that led into dark murky blackness, uprooted trees that lay rotting in the swampy water, and huge cypress trees with tangled moss clinging to their limbs, making the entire area look primeval and wild.

The ship sailed onward, into the Barataria Sound, past Grande Terre, where the infamous Jean Lafitte, one of the deadliest pirates in the West Indies and the Gulf Coast area, took refuge with his band of cutthroats.

Hour after hour the ship plowed northward. The swamps and waterlogged forest seemed to effortlessly slide by. On either side of the cleared land by the river stood row upon row of cotton stalks heavily loaded with their yellow blooms, which would soon make bolls and then ripen into long lines of snowy white cotton.

The southern sunset came abruptly; with a sweep of a dark brush, all gold, pink, and hazy purples were wiped from the sky and the thick night came down among the rising din of screaming whistles and bells as the river traffic increased.

By the time the *Blue Diamond* nosed into the wharf with a shudder and a thump, a bright moon shone over the crescent city, shining on its harbor and teeming streets like an unwavering beacon. There was a rattle of ropes as the last of the sails was lowered and the gangplank clattered into place.

Christopher smiled when his rented carriage turned up the long road that led to his home, which stood majestically among many towering oak trees. He could not help but wonder what Celeste had thought the first time she had seen his home. Remembering how greedily her eyes had lit up over the presents he and his grandfather had given her, Crescentview must have made a grand impression. It stood three stories high, and the front porch pillars were so huge that he could not begin to wrap his arms around one.

When the carriage pulled to a stop, Christopher climbed out and pressed some money into the driver's hand. "That's all right, I can manage this by myself," he said when the driver started to assist him. He hefted his small seaman's trunk atop his shoulder and hurried toward the front door. Then, the smile quickly faded from his face and he stopped short. His mouth became dry with fear and dread knotted in his stomach like a hard ball, for hanging on the door was a black wreath, a mourning wreath.

Dropping his trunk, he raced for the door, flung it open, and ran inside. Sitting, half asleep in the foyer, was George, a servant who had been with the Phillips family for as long as Christopher could remember.

"George?" he asked fearfully. "What's happened?"

George came awake with a start, his rheumy eyes watering even more at the sight of Christopher. "Mister Chris! Thank the Lord, you've finally come home! The Missus 'structed me to stay down here every night and watch for you." His chin trembled. "Somethin' terrible done happened!"

Christopher was beside himself with worry. "What is it, George?"

The old Negro shook his head sadly. "The Missus said she'd tell you. She said to go on into your papa's study and for me to fetch her as soon as you got here." Huge tears ran unashamed down his wrinkled cheeks. "But it's bad, Mister Chris! Oh, Lordy, it's bad!"

Christopher knew it was useless to press for information from George. If his grandmother had given the old man instructions, he would follow them to the letter regardless of what anyone said.

For what seemed like an eternity, Christopher waited, daring not to think about which loved one he had lost as he paced back and forth across his father's study until, finally, the door opened and his grandmother entered. His heart lurched at the sight of her. She looked so old, so frail, so alone, he realized immediately that it must have been his grandfather who had passed away. He crossed the room quickly and took her hand in his. "Grandmother . . ."

Gazing up at him with tears in her eyes, she gently pressed her fingertips against his lips to silence him. "Chris, I would give anything in the world not to be the one who had to tell you this." She gestured toward the sofa. "But, please, first let us sit down. I haven't been

203

feeling very strong lately."

Realizing she had to do this in her own way, in her own time, Christopher did not press for any details. He already felt the loss, and it tore at his heart like a burning pain.

Clutching her handkerchief tightly in her veined hands, she spoke softly, "So much has happened, I scarcely know where to begin. For days now, I have thought about how I would tell you—I even prepared a little speech—but now I think I have forgotten every word. There is no easy way." She paused and bit her bottom lip to keep it from trembling so. Tears blinded her eyes and choked her voice. "Two months ago . . . while on . . . the way . . . back from Martinique . . . the *Emerald Tempest* . . . was caught in a . . . terrible storm and was lost at sea. All hands and . . . crew were lost, also all of the passengers, except for your fiancée. Celeste was the . . . only survivor."

Christopher reeled from the impact of her softly spoken words. "What?" Exhaling a great breath of air, he sagged against the back of the sofa. He swallowed hard and turned his face aside while struggling for control of his emotions. He had expected to hear that his grandfather had died . . . but not news like this. It was too horrible to fully comprehend.

Rising blindly, Christopher walked over to a glass case where tiny replicas of every ship in their line were proudly displayed. After his grandfather had retired from the sea, he had painstakingly carved them, adding billowing white sails, braiding string so that it resembled rope, and added each precise detail to every ship until it looked exactly like the original. He stared at the replica of the *Emerald Tempest*, his expression one of mute wretchedness. He stood with his hands shoved into his pockets, his shoulders hunched forward, as the face of his father, his grandfather, and all the faces of the crew passed before his eyes. It was a deep loss that would take a long time for him to accept, if he ever could.

Jeannine's voice choked in despair, "I doubt if we will ever know all the details, and in a strange way, for that I am thankful. How Celeste survived we will never know either, but I do feel it was a miracle. She was rescued three days later, more dead than alive."

Christopher whirled and spoke bitterly, "I don't want to hear about Celeste right now, Grandmother! Your husband—my grandfather—your son—my father—and men—good men, some I've known since I was a small boy—died with that ship, and you expect me to be thankful"—he gestured wildly, groping for the right words to explain his feelings—"that a young twit of a girl somehow survived this terrible tragedy? I am sorry, Grandmother, even if she is my fiancée, I can't find it in my heart to do that!"

Suddenly, noting the pain and heartbreak evident on his beloved grandmother's face, he rushed to her side and gathered her gently in his arms. "I didn't mean to lash out at you," he whispered, his misery like a steel weight. "Here I've been, thinking only of my pain, and you have had to face this all alone, without anyone by your side."

"Hush, love," she murmured softly, hugging him close to her. "At first, I admit to having the same thoughts about Celeste, too, but I soon realized it was only my grief, only my anger over having suffered such a loss. Later, when you have had time to think, you will believe differently, too. But for now, please, just hold me tightly and allow me to hold you. We Phillipses have always been strong, but I suspect our strength comes from each other."

"Oh, Grandmother, we are going to miss them so much!" Christopher wished desperately to be a small boy again, so that he could bury his face in her lap and cry until the pain was gone, but he also knew his loss went far beyond what tears could repair.

It was difficult at first, but the longer they talked the easier it became for them to share small unimportant events that had happened over the years. One moment they would laugh over some amusing anecdote, and the next moment their eyes would grow misty over a past remembrance. It was difficult for them, but together they took a step forward toward the realization that life goes on regardless of one family's pain and tragic loss.

It was much later before Jeannine could bring herself to tell her grandson what else had happened. "Chris," she began slowly, "I hate to add another burden on you —especially after such devastating news—but it is something you have to know. It cannot wait."

He had been about to pour them a snifter of brandy. Turning to face his grandmother, the expression on his face revealed his concern and reluctance.

"Please, do not look so stricken. It is not as bad as I made it sound," she hurried to say. "I believe the . . . situation was handled in the only possible, logical way it could be handled." She patted the arm of a chair sitting next to the sofa. "Come, sit down, and I want you to pay close attention to what I have to say."

Christopher did as she requested and, with guarded eyes, watched her closely. He took a deep breath and said, "Somehow, I have the feeling I am not going to like what you are about to tell me."

"I doubt if you will. Nevertheless, I believe you will agree that we handled the problem correctly." She gazed directly at him, not wanting to delay it any longer. "Do you recall the details concerning that stipulation in your grandfather's will, the one that dates back to his grandfather?"

Christopher could have sworn his blood had been replaced by ice water. He did remember, he remembered it all too clearly. He mouthed the words slowly, "Yes, I do. The last surviving male has to be married by the age of thirty or the entire fortune will revert to . . ." Stunned, he stared at his grandmother. "Are you trying to tell me Nicholas, that . . . dirty son-of-a . . . that he laid claim to what is mine?"

"Oh, he tried to. He and his attorney arrived early that morning, the day of your birthday, with all of the necessary papers in hand. Nicholas was barely able to conceal his glee over the thought of getting his hands on all of that money." She shrugged with satisfaction. "If he had not been so greedy and had waited until the day after, there would not have been a single thing we could have done, because quite frankly, I had forgotten the date—and I am ashamed to say, I had even forgotten about the stipulation."

He swallowed with difficulty and found his voice. "I take it you were able to do something to stop him. But how? I thought the stipulation was ironclad."

Jeannine stared at him boldly, defying him to complain. "I explained the situation to Celeste and convinced her to marry your proxy."

"You did what?" he asked incredulously.

"A proxy marriage . . . it is very legal . . ."

Christopher ran his hand through his hair. "I know what a proxy marriage is, it's just that it took me by surprise." He thought about it for a moment then shrugged. "Well, I suppose it doesn't make much difference. We were going to be married anyway, except . . ."

"Except what, Christopher? Surely you do not object, do you?" she asked, suddenly uncertain.

He looked at her sharply. She never addressed him

by his complete name unless she was extremely concerned. He hurried to reassure her, "Oh, no, Grandmother, I don't object. It's just that"—he gave a humorless laugh—"the only reason she and her father were coming to New Orleans on the *Tempest* was because she insisted upon having a huge, fancy wedding. I think it is kind of ironic the way it turned out. Not only was a fancy wedding impossible, she had to marry my proxy as well." He sighed. "But, considering the fortune involved, I imagine she was quite willing to forego a fancy ceremony."

Confused, Jeannine frowned. "That was not the impression she gave me."

"You mean she would have rather had a fancy wedding even if it left us penniless?" Astonished, he shook his head. "That sure doesn't sound like her."

"No, you misunderstood. The impression she gave me was . . . reluctance to marry you because you might not approve. In fact, I had to—as you might say—do some tall talking just to convince her."

"Celeste? You have to be kidding!"

"No, I am serious."

He slowly raised his brows as if not quite able to believe what he had just heard. "It sure doesn't sound like Celeste."

Deeply concerned, Jeannine placed her hand on his arm. "Christopher, I realized from the very beginning you were reluctant about this arranged marriage, and that you only agreed to it because you thought it would please your father and grandfather." She paused, thinking about the baby Celeste carried. "From what I was led to believe, you and Celeste became rather . . . shall we say, well acquainted while you were on Martinique. But now, from the way you talk, I am not so sure. Tell me, and please be completely honest not only with me but with yourself. Do you have any feelings at all for this young woman?"

Again, Christopher ran his hands through his hair as he tried to weigh his feelings. There were so many conflicting memories. "If you are asking if I love her, no, I don't," he finally stated bluntly. "My idea of love between a man and a woman is something that does not happen in a day, a week, or a month. It is a relationship that builds over the years into what you and Grandfather shared."

"We were very happy together, but I think you are a little too idealistic."

He gazed at her, sincerity shining from his eyes. "Maybe so, but during the voyage home, I tried not to even think about her, and when I did it was"—he shrugged helplessly—"trying to think of a way to call off the wedding." He shook his head. "Celeste is a hard person to get to know. While on Martinique one minute, I would think she was a selfish, greedy person—all of the qualities in a woman I detest—then the next minute, she was caring and compassionate. She is a mystery to me, Grandmother, a complete mystery."

She wrung her hands together worriedly. "After hearing how you feel, I almost regret . . ."

". . . arranging my proxy marriage?"

She nodded.

"Don't." He gently patted her hand, pushing aside the memory of that night he and Celeste had shared. Regardless of how magical it had seemed, one drunken interlude could not change how he truly felt. "I realize this probably makes me sound cold and callous, especially after telling you how I really feel about her, but under the circumstances, I would rather return to find a wife, even if she is Celeste, than return and discover I didn't have a penny to my name. And knowing dear cousin Nicholas, there is no doubt in my mind he would have taken everything he could have gotten his hands on."

Jeannine was still not convinced. "That makes me feel a little better, but not much. I just had to do something, Chris. I could not stand idly by and allow Nicholas to claim everything you have worked for all of your life. Of course I realize you cannot claim all of the credit for the success of the Phillips shipping line. Your father and grandfather worked hard, too, but I also know it has been fifteen years since William actively worked in the business, and your father"—she smiled at the memory—"well, Edward loved the sea, period. He never cared about expanding the business the way you did."

It hurt Christopher that his grandmother was so worried. Again, he tried to reassure her, "I know you did what you thought best, Grandmother, and I appreciate it. It was the only possible thing you could have done under the circumstances. And as for me and Celeste, don't worry about us. Everything will work out fine, you'll see."

"I hope so, Chris," she said slowly, thinking about the baby and wondering what his reaction would be when Celeste told him. Suddenly, Jeannine hoped the girl would wait a week or two before telling him about the child. It would give him a little time to adjust, time to deal with his father and grandfather's death, his marriage, the entire way his life had changed in such a short time.

Christopher gently caressed her cheek. "You have to be tired. You should go back to bed and try to get some rest."

"Yes, I am tired," she admitted. "However, I think there is something else you should know."

His brows drew together in an agonized expression. "Grandmother, unless it is terribly important, I had just as soon not hear about anything else tonight."

"It is important, not devastating, but important. It concerns Celeste. And it's only a word of caution, but . . . you must be careful what you say to her. She has been through a terrible ordeal herself. Even though she has been here nearly two months now, she only became aware of her surroundings a couple of weeks ago. At first, Dr. Blackmon thought she was in a coma, but her symptoms puzzled him. After reading through some of his medical journals, he decided that she was not in a coma; instead, her mind had withdrawn within itself as a protective measure."

"I am not sure I understand, Grandmother," Christopher said slowly. Then, his eyes widened. "Are you trying to tell me she is insane?"

"Oh, heavens no!" Jeannine waved her hand as if to push aside that silly a notion. "The way Andrew explained it to me, Celeste suffered such a . . . terrible ordeal, her mind could not cope with all of the horrors she witnessed. It was only after she became comfortable with her surroundings that her mind came to realize she was safe and that it was all right for her to accept reality again." Tears glistened in her eyes at the memory. "Chris, I felt so sorry for her when she finally awoke; her first conscious thought was that she was dead. And the first thing she asked was if I were an angel." Jeannine sorrowfully shook her head. "It was so pitiful."

The enormity of all that Celeste must have suffered swept through Christopher. Pity for her filled him. His expression was guarded as he asked, "Do you think I should wait a day or two before I see her?"

"Definitely not! What that girl needs the most right now is what I needed a short time ago." Jeannine, knowing they had been intimate, did not feel reluctant to offer her suggestion. "She needs to be held, to be

211

consoled, to feel loved, and to be comforted. And, I might add, it certainly would not hurt you either. You admitted to me that you do not love her. But if the two of you are able to share your grief, perhaps that will be the beginning of a bond between you, a bond you will have in the future . . . if you are to expect any happiness." Using her cane for support, she slowly rose to her feet. "You think about what I said, and if you decide I am right"—she attempted a smile—"then I am sure you will know what to do. And by the way, if I may be so bold as to add, physically, there is nothing to prevent you and her from . . . doing what comes naturally between a man and a woman."

"Grandmother!" It surprised Christopher that she would speak so openly about such a relationship.

"Don't look at me that way, young man! I was married to your grandfather for nearly fifty years. And while I fully realize women are not supposed to talk about such things, William and I shared a very pleasant . . . relationship together. I will also state the very closest moments in our personal lives came during times of crisis. We found comfort in each other. That is why I feel it is so important that you go to her now. And, if you have as much intelligence as I think you do, then I feel you should know that I had her moved into your bedroom. I felt she would be much more comfortable there." She caressed his cheek, then lovingly kissed his forehead. "As for me, I am tired now. Good night, my love." With amazing ease, she turned and quickly left the room.

Christopher stood there for a moment, carefully considering everything his grandmother had said. Perhaps she was right. Perhaps he did need Celeste now, maybe not in an intimate way—making love to a woman was the last thing he had on his mind right now. News such as he had received tonight had a way of cooling even the most passionate ardor. Still, as his grandmother had said, if they were able to share their grief, it could be the beginning of a tender relationship between them. And, feeling about her the way he did, if this marriage was ever to be anything like his grandparents', then he should do everything within his power to make it successful. Without giving himself the chance to change his mind, he strode quickly across the room, out into the foyer, and up the long winding staircase.

Chapter Fifteen

Finding a candle on the table that stood in the hall beside his bedroom door, Christopher lit it, then opened the door and entered. He could see Celeste lying on her side, her arm wrapped snugly around a pillow. Even though the night was warm, the heavy drapes had been partially drawn and they only moved slightly from the nighttime breeze. It did not surprise him that the room had been deliberately darkened against the moonlit night. He had heard too many times about men surviving from a shipwreck; they would complain of the salt water stinging their eyes, irritating them, and after days of being in a lifeboat or a raft under the burning sun, their eyes would be sensitive to light for a long time thereafter.

He quietly walked over to her bedside and gently touched her arm, but she did not stir. Under the flickering light of the candle he noticed a small vial of white powder sitting on the night table, and his lips settled in a grim line. Celeste was just the kind of woman who would turn to something like laudanum to ease her misery. Then, he instantly felt ashamed for his thoughts. Not having seen the horrors she had witnessed, perhaps he should not be so quick to judge.

Christopher weighed the advice his grandmother had given him against his own feelings of weariness and decided not to make a further attempt to wake her. There was a small voice that nagged at him, saying if Celeste did awake, there could be a strong possibility she would expect him to consummate their marriage, and he realized he had absolutely no desire for a woman tonight. Christopher chortled to himself but it was without humor. It was certainly the first time he had ever had that particular feeling!

He opened the drapes further to allow more fresh air to enter, then walked softly to his side of the bed, blew out the candle, and got undressed.

He lay on his back with fingers entwined beneath his head, gazing at the shadows dancing on the ceiling. Three tall trees stood outside the bedroom windows and their limbs began to sway as the wind rose slightly. A faint smile pulled at his lips as he remembered the countless hours he had lain in this same bed and watched the shadows gradually change shape, becoming knights riding their magnificent armor-plated horses as they searched for fire-breathing dragons. Oh, the wars that were waged, battles that were lost and won in the blinking of an eye. Then, almost magically, the horses would change into heavily armed men-of-war and the knights into fierce pirates. Everyone thought he had inherited his love for the sea from his father, and perhaps, in part, he did. But only Christopher knew the entire truth. His love for the sea and exciting adventure stemmed from the battles his imagination had waged on the ceiling.

Then Christopher's smile faded as he remembered his grief with painful clarity. He knew it was wrong to avoid facing the truth, but for a moment he wished he had never returned home. There was an intense longing in him to feel the wind once again in his face, the taste of the salty water upon his tongue, to escape the painful realities of life and death. If there were any possible way, he would have gone immediately back to his ship, set sail, and not returned until he felt he could cope with all of his feelings. But that would have been the coward's way out. He was a man, the only man of the family now, and there were certain responsibilities he had to face whether he wanted to face them or not.

He turned his gaze toward Celeste, unconsciously noting how the moonlight shone on her dark hair. He was momentarily reminded of Martinique, a dimly lit stable, and an incredibly passionate, loving woman. But there was something about that night that nagged him. It was not a constant thing, but it lay just beneath the surface where he would think about it occasionally, then put it aside when he could not remember. Christopher supposed if it had been important, he would have remembered regardless of how much he'd had to drink.

Then, the room darkened as a black cloud scudded across the face of the moon and lightning cracked through the sky. The wind outside became stronger and its voice whispered, then screamed through the heavy ladened limbs of the giant oak trees. In the distance, a roar of thunder sounded.

She moaned and snuggled closer to her pillow. Her breathing became more ragged and she stirred fretfully. Then, when a fierce bolt of lightning struck a tree somewhere near the house and thunder grumbled louder, pitiful sobs tore from her throat. She flung the pillow from her embrace and sat bolt upright in the bed. "No! No!" she screamed hysterically, clamping her hands over her ears. "Make it stop! Please make it stop!"

Realizing the approaching storm was the cause of her nightmare, Christopher gathered her close and she clutched at him frantically. He could feel her heart beat savagely against his chest.

"Hush, my sweet," he whispered softly, pulling her down close beside him and deeply breathing the delicate fragrance of her hair. "It's nothing but a thunderstorm, that's all; just a thunderstorm. There's nothing to be afraid of."

Having taken a headache powder earlier, Dionne found it difficult to come fully awake. "Christopher?" she murmured groggily. "Is it really you, or am I dreaming?" She opened her eyes to see the familiar countenance that had been so vivid in her memory, and an elated feeling washed over her. She had not had a moment's peace knowing he was somewhere out there on that devil sea. The fear for his safety had been almost as strong as her grief.

"You are not dreaming, it's really me," he replied in a gentle voice, reasssuring her as though talking to a child.

"B—but . . . how . . . when? . . ."

"I just returned a short while ago. I spoke with Grandmother and she told me everything." His arms tightened around her when lightning struck again and she trembled from stark terror.

She sobbed raggedly. A great need burned within her to pour out the misery she had been attempting to hide. "Oh, Christopher, it was horrible! It was all so horrible!" Dionne's recollection of the tragedy was so strong it didn't occur to her that Christopher thought he was holding Celeste. The only thing she could think of was how terrible it all had been, and how comforting and consoling it now felt for someone to hold her. His arms felt so good that it was almost like she had been invited home again after a long, lonely exile.

"I know, I know, and I am so sorry," he murmured gently, amazed over how she fit so perfectly in his arms. "Now hush and go back to sleep. There is no need to worry. I am here and I will keep you safe."

218

"Oh, but Christopher, they are all gone!" she cried in anguish. "Andre, your father and grandfather . . . everyone . . . they are all gone!"

Christopher did not answer immediately. There was nothing he could say, his throat having become too tightly constricted. Not wanting her to know he did not trust himself to speak, he pulled her even closer and buried his face in the velvety softness of her skin. He could feel her breath, feathery soft against the mat of hair on his chest. He could not help but marvel at the feeling that it was as though Celeste had been made for him, for she fit against him pefectly, her gentle curves just right for the length of his hard, muscular body. He'd only experienced this particular feeling once before and it had been that night in the stable. But instead of arousing him now, it merely made him feel more compassionate, more sensitive to all of the horrors she had suffered.

Feeling his arms tighten around her, Dionne's eyes widened as she floundered in an agonizing maelstrom. At last she had come fully awake and now realized Christopher thought he was holding Celeste in his arms. She bit her lip until it throbbed like her pulse, then she trembled, not knowing if he meant to claim his husband's rights or not. Dear Lord, what would she do if he did? How could she allow him to make love to her with him believing she was Celeste? What would she do when he learned the truth? She had no way of knowing, but one thing was certain: Regardless of his reaction, she was in for heartbreak.

Dionne had time to think, to reflect during the past two weeks, and had reached a startling and even strangely frightening conclusion. That first time they'd met, it had not been dislike she'd felt for him; instead, it had been a deep attraction. To claim dislike for him had only been her way of protecting herself against being hurt. Then later, when she discovered he was Celeste's betrothed, she had attempted to put him firmly from her mind, but it seemed as though she refused to leave it alone. That night in the stable was proof positive that she cared deeply for him. While she had almost convinced herself it had only been the heady effects of the wine, deep down inside she knew she could have somehow resisted—if she had wanted to badly enough—and she could have done it without making him suspicious. Oh, she could stand and claim, until the end of time, that she'd had no idea what Celeste was planning, but her conscience knew differently. She had coveted another woman's man, and now she and her child would have to pay dearly for that sin. There was no doubt in her mind that he would hate her as soon as he learned her true identity, if for no other reason than that she had lived and Celeste had died.

Christopher felt her grow more tense in his arms and that was disturbing to him. "Relax, Celeste," he whispered, and caressed her gently. "Go back to sleep. I am not going to . . ." His voice faltered. "Tonight, I just want to hold you."

Dionne had been so wary that she did not realize she had been holding her breath. Grateful that Christopher was the sort of man who would have thoughtful consideration for a woman, she breathed a deep sigh of relief as her mind quickly raced. I should tell him now, this very minute. It would be the perfect time to tell him the truth.

Slowly building courage from somewhere deep inside, she lay there for a few minutes more, then hesitantly began, "Christopher . . . please, I have to . . . talk to you." She paused for a moment, waiting for him to answer. "Christopher? Please, it is so important." Again she waited, but her only reply was the wind moaning through the treetops. Then, she heard his even breathing and realized, with dismay, that he had already fallen fast asleep.

Dionne winced painfully as a bright burst of sunlight hit her across the face. Raising a hand to cover her eyes, she discovered it did not provide much help and struggled to move, but it was as if a strong band of steel held her immobile. It was not until she felt the tightening of Christopher's arm that she came fully awake. In a rush, the events of the past few weeks came flooding back to her, causing her to blush shamefully at the terrible scheme she intended to employ if Christopher did not immediately agree to her wishes. She felt a wretchedness of mind that almost equalled the agony of her suffering the grief and distress of the shipwreck.

Cautiously, so as not to waken him, she turned her head slightly to study him, as though somehow half hoping to find him changed; but he was not. Though the tiny lines around his mouth and eyes were not so pronounced in his sleep, there was still an arrogance about his dark, handsome features that could not be denied. Just the sight of him made her heart pound viciously beneath her breast. She tried not to think of what the future might have held for them if only the circumstances had been different.

For all intents and purposes, last night was her wedding night and this was the morning after. How disappointing. This was never how she had imagined it would be. Dionne sighed wistfully, her heart aching at the depressing thought. If she had been a wife of his choice, she would have awoken happy and contented instead of feeling sorrow and fear. He would have had one arm wrapped possessively around her, one hand tangled in her cascading mane of hair, and his lips would have been nibbling at the lobe of her ear.

Then, Dionne tensed with shame. Stop that! Stop allowing your mind to torture you this way. Those daydreams are nothing but wishful thinking. If worse comes to worse, and if you have to issue those ugly threats, you will be fortunate if he even looks at you in the future, much less holds you in his arms! Don't be a fool, Dionne! Don't allow your whimsical daydreams to lead you astray. You are in for so much heartbreak as it is, without asking for more. She turned troubled eyes toward him. Christopher, wake up, she silently pleaded. Please wake up. I want to get this terrible thing over and done with!

As if in answer to her prayer, Dionne felt him move. She swallowed hard, knowing she would soon be faced with the startling moment of truth. It was something she would have gone to any lengths to avoid, yet that was impossible. Her day of reckoning had come.

For the past hour Christopher had been slowly awakening. His eyes had opened when the faint blush of dawn had touched the sky, but he was too weary to rise. Instead, he had snuggled back into the lulling security of the gray area between sleep and awareness that he always found so peaceful, comfortable, and strangely reassuring.

Now that Celeste was beginning to stir, he pulled her closer to him. "Good morning," he mumbled sleepily, and brushed his lips across her cheek.

He opened his eyes, then closed them. Then, when they popped open again, his expression was full of disbelief. Now that the room was well lit, he could tell immediately who was beside him. "Dionne!" he uttered incredulously. "What in . . . the hell? . . ." Not only was he completely baffled, he felt numb as well.

Mustering dignity she did not feel, Dionne quickly

threw back the sheet, hurried to the windows, and closed the drapes. She tossed a robe over her shoulders, then sank slowly onto a chair and clasped her hands tightly together to prevent them from trembling so badly.

For a moment, her mouth worked but no words would come. Then she gave a feeble smile, and when she finally found her voice, it was high and squeaked with nervousness. "Good morning, Christopher! How are you today?" Immediately realizing how terribly inappropriate that sounded, she groaned miserably and pressed her hand against her forehead, thus covering her eyes, too.

Christopher could only sit there, his mouth hanging open with astonishment. After what seemed like an incredible amount of time, he finally managed to sputter, "What in the hell are you doing here?"

Awkwardly, she cleared her throat and wished she were a million miles away. Dionne knew she was facing double jeopardy: having to be the one to tell him Celeste had perished in the shipwreck, and that she was now his wife. "N—now, Christopher, I realize this will come as an incredible shock to you, but please, I hope you will remain calm, and . . . please allow me to explain."

He folded his arms and still continued to sit there, but his expression of astonishment had faded. In its place was a dark rage, slowly building. His voice was cold, his words precise and deliberate, "I am calm! And I am waiting for an explanation."

Dionne swallowed hard. Her eyes were two large fathomless orbs of fear, and they were also filled with obvious dread.

"Well, I am waiting!" he demanded again. "What are you doing here?" Fury tugged at his heart and mind. He all too well recalled what his grandmother had told him about Celeste surviving and about the proxy marriage. But since Dionne was here instead of Celeste, it could only mean one thing! Still, something inside him demanded to hear the spoken words.

She pulled her gaze from his. "Th—this is very difficult and I am not sure where to start."

"Try at the beginning!" he insisted, his anger building. He tried not to think what her answer would be, but as each suspicious thought flashed through his mind, a knot formed and grew larger and larger in the pit of his stomach.

She took a deep, trembling breath. "Christopher, Celeste did not . . . survive when the ship sank."

Christopher could not begin to describe the emotions that tore through him: remorse, regret and, strangely, even a flicker of relief, but he found that disturbing and quickly pushed it aside. After learning about his father, grandfather, the entire crew, and the ship, there was a place in his heart that was completely numb, and any other news now seemed inconsequential regardless of how devastating it should have been. "All right," he said coldly. "So she did not survive. What are you doing here?"

Completely shocked by his reaction, Dionne could only stare mutely at him. Even with as much reason as she had to hate Celeste, she still regretted her death.

"I asked a question and I demand an answer!"

Dionne was aghast. "How can you be so callous!" she asked with disbelief. "I just told you that Celeste is dead and you showed no more emotion than if I had said"—she gestured wildly with her hand—"the sun rises in the east! How can you sit there and act so unfeeling?"

"How I can sit here, or what I do or do not feel, is no concern of yours!" he muttered coldly. "I will say I sincerely regret that Celeste lost her life. However,

224

when I returned home last night I also learned that my father, grandfather, and the entire crew of the *Emerald Tempest* were gone. I knew every man on board that ship and was proud to claim every one of them as my friend. And now simply because I have learned one more person has died does not mean I will fall to my knees in agony and beat my chest until my hands bleed, or throw myself out the window because I cannot stand the loss. How I deal with my own personal grief is my business and mine alone!"

She immediately felt ashamed. "I'm sorry . . . I . . . did not realize . . . you just . . . seemed to take the . . . news so indifferently . . ."

"Whether I act indifferent or not is no concern of yours either. What is my concern is why you are here!" He knew why she was here, and the fact that she had tried to play him and his grandmother for fools made him seethe with mounting rage. If she thought she could get by with impersonating Celeste here, the way she had in Martinique, she was insane. Surely the bitch realized he would have known immediately she was not Celeste! What was her game? What kind of devious scheme was she trying to pull?

Dionne made a quick involuntary appraisal of his features and decided not to allow his blustering manner to intimidate her. "How do you expect me to explain anything when you are screaming like an uncivilized heathen?"

An eyebrow raised in contempt. "It pleases me to know I am now an uncivilized heathen. Is that a step up from being a barbarian?"

Dionne tried not to allow his reference to the past sway her. Forcing sarcasm into her voice, she sniped, "I don't know yet, I haven't decided."

"You haven't decided? Well, that just tickles the hell out of me!"

Christopher angrily threw back the covers, slipped on his trousers, and walked over to the windows. He parted the drapes with his hand and peered outside, catching Dionne completely off-guard when he turned and asked, in a cold, deliberate voice, "I want to know why you are pretending to be Celeste."

Dionne lowered her eyes and answered, in a barely audible whisper, "I can assure you, it is not by choice."

"What's that supposed to mean?"

Instead of answering, she raised her chin defiantly. "I am not happy with this situation either. If I may be so bold as to suggest we behave like a lady and a gentleman and speak calmly and rationally to each other, perhaps everything can be explained to your satisfaction. If not, then I will be more than happy to leave."

Hearing a noise outside the door, Dionne stood and gave a weak smile. "If you will please excuse me, I believe that was Berta bringing a pot of coffee." She walked across the room with stiff dignity and returned momentarily, carrying a tray laden with a carafe, a warmer, and a coffee service. Dionne trembled so badly the carafe actually rattled against the cups as she filled them, then handed one to Christopher. "If my memory serves correctly, you take your coffee black, do you not?"

Accepting the cup, Christopher's lips curled into a sardonic smile. "I must say, you've certainly settled into my home very comfortably. Not only have you apparently fooled my grandmother, you have our servants waiting on you hand and foot." He raised the cup in a mock salute. "I offer my congratulations."

Dionne's eyes narrowed with anger but she held her tongue. During the time Andre had been recovering from his stroke, they had played numerous hands of friendly poker and she had learned the game well. She

226

knew it was a mistake to reveal her hole card too soon. But this was not a friendly game, and the stakes were much higher than she had ever played for before. The future of her child was at stake and she knew one mistake could be disastrous. There could be no bluff run here. She either had to play the cards in her hand to the best of her ability or fold them. And folding them was something she could not afford to do.

"If I recall," she began slowly, "we were about to have a civil discussion, were we not?"

"That is not exactly how I remember it." Staring at the ceiling, he squinted his eyes and arrogantly pretended to try and recall what had been said. His tone of voice was extremely sarcastic. "Let's see, the way I recall it, you were going to behave like a lady— that is, try to be that which you are not—and explain to my satisfaction why you are pretending to be Celeste. And, to the best of my knowledge, you also said if you could not explain all of this nonsense to my satisfaction, then you would gladly leave." He slammed his cup down on the table and roughly grasped Dionne by her arms. "I believe I can offer an even better suggestion," he muttered satirically. "Celeste told me what a liar and cheat you are, and I am not in the mood to hear lies today. So let's forego all of the preliminary explanations. Let's pretend I have already heard them. So that brings us to the point of your departure." Christopher was so angry that his face was white with rage. "I will give you one hour to vacate my home, and if you are not gone by the time that one hour is up, I will personally throw you out!"

Dionne wrested herself from his grasp. She felt stripped of pride. Tears filled her eyes as her face flamed with humiliation. She would have liked nothing better than to do as he ordered. It was only through sheer determination that her child would carry his rightful name that she allowed herself to issue an ultimatum.

Dionne raised her head proudly and stared directly into Christopher's eyes. It took every ounce of her willpower to keep her voice steady. "Very well, since you refuse to listen to reason, I am sure Monsieur Nicholas Dumont and his attorney will be delighted to hear my explanations!"

Chapter Sixteen

Christopher inhaled sharply at this. His mouth took on an unpleasant twist and his eyes glittered coldly. "What did you say?" he asked, his tone incredulous.

Dionne deliberately hardened her voice. "Out of respect for your grandmother and for the kindness she has shown me, I will repeat what I said—just in case you decide to change your mind about asking me to leave!" she added sarcastically.

"You don't have to repeat it. I heard what you said. I want to know what in the hell you meant by it?"

For a moment, his heart raced as he considered the repercussions if she carried out her threats. He did not like the possibilities that suddenly flashed through his mind.

How Dionne longed to bury her face in her hands and cry bitterly for what she was about to do, but she could not. God forgive her, she could not. She had to put her unborn child first, regardless of how much it hurt, regardless of how much it would make him hate her.

"I thought I made myself quite clear when I said I was sure Monsieur Dumont and his attorney would be delighted to listen to my explanation," Dionne stated matter-of-factly.

"You wouldn't dare!"

"Oh, wouldn't I?" Tossing her head flippantly, she taunted further, "I am sure they will be delighted to hear that our marriage is not, shall we say, entirely legal, since I am Dionne Martin and not Celeste Debierne!" She smiled with mock sweetness. "Tell me, Christopher, what will happen to your inheritance then? How will you feel when Monsieur Dumont lays claim to the entire fleet of the Phillips Shipping Line and to all of its assets?"

Christopher clenched his hands into fists. His nostrils flared with rage. "Damn you, Dionne! Damn you to hell!" Then, realizing he could not allow her to know how important the shipping line was to him, he tried to bluster his way through. He threw back his head and let out a great roar of laughter. "Go ahead and tell them." He tried to shrug indifferently. "Money is not important to me!"

She dismissed that declaration as though it were as important as a grain of salt. "You know, Christopher, I find it amusing that men and women of considerable wealth will go to great lengths to claim they do not care for money and the luxuries it will buy. But do you know what? I have never heard a poor man make that sort of statement. However, there is a slim possibility you are telling the truth; you may not care for the money. But I will wager you do care for your fleet of ships and it would be foolhardy of you to allow me to walk through that door. Am I not correct?" she asked, with a raise of her keenly arched brow.

Sighing heavily, Christopher sat down and stared dejectedly at the floor. He was too weary to fight her. Dionne's assumptions had been correct: He could not allow her to go to Nicholas. He finally raised his head, his voice resigned. "All right, you win. What is the price I have to pay for your silence?"

Dionne knew she should have felt triumphant in her

230

victory; instead, it was a mixture of relief and despair. Nevertheless, she could not allow him to see her true feelings. She swallowed hard, lifted her chin, and boldly met his gaze. "I believe the price is a small one to pay, especially considering what is at stake." Instead of gloating, she found herself wanting to explain as much as possible. "I'm sure you realize it was your grandmother who suggested we marry by proxy so that Nicholas could not inherit your fortune."

"Oh, is that so?" he questioned doubtfully.

"Yes, it is."

"And you agreed?"

She shrugged. "Isn't it rather obvious?"

"It's obvious that you are nothing but a damned liar!"

Angrily, Dionne stood and placed her hands akimbo. "I am not a liar!"

"Then why does she think you are Celeste?"

"I tried to tell her my real name."

His lips curled into a sarcastic grimace. "Oh, sure you did! I can just imagine how hard you tried to convince her!"

It was plain to Dionne that she was getting nowhere fast by arguing with him. "Do you want to hear this or not?"

He glared at her hatefully. His mouth worked, but he was so angry that words would not come.

"Well?" she snapped impatiently. "Do you or not?"

"After your threats to go to Nicholas," he sputtered, "I don't have much of a choice. Go ahead, tell me. But I have a feeling it will cost me dearly!"

"For the first time this morning, Christopher, I agree; you don't have much of a choice. As for costing you dearly, I suppose that depends upon how one looks at it."

Christopher rolled his eyes and grumbled to himself,

"She agrees with me! That is one consolation at least!"

Dionne decided to ignore his sarcastic remarks. If they continued down that avenue, they would never reach an agreement. "The way I see it, we are man and wife. However, since I am not the person . . ."

Christopher rudely interrupted, "I am not stupid, Dionne. I fully understand the problem. If anyone discovers you are not Celeste, then they will also realize I am not legally married, and then Nicholas can step in and take everything I own—which I am not about to let happen—so why don't you just tell me your price so we can get this over with!"

She glared at him. "All right, I will. I want your name for two years."

When she said nothing further, Christopher looked at her expectantly. "And? . . ."

Confused, she asked, "And what?"

He sighed heavily, rolled his eyes, and impatiently drummed his fingers on the arm of the chair. "What else do you want? Surely that is not all?"

She nodded. "Basically it is. Not only should two years satisfy any stipulation in your grandfather's will, but it should give me plenty of time to prepare a life for . . . me and my . . . child," she added, her voice dropping to a barely audible whisper.

"For you and your what?" Christopher was incredulous. "You mean you are going to have a baby?"

Not trusting her voice, she could only nod her head. But her eyes remained locked on his face, for she was anxious to see his reaction.

Christopher ran his fingers through his hair. This news certainly cast a different light on the situation. "So that means the child will have my name as well," he said thoughtfully. His eyes narrowed as he considered the problems that could arise in the future.

"Yes," she murmured softly.

"What about the child's father? Won't he have something to say about this or doesn't he know?"

"I feel c—confident the child's father will never . . . claim my baby. A broken sob caught in her throat. "I realize you do not think too highly of me, but it is important—at least important to me—that I tell you, that you believe me when I say, I love my baby's father." She looked longingly at Christopher, fervently wishing she could tell him the entire truth but knowing he would never believe her.

Christopher found it so disturbing to look directly in her eyes that he had to lower his gaze. He had never seen such anguish before. Why, the little fool did love Louis Fairmount! he thought to himself.

Not knowing what to make of his silence, Dionne hesitantly continued with her proposal, "At the end of two years, I will only ask for a . . . small amount of money so that my child and I can go far away from here and attempt to build a new life. And I promise, I will never make any additional claims on you or any member of your family."

"And that is all you want for your silence?" He found that hard to believe.

"Yes."

Christopher's earlier sarcasm returned, but it was not as vehement as before. "I am not so much of a fool as you think, Dionne. That is what you say now. But later, if your child carries my name, there is nothing to stop you from claiming he or she is my legal heir. What if some time in the future I remarry and father children of my own? Then, when they are grown, your child could step in and claim what is theirs. No, no. Good try, but it won't work."

Dionne moved to the window so that he could not see her agonized expression. "But, I've given that considerable thought, too. I will sign papers denying

233

any and all future claims to your wealth—as long as my child is not branded as a bastard. You can word the paper any way you want to and I will sign it. My child's future is what this is all about, anyway. I was a bastard, and I still remember how cruel people can be. I do not want that for my baby."

Christopher thoughtfully stroked his chin. He did not have much choice. He could either do as she demanded or lose everything he owned. He tried not to sound too eager. "I suppose legal papers could be prepared to that effect." Then he walked over to where Dionne stood and forced her to look at him, his eyes stripping her of any remaining pride. "Celeste warned me that you are a liar. If I find out that you are lying to me now, heaven won't be able to help you!"

Dionne wanted to scream the truth at him, that Celeste was the liar, not she! That she had twisted and turned everything to her own advantage. That she used people then casually discarded them as though they were nothing but pieces of garbage. But, she realized the entire truth would do more harm than good. For now, it appeared she had won a name for her child and that was more important than anything else in the world. She defiantly raised her chin. "Well, what is your decision? Do we have a bargain or not?"

"Yes, we have a bargain!" he growled.

"Do I have your word of honor?" she pressed.

He crashed his fist against a table and glared at her with contempt. "Yes, damn it, you have my word of honor! But I think we need to get something straight between us right now. I will not allow you to bring shame on my family's name or on any member of this household. Since you are going to be my wife and will carry my name for the next two years, I will not tolerate you embarrassing me or my family! That means you will not have affairs with other men and you will

234

conduct yourself like a lady! Do I make myself clear?"

Dionne gasped with shock at his crudity. He spoke as though she were about to run naked from the house and find the first available man! God forbid! She bit her lip to keep from shouting at him.

Christopher, seeing her despair, chortled triumphantly. "Well, what is your decision? Do we have a bargain or not?" he parroted her words.

Realizing he was deliberately taunting her, Dionne's face turned ashen. "Yes," she choked, "we have a bargain."

"But do I have your word of honor?"

"Yes!" she shouted.

Christopher's face was livid with rage. "That is certainly a surprise," he drawled sarcastically. "How does a woman like you have honor?"

"What do you mean . . . a woman like me?" Her voice was as cold as ice.

He raked her full length with a frosty perusal. "I believe in a few months it will be quite obvious."

Dionne wanted to hit him so badly she had to grasp the back of the chair to keep from doing so. "If you are referring to the fact that I am pregnant, may I remind you that it takes two to make a baby! And, besides, I suppose you expect me to believe that you, at age thirty, are completely innocent! That you have never made love to a woman!"

"Well . . . that's different!" he sputtered indignantly. "I am a man."

"I see no difference," she retorted angrily.

Christopher, finding her accusations a little too discomfiting, threw his hands in the air. "I am tired of this arguing. I need to see my grandmother and inform her of this . . . development. I regret having to tell her about it, but I see no way to keep the truth from her. Two years is too long to try and live a lie. Besides, she is a very smart woman. She would soon become suspicious."

"Yes, I agree, but I insist upon being present when you tell her." Even though she had only been there for a short period of time, she had grown quite fond of the woman and did not want Christopher to present only his side of the story.

"Very well, I have no objections. I'm sure you know where her room is. You can join us as soon as you have dressed." He started for the door.

"Christopher, wait."

He turned, his brow rising questioningly.

"I—I have nothing to wear. The doctor allowed me out of bed for the first time only yesterday. Besides," she gestured at him, "shouldn't you put on your boots and a shirt?"

It was only then that Christopher realized he had not dressed yet. Mustering dignity by shooting her a glowering look, he marched to his wardrobe and removed clean garments. He disappeared behind a dressing screen, reappearing in a few minutes completely dressed except for his boots.

"If you intend to come with me, I suggest you make yourself as presentable as possible."

She straightened her robe, tying it firmly around her waist with the sash, then hurried to the dressing table for her hairbrush.

While tugging on his boots, he looked at her sharply. "I will also speak to Grandmother about purchasing you whatever you need. Now that I am home, there will be a memorial service for my father and grandfather, and if the doctor allows you to attend, you will need something decent to wear. Now that you are my wife, certain things will be expected of you."

"Christopher, may we . . ." Dionne broke off abruptly, biting her lip, tears beginning to stream

236

silently down her pale cheeks.

"Madame, if you think tears will soften my heart, you are badly mistaken."

Dionne slammed the hairbrush down on the dresser top and whirled to face him. "The tears are for my benefit, not yours! Do you have the audacity to believe you are the only person who hurts? Who has suffered a loss? Your father and grandfather were very fine men. I know you loved them and I know you will miss them. But other people died in that shipwreck! I lost my family, too! Andre and Nigel and . . ." She sniffed and wiped her eyes. "There is one thing I will promise you, though. You will not see me cry . . . ever again!" She tried desperately to keep her bottom lip from trembling. "I only thought that . . . when you mentioned a memorial service for your family, we might have one for Andre, too."

Christopher immediately felt ashamed. Regardless of his personal opinion of Dionne, she had cared deeply for Andre Debierne. Although he had not known him long, he had grown fond of the old man, too. "I'm sure something can be arranged," he said softly. "And, Dionne, in spite of what is happening between us, I want you to know I am sorry about Andre. I am sure you thought a lot of him."

Dionne took short, quick gasps of breath, as though to inhale deeply would cause the dull, throbbing ache in her heart to stab more painfully, hurting her beyond what she could bear.

He glanced at her and, under the circumstances, approved of her appearance. Assuming she did not know her way around the house since she had been confined to bed, he asked bluntly, "Do you know where Grandmother's room is?"

"No."

"Then come with me."

237

Only the rigid way Christopher held his shoulders betrayed his anger and frustration, and he walked swiftly to the door, down the long hallway and winding flight of stairs. Dionne stayed right behind him, having to take two steps to his one as his long legs quickly shortened the distance.

At first she was puzzled by the fact that Madame Phillips's bedroom was on the lower floor. The weather in New Orleans was much like Martinique, in respect to being hot and sultry, although she understood New Orleans did have cool, sometimes even cold weather in the winter. Bedrooms in warmer climates were almost always located in the upper parts of the house so that they could get any breeze that stirred. Then, Dionne realized that since the woman had to walk with the assistance of a cane, she must have moved to the lower floor as did Andre when he had his stroke. With a slight sting to her conscience, she also realized what a chore it must have been for the older woman to climb the stairs each day to visit with her.

Not having been downstairs before, Dionne's eyes widened at all the luxurious furnishings and the elaborate oak woodwork, although by having to keep up with Christopher, she barely had a chance to notice any of the elegant detail. She made a mental note that, as soon as their lives settled into a normal routine, she would explore every nook and cranny of the huge, palatial mansion.

Christopher finally stopped in front of a door and rapped softly. Dionne breathed a sigh of relief when she heard Madame Phillips give permission for them to enter.

Jeannine Phillips was sitting in bed, propped up by many white, fluffy pillows. She set her cup and saucer on the lap tray and greeted them with a charming smile.

"Why, Chris, Celeste! What a pleasant surprise!

238

Would you like to join me for breakfast?" Not waiting for an answer, she sent her maid, Bella, to the kitchen for additional trays.

Noticing the grave expression on Christopher's face and the girl's slightly swollen eyes—from crying, no doubt—Jeannine's smile quickly faded. "Is something wrong? Child, what are you doing downstairs? I know the doctor said you could get up, but I do not think he meant you could run all over the house."

Christopher gave Dionne a warning look to keep silent before he brushed his lips across his grandmother's forehead. "Now, Grandmother, don't get yourself all upset."

"Young man, I am not upset, but you know how I dislike for you to talk to me in that condescending tone of voice." She stared at Christopher intently as he sat at the foot of her bed. "I can feel it in my bones. Something is the matter and I want to know what it is."

Dionne's courage was quickly faltering. She took a chair close to Jeannine's bedside and hesitantly raised her eyes to meet Christopher's. Now that she was here, she almost wished she had stayed in her room and talked with the woman later.

"Yes, Grandmother, something is wrong. Something is very wrong," Christopher admitted reluctantly.

Impatiently, Jeannine crossed her arms and directed a curious gaze between her grandson and his wife. "Is it so bad you cannot find the courage to tell me?"

"Courage has nothing to do with it." Christopher rubbed the back of his neck while trying to find the right words. His hesitation stemmed from the fact that he feared his grandmother would blame herself for this predicament he was in. Then, realizing his continued silence was even more distressing to her, he gestured toward Dionne and stated matter-of-factly, "Grandmother, she is not Celeste Debierne."

239

Startled by the news, Jeannine blinked, then glanced sharply at Dionne. "W—why, who are you, child?" she asked, her face as grave as the girl's she questioned.

Feeling very ill-at-ease, Dionne shifted on the chair and replied in a small voice, "My name is . . . was . . . Dionne Martin. I was the Debiernes' housekeeper." She lifted her chin boldly. "No, I was more than just a housekeeper. The Debiernes were like my own family."

Jeannine appeared to accept that information calmly. The remembrance shone brightly in her eyes as she recalled that day she talked with the girl and presented her plan for a proxy marriage.

"Why, I remember you trying to tell me you were not Celeste, but I would not listen. I was so worried about Nicholas, I simply passed it off as you having a loss of memory." Then, the enormity of the situation settled over her and her eyes grew wide with concern. "Oh, dear, this does present a problem! If you are not Celeste, then Christopher does not have a legal wife— or at least I do not think so. And if he is not married, then Nicholas can still lay claim to . . . oh, dear . . ." Her voice trailed off.

Strangely, Dionne received no great amount of satisfaction when Christopher glanced at her in surprise. It was enough that he knew she had tried to tell his grandmother the truth.

Christopher took his grandmother's hand in his, hoping to reassure her. "Yes, it does present a problem—or rather it did—but I think Dionne and I have reached a workable solution." He was not about to upset his grandmother with all the details of the ugly scene that took place between him and Dionne earlier, even if it meant he had to pretend things he did not feel.

Obviously upset, Jeannine pressed her hands to her temples. "Well, for heaven's sake, will you please go ahead and tell me?"

He cleared his throat, his tone of voice unusually calm as he continued, "As I said, I believe we were able to work it out. I am not going to debate the fact of whether our marriage is legal or not. My proxy married a woman in good faith, and as far as I am concerned, I am legally married. And I am sure an attorney and a minister could have a lengthy debate whether Dionne is married or not. While it is true she used an alias, she still spoke the vows, not anyone else. So, regardless of the legalities involved, it looks to me like we are married." He nodded toward Dionne. "We discussed our mutual problems, and we have decided to continue with our marriage for a period of two years. Now, we realize you may think this is not the proper thing to do, but considering the problem will still exist with Nicholas if I don't have a wife, it is really our only solution. We figured two years would be an ample amount of time to satisfy the courts, then we will dissolve the marriage. In exchange for all of this, Dionne's child will have a legal name—or at least the child will not carry the stigma of being a bast . . . of not having a father. After the two years are up, I have agreed to give Dionne enough money to establish a life for her and her child somewhere far away from here." He took a deep breath. "So, there you have it, all in a nutshell."

Dionne could only stare at Christopher in amazement. He had been so outraged and angry earlier, but now he sounded as though not a cross word had passed between them. Apparently he did not want his grandmother to know exactly how upset he had been.

Jeannine thought about what he had said for a moment, then turned her attention to Dionne. "I can certainly understand why Christopher is so agreeable to this solution, but why are you? Two years of your life is a long time to give under these sort of circumstances."

Dionne nervously wet her lips. "Yes, Madame

Phillips, I agree. Two years is a long time. Nevertheless, I feel it is a small price to pay for my child's future. This baby is all I have in the world, and I will do anything within my power to protect it."

"I take it, then, that the child does not belong to my grandson."

Christopher injected quickly, "No, Grandmother, it does not belong to me."

Jeannine heard what Christopher said, but her eyes were fastened on Dionne's face. There was something about the girl's expression when Christopher denied the child that disturbed her. But Jeannine quickly decided to make no mention of her strange feeling. She thought it best to let that particular matter drop for the time being.

"I suppose I am still confused. Am I correct to assume we three are the only people who know about your real identity?"

"Yes, Madame," Dionne replied.

"Then I am still not satisfied with your answer. Why are you willing to invest two years of your life married to a man you do not love and who does not love you, when you could wash your hands of this entire situation, go off, and start a new life immediately? No one would have to know the child did not have a father."

Dionne could never tell Jeannine the real reason she demanded to stay married to Christopher . . . that her child deserved to have its rightful name and this was the only way she could make sure of it. It was a secret that would have to remain locked in her heart forever.

"Madame Phillips, I will be completely honest with you. You see, my mother . . . was not married to my father. Where I was raised, everyone knew I was a bastard. I still hear people's cruel taunts in my mind, and I will do anything within my power to see that

242

that does not happen to my child." She took a deep, shuddering breath. "I have given this considerable thought, because I knew I would have to face this when Christopher returned from Brazil. If you will think back to the day when you told me about Nicholas and the problems concerning Christopher's inheritance, that is also the day I learned I was going to have a baby. Oh, I realize I could pretend to be noble and claim I did it entirely for Christopher, but we all know I would be telling a lie. I will admit, I panicked. To be blunt; I married Christopher so that my child would have a name. However, since then, I have had time to think. The way I figure it, I am trapped as much as Christopher is. If the truth is revealed, he loses his fortune and my child will have to carry the stigma of being a bastard for the rest of his or her life. Living here for two years is strictly my idea, my demand, because if I suddenly disappeared, I am sure your dear cousin Nicholas would be greatly suspicious, suspicious enough to start digging, and there is no telling what lengths he would go to to reveal the truth. So, the way I see it, if Christopher's lie is discovered, mine will be, too."

Jeannine leaned wearily against her pillows. She had been watching the girl intently, guessing the depth of her pain and feeling a momentarily flash of guilt at the possible hurt she had caused her by insisting she marry Christopher by proxy. The fact that the child was not Christopher's suddenly seemed unimportant. And even though she had been with another man, there was something about this young woman that commanded her respect. One thing Jeannine was certain of: It was a feeling she had that insisted this girl was not bad or evil. Perhaps Dionne's love had been misguided, but that was a mystery, too. She could have sworn this girl was in love with her grandson. How it would all turn out

243

only time would tell, but for now, they would all have to take it one day at a time.

She turned troubled eyes to her grandson. "Christopher, do you have anything to add?"

He shook his head then shrugged. "No, Grandmother, I believe she fairly well said it all." He sighed heavily. "I just wish these two years were over with."

Dionne's mouth tightened. Two years. It seemed so long, yet such an incredibly short span of time. Oh, if there were only someone she could talk to. If she could only confide in someone and tell them how she had fantasized about the future. For the past few weeks she'd had such hopeful dreams: how Christopher would return home from the sea, take one long look at her, and realize it was she whom he had loved all along; that it was she whom he had made sweet love to that night in Martinique, and now, the fact that she carried his baby from the results of their lovemaking made him the happiest man in the world, and they would live the rest of their lives in rapturous splendor.

Dionne stared momentarily at Jeannine and realized she could tell the woman all of this, and perhaps she would understand and maybe even believe her. But Christopher would not. Celeste had filled him so full of her lies that he would think she was deliberately trying to pass the child off as his, then that would harden his heart against her even more than it was now. No, like it or not, it was a secret she would have to keep for the rest of her life.

Jeannine frowned. "Wait a minute, I've thought of something that could cause a problem; in fact, there are two things that worry me."

"What are they?" Christopher asked.

"Her name. What are we going to call you, child?"

Dionne shook her head, her hazel eyes wide with alarm. "I don't want to be called Celeste. She is dead."

"Well," Jeannine said thoughtfully, "I suppose we could call you Dionne, and if anyone asked any questions, we could tell them Dionne is your middle name and that is how you prefer to be addressed. Is this agreeable to the two of you?" Seeing them nod, she spoke about her other worry. "What will we do if someone from Martinique sees Dionne and recognizes her? How will we explain it?"

"This is one of the problems that comes up when people are caught in a web of tangled lies," Christopher muttered darkly. He thoughtfully stroked his chin, searching for an answer. "Dionne bears an uncanny resemblance to Celeste. I mistook her for Celeste several times myself." Then, remembering how Dionne was always masquerading as Celeste, his lips settled into a thin white line and he glared at her, daring her to dispute him. "I just remembered something. Celeste told me they were always switching identities and no one ever caught on to what they were doing. So I don't see that that will be a problem. But to be on the safe side, I will cease all business activities with Martinique. It will not be too much of a financial loss."

Christopher's angry expression and Dionne's painful one did not go unnoticed by Jeannine. But again, she decided not to mention it. It was something to be stored in her mind and used for reference when and if it became necessary.

Christopher stood and kissed his grandmother on her forehead. "If you don't mind, I am going to skip breakfast. There are several things I need to do, but I promise to return in time so that we can have dinner together." He took Dionne by her arm, clearly indicating she was to leave too. "And I am sure you are very tired, Dionne, and would like to lie down for a while." He pasted a smile on his lips. "Grandmother, please have Bella bring her tray upstairs."

Once they were in the hall, Dionne placed her hand on Christopher's arm. "Please, I want to . . ."

"Be quiet, Dionne!" Glancing about carefully, he lowered his voice and said, "We will speak about this in private, not out here in the hallway where any of the servants could easily overhear. Come on to the bedroom; there is one more thing I want to get straight with you." He spun on his heel and marched staunchly away.

Dionne said not another word until Christopher closed the bedroom door firmly behind them.

"Christopher," Dionne began hesitantly, "I want to thank you for not telling your grandmother that I threatened to go to Nicholas. . . ."

"You can drop your act. This is me you're talking to, remember?" He pointed his thumb at his chest. "My silence had nothing to do with you. I didn't tell Grandmother because I didn't want to upset her. I figure she feels guilty enough as it is, although none of this is her fault."

Dionne wanted to scream at him that it was not her fault, either, but she held her tongue.

Christopher stared at her hard, his eyes as cold as shards of ice. "When we are in my grandmother's presence, we will behave in a civilized manner toward each other, but if by chance we are alone together, just stay out of my way. The less I see of you, the better." He glanced about the bedroom. "This is my room. It has been since I was a small boy. I do not intend to give it up now. There is a room adjoining it. I suggest you gather what possessions you have and move in there. If I had my preference, you would stay in the room at the far end of the hall or maybe even on the upper floor, but since we have to at least pretend to be husband and wife, adjoining rooms are not unusual. But I do expect you to keep that door closed because this room, madame, is off limits to you!" With that, he stomped angrily from the room and slammed the door soundly behind him.

Dionne stared after him with sad, troubled eyes. Then suddenly, without warning, large tears began spilling down her lovely but drawn face. She sank wearily onto a chair and cried until there were no more tears left.

Chapter Seventeen

Three weeks later brought the day of the memorial service for all those who had lost their lives on board the *Emerald Tempest*. It dawned hot with a hazy mist over the thriving city.

The Phillips family had long ago delegated a special plot of ground on the huge estate for their crew's personal use whether it be for their immediate families, or for a member of the crew who had died at sea, or simply from old age or illness. It was there that Christopher had a huge marble stone erected with his father's name chiseled at the very top, then each member of the crew listed in order of rank or longevity with the shipping line, all the way down to the cabin boy's name. In their family's private cemetery, an individual stone for his father had been placed beside the grave of his mother, who had died in childbirth. There were also individual stones for his grandfather and Andre. He thoughtfully arranged for small stones to be placed in the servants' plot for the two members of Andre's household who had lost their lives during the tragedy.

At the beginning of the week announcements had been sent, inviting distant family members and personal friends to the memorial service. And now Crescentview was a beehive of activity, since all the guests had arrived.

Feeling completely inept and frustrated, Dionne sat on the chair in front of her dressing table and stared miserably at her reflection in the mirror. The memorial service was due to begin in only a matter of minutes and she was not dressed yet, nor would she be able to finish dressing without some assistance. The only black dress that had been purchased for her was a beautiful yet simple gown, but the buttons and hooks were all in the back and she found it impossible to fasten them. All the female servants except for Bella, who was Jeannine's personal maid, were downstairs seeing to all the family friends and distant relations who had come for the services, and there was not a soul available to help her.

Hearing a sharp rap at the door, Dionne breathed a sigh of relief, then hurried over to open it, fully expecting to see either Berta or Bella. Instead, Christopher stood there, his arms crossed, with an impatient look on his face.

"Aren't you ready yet? Everyone is downstairs waiting for you."

"No, *Ciel defendre,* I—I cannot fasten my dress and I have not seen a servant for the past hour."

"Well, here," he grumbled, pushing open the door and entering, "let me do it then." Once inside, he closed the door, leaned his head against it, and sighed heavily. "It's no wonder you haven't seen a servant. They're all down there running their legs off waiting on all those people." He looked at Dionne curiously. "Didn't you help Grandmother address the invitations?"

Dionne was surprised. This was the first time since the morning after he had arrived home that Christopher had spoken to her with a civil tongue outside the presence of his grandmother. He had been so cross with her that she had even been taking her meals in the privacy of her own room. This was certainly a change, and she was not about to complain.

"Yes, I did," she managed to answer in what she hoped to be a steady voice.

"How many were there?" he asked, his brows knotting into a weary frown.

"I think about fifty. Why?" She looked at him suspiciously. If a mistake had been made, would he blame her for it?

He shook his head, looking completely bewildered. "There have to be at least two hundred people down there. Where in the world did they all come from?" He did not wait for Dionne to reply. "I guess when one person received an invitation, he figured the entire family was invited. And if I were a betting man, I would wager every man down there is smoking the most inexpensive cigar he could find, and not only that, every woman must have doused herself with an entire bottle of cheap perfume. I've been down there for what seems like hours, and I think every man who has shook my hand has waited until he's right in my face before he exhaled his cigar smoke, and every woman who has doused herself the heaviest with perfume has insisted upon hugging me!" He wrinkled his nose and blew heavily through his mouth. "It has given me a terrible headache and a queasy stomach to boot."

Dionne looked at him sympathetically, then she set her chin with a firm determination. Perhaps there was something she could do to make him feel better. Their personal situation could not be much worse and this might even help ease the tension between them. What would it hurt to try? All he could do was grumble and glower at her the way he had been doing the past few weeks.

Taking him by the hand, Dionne began leading him

251

toward a chair by the open window. "Come over here and sit down for a moment. I think I have something that will make you feel better."

"But . . . all of those people are waiting. I have to get back down there. It's past time for the service to start."

"Perhaps so, but they will not begin without you and a few more minutes will not hurt." Her eyes suddenly widened with worry. "If it is as bad as you say, how is your grandmother holding up to all of that?"

Christopher chuckled wryly as he settled his long frame into the chair. "She wisely beat a hasty retreat to her room several hours ago, and if I might add, not a soul seems to miss her!" Apparently forgetting about his animosity toward Dionne, he turned around in the chair to face her and spoke in an astonished tone of voice, "Tell me something, do people only come to funerals to eat? Don't get me wrong, I have never objected to what anyone eats in my home, but they sort of remind me of a herd of cattle grazing. And not only that, other than when they have attacked me, I've not heard one word of sorrow." He flung his arm with disgust. "It's more like a festive occasion to them!"

"I know," Dionne soothed. "But I'm sure they don't mean to be unkind. It's a shame, but it seems like some families and friends do not get together anymore except when there has been a death."

She handed him a cool glass of water and sprinkled a small amount of her headache powder in it. "Here, drink this. It will help ease your headache."

He peered at the glass, his eyes hardening and the muscles in his cheeks flexing immediately. "Laudanum? No, thanks, I don't take stuff like that," he stated adamantly. "And by the way, I doubt if it is very wise for you to keep taking it. It's easy to become addicted to drugs like that, and besides, I doubt if it is good for that baby you're carrying. I've heard of a few instances when a baby was actually born addicted to laudanum and even other drugs, too, especially if its mother became too dependent on them."

Dionne gasped. "But it is not laudanum, or at least I do not think so. Dr. Blackmon gave it to me because my eyes were irritated so badly they made my head hurt. Surely he would not give me a dangerous drug?" She looked at him anxiously. "Please taste it and see if it is laudanum, and if it is, I will throw it away because I would never do anything intentional to harm my baby." His news had frightened her so badly that she could actually feel her heart pound furiously.

Christopher wet the end of his finger and stuck it into the drug vial, then he touched it to the tip of his tongue. "No, it isn't laudanum," he said slowly, feeling a little surprised over the relief that quickly swept over him. "But I am sure if Dr. Blackmon gave it to you, it's safe for you to take."

Dionne eyed the bottle suspiciously. Regardless of what Christopher said, she was not about to take any more of it.

He turned the glass up, drinking the contents more to reassure Dionne than to ease his headache, and that surprised him, too. He had been telling himself for the past few weeks he did not care how she felt, and now he found it to be a little discomfiting to discover differently.

Dionne, still determined to ease his discomfort, quickly urged him to slip out of his jacket. She then opened a tin of soda crackers and handed him a few. "Every now and then my stomach feels a little unsettled. I've found if I munch on crackers and sip a glass of lemon water, it helps to relieve my nausea."

Christopher looked at the crackers skeptically. "Are you sure?"

"Yes, I am positive." She quickly filled a glass with

lemon water. "Here, drink this too."

Dionne stepped behind the chair so that he would not see her smile. Regardless of how arrogant and presumptuous he behaved at times, he still enjoyed being petted and fussed over, even if it was by her hand. She made a mental note to remember that in the future. What was the old saying? "One could catch more flies with honey than with vinegar," and Dionne felt confident she could supply as much honey as was necessary if it would help relieve the tension between them.

Since Christopher appeared to be in such a mellow mood, she decided to push her luck to the very limit. She filled her porcelain wash pan with water, and dampened a cloth, folded it, then pressed the cloth to the back of Christopher's neck. "This will relax and help cool you off. I can imagine how hot it was downstairs with all those people milling around."

"Yes, it was hot down there," he admitted. "It was worse than being in the cargo hold of my ship in the dead of summer." He began to flex his shoulder muscles as if trying to relieve a cramp.

"Here, allow me to do that." Dionne was quick to offer to massage his shoulders. She slipped her hands underneath his collar and began to expertly knead his tense muscles. "I used to do this for Uncle Andre all of the time," she quietly reminisced. "He claimed it always made him feel so much better."

Christopher closed his eyes and sighed heavily. "Mmmm, I have to admit, it does feel good." Then his head jerked as though he had suddenly remembered his vow to stay as far away from Dionne as possible. His tone of voice instantly hardened, "I think we've wasted enough time up here. Everyone will be wondering what's happened to us."

"But . . . do you feel well enough?" she asked worriedly.

He looked up at her and was amazed at how sincere she appeared to be. There was nothing but kindness in her eyes and that surprised him, as he had been deliberately treating her cold and aloof. "Yes, I feel much better. Thank you."

Rising from the chair, Christopher quickly adjusted his shirt and slipped on his jacket. He muttered gruffly, "Turn around and let me fasten your dress."

The moment Christopher touched Dionne he felt a sudden tremor of sensuality run through him. He felt her start slightly and realized she had experienced the same tingling sensation. Surprised to find his mouth had suddenly gone dry, Christopher swallowed hard. He brought his gaze up and saw Dionne in the mirror, noting that her face had suddenly blanched. For a moment, their gaze locked and held, then Dionne shyly lowered her lashes.

Christopher dropped his hands as though he had been burned. Awkwardly clearing the knot that had quickly formed in his throat, he muttered in a hoarse whisper, "We had better go. Everyone is waiting for us."

"Yes," she murmured softly, "I suppose they are."

Coming to the end of the staircase, Christopher's features immediately tightened when he saw Nicholas hurrying toward them. He took Dionne's arm and whispered in a barely audible voice, "Watch yourself; be careful what you say. Here comes dear cousin Nicholas."

Dionne had seen the man, too, and although the expression on his face was friendly, it did not match the dark gleam in his eyes. She could feel her knees begin to tremble.

"Christopher," Nicholas said, shaking his hand, "I'm sorry we have to meet under these trying circumstances." He took Dionne's hand and pressed it to his lips. "I must say, my dear, you are looking much better than when I last saw you."

Dionne resisted the overwhelming impulse to yank her hand away. All too well, she remembered the darkened room, the hastily spoken words that made her Christopher's wife, but most of all, she remembered the black scowl that had been on this man's face. It had frightened her then, and he frightened her now.

Forcing herself to be polite, she murmured, "Th— thank you, Monsieur Dumont. My health has improved greatly."

Nicholas's smile did not reach his eyes as he pulled a woman to his side. "Christopher, Madame Phillips, I do not think you have had the pleasure of meeting my wife. We were married a few days before your proxy marriage. Lorraine, this is my cousin, Christopher Phillips, and his bride, Celeste."

Dionne glanced at Christopher and nervously wet her lips. "Please, monsieur, I prefer the given name of Dionne instead of Celeste."

"Oh? But I thought Celeste was your given name," he said slowly.

"Y—yes, it is. But Dionne is my middle name and I prefer to be addressed by it rather than my first name."

Christopher, afraid that Nicholas would become suspicious by Dionne's apparent nervousness, politely nodded his head at his cousin's wife. "I didn't know Nicholas was married. It is my pleasure, madame."

The woman eyed Christopher appraisingly, boldly taking in his masculine physique and handsome features, but when she looked at Dionne, her eyes filled with scorn.

"So," she drawled slowly, "you are the woman who appeared so conveniently, just in time to prevent my husband from claiming his rightful inheritance. Tell

ACCEPT YOUR FREE GIFT AND EXPERIENCE MORE OF THE PASSION AND ADVENTURE YOU LIKE IN A HISTORICAL ROMANCE

Zebra Romances are the finest novels of their kind and are written with the adult woman in mind. All of our books are written by authors who really know how to weave tales of romantic adventure in the historical settings you love.

Because our readers tell us these books sell out very fast in the stores, Zebra has made arrangements for you to receive at home the four newest titles published each month. You'll never miss a title and home delivery is so convenient. With your first shipment we'll even send you a FREE Zebra Historical Romance as our gift just for trying our home subscription service. No obligation.

BIG SAVINGS AND **FREE** HOME DELIVERY

Each month, the Zebra Home Subscription Service will send you the four newest titles as soon as they are published. (We ship these books to our subscribers even before we send them to the stores.) You may preview them *Free* for 10 days. If you like them as much as we think you will, you'll pay just $3.50 each and *save $1.80 each month* off the cover price. *AND you'll also get FREE HOME DELIVERY.* There is never a charge for shipping, handling or postage and there is no minimum you must buy. If you decide not to keep any shipment, simply return it within 10 days, no questions asked, and owe nothing.

MAIL IN THE COUPON BELOW TODAY

GET FREE GIFT

To get your Free ZEBRA HISTORICAL ROMANCE fill out the coupon below and send it in today. As soon as we receive the coupon, we'll send your first month's books to preview Free for 10 days along with your **FREE NOVEL.**

——— F R E E ———
B O O K   C E R T I F I C A T E

ZEBRA HOME SUBSCRIPTION SERVICE, INC.

YES! Please start my subscription to Zebra Historical Romances and send me my free Zebra Novel along with my first month's Romances. I understand that I may preview these four new Zebra Historical Romances Free for 10 days. If I'm not satisfied with them I may return the four books within 10 days and owe nothing. Otherwise I will pay just $3.50 each; a total of $14.00 (a $15.80 value—I save $1.80). Then each month I will receive the 4 newest titles as soon as they come off the press for the same 10 day Free preview and low price. I may return any shipment and I may cancel this arrangement at any time. There is no minimum number of books to buy and there are no shipping, handling or postage charges. Regardless of what I do, the FREE book is mine to keep.

Name _____

(Please Print)

Address _____ Apt. # _____

City _____ State _____ Zip _____

Telephone ( ) _____

Signature _____

(if under 18, parent or guardian must sign)

Terms and offer subject to change without notice.

Get a Free
Zebra
Historical
Romance

*a $3.95
value*

me, dearie, which brothel did they pull you out of?"

Both Christopher and Nicholas opened their mouths to protest, but Dionne placed a restraining hand on her husband's arm. As she slowly appraised Lorraine, noting her flaming red hair—too red to be natural— her heavily made-up face, and her tawdry, tasteless clothing, she did not have to pretend her dislike for the woman.

Dionne forced a syrupy sweet tone to her voice, "Considering the conditions of the will, it is quite apparent that mine and Christopher's marriage was no more convenient than yours and Monsieur Dumont's. But at least Christopher and I were betrothed far before then. As for the other matter you mentioned, I assure you, I have never seen the inside of a brothel." She deliberately allowed her gaze to rake the woman with disgust. "However, it is extremely evident that you cannot make that claim."

Lorraine clenched her hands into tight fists. "Why, you little . . ." Then she caught herself and laughed, its sound ringing out loudly and coarsely. She arched one brow and tossed her head defiantly. "It so happens I come from a very fine family and my brother is the most highly respected attorney in all of New Orleans. But then I am sure you never knew what a respectable family was. That is, not until you wheedled your way into this one." She placed her hands akimbo. "I know a twit when I see one, and I can assure you one thing. . . ."

"Lorraine, will you please shut up!" Nicholas hissed angrily, pulling at her arm.

Christopher placed his arm around Dionne protectively. When he spoke, his voice was as cold as ice. "Madame Dumont, may I remind you that this lady is my wife and that you are in our home. You can either speak to her with respect, or not trouble yourself to speak to her at all." He glared at Nicholas. "And I suggest you do not bring your wife back into this house until she has learned some manners! I will not have my wife or anyone in this household spoken to without proper respect."

"Yes, Christopher, of course." Nicholas then bowed curtly to Dionne. "Madame Phillips, I offer my most humble apology." His face dark with rage, he roughly grabbed Lorraine's arm and half dragged her away.

Christopher turned to Dionne, an expression of awe gracing his face. He murmured softly, "Very well done. I was proud of the way you handled that situation."

Dionne, trying not to show how pleased she was over Christopher's surprising reaction, accepted his praise with a faint smile.

"I had intended to leave you here while I go after Grandmother, but now, with that—that barracuda loose in the house, I am a little reluctant."

"No, please go on and get her. I have caused enough of a delay as it is. I'll be fine, and I will be right here waiting for you."

"Are you sure?" He grinned and motioned with his head. "The barracuda might return."

Dionne could not suppress the laughter that bubbled in her throat. "I am positive. Besides, I believe you firmly put that woman in her place."

Christopher chuckled. "You didn't do so bad yourself."

Dionne watched Christopher until he disappeared down the long corridor leading to his grandmother's room. For the first time since he had returned, the smile on her face was not forced. Sighing hopefully, she felt at long last a step might have been taken in the right direction. She hoped so. Oh, God, she hoped so.

Chapter Eighteen

Christopher sat in the study, his elbows propped on the arms of the chair, his head bowed, resting on the steeple his fingers had formed. He could not understand why he felt so perplexed. His and Dionne's agreement had been to stay out of each other's way except when they needed to pretend to be a happily married couple. And now that he needed her, he was reluctant to ask.

Several of his distant relatives had come from out of town to attend the memorial services and would not be leaving until early in the morning. Even Nicholas and his wife were staying overnight, although Christopher felt they could have easily returned to their own home after the services without any inconvenience.

Christopher strongly suspected Nicholas or that wife of his had been making sly innuendos about the strange circumstances surrounding their marriage. Too many people had asked too many prying questions about his bride: when they had met, where she was from, and also numerous other questions. While he had never been one to care one way or the other what people said or thought about his reputation as a bachelor, he did not want a hint of scandal to touch him now that he was married. He felt it had something to do with his family's honor. As much as he disliked asking her,

Christopher saw no other way to put their questions to rest than to request that Dionne come down, mingle with his relatives, and join them for dinner.

It wasn't that he felt Dionne could not handle the situation. Quite the opposite, for she had definitely put Lorraine Dumont in her place and there was not a doubt in his mind that she could do the same with anyone else if the need arose.

However, his reluctance was that he simply felt too uncomfortable around her. No, that was not entirely true. He felt too comfortable and too confused around her. For instance, earlier today, when she had given him those crackers and lemon water and had massaged the tension from his neck and shoulders, it had been such a natural, caring reaction one person would expect from another that he had not even thought about it until later. Could it have just been her way of trying to get on his good side? No, he did not think so. He had always taken a lot of pride in his ability to judge other people, and now that he was being completely honest with himself, there was something about this situation with Dionne that puzzled him. On the one hand, he knew she was a devious, scheming woman who would go to any lengths to get what she wanted. But on the other hand, he had a feeling—no, it was stronger than a feeling; it was a gut-wrenching instinct that she was not the sort of woman Celeste had claimed she was. So, what did that make Celeste?

But if he were to trust his instincts, how could he disallow the fact that Dionne was pregnant? That in itself told the entire story. Good, decent women did not sleep with a man before they were married.

Then, Christopher felt all color drain from his face as he remembered the night he had spent with Celeste. How could he judge one without judging the other? He was as much, if not more to blame for what had happened with Celeste, so what gave him the right to think it was any different with Dionne?

The way he figured it, her troubles stemmed from the fact that she had impersonated Celeste. If she had not done that, then from all he had heard about Louis Fairmount, he would have never given Dionne, a simple little housekeeper without a penny to her name, a second look. Maybe Dionne did love Louis. Maybe that was why she had done what she did. So how could he really fault her for that? Who was he to judge? After all, there had even been wars waged between great nations over that fickle emotion called love.

Christopher propped his hands behind his head and leaned back in his chair, trying to imagine what must have taken place between Dionne and Louis.

In his mind's eye, he could see Louis somehow discovering she was not Celeste, then more likely he had spurned her. To the best of his recollection, Dionne had never said why she was on board the *Emerald Tempest*, so Louis might have even threatened to expose her. Perhaps that was why she had decided to leave Martinique. He shrugged, doubting if he would ever really know the reason why she was on board the ship. It would probably remain a mystery. Which, brought him to the point of why Dionne had been brought here to Crescentview after being pulled from the sea.

His grandmother had told him what the captain had said; how the girl had babbled incoherently about the *Emerald Tempest*, the hurricane, and Christopher. Why she had been babbling about him he did not know and probably never would. The captain of the *Storm Tide*, knowing the Phillipses and the names of their ships, contacted Jeannine immediately after docking.

261

The letters his grandfather had written home describing his future granddaughter-in-law had led his grandmother to believe that it was in fact Celeste who had survived the terrible disaster. But the girl had been in such a delirious state for so long afterward that there had been no way to question her, and there had really been no reason to. Then, faced with the sudden dilemma concerning Nicholas and the loss of his inheritance, there seemed to be no other choice than to approach the girl with what appeared to be the only solution to their problem. However, his grandmother staunchly insisted the girl had been reluctant to enter into the proxy marriage until she discovered she was going to have a baby.

Christopher sighed heavily. Knowing now what he did about Dionne and her fear that the child would be branded as a bastard, it was no wonder that she had agreed to marry his proxy. How could he fault her for that? Even wild animals were fiercely protective of their offspring. Should he expect a human to behave differently? Also, he could not deny the fact that if Dionne had not agreed to marry him, where would he be today? Perhaps, instead of such animosity, he should be feeling gratitude.

Still, theirs was not a marriage and it never could be one. It was just a farce and that is all it ever would be until it could be dissolved. But, perhaps if he tried to look at it differently, it would make the next two years easier on him and Dionne, too. It was difficult to admit, but this entire situation could not be that easy on her either. However, with all the ugly accusations he had said when they had made their agreement, and considering how he had been avoiding her, if they were ever to have a halfway amicable relationship, he figured he would have to make the first goodwill gesture. Christopher rose slowly from the desk. One thing was certain: He could not do it sitting in the study.

"Why, Christopher!" Dionne said, unmasked astonishment sweeping across her face as she clutched her dressing robe tightly around her. "I did not expect to . . . see you again . . . today."

She wished now that she had remained dressed, but the black gown had been so hot, and besides, it was the only one she had and it was possible she would have to wear it again before it could be laundered.

"May I come in?" he asked.

"Y—yes, of course." She opened the door to allow him to enter. This was certainly a surprise. For three weeks he had ignored her, and now this was twice in one day that he had come to her room. Of course, she could not consider the first time to be a cordial visit, and maybe not this one, either. It all depended upon what he had on his mind, but from his expression, he appeared to be in a personable mood.

Christopher took a deep breath and shifted uneasily on first one foot then the other. "May I sit down?"

"Y—yes, of course." Dionne suddenly wished she could think of something clever to say instead of stupidly repeating herself.

Christopher quickly crossed the room and sat on one of the chairs at the window overlooking the garden. This had been his governess's room when he was a small boy and it had been decorated with a woman's needs in mind. He was thankful for that now. Dionne hesitantly selected the chair right across from him.

His brow narrowed when he noticed that her faint smile held a touch of sadness, then upon closer scrutiny, it was evident her eyes were slightly red and swollen. "Have you been crying?" he asked bluntly.

The tensing of her jaw betrayed her frustration over his having noticed the condition of her eyes. She stared at him, suddenly defensive. "Yes, I . . . have. I have been thinking about the . . . memorial services. I will miss Uncle Andre. I will miss him very much," she added sadly.

"Yes, I am sure you will," Christopher responded softly, hoping she would not dwell on the subject. He did not want to think or talk about the memorial service or anything else that pertained to sadness.

Dionne tightly clasped her hands together while trying desperately to think of something to say. "How is Jeannine? Is she holding up under the stress well? I did not see her again after the services were over."

"Grandmother went straight to her room afterwards, but I believe she is doing fine, although I think the past few days . . . well, actually the past few months are beginning to take their toll." His brow furrowed with worry when he thought about how wan she looked lately.

"If only she had something to keep her mind occupied, perhaps she would not be so depressed," Dionne mused.

An idea suddenly struck Christopher. It was perfect! Not only would it give his grandmother something to do, but it would also be a way to make a friendly overture toward Dionne without it being so apparent. "I hoped you would say something like that."

Dionne looked at him curiously. "Oh? Precisely what do you mean?"

He shifted uneasily, finding her intent gaze to be very distressing. "I guess I might as well come right to the point. Regardless of the situation between us, Grandmother is very fond of you. She made that clear from the beginning, and even under the circumstances, she seems to be excited about your baby. I realize there are certain things a child will need, so as soon as the two of you feel up to it, why don't you go into town and buy whatever you are going to need for the baby? Ask her to go with you. I know she likes to sew, and I am sure she will be more than willing to help. In fact, she would probably love to do it. Besides, it should keep her busy for a while."

Her face paled at the suggestion. It all sounded very nice, but how was she supposed to go shopping without money? As cold as he had been toward her, she was not about to ask him for any. She had a tidy little sum saved, but it was in the bank in Martinique, and it would be far too dangerous to try and withdraw it now.

Christopher, as though reading her mind, continued, "There are several shops where I have charge accounts, or I can give you the money. Either way, it does not make any difference to me."

Dionne began playing with a tiny piece of thread that had not been clipped from a seam.

Seeing her reluctance, Christopher stiffened. What's wrong? Don't you want Grandmother to accompany you?" he asked, suddenly suspicious.

"Oh, no! It isn't that." Feeling embarrassed over what she had on her mind, she lowered her gaze. "It's . . . just . . . I am not too fond of accepting money from you—especially for the baby's clothing. Somehow, it just doesn't seem right."

"Dionne, look at me." Christopher reached out and cupped his hand under her chin and lifted it. "I am going to be honest. I'll have to be honest and to admit that it grates on me personally that a child who does not belong to me will carry my name. However, I am not an ogre who devours innocent children. None of this is your baby's fault." He gestured with his hands. "For God's sake, it can't help any of this. And as for being reluctant to accept money from me to buy things you will need, what do you expect me to do, let it go naked?" He laughed, disgruntled. "Not hardly. And that goes for you, too. Anything you need, buy it. I've never been a stingy person and I don't intend to start now."

Slightly wary of his sudden change of attitude, she looked at him a little defiantly. "Aren't you afraid I might abuse your generosity?"

Christopher returned her stare, a slow smile spreading across his face. "No, I'm not."

Finding his smile a little too discomfiting, she rose from the chair and turned her attention to the window. For days she had prayed that he would come to her room and visit as they were presently doing. But now that he was actually here, she could not help but wonder why. Had he really had a sudden change of heart, or did he just merely need something? Then, Dionne took a deep breath and placed what she hoped to be a pleasant smile on her face. What did it matter if he did want something from her? Regardless of the reason, at least he was here and they were speaking on friendly terms; that was the most important thing right now. She would have to try and remember not to be too impatient.

As Christopher sat watching her, strange and disquieting thoughts began to race through his mind. He remembered how she tilted her head a certain way when she laughed, and how that laughter always seemed to touch her pretty eyes. And, no doubt, her eyes were pretty. It was amazing how they seemed to change color with the different garments she wore. Today, wearing the black gown, they had appeared to be as dark as fathomless pits, but tonight—perhaps it was her green dressing gown—they seemed to shine like emeralds. Without warning, Christopher could feel his heart begin to beat with a rapid tempo.

Dionne turned and the smoldering flame she saw in his eyes startled her.

Quickly coming to himself, Christopher pushed those thoughts from his mind and stood. His voice sounded gruff, even to his ears. "I would like for you to come down and join us for dinner. Grandmother went to her room early, and since a few of the guests are staying overnight and some just staying for dinner—I believe the cook counted twenty—I need your presence down there. I realize you are still not all that familiar with the house, so I have instructed Bella to prepare as many guest rooms as necessary."

She stood still, hiding her inner turmoil with a deceptive calmness, for Christopher had changed right before her very eyes. One moment he appeared to be so friendly and relaxed, and yes, there had even been a slight flicker of desire burning in his eyes. But now, it was as though a black curtain had fallen over his features, masking his thoughts and leaving behind the dark scowl she had grown so accustomed to seeing.

Forcing her voice to remain steady, she replied, "Very well. I will be down as soon as I've dressed."

"Just a word of warning: Be careful. Nicholas and that—that wife of his are still here. I was informed a while ago they intended to spend the night."

"Oh, dear," she said with a chuckle, trying to recapture their light mood. "Would it be possible for me to have a headache?"

"Do you?" Christopher asked, his jaw tensing.

"No."

"Then, madame, I suggest you stick to our bargain," he muttered tersely as he stood and walked toward the door.

"But I was only teas—" Her lips settled into a grim line. "Your suggestion was not necessary. I fully intend to live up to my word."

Christopher stopped in midstride, turned, and retorted curtly, "See that you do, madame, see that you do."

Dionne could only stand there, clenching and unclenching her hands while taking several deep breaths, trying to calm her nerves as she heard his footsteps disappearing down the hall. His words had been so cold and unfeeling that she wondered how she could have ever hoped they might at least become friends. It seemed as though each time he tried to forget and relax with her, his memory would scream in protest, then his anger would return stronger than before. She sighed deeply and uttered a silent prayer for strength.

Dionne pasted a smile on her face and slowly descended the stairs. For one brief moment she had to stifle the impulse to turn and flee back to the safety of her room, for silence slowly fell over the assembled guests as though it were a wave washing across sand. Swallowing hard, she drew a deep breath, then continued down the spiraling staircase.

Seemingly from out of nowhere, Christopher appeared and took her arm. "Good evening, my dear. You look lovely tonight . . . as usual."

She glanced at him sharply and was surprised to see laughter in his eyes. She did not know whether his amusement was directed at her or for the act they would have to perform. She quickly decided that if he were mocking her, she would not be bested. Forcing her voice to sound as charming as possible, she batted her eyelashes and smiled at him. "Why, thank you, Christopher. And, may I return the compliment?"

He did look handsome. He wore a black coat and trousers, and a light sky-blue shirt with a matching silk brocade vest. With his raven's hair and deep blue eyes, his wide shoulders and narrow hips, he presented a strikingly handsome figure of masculinity.

Nodding his head with acceptance, he began making introductions. Dionne followed, her mind soon whirling with all of the names.

"Dionne, this is my mother's Aunt Molly, and her husband Alfred Henderson. My father's second cousin, Frank Mitchell, and his wife, Mary. Another second cousin, Andrew and Lavada Neckar."

The names and faces all passed before Dionne in a mindless blur. Her arm quickly became weary from shaking everybody's hand.

"Hey, you scamp, don't forget me!" a feminine voice said from behind.

Christopher turned and he blinked, then he laughed with delight. "Rosalyn! Is it really you? How good it is to see you again! It's been what—at least ten years since we've seen each other?" He stepped back and surveyed her admiringly. "I must say, you're all grown up now, and if I may be so bold as to add, very nicely too."

Dionne found herself tensing over Christopher's reaction to seeing the young woman. She felt tiny fingers of jealousy grabbing at her heart.

The woman laughed and tossed her dark mane of hair, her warm brown eyes shining with affection. "Well, what did you expect? Did you expect me to stay a little brat all of my life?" Her eyes narrowed teasingly and her voice held a challenge, "Betcha I could still beat you climbing a tree though!"

Christopher bantered good-naturedly. "The only times you won were when I let you win."

"Oh, sure, that is what you claim now, but you and I know otherwise!"

Still laughing, Christopher introduced the women. "Rosalyn, this is my wife, Dionne. Rosalyn is my mother's baby sister," he explained.

Breathing a small sigh of relief, Dionne extended her hand, immediately liking the young woman whom she judged to be close to her own age. Rosalyn smiled and greeted her more warmly than anyone had thus far.

Christopher reminisced, "Rosalyn was a daring little tomboy who followed us boys around like a lost kitten." He chuckled at his memories. "We had a tree house once and she begged and pleaded until we let her come up. . . ."

"Yes, then you tied me up, then ran off and left me there all alone! I'll bet you had to stand up and eat for a week after your grandfather got a hold of you!"

Christopher shook his head. "No, it was more like two weeks, but it was worth every minute of it." His voice became soft. "I'll have to admit, even though I was twenty at the time, I missed you when Pap sent you back east to school. Pap was what I called my other grandfather," he told Dionne.

"Yes, and I was twelve and I thought my heart would break." She looked at Dionne. "No one will ever know how much I loved this scamp. I used to lie in bed at night and hope I was adopted just so I could marry him when I grew up."

"Well, I'm sure glad it turned out differently," a man said as he took a place beside Rosalyn.

"Robert! I thought you were getting some lemonade." Rosalyn hooked her arm in his. "Christopher, Dionne, this is my husband, Robert Brooks. We have been living in Boston ever since we were married over two years ago. We have just been in New Orleans a month now, and when I heard about the . . . *Tempest*, naturally I sent our condolences to your grandmother, but we decided not to call personally until you had the memorial service. I was very sorry to hear about . . . the terrible tragedy. Christopher, I know you were very

270

close to your father and grandfather . . . and, Dionne, I'm sorry about your father, too."

All that Dionne could trust herself to say was, "Thank you. You are very kind."

Rosalyn, trying to turn to a lighter subject, pretended to frown. "Now that I have had a chance to think of it for a moment, I suppose we had better postpone that tree climbing contest for a while because Robert and I are expecting our first child in about five more months."

"Well, may I offer my congratulations." Christopher heartily shook Robert's hand.

Dionne waited expectantly, wondering if he would mention anything about the baby she carried, but when he said nothing, she tried not to be too disappointed.

At that time, George announced that dinner was served. Christopher turned to them and asked, "Will you please join us at the head of the table?"

Both Rosalyn and Robert began shaking their heads. Rosalyn spoke up, "We are not staying for dinner. We are going on home. I just wanted to stay long enough to speak to you alone." She gestured at the noisy people heading toward the dining room. "Considering all that you have been through today, looks like they would have more consideration. And if you don't mind my saying so, I am sure both of you are exhausted. You should just go on to your room and get some rest."

Christopher sighed. "I would like to, but dear ol' Nicholas hasn't changed a bit. He is still up to his dirty little tricks, or so I've heard."

"Yes, so have I." She patted Dionne's hand. "Don't listen to a word he says. He made it a point to tell me all about your proxy wedding . . . and tried to make it sound as . . . ugly as possible. But even though it was under tragic circumstances, I still think it is terribly romantic. However, I think you should be warned. Nicholas's wife is—is . . ."

"Christopher referred to her earlier as a barracuda," Dionne said, in a lowered voice.

Rosalyn threw back her head and laughed. "It fits! It fits perfectly!"

Taking his wife's hand, Robert said, "We have to be going now, Rosalyn. Christopher, Dionne, it has been a pleasure meeting you. Hopefully, next time it will be under different circumstances."

With Rosalyn and Robert being the only friendly faces she had seen, Dionne hated to see them go and was pleased when Christopher issued an invitation for them to return as soon as possible.

Christopher then turned to Dionne and presented his arm. His eyes suddenly looked bleak and tired. "Well, Madame Phillips, are you ready for this?"

"No, but unfortunately it looks as though I have no choice. I feel like a Christian about to be thrown to the lions."

"Madame, those are my sentiments exactly!"

Biting her lip, Dionne looked away, wondering how he meant it. If he thought her to be a hungry lion, or his relatives . . .

Chapter Nineteen

"I must say, I am extremely disappointed," Lorraine's brash voice rang loudly. "All of my life I have heard how wealthy the Phillipses are, and how their women wear so many jewels that they practically blind everybody within a fifty-foot radius."

"Lorraine! You are behaving so rudely!" one of the women admonished. "Shame on you!"

Ignoring the woman, Lorraine's eyes narrowed as she chuckled sarcastically. Then she raised her voice to make sure all the women standing nearby could hear her very clearly. "Not only does she not wear jewels, she doesn't even wear a simple gold wedding ring . . . and just married, too. Isn't it a shame!" She spitefully clicked her tongue. "And someone really should take the poor thing under her wing and show her how to dress properly. Why, she is wearing the same gown that she wore to the memorial service! Apparently she doesn't know that is not the proper thing to do. I know I would not be caught dead wearing the same gown to two separate occasions held in one day!"

Dionne could not help but overhear Lorraine Dumont, and her face paled at the woman's rude comments. She glanced down at her bare left hand and self-consciously hid it among the folds of her dress.

Everything had gone so well at dinner. The food had

273

been delicious and the conversation had been kept in a lighter vein. But now that all the women had congregated in the parlor while the men disappeared into the study to smoke their cigars and have a glass of brandy, Dionne found herself in the center of many unfriendly faces. It wasn't that they were actually unfriendly, Dionne decided. But they were definitely curious and everybody had lowered their voices expectantly when they overheard Lorraine making her unkind remarks. It was almost as if they were eager to hear an argument.

Determined not to let the woman turn this into a spectacle, Dionne continued to chat with one of Christopher's distant aunts.

"My dear, are you just going to ignore what she said?" the elderly lady asked, surprised.

"Yes, I see no reason to add fuel to her fire. It is very plain to me that she is spoiling for an argument. And after today, I am simply too weary. Besides, everything she said was the truth. I am wearing the same gown that I wore to the memorial service. You see, all of my clothing was lost when the ship sank, and I have barely had the time to purchase absolute necessities, much less anything else. And as for a wedding ring, no, I do not have one as of yet, although I am sure Christopher will remedy that situation just as soon as possible. Bless his heart, he has been so busy making preparations for the memorial services and his own personal business, I am sure he has not had time to think about it. Besides, I believe what he feels for me in his heart is more important than a little band of gold. Do you not agree?"

Dionne smiled sweetly as the little old lady bobbed her head and leaned closer and closer, eager for bits of gossip or information that she could use later.

Dionne fully realized she was answering each and

every one of Lorraine's spiteful charges without it appearing so obvious. She continued, "As for not wearing jewels, considering the occasion, I personally believe it would be in poor taste if I wore them. I feel it would be showing a lack of respect."

The woman kindly patted her hand. "I agree, my dear, I agree." She hurriedly fluttered her fan, looking anxiously around for a familiar face so that she could relate what Christopher's little bride had told her. Seeing someone she knew, the lady raised her fan and waved it. "Yoo hoo, Molly! Excuse me, dear," she told Dionne and was off in a rush.

Lorraine was furious Dionne had ignored her remarks. She sat watching her, seething with rage, and trying to think of something to say that would really embarrass the little twit. Damnation! If only the little hussy had drowned with the rest of them, she would be standing in her shoes right now! Lorraine lifted one brow scornfully. But one thing was definite: She wouldn't be wearing a dowdy black gown like that, though.

Berta, serving tea and sugar cakes to the ladies, had overheard everything that spiteful Dumont woman had to say about her new Missus. She made it a point to go over and offer her some tea, just to try and get her mind off Missus Dionne.

"Go away, girl," Lorraine grumbled. Then, suddenly changing her mind, she called her back. "Do you have something besides tea?"

"Sugar cakes, ma'am," Berta said with a curtsey.

"No, you stupid fool, I meant something stronger than tea! Wine or perhaps even whiskey?"

"Oh, no, ma'am. Madame Phillips tol' me to keep the liquor cabinet shut tight."

"Oh, she did, did she?" Lorraine did not know the servant had been referring to the elder Madame

Phillips. She pressed her lips together in anger and glared at Dionne. "I think I'll give that little snip a piece of my mind!" She pushed Berta aside and moved abruptly toward where Dionne was standing talking to another woman.

Berta had seen the murderous gleam in the woman's eyes. She beat a hasty retreat to find Christopher.

Lorraine crossed her arms and stood behind Dionne, smirking, until the other woman saw her and motioned for Dionne to turn around.

A cold chill crept over Dionne when she saw the dark scowl on Lorraine's face. Struggling to keep her voice at a calm, even tone, she asked, "Yes? Is there something I can do for you?"

"The servant said that you ordered the liquor cabinet locked. Don't tell me that the Phillipses are now so destitute that all they can serve is weak tea!"

Dionne gasped. "I beg your pardon?" This woman had gone just about far enough.

"What's the matter, honey? Are you deaf as well as dumb? I said I wanted something to drink other than that watered-down tea you are trying to push off on us." Lorraine triumphantly glanced around the room now that it had grown deadly quiet. "You certainly have a lot to learn, dearie. This is the poorest excuse for a party I've ever seen!"

"That is where you are wrong, Madame Dumont!" Dionne muttered angrily. Sparks flew from her eyes as she glared at the woman. "This is neither a party nor a social gathering. My husband and I are not entertaining anyone. It so happens we are in mourning, and I should not have to remind you of that fact! Tonight is nothing but a gathering of friends and family members of the people we honored today, the people who lost their lives so tragically. Christopher and his grandmother opened up their home to you as a kind gesture, and you repay their hospitality by flinging insults and making malicious remarks. I will not have it! If you cannot conduct yourself like a lady and show my husband's family the proper respect due them, then I strongly advise you to leave this house immediately!"

Lorraine tossed her red hair defiantly. "Can you imagine the nerve this little snip . . ." But as she slowly looked around at all the accusing faces, her voice faltered. She nervously wet her lips. "Why, I've never been asked to leave anyone's home before."

Dionne remained unmoved. "Madame, I believe there is a first time for everything!"

Lorraine gave Dionne a withering look and staunchly left the parlor, only to run into Christopher face to face after she had slammed the doors.

"You ought to teach that wife of yours some proper manners!" she grumbled and tried to push past him.

"Oh, no. Not so fast." He caught her arm. "I think it is time we get this settled. I stood out here and overheard every vicious remark you made, and I am aware that Nicholas has made a few himself. Do you see that door right over there?" He pointed his finger. "That is my private study. Your husband is in there waiting until I can say good night to all my guests. You would be wise to join him."

Lorraine jerked her arm loose from his grasp. She stared at him with pure hatred shining from her eyes. "Maybe my husband won't take it so kindly how you've manhandled me! He just might demand satisfaction from you!"

A cold, diabolical smile spread slowly across Christopher's lips. "That, madame, is up to him. However, before you start making rash challenges or before you get Nicholas into more trouble than he can get out of, I suggest you ask him about my prowess with dueling pistols or a foil. Unless you want to suddenly become a widow, I think you might have a change of heart. Now, I suggest that you join him before I have a chance to change my mind. If I do, I may not be so generous!"

Lorraine started to make a snide remark, but when she saw the dark, foreboding expression on his face, the words died on her lips. She turned and scurried across the floor.

Christopher walked over to where Berta stood waiting with a wide smile on her face. "Berta, I want you to go get the other servants and be prepared to escort our guests to their rooms. I think it is time to put an end to all of these goings-on tonight."

"Yes, sir, Mister Chris, and it's not a minute too soon if you ask me!" she said with a firm nod of her head.

Christopher quickly gave George instructions what to tell the men who were all in his father's study, then he swung open both doors leading into the parlor, noting with silent satisfaction that Dionne seemed to have fared the storm that Lorraine had left behind in her wake. He walked inside. Christopher charmingly took the hands of the women who would not be spending the night at Crescentview and led them out to the foyer. He told them how thoughtful they had been to come and to please come back and visit as soon as possible. He politely informed the other ladies that servants had been stationed outside to show them to their rooms. He also told them that breakfast would be served promptly at seven o'clock but not to expect him or his wife to be present. In the space of less than ten minutes, the room had been cleared. It was then that Christopher sagged wearily against the door and breathed a deep sigh of relief.

Dionne had been busy shaking hands and bidding the women good night. Seeing the obvious look of relief sweep over her husband's face, she sat down on a chair and, with a smile too wide to conceal, began applauding. "May I offer my sincere congratulations." She chuckled easily. "I have never seen a room cleared so quickly."

He grinned, reminding her of how a little boy looked upon receiving praise. "It did smack of brilliancy, didn't it? However, I can't claim the credit. I've seen my grandfather do it several times, and I have to admit, that particular ploy has never failed yet." He sauntered toward her. "Besides, I don't think you did so bad yourself."

"But it was all your idea."

"I was not referring to that. A short while ago Berta came for me while we were all in the study. She said that redheaded woman looked like she was about to tear you apart. Deciding that was my perfect opportunity to portray a knight in shining armor, I came to rescue the sweet damsel in distress." The smile in his blue eyes contained a sensuous flame as he put his hand on her shoulder in a possessive gesture.

Dionne found his touch so distracting that she could hardly lift her voice above a whisper. "Then why didn't you?"

Lightly he fingered a loose tendril of hair on her cheek. "Because the lady did not need rescuing. I found that she had managed to tame the dragon all by herself." He was held mesmerized by the sheer loveliness of her eyes.

Dionne reveled in his open admiration for her. Her heart slammed erratically against her breast. A soft, loving curve touched her lips as she murmured, "I hated to lose my temper in front of the other guests."

Christopher was barely conscious of his actions as he lowered his head and leaned forward. Then, upon realizing what he was about to do, he caught himself and stiffened. Instantly, his manner changed. The muscles in his jaw flexed and a frown crossed his face as he said gruffly, "If you had allowed her to get by with that, you would have never known a moment's peace." He took her by the hand. "I want you to come with me. Nicholas and Lorraine are in my private study waiting on us. Hopefully, we can put an end to all of this nonsense."

Trying not to reveal how his actions had unnerved her, Dionne swallowed with difficulty and managed to find her voice. "What do you intend to do?"

He ran a trembling hand through his hair. "I'm not sure yet. I only know we have to do something to put an end to the trouble they are trying to cause. I would just as soon have a confrontation now and get it over and done with."

Dionne silently agreed. Although she dreaded the thought of facing that woman again so soon, Christopher was right. They had enough to worry about without having to wonder from which direction they would strike next.

Christopher turned to her. "By the way, my study is very small. The only furniture in there is my desk and chair and three additional chairs. I don't want you sitting with them. I think we would make a more formidable impression if you stood beside me." He gave Dionne a reassuring smile before opening the door.

Upon their entering the tiny study, Nicholas immediately jumped to his feet. "Christopher, I must protest the outlandish way your wife spoke to mine."

Christopher's eyes narrowed angrily as he glared at Lorraine. "I see you do not know how to accept good advice, madame!"

Nicholas's eyes were wide, not from anger but from fright. "She even said you mentioned a duel!"

"Your wife lies! I made no mention of a duel, she

did! Just as she lied about Dionne verbally attacking her! However, if this unwarranted persecution of my wife continues, I may be forced to seek satisfaction on the field of honor."

Suddenly, even more frightened, Nicholas eased back into the chair. "Y—you know I would not be a m—match for you in a duel."

"Precisely. That is why I demand this persecution cease immediately."

Lorraine could not remain silent any longer. "But you cheated us! How can you expect us to sit idly by while you enjoy the fortune that should belong to us?"

"How so, madame?" Christopher eyed her coldly.

"B—because the inheritance would have belonged to Nicholas if—if"—she gestured wordlessly at Dionne— "this creature had not been pulled from the gutter and married to you in the nick of time! Why, look at her! One can tell at first glance she's not a woman of quality! Why, her skin is as dark as a—" Her words trailed off, but the light that suddenly gleamed in her eyes was that of pure joy. Quick to seize upon the idea, she excitedly turned to Nicholas. "This is it, Nicholas! We have been searching for a way to discredit this marriage, and now we have the ammunition to do it!" She tossed her head triumphantly and stared gloatingly at Christopher. "You might as well kiss all of this good-bye, because within a matter of days it will all be ours!"

"Madame, what in the hell are you raving about?" Christopher demanded to know.

Nicholas squirmed uneasily. "Yes, Lorraine, what is it?"

Now that Lorraine felt she had the means to acquire Christopher's fortune, she stood and strutted back and forth across the floor, thoroughly enjoying the power she felt she held in her hands. She gestured to Dionne who stood quietly, watching every move she made.

"Look at her, Nicholas. Isn't it quite apparent that the little twit is dark, far too dark to be a woman of quality? There is no doubt in my mind that she has colored blood in her veins."

Dionne gasped with horror. "No! That's not true!" She clamped her lips tightly together when Christopher gestured for her to remain quiet.

Lorraine continued viciously, "You know the laws in this state. It is illegal for a white person to marry a person of color. So that means his marriage is not legal. With this information we can go to my brother, he can petition the courts, and this house . . . everything will be ours!"

Christopher half rose out of his chair, then thought better of it, for he knew if he ever got his hands on Lorraine, he would probably kill her. "Madame!" his voice thundered loudly. "You have pushed my patience to the limit. If I hear one word of that nonsense uttered outside the walls of this room, I will have your head on a platter!"

Lorraine smirked. "Are you threatening me?"

A satanic gleam emitted from Christopher's eyes. "No, madame, I just made you a promise!"

Wetting her lips nervously, Lorraine glanced at her husband. "Are you going to let him get by with talking to me like that?"

"Shut up, Lorraine," he muttered, his eyes never leaving Christopher's face. He felt torn. If by chance there were truth in what his wife said, he could stand to gain all of this. But, if the accusations proved to be false, he could very easily pay the ultimate price. There was no doubt in his mind that Christopher would call him out on the field of honor and he knew he was no match for his cousin's skills with the pistol or a foil.

"Nicholas, I urge you to use your common sense," Christopher said staunchly. "My wife's blood runs as pure as mine or yours, and it can be proved if necessary. Witnesses can very easily be brought from Martinique where she was born and raised.".

"B—but she is dark."

Christopher folded his arms together and leaned back in his chair. "Yes, she is darker than most women. But need I remind you that she recently survived a shipwreck? Use your common sense, man. She was on that raft for days under a merciless sun!" He chortled defiantly. "I believe a long, drawn-out court battle is unnecessary. I can offer a solution to this and everything can be settled in four days' time."

"How?" Nicholas asked, still feeling uneasy, wondering if his wife had pushed Christopher too far.

"I suggest we set sail tomorrow, and when we reach the middle of the Gulf of Mexico, we put your wife adrift on a raft without a morsel of food or a drop of water. Then, after three days, we will rescue her. If her skin is not as dark as Dionne's, I will gladly sign over everything I own to you. However, if I win the agreement—and there is no doubt in my mind that I will—I shall feel that my wife's reputation has been irrevocably damaged and I will seek satisfaction. Again, that is no threat; it is a promise!"

Nicholas glanced about nervously. He had personally seen shipwreck survivors before, men who had previously worked out in the sun and whose skin was accustomed to the hot rays, and they had been brought in from the sea in terrible condition. Also, considering the fact that all genteel women went to great lengths to avoid direct sunlight, it was certainly no wonder that his wife now had a tawny complexion. Since he was not about to accept Christopher's outrageous suggestion to cast Lorraine adrift on a raft, he knew if they persisted with this threat, there would be a court battle, for there was no way Christopher would hand over his fortune without a fight. They would lose for sure, because that girl had no more colored blood in her veins than he did. Besides, the frightening thought of what would happen if his cousin did call him out on a field of honor was enough to make him think twice.

"Now, Christopher, I believe Lorraine has been a little too hasty with her accusations."

"Well, I don't think I have been too hasty!" Lorraine snapped imprudently. "And I will personally see to it that all of New Orleans knows about this juicy tidbit of information before the day ends tomorrow!"

Seeing Christopher's angry scowl and having had enough of her waspish tongue himself, Nicholas leaped from his chair, grabbed Lorraine by her shoulders, and shook her furiously. "I have pleaded for you to behave yourself, but you insist upon refusing. If you open your mouth one more time, so help me God, I will take Christopher up on his offer. We will set sail tomorrow! However, I will not be as generous as my cousin. I will demand we return to New Orleans immediately, and you will be left on that raft until the end of time!" His voice screeched with anger. "Now, I have listened to enough of your accusations! The woman has no more colored blood than you, and I had better not hear anything else about it! My life is not what I expected, but I do not want it to end in the dust of a dueling field! Do you understand me?"

Lorraine's eyes widened with surprise. She had never seen Nicholas this angry before. "Y—yes, Nicholas," she stammered. "I was only trying to help!"

"You have a poor way of showing it! All you have succeeded in doing is almost getting me killed! God only knows I have enough to worry about from my enemies without you turning my family against me!"

He roughly shoved her into a chair and turned to Christopher. It was difficult to read his expression, as it was so filled with fear and anguish. "You've got to listen to me. You have to understand why I was so desperate for money, why I am still so desperate."

"No, you're wrong, I don't have to listen to a word you have to say," Christopher said firmly. "But . . . I suppose I will, even though you don't deserve it." In truth, he was anxious to know the motive, other than greed, behind Nicholas's desire for his money.

Nicholas was downcast, completely dejected as he began, "Lorraine and I were already married when I learned the *Emerald Tempest* was overdue. New Orleans had caught the storm's fury, and I heard down at the docks folks around feared the ship had gone down in the storm. Then, when the *Storm Tide* brought her in"—he motioned toward Dionne—"the captain said it looked like she was the only survivor. Realizing in all likelihood William and Edward were dead, it was then that I got to thinking and remembered the old clause in the will. It's not that I wanted to take what was yours, Christopher, and that's the truth. It's just that . . . I've had a bad run of luck at the gambling tables here lately, and if I don't raise some money soon—a large amount of money—they've threatened to kill me, just to make an example out of me. I told the story to Lorraine's brother—I'm sure you know him, he's been my attorney for a good while now—and he thought I had a good chance to claim the inheritance. Then when we found out she was your betrothed and your grandmother arranged that proxy marriage . . . well, that pretty well nipped my plans in the bud." Nicholas clutched at Christopher's desk. "You have to believe me when I say I only came out here today to . . . well, other than pay my respects to your family, I intended to ask if I could borrow some money. That's all, I swear to God that's all!"

Christopher was confused. "Then what was the

purpose of all those insulting remarks and sly innuendos?"

"Well, it was like this." Nicholas rubbed his chin. "When we got out here, Lorraine and I heard rumors—seems like someone overheard a couple of your servants talking—that you didn't have a real marriage, that you didn't share meals, and you certainly didn't share a bedroom. Lorraine and I talked and we decided that you might not even . . ."

Dionne placed her hand on Christopher's shoulder possessively. These people had made her so angry that she momentarily forgot herself. Her voice was heavy with sarcasm, "Monsieur Dumont, let me assure you that we do have a marriage. I will also assure you that my husband is a kind and considerate man. I have been through a great deal lately, and even though we do share separate rooms, they are adjoining. In fact, in about six months from now, the proof of how real our marriage is will arrive!" Realizing what she had just said, Dionne's eyes widened with horror. "Christopher! I'm sorry! I did not mean to blurt . . ."

"That's all right, my dear." He patted her hand reassuringly. "You didn't tell them anything they won't discover in a few months anyway."

Trying not to show his worry, Christopher threaded his fingers through his hair. He had to think of something so that Dionne's pregnancy would not create a new scandal. He did not doubt for a moment that once Lorraine began counting on her fingers, they would be in for a new round of her witch's tongue. Then he smiled as an idea struck him.

Forcing a gruff tone to his voice, Christopher leaned forward eagerly. "So, you have doubts as to whether or not we have a real marriage?"

"W—well, yes, that is until she said what she did."

Christopher's mouth spread into a thin-lipped smile.

"I am curious, Nicholas, what makes you think that proxy marriage was our first ceremony? Did you ever stop to consider we could have been married on Martinique?" He placed his arm around Dionne's waist to offer reassurance when he felt her grow tense over his false implication. "Did you ever stop to consider my grandmother knew nothing of what had already happened on Martinique when she proposed our proxy marriage? Did you ever stop to consider that our marriage by proxy was not necessary?" He shrugged and chuckled wryly. "However, I suppose, under the circumstances, I should be thankful the ceremony was held because any papers Dionne might have had in her possession were lost when the *Emerald Tempest* sank, and there would never have been a way to prove it one way or the other."

It was suddenly difficult for Dionne to keep a straight face. Although Christopher had never said they were married at an earlier time and place, he implied it in such a clever way that there was nothing else for Nicholas and Lorraine to think.

"You are right, Christopher, I never even thought about that possibility. But you have to believe me. I never would have done any of this if I had not been so desperate." He raised his head bleakly. "They are going to kill me. You are talking to a dead man!"

"What would it take to pay off your gambling debts?" Christopher asked abruptly.

Nicholas loosened his shirt that had suddenly grown tight around his neck. "I owe close to ten thousand dollars," he said in a small voice.

Christopher whistled through his teeth. "That is a sizable amount!"

"Yes, it is. It's more than I can hope to raise." He started to get to his feet.

"Wait a minute," Christopher said with a wave of his

hand. "Sit back down." He removed two cigars from his desk drawer, handed one to Nicholas and lit the other, then waited until blue smoke curled about his head before speaking again, "I'll tell you what I am going to give you, and it is something few men ever get. It is called a second chance. How would you like an opportunity to start all over again?"

"I would grab at it," Nicholas said in earnest.

"We opened several warehouses out in San Francisco recently and I need a man to help watch over my business interests out there. If you agree to take the position, I'll pay off your gambling debts here and also give you enough money to build a decent house and I will pay you a decent wage. Now, a word of warning. I will not give you a lot of responsibility at first. But later, if you prove worthy, you'll be given more responsibility and more money as you deserve and earn it."

Lorraine was unable to remain silent any longer. She protested loudly, "I'm not about to leave New Orleans! Why, that is still a heathen country out there! Why . . ."

"For God's sake, Lorraine, shut up!" Nicholas shouted. His nostrils flared with rage. "It's my life on the line here, not yours! He's giving me a chance to make a fresh start and, by God, I'm going to take it whether you go with me or not!" He extended his hand to Christopher. "I gladly accept your offer."

"Don't you want time to think about it?"

"There's nothing to think about. If I stay here, my life is not worth a plugged nickel. And don't worry about my wife." He glared at Lorraine. "I'm sure she will agree to go with me as soon as she has time to think it over."

Christopher pushed back from his desk. "The *Black Pearl* sets sail for San Francisco in three days. Can you be ready by then?"

Nicholas chortled humorlessly. "I can be ready in the morning . . . tonight, if necessary."

"I have to go down to the docks tomorrow and take care of some business. Why don't you come by my ship, the *Blue Diamond*, and I'll go over all the details with you and explain exactly what your duties will be."

Nicholas grinned. "I'll be there first thing in the morning. Come on, Lorraine, we can see ourselves out." He paused at the door. "Uh, Christopher, about those gambling debts . . ."

"We will take care of those tomorrow. I think it would be to my advantage to go with you to see the people and tell them I'll stand good for what you owe. But I will not pay one dime until you've set sail on the *Black Pearl*."

"Well, I suppose that is only fair." Unable to hide his relief, he nodded his head. "Good night, and I will see you tomorrow, Christopher."

After the Dumonts had gone, Christopher looked up at Dionne and smiled. "Madame, all of this has left me weary. Will you join me for a glass of wine?"

Trying not to think about another time when they had shared wine, Dionne gave a hesitant smile. "I would be happy to."

"Let's stay right here. You sit down and I will pour it. I know you're bound to be tired."

"Yes, I am tired," Dionne admitted with a sigh. "But I think I am even more amazed."

"At what?"

"At you. I discovered tonight that you are a very compassionate man. It was generous of you to not only offer Nicholas a position in your company, but for you to pay off his gambling debts as well, especially after what he and his wife attempted to do. I doubt if I could have been so charitable."

He handed Dionne a glass of wine and allowed his hand to linger near hers. "It is worth it for the peace of mind we'll have. Don't misunderstand. I didn't like what they tried to do, but if they are in San Francisco, at least they won't be able to start any rumors."

She bit on her lower lip and stole a look at him. "Christopher, I'm sorry I blurted out what I did about the baby. I was just so angry. . . ."

"There's no need to apologize. Like I said, everybody will know before too long. What I told them was something that just came on the spur of the moment, but I think we should consider sticking to that story—for the sake of your child, and I suppose it will help our pride just a little bit too."

Deeply touched by his kind gesture, she smiled and murmured, "Thank you."

Suddenly feeling uncomfortable, Christopher drained his glass and rose to his feet. "Shall I walk you to your room?"

"I would be delighted," she replied, resisting the impulse to smooth back an errant lock of hair that had fallen over his forehead.

As Christopher held out his arm for her, his eyes narrowed, then he frowned. "Now I know what's been puzzling me about you. Your locket is gone, your pendant watch."

Dionne's hand went to her neck, and she smiled sadly. "Yes, it was lost. . . . I lost it when the ship . . . sank."

"I'm sorry." The muscles in his cheeks flexed tightly. "I know how you cherished it. It was a gift from your mother, wasn't it?"

"Yes," she answered softly and slowly raised her eyes to meet his.

Without warning, Christopher lost himself in the soft liquid eyes that beheld him. Again, he was barely conscious of his actions as he leaned forward. Even if he had wanted to, he could not have stopped, for he felt drawn to her. His hands slipped through her hair at the nape of her neck and gently pulled her to him. Then his mouth found hers. He felt her lips slacken and begin to tremble, and then open as his mouth moved over hers. He tasted response, sweet and warm, and grew acutely aware of the frantic beat of her heart against his chest. She seemed to fit perfectly in his arms, and her lips felt as though they had been molded for his kisses. He marveled at the feel of her body pressed close to his. Strangely, it was almost as if they were part of one being, yet completely separate entities. Then, realization swept over him that another man had held her in his arms before, another man had known her sweet lips and all of the mysteries she concealed.

Releasing her abruptly, he staggered backward, the expression in his eyes that of painful agony. Then turning, he quickly left the room as if the devil himself gave chase.

Chapter Twenty

Dionne sat beneath one of the huge oak trees, pinching off tiny pieces of bread from a loaf and tossing the crumbs to a few chattering squirrels that played upon the huge well-manicured lawn. She then turned her attention to a hummingbird as it beat its tiny wings while hovering near a jar of honeyed water that had been set out for that purpose. Her eyes widened with alarm when she saw a large tabby cat crouching low on his haunches sneaking silently up on the bird. Shouting loudly, Dionne clapped her hands together and shooed the bird away. The squirrels, also frightened by the sudden noise and perhaps even sensing the danger from the cat, scurried across the lawn and hurriedly scampered up the surrounding trees. Instead of running, the cat turned toward her, arched its back, and hissed angrily.

"I believe you have made an enemy," Christopher said, smiling as he joined her on the ground. "You scared off his dinner."

Dionne tried not to show her surprise over seeing him as she replied, with a grumbling chuckle, "I should hope so!"

She was amazed at his nonchalant audacity. It had been nearly a week now since the memorial service, and this was the first time he had made any attempt to even acknowledge her presence, much less speak to her. He behaved as though he could walk in and out of her life without any thoughts of her feelings. Dionne looked at him with an air of defiance. If he wanted to act so nonchalant, so could she. She would give him a taste of his own medicine and show him how it felt.

Acting as though they had been talking for hours, she said easily, "I suppose I should not admit this to anyone, but I have never really liked cats that much. I guess it stems from all of the many superstitions that were so prevalent on Martinique."

There was a faint glint of humor in his eyes as Christopher plucked a blade of grass from the ground and stuck it in his mouth, then leaned back on his elbows. "Superstitions are nothing but nonsense."

"I disagree. I think there are more to them than people care to admit. When I was a little girl I used to slip out of my room and sneak out to the workers' camp and watch them perform their secret religious rites—that is, the workers who were not Christians. There was one old Negro woman who terrified me. She came from Haiti and I honestly believe she was what they call a voodoo woman and she was always surrounded by cats!" Dionne shivered from the memory.

Christopher laughed at her. "And you call that superstitious? She was probably nothing but an old woman who loved cats."

Dionne's expression told him she was not convinced. "You can laugh at me all you want to, but one night she saw me hiding in the bushes. I noticed as she was dancing she kept getting closer and closer, but I was too frightened to run. Then, all of a sudden, she grabbed me, shook me really hard, and muttered something in her native tongue. She then turned me loose and let out the most piercing scream I've ever heard in my life. I ran as though a million devils were chasing me.

Needless to say, I never went back down there, but for weeks afterwards I had the most terrible nightmares you could imagine."

"Since you don't like cats, do you like dogs?"

"I don't know," she admitted reluctantly. "I've never been around them much. Uncle Andre wasn't much of one to have pets."

"You mean you've been here all of this time and you've never met Katie?"

"Who is Katie?"

He grinned. "Instead of telling you about her, I'll just introduce you." He stuck both small fingers in his mouth and gave a shrill whistle. Within moments, a huge black dog came sprinting around the corner of the house. "Come on, Katie, come on, girl!" He began patting the sides of his legs.

The dog landed with her front paws on Christopher's chest and knocked him backward, then began licking at him and happily wagging her tail.

Dionne edged cautiously away. Her eyes were wide as she asked, "D—does she bite?"

Christopher pushed the dog away and sent her chasing a stick he threw. "Only if I tell her to, but under normal circumstances the biggest problem with Katie is to keep her from licking you to death." The dog brought the stick back and he threw it again, only this time farther away. He chuckled easily. "Your encounter with that cat brought back a memory when I was a little boy. My father never liked to have a female dog. He claimed that a bitch was . . ."

"A what?"

Christopher glanced at her and, realizing she knew nothing about animals, patiently explained in his smooth, mellow voice, "A bitch is how one refers to a female dog. Anyway, my father never liked bitch . . . female dogs. He claimed they were too much trouble, they were always in heat or having puppies or something. But somehow he got hold of Katie's dam's mother. . . ." He paused and, before Dionne could ask, offered an explanation, "Katie's grandmother's name was Blackie, and he decided to keep her. I couldn't have been over four at the time, but I remember getting all excited over having a girl dog. I ran into the house as fast as my legs could carry me, shouting for my grandmother, yelling at the top of my lungs that Blackie was going to have kittens!"

Able to see it exactly how it happened, Dionne giggled, thoroughly amused. "Oh, no, you didn't!"

Christopher chuckled easily. "Yes, I did." He glanced at Dionne. "I'll give you two guesses what we named Blackie's first pup."

Dionne, still laughing, shook her head. "Don't tell me you named her Kitty?"

"I'm afraid we did!"

They laughed for a few minutes, then Christopher told her about several other incidences that had happened when he was a child. Then suddenly, without warning, his manner grew somber. "Dionne, about the other night."

She tensed and held her breath, knowing he was about to mention that tantalizing kiss they had shared. However, she did not know what she would say or do. She had thought about it often over the past few days, reveling in the way it made her feel. Then, when he had purposely avoided her, she did not know what to think. Could it have been nothing but a deliberate ploy to keep her in turmoil, to keep her confused?

To her surprise, he said nothing about the kiss. "Don't ask me how, but I heard that Lorraine deliberately taunted you about not having a wedding ring." He reached into his pocket and removed a tiny red velvet jewelry sack. Handing it to her, he said, "I hope this is suitable. It may make us both feel more respectable."

Dionne opened the sack and gasped, for it contained a delicate gold band. Wondrously, she removed the ring and slowly raised her gaze to meet his.

"Go ahead and see if it fits," he urged.

For one brief moment she had hoped Christopher would offer to put it on her finger and tried not to show her devastation when he did not. She supposed it would have been the same thing as his ready acceptance of their marriage, and with a sinking heart, she knew he would never do that. Quickly blinking back her tears of disappointment, Dionne slipped his ring on her finger and held up her hand so that he could see it.

"Yes, it fits perfectly," she said softly. "Thank you. It was very thoughtful."

Christopher stiffened, sensing her disappointment but not knowing the reason why. He had thought it would please her. Women! The more a man tried to figure them out, the more mysterious they became! Then, he realized the wrong person had given her the ring. If the baby's father had given it to her, she would have probably squealed with joy.

He tried not to show his bitterness as he said, "I guess you might like to know that everything went smoothly and Nicholas and that wife of his are gone. They sailed on the *Black Pearl* a few days ago. We don't have to worry about them anymore."

"That is a relief," she admitted. "I am sure if they had stayed, Lorraine would have kept pushing at Nicholas until they started to dig for information."

"Yes, I suppose they would have," he said, abruptly standing. He started to walk off without even saying anything else, then he stopped and turned slowly. "If you feel up to it tonight, will you join me and my grandmother for dinner? This being my last night at

297

home for a while, I think she has something special planned."

"Your last night home? But I didn't know you were leaving!" Dionne quickly scrambled to her feet. Then, not wanting him to think she was too anxious, she stammered, "Are you sure it's wise to leave?" *Oh, no! Please don't go, please stay here with me!* she wanted to cry in protest.

He frowned. "Why do you ask?" He had to fight against the impulse to brush back a tendril of her hair that had loosened and fallen to her neck.

"I . . . simply thought you might be hesitant to leave your grandmother. I know for a while there you were worried about her health."

"Thank you for your concern about her," he said sincerely. "I spoke to Dr. Blackmon and he said she was as sound as a dollar, but if it makes you feel any better, I also talked to Grandmother and asked her feelings about the matter before I made a final decision."

Christopher all too well recalled the conversation he'd had with the doctor. Not only had his grandmother's health been discussed, but Dionne's as well. The doctor had been concerned he might be reluctant to have marital relations with her since she was pregnant. He had assured him that as long as Dionne remained healthy, it would be perfectly all right until the seventh or eighth month of her confinement. Of course the doctor had no idea of the extent of their physical relationship.

"W—will you be gone long?" Her voice was suddenly bleak.

He slowly walked back toward her, battling the strong urge to take her in his arms and kiss away the loneliness that had immediately appeared in her eyes.

"No, not long. Sometimes it will only be for a couple of weeks, and other times it will be for around a month."

She struggled not to show her despair. "You have more than one voyage to make?"

"Of course I do," he said, as if the answer was obvious. "It is time for cotton to be picked, then after it is ginned it has to be taken to market. The *Blue Diamond* alone has between twenty to thirty shiploads of cotton to pick up along the Gulf Coast. It used to be that I seldom came home during this time of the year, but now that Grandmother . . . is alone, I figured I would come back to Crescentview after each voyage and make sure she is getting along all right." Christopher could not admit that he was hesitant to leave her for any long periods of time either.

Dionne wanted to plead with him to stay. Even if he did ignore her, even if he did go out of his way to avoid her, at least she was able to catch a glimpse of him each day. How could she face not seeing him? She had to know more of the details, she simply had to! "You said . . . the voyages would last from two weeks to a month?"

"Yes. Some of the cotton has to be brought here to New Orleans and that usually takes around a couple of weeks, but when I have to take a shipload to New York, it takes a good month."

"I see," Dionne said and slowly lowered her head, afraid she would lose control of herself if she looked at him.

Suddenly finding this conversation too uncomfortable, Christopher turned once again, but then her voice called him back.

"Christopher, I . . . will miss you," she murmured softly.

He started to smile, then it was as if he suddenly

299

caught himself. Instead of smiling, he nodded curtly, spun on his heel and, with long fluid strides, quickly disappeared into the house.

Unable to sleep, Christopher lay in his bed trying to sort through all the confusion that kept hammering through his mind. He found it difficult to admit his true feelings, even to himself, but this was something he could no longer ignore. Even though he had fought against it with each breath he took, tender emotions were beginning to stir in his heart for Dionne. But how could that be? How could he begin to fall in love with a woman when she was in love with another man, when she was carrying another man's child? That thought was sobering. If only he could find a way to convince his heart the truth that he knew in his mind, he could walk away from her without a moment's hesitation. But that was the problem; human hearts did not listen to reason or logic. Why did it seem as though his emotions had taken off on their own precarious path without thought of the outcome?

He sat up on the side of his bed, resting his forearms on his thighs, his shoulders slumping with dejection. How could he face the long months ahead feeling this way?

Suddenly, without even stopping to think of the possible consequences, Christopher rose and strode hurriedly toward the door leading into Dionne's bedroom.

From the moonlight that streamed through the open window, he could see that she had thrown her cover off in her sleep. His breath caught in his throat. One strap of Dionne's nightgown had fallen from her shoulder, exposing a generous amount of her full, ripe breasts. Somehow, the undergarment had ridden up, too, displaying a flash of leg and thigh. He groaned as he felt his loins quicken and his manhood harden. Slowly, he lowered his hand and touched her shoulder.

She stirred sleepily, then upon seeing Christopher standing by her bedside, she came instantly awake and bolted upright. "C—Christopher?" she asked almost fearfully. "W—what are you doing here?"

Instead of answering immediately, he sank slowly down on her bed and grasped her velvet-soft shoulders with his hands. *"I want you. I need you,"* he breathed huskily. Without giving her a chance to refuse or willingly submit, Christopher turned her lovely countenance up to his and kissed her, claiming her lips demandingly. The instant they touched, he was lost. He could not have stopped, even if he tried.

Dionne did not have time to protest, even if she had wanted to. One moment she had been sound asleep, and the next she had found herself in the arms of the man she loved with all her heart and soul. She had prayed for this moment and now that it was here, she yielded completely without a thought of what tomorrow would bring.

He kissed the trembling corners of her lips, thrilled by how they quivered beneath his mouth. Then, he teased them gently with his tongue. He traced the outline of her lips as though he were memorizing every curve, every detail of their so sweetly vulnerable shape. He parted her mouth, forcing it open with his tongue, and ravaged it tenderly, caressingly, tasting every drop of the honeyed nectar within, savoring it lingeringly until the fire in his blood drove him to be more demanding.

She threaded her fingers through his ragged mane of hair and answered his sweet, demanding kisses without a moment's hesitation.

Dionne's mind was blank except for a heady swirl of dizzying sensations that flooded through her like a maelstrom, sweeping all thoughts of sanity away. Her mouth grew warm, tingling inside where his tongue had pillaged it, devoured it, as though he could not get enough of her. And, like a fragile piece of silk, she was engulfed in the raging flames of emotions he unleashed inside her.

Christopher's mouth found the small, soft sensitive place on her shoulder and teased the spot relentlessly with teeth and tongue as she made soft mewing sounds of delight beneath him.

Her blood was like quicksilver as it pounded like a wild, raging river through her veins.

He could feel the pulse beating erratically at the hollow of her throat when his lips kissed her there.

Christopher's palms cupped Dionne's breasts, tightening gently upon the full ripe mounds that filled his hands. Lightly, he brushed her nipples, over and over, until they were hard little peaks of excitement, aching for his caresses. His deft fingers slid slowly over the darkened crests; his thumbs flicked at the tiny buds. He took one small button in his mouth, and he gasped from the sheer pleasure of it. Languidly, he sucked until soft moans of delight emitted from her throat. His teeth closed gently around the dark tip, nuzzling it, nibbling it. His tongue teased it, taunted it, swirling about it in the most sensual manner, sending ripples of ecstasy racing from it in all directions.

His lips then closed over her other nipple, stimulating it exactly as he had done with its mate.

Dionne cradled Christopher's head, stroking his black hair with trembling hands as his tongue languidly titillated her nipples until liquid flames of fire coursed through her body, blinding her to everything but her need for him.

His hand traveled deliberately down the length of her to her belly, then slipped down to her legs, his

302

fingers teasing like silky feathers trailing along the insides of her thighs, then back up and down again, tormenting her with rapturous delight.

Then, his fingers slipped in to stroke the length of her with small fluttering movements that made her loins quicken unbearably. The little flower of her secret place budded beneath the heat of his fingers, its delicate petals furling and unfurling until it suddenly blossomed wildly.

A throaty moan of passion escaped Dionne's lips. She trembled uncontrollably at the delicious sensations he was arousing in her as he opened the gentle swells of her womanhood, caressing her rhythmically until she was wet and warm where he touched her, and she yearned for him to fill her completely, to make her his once more.

Christopher too felt the need to have her, to possess her, to at last make her his. His raging desire was one without reason, without sanity.

He rose and poised above her, and began the wondrous descent into the beckoning chasm of her soul. The walls of her hot, scorching flesh closed around him, burning, searing until a fine sheen of perspiration beaded over his entire body. His masculinity throbbed, pulsating from the heat. Then, slowly, when he could trust himself to move, he began to thrust in and out of her, his body keeping time with the rhythmic, yet primitive sounds of their gyrating tempo.

Dionne clung to him, her arms wrapped about his back so that she could feel the rippling of his corded muscles. Her breasts tingled against his hair-roughened chest. She arched her hips and met each of his thrusts with thrusts of her own. Her womanhood caressed and stroked his maleness until he was driven beyond the realms of sanity.

Their heat built, shrouding them with its intensity,

its volcanic eruption. Over and over they joined and blended together until, finally, they soared to the heights of ecstasy and far beyond the grasp of mortal men.

Then slowly, oh so slowly, everything drifted back into place, and deeply contented, they fell asleep in each other's arms.

Dionne slowly came awake as the brilliant sunlight streamed through the windows to disturb her blissful dreams. She sat up in bed and stretched languidly. Then, the memory of Christopher's wonderful love-making came back in a heated rush. Gasping with joy, she turned suddenly, but to her dismay only the outline of where his head had lain on the pillow was what remained. He was gone.

Leaping from bed, she flung open the doors leading to his room and discovered that it, too, was empty. Then, with a sadness she did not know possible, she walked slowly back into her room and sank onto a chair by the window. She stared pensively outside. In her heart she knew he had set sail with the early morning tide and he had not even told her good-bye.

Then Dionne caught sight of a small red velvet jewelry sack lying on her night table. She frowned, for she knew that she had placed the velvet bag that held her wedding ring into a drawer the day before. With trembling hands, she picked up the bag and opened it.

"Oh! That dear sweet man," she murmured as she removed a pendant watch from the sack, a pendant watch exactly like the one her mother had given her years before. Clasping it to her breast, tears of joy filled her eyes and a happy smile touched her lips. Dionne knew this was his way of saying that she had a chance to capture and hold his heart.

Chapter Twenty-One

Carrying a small tray laden with a coffee carafe, cups, a warmer, and a flaky croissant, Berta walked into the parlor and set it on a serving table. She looked at Dionne, who paced restlessly in front of the double French windows, and smiled fondly. "I declare, Missus Dionne, you're more nervous than a long tail cat in a room filled with rocking chairs! And if you keep up with that pacing, that child of yours and Mister Chris's is gonna be born wearing walkin' shoes!"

Dionne gasped. "How did you know I am going to have a baby?" She looked anxiously down at her abdomen. Except for a thickening of her waistline and a slight rounding in her stomach, one could scarcely tell she was expecting.

The servant laughed infectiously. "It's just something a body knows, Missus Dionne. I know you not showing yet, leastwise not much, but I reckon part of it's got to do with your rosy cheeks, the lilt in your voice, and the way you walk." She laughed again. "I 'spect even a blind man could tell." Berta did not deem it necessary to tell the little missus that she had overheard the doctor and Missus Phillips talking when the girl finally woke up from that deep sleep she had been in. Besides, hardly a thing went on around Crescentview that she didn't know about.

Dionne chuckled. "I had no idea it was so obvious."

"Well, it is. And from the looks of you, the way you carrying that babe in the backside, I 'spect you best be thinking of boys' names. 'Course, I spent most my years takin' care of Missus Phillips and ain't hardly been 'round babies in a long spell, but b'fore I came here, I did help bring a few into this ol' world . . . and it's just somethin' a body knows. Yep. Be nice to have another little Mister Chris runnin' around here." She shook her head and clicked her tongue. "But let me tell you, that boy was a handful! What that child couldn't get into just hadn't been thought of!" She placed her hands akimbo. "Now, why don't you come over here and rest your feet a spell and have a cup of this here coffee. Cook made it 'specially for you, and these croissants . . . mmmm, they are delicious! And you quit pining for Mister Chris. He'll be back home 'most any day now." She began dusting the tiny porcelain figurines that filled an enormous glass-enclosed cabinet.

Dionne poured a cup of coffee and laced it heavily with sugar. She stood in front of the windows and looked outside. The sky was gloomy and dismal, a damp blanket of heavy gray. It was not actually raining, but the sky was so thick that moisture seemed to drift down from nowhere. Even the Crete myrtle trees with their pink autumn flowers did nothing to cheer up the dreariness. And what had happened to the huge oak trees? One night she had gone to bed and the leaves had been gold, brown, green, and orange, and the following morning the limbs were practically bare.

Bare, that is how she felt, stripped to the bone and left defenseless. *I want you, I need you,* Christopher had said that night, but not one whispered word of love had been mentioned. Not that she had expected it any more than she had expected Christopher to come to

306

her bedroom burning with desire. A nagging voice kept harping at her over the past four weeks, a nagging voice asking, "Who did he make love to, Dionne? You or Celeste? Or was it perhaps some other faceless woman you know nothing about?"

At first, she was so elated he had come to her. But now Dionne did not know how she felt, except that the love she had for him burned even more fiercely than before. Nagging worries had entered her mind that she could be confusing a strong physical attraction for love. But after thinking about it for a while, she pushed those thoughts aside. Oh, she was definitely physically attracted to him. What woman would not be? He had a body suitable for a pagan God and he was so handsome. But there was something inside him, something very special that made her long to cuddle him and hold him close; not for one day or for one night, but for an entire lifetime.

Berta thought all of her anxiety came from her wanting Christopher to hurry home. She wanted nothing else but for him to walk through the front door this very minute. But there was also a dread. A huge, frightening dread that he would look at her and all that she could see in his eyes would be scorn. If that happened, how could she accept it?

Berta's words broke into her tortured thoughts. "Ol' Berta will be the first one to admit being surprised how that Katie dog took up with you!" She nodded in the direction of where Katie lay in front of the fireplace. She rolled her eyes. "Even more surprised when Missus Phillips let you bring that animal in the house!"

Dionne looked at Katie and smiled. She smacked her lips, and the dog came immediately to her side and obediently sat down. Dionne's hand automatically reached down to stroke her affectionately. "But she was so wet and miserable-looking the other day, I didn't have the heart to leave her outside. Besides, she's a good girl, aren't you, Katie?"

The dog whined and beat the floor with her tail.

"Leastwise you and George gave her a bath and she smells clean now!" Then Berta's expression turned real serious. "But what if she . . . what if she . . ."

"Katie hasn't yet, has she?"

"Well . . . no, I reckon not. Leastwise I ain't seen it if she has."

"And I don't think she will, not if we let her outside regularly. I've been letting her out first thing in the morning, a few times during the day, and the last thing at night. But if I'm not around and if you see her standing at the door, be sure and let her out, and tell the other servants, too."

"Oh, yes, ma'am, I sure will!"

From the height where Christopher stood on the quarterdeck, he could see a jumbled, animated bustle of activity on the wharf. But the New Orleans docks were always like this during this particular time of the year. Noticing black stevedores had just started to unload the ship in front of them, Christopher's mouth settled into a grim line as he realized it would be a while yet before the *Blue Diamond* could be unloaded and he could leave for Crescentview.

Whirling about, he had to shout to his first mate in order to be heard above the din of noise. "Barney, have you seen that cabin boy anywhere?"

"Nay, Cap'n," the red-haired Scotsman replied. "The last I seen o' him, cook had him cornered in the galley, scrubbing pans he was."

"Jake," Christopher called to one of the crewmen, "find the cabin boy and have him come up here on the double."

"Aye, Cap'n."

In only a matter of a few minutes, the boy arrived breathlessly on the quarterdeck.

Christopher, feeling his shirt getting moist, adjusted his raincoat. "Billy, after we start unloading, I want you to keep a close eye on the cargo hold, and when it's almost empty, go down to the galley and heat some bath water. Then I want you to lay out clean clothes for me."

"Aye, aye, Captain," the young boy said, saluting smartly, then scrambling back down to the main deck.

Christopher could not help but smile over the boy's eagerness to please, this being Billy's first voyage. He recalled the first time he had sailed with his father as a member of the crew. All of the men had been so patient with him, showing him how to tie knots and how to help hoist the sails. But the most important chore he had learned to perform on that voyage was how to swab the deck. His fondest memories of those early years was when the crew gathered on deck at night and told their mariners' yarns about the old days. He realized later that the men had stretched the stories, making themselves appear to be over ten feet tall and their adventurous feats next to impossible. To hear them tell it, it had been a crewman working for the Phillips Shipping Line who had parted the Red Sea, but, of course, they had been eager to impress their captain's son.

Eagerness. That is what he had felt all week long, but now that they had docked and it was almost time for him to return home, his eagerness seemed to have been replaced by . . . No, he was not frightened! Christopher tensed over that unwarranted thought. He had not been frightened since he was a small boy, and now that he was a man, he certainly was not about to let concern over a woman make him quake in his boots. If he only knew how Dionne felt over his having made love to her. . . .

"Cap'n, Cap'n," Barney repeated, trying to get Christopher's attention.

"Yes, what is it?" he asked, tearing his mind away from those thoughts.

"I said, if ye like, me and the mon can handle things here." He gestured with his hands. "Be gone to ye wee lass."

Christopher shook his head. "No, you and the men are just as tired as I am, and are probably just as anxious to get home yourselves."

Barney adjusted his eye patch. "I have me doubts about that, mon. All I have to look forward to is me rented room, a bottle of good Scotch whiskey, and a paid woman." He grumbled, "Come to think on it, I may just find the bottle of whiskey and sleep on board tonight."

Christopher clasped his friend on the shoulder. "Barney, my man, if I were wise, I should consider doing the same thing."

It was nearly midnight before Christopher stepped out of the hired carriage and started up the walk leading to the house. Everything had certainly changed during the long month he had been away. Leaves had turned and already fallen, and with the thick overcast skies and dark house, it looked empty and uninviting. He wondered if that would be his reception once he got inside.

Trying to be as quiet as possible, he opened the front door and went directly to his room. There, he slipped out of his boots and fumbled around in the darkness for a bottle of whiskey he kept on his escritoire. He pulled the cork from the neck and drank right out of the bottle, then, throwing back the coverlet on his bed, he piled all of the pillows against the headboard, lay down on the bed, and propped against them.

"Damn! It's cold in here," he muttered to himself and took another drink of whiskey instead of snuggling underneath the covers.

This time of the year the fireplaces were not lit on a regular basis and the room was chilly. The ceilings were high so that the rooms would be cooler during the hot summer months, but when it did turn cool, especially with it raining and drizzling for days on end, the entire house seemed to be colder than it normally would have.

Sighing heavily, Christopher sat up on the side of the bed and placed the bottle of whiskey on his night table. He did not want anything to drink, but his memories kept torturing him. He stared hard at the closed door leading to Dionne's room. It looked as tall and as formidable as the White Cliffs of Dover.

Then, remembering how she had looked that night he had gone into her room, how she had been lying there with her cover kicked down to the foot of her bed, Christopher wondered if she was uncovered now. He saw her in his mind's eye, cold, shivering, too sleepy to awaken, and lying there uncovered, catching her death.

"Guess I should look in on her and make sure she is under the covers," he grumbled under his breath.

Getting up and padding softly across the floor, Christopher opened the door. It was so dark that he advanced cautiously. Then, everything seemed to happen at once. He stepped on something warm and furry, the floor moved out from beneath his feet, there was a whine, a yelp, then a bark, then Christopher found himself sprawled in the middle of the floor.

"Damn it to hell! What in the hell is going on in here?" he thundered.

Dionne awoke immediately. Someone was swearing

and cursing, and Katie was yelping from pain. She found the matches on her night table, struck one, and lit the lamp. Holding it beside her head, she peered into the darkened room. Her eyes widened when she saw Christopher lying on his backside and Katie hobbling on three legs and whining.

"Katie! Girl, are you hurt?" She flew out of bed and hurried to the injured animal.

Christopher turned his head sharply. "Katie? What's she doing in here?"

"Keeping me company," Dionne said over her shoulder as she knelt beside the dog.

Blinking nonplussed, Christopher, still sprawled in the middle of the floor, sputtered, "Madame, I should hope you would be concerned if I were injured!"

"Are you?" she asked pointedly.

"No."

"Then please help me look after Katie."

Feeling slightly ashamed over his misalignment of concern, Christopher hurried over to his dog. After gingerly testing her front paw, he said, "I believe she is all right. I doubt if there is any serious injury." By now Katie was standing on all four legs and wagging her tail happily.

Dionne, clad in her thin nightgown, suddenly felt shy. "Th—that is a relief," she murmured softly.

Christopher ordered Katie to go lie down as he helped Dionne to her feet. "What is she doing in here, anyway?" His eyes widened upon being able to see through Dionne's gown. Without warning, he could feel his blood begin to race through his veins.

Aware that she was clad in only a sheer nightgown, Dionne quickly slipped on her robe. "Katie and I have become very good friends while you have been gone. Each day she accompanies me on my walks. I throw sticks and she chases them, but . . . the weather has

312

been so nasty the past few days ... and I saw her standing out on the front porch looking so cold and lonely, I simply had to bring her in. George helped me bathe her. ..."

"You gave her a bath?" he asked with surprise.

"Yes."

"And she let you?" He remembered trying to give her a bath two summers ago and deciding then never to attempt it again.

"Yes, of course she did."

"And Grandmother did not object when you brought her in?"

"No. In fact, if the truth were known, I believe Grand'mere is as fond of Katie as I am."

"Grand'mere?" He knew that was the French word for grandmother and wondered why Dionne was calling her that.

"Yes ..." she said hesitantly. "That ... is what ... she asked me to call her."

"Oh, I see."

Feeling extremely self-conscious, Dionne turned away from him and asked, "Have you been in long?"

"Here at the house, no, but the *Blue Diamond* arrived in New Orleans late this afternoon."

"I—I see." She lowered her eyes, wondering where he had been but too afraid to ask; too afraid he would tell her what she did not want to hear. But the image of a faceless woman suddenly appeared in her mind.

For a moment, Christopher was amused over the fact that he could read her emotions so clearly. Then his amusement quickly turned to aggravation. Did she know what he was thinking too? Were his emotions so apparent? Much to his surprise, he found himself explaining, "No, I don't think you do see. I had to remain with the ship until she was unloaded. There was another ship in front of us and we had to wait. We just finished a short while ago."

It was difficult for Dionne to keep the relief from being too evident in her voice. "Then you must be starved half to death. Would you like something to eat? I am a better cook than you might think."

As he lowered his eyes to meet hers, his breath caught raggedly in his throat. He had never seen Dionne look lovelier. Blood began to pound hotly through his veins. "No, I'm not hungry. At least . . . not for food."

Suddenly, he drew her into the circle of his arms. The feel of her body was so good next to him. His lips touched her forehead lightly, barely perceptibly, covering her brow and hair with surprisingly gentle kisses.

Dionne pulled away slowly, an unconsciously seductive smile playing on her lips as she realized suddenly, elatedly, that all of Christopher's mocking coldness was nothing but a facade. Those words, *I need you, I want you,* had not been uttered by the driving force of passion and nothing else. There had been feelings behind those words! He did care for her! Perhaps he could not bring himself to admit it just yet, but he cared! And he wanted her, just as she wanted him!

She knew almost instinctively what she looked like to him at that moment; yet instinct was not necessary, for she could see herself mirrored in the fathomless darkness of his deep blue eyes. For a woman she was reasonably tall, but not too tall. Slender, but not too slender, for the child growing within her had filled her proportions out to that of complete womanhood. Her legs came together in a triangular shadow beneath the filmy whiteness of her nightgown and her breasts were a perfect outline, slightly darker in the center where erect nipples teased the sheer fabric.

A cold draft chilled the air, but Christopher's eyes were hot and searing on her body, warming every inch of skin they caressed. An answering heat seemed to surge through her veins, burning her breasts, her belly, her limbs, and especially that secret spot between her thighs where she longed to feel his strength.

Dionne held herself away from him for one brief second, conscious that he had not reached for her again, conscious that perhaps he had changed his mind. But then, the flame that still glowed hotly in his eyes told her she had been mistaken, that his need was her need, her longings his longings. Slowly, achingly, she opened her arms and went to him.

A husky moan escaped his lips as he buried his face in the silky softness of her neck. The delicate fragrance of her hair further inflamed his blood. Rough masculine cheeks rasped her tender flesh, a male mouth, hard and hungry, opened to greedily taste the sweetness of hers.

They needed no tender words, no sweet caresses to arouse them; their passion was abrupt and raw, soft and gentle, two completely different elements, yet strangely they were a savage mixture of both.

Strong arms rippling with muscles easily lifted her and carried her to the bed. Hands—wanton hands— tugged at his clothing, helping to rip it off.

Dionne thrilled to the hard muscles of his chest and shoulders, the lean hardness of his thighs as he forced them between her legs, urging them apart. There was a small amount of pain when he entered her, for she was almost new to lovemaking, but the pain was fleeting, almost over before it began. And soon she found herself being swept along on tides so swift and turbulent that she could think of nothing, feel nothing but her need for the sweet fulfillment that erupted in her body at last, leaving her weak and shivering in its wake.

Afterward, lying so contentedly beside him, their arms still entwined around each other, it seemed to Dionne that her heart would never cease its wild assault against her breast. How gentle he was, holding her tenderly, so lovingly, now that their passion was spent. She marveled over the rapturous ecstasy they had just shared.

Then, as ragged pulses slowly abated, and his soft murmuring kisses became even more gentle and even more loving, the flames of crimson desire slowly came back to life and they knew each other once again.

Dionne awoke long before Christopher. After rising and attending to her early morning needs, she went back to bed and snuggled contentedly in his arms as the faint blush of dawn appeared on the eastern sky. She thought how poetic it almost was: Crescentview had been so heavily laden with misery it was as if the sky itself had been mourning for his return, and now that he was here, the sun had burst brilliantly through and chased the gloom and despair away. Nevertheless there was a dark shadow hanging over her paradise. He still had not said the three magic words, *I love you,* even though seemingly they had shared more love and happiness than some men and women shared in an entire lifetime.

Just be patient, Dionne, be patient, she told herself. *And in time, it will come . . . it will come.* She closed her eyes and slowly drifted back to sleep.

"Good morning, Missus Dionne, are you gonna sleep all day?" Berta asked as she bustled into the room carrying a breakfast tray. She stopped short when she

316

saw Christopher lying in bed with his arms wrapped all around her mistress. "Why, Mister Chris! I didn't know you was back home! Lordy, let me get Missus Dionne all fixed up with her breakfast and I'll go tell Missus Phillips that you've done already snuck in on us in the middle of the night!"

"What time is it, Berta?" Christopher asked, sitting up in bed and yawning sleepily.

"It'd be 'bout seven o'clock."

"Then it is too early to wake my grandmother. I'll go in and see her in a little while." He stole a glance at Dionne and smiled when he saw her blush shyly.

Dionne's eyes took a hesitant path to Christopher, a pale blush stealing across her face as she saw his naked torso in the light of day for the first time. She marveled at the sight of his wide muscular shoulders and chest, at how his hair crisped and curled and grew in mass profusion across his chest, then swept down past his taut stomach and disappeared beneath the covers. His eyes mockingly caught and held hers, for he realized her embarrassment, yet his chest swelled with pride over the admiring way she beheld him. Dionne blinked, blushed, then slowly lowered her lashes. Suddenly, anxious to do something other than look at Christopher, she slipped on the bed jacket that Berta had handed to her before she began stoking the embers in the fireplace and adding logs to the hot coals.

"It'll be all toasty and comfortable in here in just a few minutes," Berta said. She poured water into a porcelain wash bowl, wet a cloth and wrung it out, then handed the cloth to Dionne.

"Thank you, Berta." She had already washed her face and hands but accepted it regardless.

"I need a washcloth too," Christopher said, then waited a moment until Berta prepared one for him. "May I have some breakfast too? I'm starving!"

317

"Yes, sir. I'll fetch your breakfast just as soon as I take care of the Missus and let Katie dog back inside." She placed her hands on her buxom hips and added, "You go on ahead and start eating, Missus Dionne. If you don't, it'll get cold and there ain't nothing worse than a cold breakfast. Do you want anything else?"

"No, this is fine, Berta," Dionne said quickly. "I have everything I need. You go ahead and wait on Mister Chris."

Christopher spoke up eagerly, "Tell Cook I want four scrambled eggs, two pieces of ham about this thick"—he measured a generous space between his finger and thumb—"a double portion of grits, some fried potatoes, three . . . no, better make that four hot buttered biscuits, an orange, a big glass of sweet milk, and a pot of hot black coffee, and I wanted it ten minutes ago."

Berta's eyes widened. "Lordy, Mister Chris, where are you gonna put all those vittles?"

He patted his stomach and grinned. "Right here, Berta, right here."

"Well . . . Lordy, Mister Chris, what in the world did you do to work up such a bodacious appetite?" She blinked, then her eyes got real wide as a smile flashed quickly across her face and she began chuckling. She started for the door, still talking and still chuckling, "I might be foolish, but I sure ain't no fool. I *knows* how Mister Chris worked up that appetite. Oh, Lordy, I *knows* how he did it!"

Dionne was mortified. She rubbed her hand across her forehead, mostly to hide her face from Christopher who was silently laughing. She could tell he was laughing; the entire bed was shaking.

She had to clear her throat twice before she could say, "I believe Berta needs to have a good talking to."

"Yes, I suppose she does," he said, still chuckling.

318

"But I hope no one takes the time to do it before she tells Cook what I want for breakfast. I think I am about to starve to death."

"Do you want part of my breakfast? I'll be happy to share." She halfway hoped he would decline, because she was hungry too.

"No, you go ahead." He sighed heavily. "I'll just sit here . . . and watch you eat." At precisely that second his stomach grumbled.

"For goodness sake, Christopher, if you are that hungry, please take my tray." Without givng him a chance to answer, she set the bed tray over his lap but quickly retrieved her coffee cup. "You can have my breakfast, but you cannot have my coffee; besides, I have already put sugar in it."

Christopher looked down and surveyed the food questioningly. It was a far cry from what he had ordered. Dionne's tray held a boiled egg, one piece of crisp bacon, a single slice of dry toasted bread, a tiny dab of marmalade, a small glass of milk, and half a glass of orange juice. It wasn't much, but he was so hungry that even the simple fare looked good. "Well," he drawled slowly, "if you insist." Then a pained expression swept across his face. "Just a minute, I'll be right back."

He leaned forward, set the tray at the foot of the bed, and before Dionne could even realize what he was about to do, he tossed the covers back and jumped from the bed. Her eyes widened, then riveted on his backside as he must have known they would. This was the first time in her life that she had seen a naked figure of a man, and although it was slightly embarrassing, she still thought he was the most beautiful creature she had ever seen. She had known downy hair covered his buttocks, having caressed them during their love-making, but the fleeting sight of such a private part of his body was very sensually stimulating. Christopher hurried back into the room a few minutes later, and she was able to see the front side of him this time. Her mouth gaped in wonder and astonishment, for that particular part of him was enormous even though it hung flaccidly between the triangle of his torso and upper thighs. Dionne wanted to look away but found she could not. Her face blazed and her mouth became dry, but still she stared at him, mesmerized.

A teasing smile pulled at the corner of Christopher's mouth as he felt her eyes hungrily devouring him. Even though the floor was freezing cold to his bare feet, he deliberately slowed his steps and fairly strutted across the room to the wash basin.

Dionne watched as he stood in front of the wash basin, washing his hands and face again. She realized the cold floor was part of the reason he began shifting his weight from one foot to the other, making his buttock muscles tense and tighten. The other reason was that he thoroughly enjoyed her watching him. It seemed to her that he stood there for an eternity, but in reality it was the mere span of seconds.

Then Christopher turned, and although he still wanted to strut slowly, he found himself hotfooting it across the cold floor. Blowing and sucking air between his lips and teeth, he muttered, "Damn! This floor is cold!"

As he climbed back into bed, Dionne realized, although a bit of shyness and reservation would still cling to her, at least for a while and perhaps for a long, long time, this was the natural order of things between a man and a woman; this was a part of life, a part of love. And, slowly, all her feelings of being ill-at-ease slipped away.

He placed the tray back over his lap and briskly rubbed his hands together. "Now, where was I?"

320

Finding no butter, he began spreading marmalade over the toasted bread. "Dionne, do you recall that conversation we had the day before I left?"

"Which conversation?"

"The one where you told me about that voodoo woman."

"Yes," she said slowly, wondering why he had brought that up.

"Are you sure she didn't place a curse on you?"

From the manner of his voice he sounded like he was teasing, for it held no barbed edge, but his words made her frown. "I'm sure she didn't, why?"

"I was gone three weeks and five days . . ."

So you counted the days the same as I, she thought, her heart soaring.

". . . and during that short space of time, you managed to steal my dog's loyalty, and apparently my grandmother has more or less adopted you because she insists upon you calling her grand'mere, and Berta, who has been a member of this household since I was a baby, completely ignores me to see to your needs first, and I have a sneaking suspicion all the other servants will do the same thing." Even though he stared at her intently, amusement danced in his deep blue eyes. "What else of mine do you want, madame?"

Dionne wanted nothing more than to murmur her true feelings. *Your heart, Christopher. I have your passion, but I want your heart, I want your love.* But she did not have the courage to speak the truth, and not wanting anything to spoil this beautiful time of natural ease between them, she decided to play his question light and carefree. "D—do you really want to know?"

"Most definitely."

"I—I'd really like part of my breakfast back," she said with mock seriousness.

Christopher tossed his head back and gave a roaring

321

laugh. He handed her a portion of the toast. "If you'll share yours with me, I'll share mine with you."

"It's a deal," she responded adamantly, taking a ravenous bite of the toast.

Christopher gazed at her, his dark eyebrows arched mischievously as he leaned forward, flicked his tongue out, and touched the tip to the corner of her mouth. When she looked at him questioningly, he laughed, touched his finger to the corner of her mouth, and murmured huskily. "There was a crumb right there. I told you I was starved. I could not . . ." He glanced away when Berta entered the room.

"Here's your breakfast, Mister . . ." Berta paused, realizing she had interrupted something. Then she grinned and, marching staunchly, brought the tray around to Christopher's side of the bed. "Cook said if this ain't enough, she'd have to send George back out to the smokehouse. And from the looks of things in here, it sure ain't gonna be enough!"

"Berta, you are beginning to behave most impertinently," Christopher growled good-naturedly.

"What's that mean?" she asked, placing her hands akimbo.

"It means you are getting too sassy."

She bobbed her head. "Yes, sir, Mister Chris, I guess I am. But it sure makes me feel good to see a pretty smile on the Missus's face, and the way you was acting there for a while, why, your face looked the same as a big ol' dark thundercloud 'fore it rained. So you go on ahead and eat your breakfast, and if you works up another appetite, then I will volunteer to go to the smokehouse myself after more vittles . . . and you *knows* how far that shed is from the house!" She hurried back to the door, stepped out into the hall, then opened the door again and stuck her head back inside. "Just wanted you and the Missus to know that I ain't

322

gonna disturb you no more this morning . . . won't let nobody else either. I'll place myself down there 'side the staircase and dares a body to get past me! I'll just dares 'em to!" she said adamantly, then firmly closed the door behind her.

Later, after they had eaten, Dionne rose and stacked their trays on a table. She deliberately moved at her leisure, not wanting anything to break the magical spell that hung over not only them but the entire room.

Christopher's eyes followed Dionne with each step she took, with each move she made. Passion began to glow in them hotly. He called her to his side and slowly slipped his arm around her waist. Although his voice was teasing, it was heavily laced with desire, "I think as sassy as Berta has been this morning, she deserves to have to make a trip to the smokehouse, don't you?"

Dionne sensually threaded her slender fingers through his hair and murmured, "Am I to understand that you intend to work up another ravenous appetite?"

"Most assuredly, madame, most assuredly," he whispered just before he pulled her down beside him and his lips closed hungrily over hers.

The days that followed quickly turned into weeks. Each time they parted was a mixture of delight and sorrow for Dionne; sorrow that he had to leave, but delight and wondrous happiness each time he returned, for he did so with an eagerness that lifted her hopes. She was also pleased to note that the door leading to his bedroom now stood open all the time.

Dionne knew Christopher had at first turned to her with only passion burning hotly in his heart, but upon each return journey, an undeniable affection appeared in his eyes and grew stronger as the weeks passed.

She was deliciously happy. It showed in her bouncy

walk, her rosy cheeks, and even in the aura that mysteriously surrounded her. She filled the long daylight hours that they were apart sitting in her room and in the parlor, sewing tiny little garments, taking long walks around the grounds with Katie always at her side. She and her grand'mere had even taken the carriage into the bustling heart of the city a few times, browsing through the many shops and stores that thrived there. Her nighttime hours were filled with dreams of Christopher and of the day that would come when she would gaze lovingly into his eyes and, instead of seeing mere affection would see love burning brightly in them.

And, as the weeks passed, her child grew beneath her heart, swelling her slender figure from a slight bulge in her belly to a rounded melon curve. Often, she caressed her burden with loving hands and prayed that the time would eventually come when she could tell Christopher the truth about the child. But, wisely, she knew before that could happen, he would have to love her as deeply as she loved him.

The *Blue Diamond* finally arrived in New Orleans. This voyage, although short, seemed to have lasted a lifetime for Christopher. Instead of staying on board the ship until she had been unloaded, he hurried eagerly down the gangplank as soon as they had docked and the ship was secured in its moorings. While waiting for a carriage for hire, he impatiently grumbled about having to do so when he owned two of them, along with an entire stable of horses at Crescentview. But, inside, he knew it would have been an effort in futility for his personal carriage to wait at the docks each day, for no one, not even he, knew when the *Blue Diamond* would arrive in New Orleans.

Finally, the carriage arrived and he paid the driver a generous amount to hurry as quickly as possible. He was eager to see Dionne, to take her into his arms and make sweet love to her. Christopher realized it was from his own impatience that the carriage seemed to take forever to reach the long drive leading to the house.

Opening the front door, he rushed inside and, upon learning Dionne was in her room, took the stairs, two steps at a time. But when he opened her bedroom door, his ardor quickly cooled, for she was standing by the window, wearing a sheer nightgown and robe, and her profile was startling. The baby she carried in her belly, the baby that had come from another man's loins, had never been this obvious before. Stunned from the impact, he could slowly feel his happy smile fading from his lips.

"Christopher!" Dionne squealed happily. She ran to his arms and smothered his mouth with kisses. "I'm so happy to see you! I've had Cook prepare your favorite dinner the past three nights just in case you were able to return early."

"We only sailed as far as Biloxi this time." He forced a gruffness into his voice he really did not feel. "But, Dionne, I feel it is only fair to tell you that I only have one more shipload to bring to New Orleans, then I will have to start taking the remaining cargo to New York."

"Let's not talk about such things right now. I just want you to hold me in your arms."

Uneasily, he pulled from her embrace. "Well . . . there will be time for that . . . later. I need to go visit with Grandmother for a while. I have been neglecting her lately. But . . . you are . . . welcome to join me if you like."

She peered up at him intently, sensing something was wrong, sensing somehow things had changed between them. But what? What had she done? A wary, hesitant smile appeared on her lips. "A—all right. A visit together with Grand'mere would be nice."

The remainder of the day seemed to stretch into infinity. Each time she tried to be alone with Christopher, he would deftly change the subject or think of something he had to do, something that could not wait.

Then, finally, when they got ready for bed, she turned to Christopher expectantly, but instead of him eagerly seeking her out, he stiffened and pulled away. "Dionne, I don't think we should make . . . love anymore. At least . . . not until after . . . your baby is born."

"But I saw Dr. Blackmon just two days ago, and he said that . . . we could . . . make love for another month, perhaps even two more."

"Perhaps so, but I am afraid I will hurt you."

So that was what had been bothering him! She breathed a sigh of relief and reached out to stroke his cheek lovingly. "It won't hurt me . . . honestly," she murmured.

"Damn it, Dionne, this is difficult enough as it is!" he growled, sitting up on the side of the bed. "Please don't make it worse!"

Still not realizing what was really bothering him, Dionne urged Christopher to lie back down. "I'm sorry. I simply did not realize you felt so strongly about it." She snuggled against him. "I am perfectly content for you to hold me close in your arms."

Christopher tried, oh, God, how he tried, but the longer he lay there holding her so close, the more tortured his thoughts became. Finally, he rolled over, seeking solace on his side, but Dionne bellied up to his back.

Christopher's eyes opened wide when he felt small,

pecking movements, much like that of a thumping finger at his back. Realizing it was the baby kicking, his blood ran cold. He flung the covers back and stood beside the bed.

"Madame," he said, his voice containing its old coldness, its old aloofness, "I cannot rest in peace here beside you, at least . . . not now. I am . . . afraid I will hurt the baby. I think it will be for the benefit of us all if I sleep in my room from now on." With that, he turned on his heel and marched staunchly into his room, firmly closing behind him the doors that had been left open.

Finding sleep impossible, Christopher restlessly paced the floor, listening to the muted sounds of Dionne's pitiful sobs as they filtered through the closed door. His insides felt as though someone had taken a sharp knife, viciously stuck it in him, and twisted the blade, showing no mercy whatsoever. But he knew he could not comfort her, for a wall had been firmly erected between them. A wall that might possibly never come down.

Chapter Twenty-Two

Even darkness could not mask the destruction that had ravaged the harbor area as the *Blue Diamond* sailed into the New Orleans port. Christopher stared intently at a burned and almost completely destroyed seagoing side-wheeler, anchored derelict in the middle of the river. No doubt the owners were preparing to tow the ship to a rarely used harbor to salvage as much as possible, then tow it on out into the deep waters of the Gulf and sink it where it would offer no hazards to other ships. He also noted grimly that many buildings and even part of the wharf had apparently been destroyed by the same fire and explosion that had claimed the side-wheeler.

"'T'would appear they've had a wee bit of a problem 'round here," Barney remarked, his Scottish brogue becoming even more pronounced, which showed his alarm. "And from the looks of it, the fire was quite recent." Some of the buildings surrounding the docks were still smoldering.

"I hope the fire didn't reach the warehouses." Christopher's jaw muscles flexed tensely. He shuddered to think what a financial loss it would be if the four huge warehouses had been destroyed.

"Aye, Cap'n. 'T'would be bad," Barney agreed, his eyes clouded with worry.

He stroked his chin thoughtfully. The calm manner of his voice betrayed none of the worries that had invaded his mind. "I suppose we had better see if we have a place to put the cargo before we start unloading the ship. Pass the order along that I want all the men to remain on board until we've had a chance to check out the situation."

"Aye aye, Cap'n." For such a huge man, Barney had the agility of a cat. He scrambled from the quarterdeck with an apparent ease and quickly passed the order along.

As soon as the *Blue Diamond* had been moored and the gangplank set into place, Christopher and Barney left the ship and hurriedly made their way past all the confusion that still abounded on the docks.

"What happened here?" Christopher asked a man who had just slumped onto the banquette, a narrow boarded walkway, and had begun drinking a tankard of beer. From the looks of the man, he had been pushed past the point of exhaustion.

The man turned red-rimmed eyes up at Christopher and shrugged wearily. "Who knows for sure? The *Annabelle* was carrying cotton and gunpowder. There has been speculation that a cheroot was carelessly thumped into the hold, landed on a bale of cotton, and it eventually set off the gunpowder. I suppose that sounds most logical. Whatever the cause, this entire area soon looked like Hades itself. When the *Annabelle* exploded, fire went everywhere. Last account I heard there were twenty-two people dead, not counting the fate of the men on board ship and hundreds of injuries."

"When did it happen?" Christopher asked softly, imagining how terrible it must have been.

"Before dawn, day before yesterday. We didn't get

330

the fire under control until last night, but all of that cotton will smolder until only God knows how long. We've been digging people and bodies out of collapsed buildings ever since."

"Is there anything my crew and I can do to help?"

"No, I don't think so. I believe the worst is over. We've just finished searching through the last building that burned." The man squinted his eyes and stared up at Christopher. "Who are you?"

"I am Christopher Phillips, captain of the *Blue Diamond.* We only reached port a short while ago."

"You own that big shipping line, don't you?"

"Yes."

"You have some warehouses too, don't you?"

"Yes," Christopher said, feeling a hard knot of dread tighten his stomach as he and Barney exchanged wary looks.

The man shook his head. "I don't think they burned. . . . I don't know, though, I might be wrong."

"That's where we were headed to find out." Christopher nodded politely. "Thank you for your time, sir."

"Wait a minute, mister," the man called when Christopher and Barney turned to leave. "You might consider arming your crew. There's been a hell of a lot of looting going on. What hasn't burned, they're stealing."

"I appreciate your advice," Christopher answered with a curt nod of his head. "Barney, you go back to the ship and start issuing weapons." His eyes narrowed thoughtfully. "Better still, go to the back of the cargo hold and break out a couple of cases of those Sharps rifles we took on in New York and give those to the men."

"Ye mean those buffalo guns?"

"Yes."

"But, Cap'n Chris, they'd blow a man to bits, they would."

"If a looter comes on board the ship, what are you going to do?"

"Kill the black-hearted bastard!" Barney answered without a moment's hesitation.

Christopher shrugged. "Dead is dead, whether you break his neck, run him through with a sword, or blow him to bits. If looters hit us and if the crew is heavily armed, a few shots and we'll be left alone."

Grinning, Barney scratched his beard and said, "Ye have a point there, Cap'n."

"I'll go check on the conditions of the warehouses and I'll join you as soon as I can."

"Aye, sir."

In spite of the seriousness of the situation, Christopher could not help but grin when he returned to the *Blue Diamond*, for Barney stood on the dock beside the gangplank, holding a rifle almost as long as he was tall on at least eight men with their hands straight up in the air.

"'T'would the warehouses be standing, Cap'n?"

"They are all right, Barney. One received a little smoke damage but that's all." He glanced at the men his first mate was holding at bay. "What's going on here?"

"Ye were right 'bout the rifles, Cap'n. Fired one shot, I did, and these sons o' whores stopped right in their tracks." He chuckled heartily. "Dinna hit nary a mon, but I blew a bale of cotton to Kingdom come, I did! What should we do with the bloody bastards, Cap'n? Shoot 'em or hang 'em?"

Christopher chewed on his bottom lip, his brow

furrowed thoughtfully. "Hanging is a tempting thought, but I suppose we had better just tie them up and leave them for the police. If we were at sea, it would be a different matter, but here in New Orleans, the authorities might frown on it if we took the law into our own hands." He called to his men who were all leaning on the rail of the ship with their rifles ready. "Jake, Robbie, bring plenty of rope and tie these bastards up and leave them right here where we can watch them. They may serve as a warning to other looters. To the rest of you, I need ten volunteers to help stand guard over at the warehouses tonight, and it goes without saying we'll have to post guards on the ship too."

The men's voices rang in a heavy chorus, agreeing to do whatever was necessary.

Christopher acknowledged their eagerness and loyalty with an appreciative smile. As soon as the volunteers had gathered around for instructions, he said to the second mate, "Rolph, do you know the warehouse manager?"

"Yes, sir, I know him well."

"Good. I've spoken to Johnson and told him I was sending help. But he has already placed some guards around the warehouses, so I don't want them to mistake your men for looters. So, Rolph, I suggest you take the men to the main office and let Johnson assign you posts. Any questions?"

Rolph shook his head and gave his rifle an affectionate pat. "No, sir, we can handle it."

After the men left, Christopher and Barney went back onboard ship. Christopher said, "You can take the first watch and I'll go down below and try to get a little rest before it's time to relieve you."

"Nay, canna do that, sir."

Having already turned to go to his quarters, Christopher spun on his heel and looked at him sharply. To his knowledge, this was the first time Barney had ever refused a direct request. Then, realizing that his friend would rather pull the second watch, the more difficult one, and this was merely his way of stating his preference, Christopher shrugged indifferently. "All right, then, I'll take the first watch and you go below and try to get some rest."

Barney did not say a word. Instead, he clamped his lips together and firmly shook his head.

Crossing his arms, Christopher studied the expression on his first mate's face. It was obvious he had his mind set on something, stubbornness emitting from him like a beacon. "I think it would be simpler if you just told me what's bothering you instead of all of this rigmarole."

A wide grin spread across Barney's face. "Thought ye would never ask, Cap'n. If ye be worried about the ship and the cargo, me and the mon can take care o' things here. Ye go on home to ye little wife. She needs ye now. Ye know it will soon be time for the babe to come. . . . Why, who knows? Ye may even be a papa already!"

Christopher retained his composure, but there was a distinct hardening to his eyes. He had only been at Crescentview twice in the past three months; three long months since he had so abruptly left Dionne's bed. The first time had been extremely awkward and unpleasant, but after what had happened the last time he had been home, going to Crescentview tonight was the furthest thing from his mind.

Everyone had been bustling around with happy smiles on their faces, talking about nothing but that baby! And from the way his grandmother had been carrying on, she seemed to have forgotten the fact that the baby did not belong to him. Even old George acted like he could not wait until the child was born. All of that had been annoying and aggravating, but nothing compared to what had happened later. Christopher shuddered from the memory. Thinking Dionne had been in the parlor, he had gone into her room looking for one of his favorite shirts. But she had been in there undressing, getting ready for dinner. The sight of her swollen belly had been completely devastating to him. It was not the *child,* but the fact that the child was *inside* of her, the fact that the *child had been placed there as a seed from another man.* A man who had known her as intimately as he had known her. In the span of mere seconds, horror had registered in Dionne's eye, horror because she had seen hatred raging in his. He had spun on his heel and left the house immediately. But every night since then, the memory of that moment had haunted his dreams. Just as he could see her in his mind's eye now. Dionne standing naked, then clutching a robe and holding it in front of her, her bottom lip quivering, her eyes misting with unshed tears, and her hand slowly trying to cover her belly, as if attempting to protect her child from his hatred. Christopher shook his head as though that would clear his tortured mind. No, he would not be going to Crescentview, not tonight. And if he had his way, he would not return home until she had that baby of hers.

"What do ye say, Cap'n? Will ye be going home?"

Barney's voice had snapped Christopher back to the present. "No . . . not tonight, Barney."

"But, Cap'n, me and the mon can . . ."

"Not tonight, Barney. Go ahead and take the first watch."

"But, Cap'n . . ."

"That's enough, First Mate!" he snapped angrily. "I gave you an order. Now, either take your post or step aside and I will place a man there who will follow orders!"

Barney's eyes widened minutely, then with a tightening of his mouth, he came to attention and saluted. "Aye, aye, Cap'n." Placing the rifle under his arm, he hurried to the quarterdeck and took his post.

Christopher immediately regretted his angry ultimatum, for Barney was not just his first mate and he was not just a member of the crew. He was his friend, a dear and trusted friend who had been with him since the beginning. What made it worse was that the men standing near them had heard the angry exchange. Christopher realized that not only had he hurt his friend's feelings, but he had embarrassed Barney in front of the crew. Reprimands aboard the *Blue Diamond* were rare because his crew was the best, and he always tried to treat them fairly. But he had not been fair to Barney. The man had only been trying to do him a favor. He had to do something, something short of an apology to make it up to Barney, but what?

Glancing about, Christopher's gaze fell on the cabin boy who was standing with his mouth agape. "Young man, do you realize you have just learned a valuable lesson?"

"Me, sir?" the boy asked, surprised.

"Yes, you," Christopher replied sternly.

The boy gulped. "What was it again you asked, sir?"

"I wanted to know if you learned a lesson from what just now happened between me and my first mate?" Christopher made sure he spoke loud enough so all could hear.

"Well," the boy drawled, "I figure what I learned is to be sure and follow orders."

"Well, yes, you should follow orders, but that was not what I had in mind."

Puzzled, he scratched his head. "What was it I should have learned then?"

"That a captain is never supposed to behave like a

pompous ass in front of his crew." It pleased Christopher to hear a few chuckles coming from the various crewmen standing guard alongside the rail.

Christopher propped his foot on the railing and stared at nothing in particular. He still had no intentions of going home to Crescentview that night, but after what had happened with Barney, it would be impossible to go to his quarters and rest. Perhaps what he needed was a bottle of good Scotch whiskey and a soft, beautiful woman. Maybe those were the diversions he needed to take his mind off Dionne and her baby. His brows drew downward in a reflective frown. That notion had come from out of nowhere, but after giving it a second thought, it was a damned good idea! The warehouses were well guarded, and the armed crew standing guard placed the ship in capable hands. Besides, with the captured looters tightly bound on the wharf in front of the ship as an example to others who might have larcenous thoughts, he doubted if there would be any more trouble around the *Blue Diamond* tonight. Without giving himself a chance to reconsider, he hurried up to the quarterdeck.

"Barney, I'm leaving the ship in your care tonight."

He grinned unconsciously. "I thought ye might be seeing it my way, sir."

"No, not quite, I'm not going home. If there is any sign of trouble here or if you need me for any reason, I'll be over on Condé Street."

"Condé Street?" Barney asked incredulously. That was part of New Orleans's infamous district. While his captain had visited those houses occasionally in the past, to his knowledge he had not been to one since he had married that lass from Martinique.

"Yes, Condé Street," Christopher repeated firmly, ignoring the puzzled expression on Barney's face. "I'll be back here at the ship first thing in the morning."

337

"Aye, Cap'n Chris."

Christopher noted with a smile that Madame Antoine's house had been painted a bright pink since he had last visited her elite establishment. What the significance was he did not know, unless it had something to do with the lovelies inside, for Madame Annette Antoine was known far and wide for her House of Delicious Delights! Thinking about the ridiculous name made him chuckle. But, there was no question about it. Madame Antoine could provide a woman for any man's needs, regardless of her color or degree of experience. He remembered one night several years ago when he had paid her a visit. There had been fifteen men standing in line for a virgin, and when he left, the line only contained one man—and no one had been sent home disappointed. He wondered then if Madame Antoine did not have some sort of magical machine in the back of the house that popped a virgin out every few minutes.

But no virgin for him; they were too much trouble. Leave those to the rutting, eager sons of the plantation owners when they came to the city with a bulge in their breeches and a pocketful of money. He wanted a soft, willing, passionate woman who had enough experience to know what pleased a man. He realized he had callous feelings about the women, but what the hell? Most of them had entered this profession with their eyes wide open. Perhaps a few did not, but there was absolutely nothing he could do about that, except avoid the houses that used devious means to get and keep their women. That was one reason he patronized this establishment. Madame Antoine treated her women fairly and, surprisingly, with respect.

Christopher rubbed the palms of his hands briskly together, smiled with anticipation, and pulled the chain hanging by the front door. Moments later he heard the rasping of bolts being withdrawn, and the door was opened by a huge Chinaman who towered even over him, and Christopher was well over six feet tall. The sight of the man was startling. He wore what Christopher believed to be harem-style pantaloons, purple in color, a wide red sash around his waist, two gold bands around his biceps, and from what he could tell, there was not one hair on the man's body, not even on his head. He remembered the man from previous visits.

"Yes, sir, you are about to enter Madame Antoine's House of Delicious Delights," the man said in his deep booming voice as he bowed and gestured grandly. He spoke perfect English. "My name is Sing Ling. I am here to help you select one of our lovelies."

Christopher felt the back of his neck tingle from apprehension as the man led him into a parlor that had been wallpapered with a bright crimson-colored brocade paper. It was definitely gaudy, but with all of the red and white couches and red and white lamp shades covering the numerous lamps, it surprisingly produced a rather pleasing effect. But still his apprehension remained, for the parlor was empty.

"Where is everybody?"

"Some of the lovelies are engaged and the others are merely in their rooms. As for the gentlemen who usually crowd in here, I suppose they are busy fighting the fire. Most of them have vested business interests in the dock area, regardless of whether they are local businessmen or if they own plantations."

"I see." He squirmed, suddenly feeling uneasy.

"What is your preference tonight, Mr. Phillips?" the doorman asked as he walked behind a white fur-covered bar, filled a glass with whiskey, and handed it to Christopher.

"Oh? So you remember me?" Christopher asked with a raise of his brow as he accepted the drink.

"Indeed, I do. Although it has been a long time since you have visited the House of Delicious Delights . . . perhaps too long. If my memory serves me correctly, your preference was Marvelous Marie, but alas, that lovely is no longer with us," he said, sadly shaking his head. Then his face brightened. "But we do have many new lovelies with us now." He produced a stack of miniature portraits from under the bar and began showing them to Christopher. "Here is Ravishing Red Robin, a beautiful Comanche Princess, but perhaps she is a little too savage for your impeccable tastes. And here is Tempestuous Teresa, a lovely quadroon. Naughty Nellie, a natural redhead, Wicked Wanda, Sinful Sylvia . . ."

Christopher shifted his weight uncomfortably, then ran a finger around the neck of his shirt as if to loosen it. "What about Rose?" he interrupted. "Is she still here?"

"Rapturous Rose? Ah, yes, but she is entertaining at the moment." Sing Ling looked at him with eyes hooded like a hawk. "Shall I make you comfortable while you wait?"

He shook his head adamantly. "No, I don't want . . . to wait." It wasn't that Christopher did not want to wait, but feeling the way he did, especially tonight, he did not want to go into the arms of a woman who had recently held another. "Do you have a lady available who has not been with someone else tonight?"

"Indeed, I do. Her name is Bashful Beverly." Sing Ling removed a cup from behind the bar. "The fee is one hundred fifty dollars. I feel I should offer an explanation, since it has been so long since you have visited us. Madame Antoine discovered this most unusual cup down at the French market. Our patrons have found it . . . rather delightful. In fact, we even had a contest to select the name for the cup. You should have been here to enter, for the winner was entitled to an entire month of free entertainment." Sing Ling chortled, his deep voice sounding almost evil. "Please insert the money into the Portals of Paradise."

Christopher looked at it, blinked, then looked at it again. The cup was not really a cup but merely a bag fashioned from pink velvet, folded and tucked to look exactly like a woman's . . . private parts! He had sailed all over the world, seeing everything imaginable and then some. But a Portal of Paradise?

Instead of tucking the money into the cup, he placed it on the bar and muttered tersely, "I believe I will pass the pleasures of the cup. But I do want a bottle of whiskey." He placed extra bills on the bar for the liquor.

Although he did not particularly care for all the gaudy frills and sensual, fantasylike atmosphere here at the Delicious Delights, the Madame made sure her women were clean and disease-free, not like some of the houses in New Orleans. And, without a doubt, the entertainment she provided pleased a lot of men and it had also made her a very rich lady.

Sing Ling palmed the money, held open a heavy curtain, and gestured grandly. "You will find Bashful Beverly behind the white door. You do not have to bother to knock. Merely go right on in."

Christopher staunchly walked past him. All this nonsense had always made him feel very uncomfortable. He paused at the door, then opened it and quickly stepped inside. The woman was lying on a bed covered with white satin sheets. She smiled when she saw him.

"Well, hello," she murmured huskily, patting the bed beside her. "Come over here where we can get better acquainted."

He grinned. Beverly was even more beautiful in real life than she was in the miniature. She had short black hair, big blue eyes, a red heart-shaped mouth, and milky white skin, but what was most impressive were her melon-sized breasts. He sauntered slowly toward her, placed the bottle of whiskey on her night table, then pulled his shirt up over his head and tossed it aside. "Hello, Beverly, my name is Christopher. . . ."

Christopher sat on the side of the bed, his shoulders slumped and feeling completely humiliated. This had never happened to him before! He had tried for what seemed like hours to have sex with this woman, but the harder he tried, the more his body refused to cooperate.

Beverly rubbed her breasts against his back and wound her arms around him. She spoke in a smooth, syrupy voice. "Now, honey, don't feel too bad. I've seen it happen to men a lot younger than you are. It just happens sometimes. Maybe you are too tired. Come on, lie back down and allow me to arouse you. I personally guarantee before you leave through that door, you will be a satisfied man!"

Not thoroughly convinced, Christopher complied with her requests. But the more she fondled and caressed, the more unwilling his body became and the more humiliated he felt. In desperation, Christopher tried to squeeze his eyes tightly shut, but to his horror, the image of Dionne appeared vividly in his mind. His entire body stiffened with rage. She was the reason why he could not function as a man!

Goddamn!" he bellowed with rage. *"The bitch has castrated me!"* He leaped out of bed and began angrily putting his clothes on.

Beverly raised to her knees and firmly planted her hands on her hips. "Why, I did no such thing!"

"I wasn't talking about you, madame. I was referring to someone else!" He yanked on his boots and stood to his feet. Reaching into his pocket, he removed some money and slapped it in her hand. "Thank you, madame. This fiasco has been no fault of yours! If I return, you have my word that the night will be spent much differently!"

Not being able to find a carriage for hire, Christopher jammed his hands into his pockets and began walking toward the ship. Damn her! Damn her to hell! Just as soon as he made sure everything was still under control at the ship, he would go home and have it out with Dionne. Regardless of their agreement, she would leave his home today! Even if it cost him every dime he had to his name, he could not allow her to cost him his manhood! With her out of the house, she would be out of his life forever. And that is how he intended for it to stay!

Chapter Twenty-Three

"Robbie, take three mons with ye to Condé Street and dona leave nary a stone unturned until ye find the cap'n," Barney said as he paced back and forth across the quarterdeck. "It be most imperative he be found and told to return to the ship. Most imperative!" He motioned with his hands. "Be gone now and be quick about it!"

The cabin boy, standing by the gangplank, cupped his hands around his mouth and shouted, "Here he comes, Mister Barney! The captain's coming now!"

Barney ceased his endless pacing, peering into the early morning fog that not only surrounded the ship, but hovered over it like a misty shroud. The captain was indeed walking toward the ship, arms swinging, long legs reaching for the next step. He walked as though he had a definite purpose in mind.

He scrambled down to the main deck, his heavy bulk making the gangplank shudder and creak as he bounded across it and ran toward his captain.

"Christopher, me lad, I was about to send a party out to find ye, I was."

Christopher's eyes locked and held with Barney's, for he had not addressed him by his Christian name in more than ten years. His eyes flew to the ship, sweeping immediately from bow to stern. Relief flickered in them upon realizing all was well with the *Blue Diamond*, the star ship of his fleet. Then, his facial muscles tensed. "What's wrong? Is there trouble at the warehouses?"

"Nay, Christopher, there be trouble at Crescentview. One of ye servants was sent with the hopes that the *Blue Diamond* had come to port. Ye be needed at home. I dinna tell 'em where ye were, though I was about to send the mons looking for ye."

Christopher quickly glanced about, looking for the messenger. Not recognizing anyone, he asked, "Did he say . . . what was wrong?"

For a mere second, Barney stared at his captain as he tried to decide what to do. He had sailed with Christopher since the first day the lad had set foot on a ship as a cabin boy. He knew him better than any man alive, and he also sensed things were not right between him and his bride. If he told him the problem concerned her, then Christopher, being the stubborn, obstinate man he was, might not think it was serious enough and might refuse to go to her. And if anything bad happened, he would regret it for the rest of his life.

Without batting his eye, Barney deliberately lied, "Nay, Cap'n. Nary a word, just that ye were needed at Crescentview immediately." He turned and shouted to the ship, "Robbie, take some mons and find ye cap'n a carriage for hire."

"Why didn't my man stay and wait for me?" Christopher asked. He had only one thought in his mind, one worry, one concern: his grandmother. She was getting well on up in years, and at this stage of her life, anything could happen. It had to be serious for Dionne to send a messenger on pure speculation they had reached port.

"I dinna know how long it would take to find ye, Cap'n, and I thought ye would prefer no one at the

346

house to know ye whereabouts."

Christopher's lips tightened. Damn everything to hell! While he had been at a whorehouse, his dear sweet grandmother probably lay dying . . . if she was not already gone. That thought was sobering.

A carriage pulled to a creaking stop and the driver leaned his head out. "I was told somebody needed a ride." Before he got the words out, Christopher had already jumped into the carriage.

"Let's go! And hurry!"

Barney called after him just before the carriage disappeared around the corner, "Send word and let us know as soon as ye can!"

Even though it was well past sunup by the time the carriage reached Crescentview, the house could not be seen from the road, for the heavy fog continued to hold steadfast, cloaking the landscape with its gray mist and spreading its eerie silence like creeping spiderwebs. Then, as they neared the house, Christopher feared the worst, for almost every window on the bottom floor was ablaze with light as were also a few on the second floor.

Having paid the driver earlier, Christopher leaped from the carriage and ran up the front steps. This seemed all too familiar, like a continuing nightmare, constantly rekindling itself by taking the people he loved the most.

When Christopher threw open the front door, it was as though time stood suspended for a mere fragment of a second. Bella, Cook, Annie, the cook's helper, George, and two young girls who helped take care of the house were all in the foyer, pacing and crying. As soon as they realized he was there, they all came at him, babbling with hysterical voices.

"Be quiet!" Christopher shouted, not being able to understand any of them. He grasped Bella by her upper arms. "How is my grandmother? Did—did I arrive . . . in time?" The servants were all so emotional it was too difficult for him to know just by looking at them.

"Your grandmother be fine, Mister Chris." Bella looked up at him and her face crumpled as tears brimmed in her eyes. "It's Missus Dionne. . . . You gotta do somethin', you just gotta! She's a-tryin' to have that baby, but he ain't cooperatin'. Oh, Mister Chris, you just gotta do somethin'!"

A gamut of emotions swept through Christopher, all the way from relief to anger. He drew a deep, shuddering breath then released it heartily. Then his mouth tightened into a thin white line as he grumbled, "You mean to say I was scared half out of my wits simply because a woman is having a baby? Good God, Bella, women have been giving birth since the beginning of time, and simply because Dionne . . ." He paused and eyed her warily, "What do you mean, the baby is not cooperating?"

All heads turned in the direction of the staircase and all eyes raised to stare somberly at the second floor when a cry came from there. It was a sound, the likes of which Christopher had never heard before; it began as a guttural moan and peaked in an agonized crescendo, then the sound became muted.

Bella, with tears running freely down her cheeks, pointed upstairs. "That's what I mean, Mister Chris. That's been going on for days now!"

"Days?" It felt as though someone had doubled up his fist and hit him in the stomach. He asked anxiously, "Isn't Dr. Blackmon with her?"

"Christopher! I thought I heard your voice! Thank God you are here!" Jeannine said with obvious relief as she appeared at the top of the stairs. She motioned with

348

her hand. "Come quickly."

His eyes never left her face as he raced up the stairs, taking them two at a time. Never had he seen her so worried and distraught. He quickly hugged and kissed her, then holding her at arm's length, he asked, "How bad is it, Grandmother?"

"I am afraid it is very serious. Dionne is having a most difficult labor." She raised her eyes to his and a sob caught in her throat. "I—I am very concerned about her, Christopher." She placed a finger across her lips. "Shhh, but keep your voice down. I don't want her to overhear this conversation."

He took her by the arm. "Then let's go to the other end of the hall so that she can't hear us." As they walked, he spoke softly, "Isn't Dr. Blackmon with her?"

"No."

"Why not?"

"We have sent for him and sent for him repeatedly, but he cannot leave the hospital. It seems there was a terrible explosion down at the docks and . . ."

"Yes, I know about that. But surely there are other doctors or midwives. . . . What about Berta? Hasn't she delivered babies before?"

Jeannine was so upset that she balled her hands into fists and gestured helplessly. "Christopher, you do not understand! There were hundreds injured in that fire and every possible person who has any medical knowledge has been pressed into service at the hospital! And, yes, Berta has delivered a few babies in her time, but they were uncomplicated births." She sighed wearily. "You have no idea how many prayers I uttered that you should arrive before you were supposed to. I have been sending George down every four or five hours to see if the *Blue Diamond* had come in yet. You being the ship's captain, I know you have a

349

certain amount of medical knowledge. . . ."

Christopher stared at her incredulously. "Are you suggesting I deliver her baby? Grandmother, don't be absurd. I've never done that before." He nervously ran his fingers through his hair. "Indeed, I do have some medical knowledge, but other than having to amputate two fingers from a man's hand, the most I have ever had to do was lance boils, bandage wounds, and stitch a few lacerations." He swallowed his worry, hoping desperately his grandmother was merely overly agitated. "Do you think you might be making more out of this than it is? After all, women have been having babies . . ."

"Damn it, Christopher St. John Phillips, be silent and listen to me!" She pointed down the hallway, her voice coming in an angry hiss, "That young woman has been in there for nearly three entire days now, in terrible agony, refusing to even accept a tiny bit of laudanum to help ease the pain because she has some fool notion that it will injure the baby, and you have the audacity to suggest I am exaggerating the seriousness of her condition!" Tears appeared in her eyes and her chin trembled. "I realize I am no great authority in this matter, but I firmly believe if she does not have that child by tonight, we will be *burying* her tomorrow!" She folded her arms and glared at him adamantly. "That is precisely how serious it is!"

Christopher could feel the blood drain from his face. It was as if a huge slab of ice had been thoroughly crushed, then gradually lowered over him, making him feel stone-cold. Dionne was dying! He had always heard that a man's entire life passed before his eyes in the split second before he died, and now his life with Dionne was flashing before his mind's eye in that brief span of time. It was all so vivid. How the sun shone on and captured the gleam of her long brown hair. How

350

the laughter reached her eyes when she smiled. The way she held her head when she spoke. The faint blush that pinked her cheeks when he walked up behind her, wrapped his arms around her, and nuzzled the silky softness of her neck. No! By all that was holy, she would not die! He would not let her die!

Abruptly pivoting on his heel, Christopher's footfalls drummed against the carpet as he marched down the hallway. There was a minute tightening of his features when he saw Katie lying prostrate beside the door. The animal, as if somehow sensing the despair, did not move her head that was resting between her front paws. Instead, she merely raised huge brown eyes and whined pitifully.

Christopher's heart wrenched at the sight of Dionne lying on the bed as he opened the door and stared at her. Her face was ashen. Her hair, drenched from perspiration, was plastered to her head, and there were flecks of blood on her bottom lip. At that moment another pain struck, and her face grimaced and contorted from the agony that tore through her.

He stood there, frozen, unable to move. It seemed as though his heart failed to beat until at last her pain abated.

Berta saw him first and wrung her hands. "Mister Chris, thank the Lord you're here!" she said excitedly.

Dionne turned and her eyes widened at the sight of him. Then she began pulling at the sheet as though trying to hide from his troubled perusal. "No, no," she muttered. "Please . . . I don't want you . . . seeing me like this. Please . . . go. Don't come . . . in here!"

Christopher crossed the room in a few quick strides, knelt down beside the bed, took one hand in his, and pressed it gently to his lips. His other hand tenderly brushed aside a damp tendril that lay across her brow. "Shhh," he crooned softly. "Everything is going to be all right. Grandmother tells me . . . the baby is being very stubborn." He attempted to smile. "Tell me, is this a trait he inherited from his mother?"

She swallowed hard and bobbed her head. "I suppose . . . so, but, please . . . Christopher, I don't want . . . you seeing me . . . this way."

"Don't worry about me seeing you; you worry about getting that baby here. Besides, how can I help if you run me from the room?"

Dionne, feeling another pain coming, turned her face away. Involuntarily, her body arched and she writhed from the intense spasm that gripped her. Christopher's eyes mirrored her torment.

After the pain had passed, he stood and turned to Berta. Taking her by the arm, they moved out of Dionne's hearing. "Do you know what's wrong, why she can't have the baby?"

Berta chewed on her bottom lip and shook her head worriedly. "I just don't knows for sure!"

"Then tell me what you do know," he urged.

She helped to explain by gesturing with her hands. "Well, like I done already said, I don't knows for sure, but those other times I helped to birth a baby, the child always came out with his face down. And . . . it 'pears to me that that child be laying wrong!"

Christopher had been watching her hands move as well as listening to what she said. "Do you mean that the baby's buttocks are where its head should be?"

"No, don't mean that t'all. The head is down, but when I feels of Missus Dionne's belly, the baby's position don't feel right to me. I should be feeling its little back, but instead, I's feeling little arms and little legs. 'Sides that, I've looked and I can see the head. I 'spect that baby is gonna have to be turned 'fore the missus can ever push him out."

He ran his hand raggedly through his hair. "Well,

then, for God's sake, turn the baby!"

Berta began wringing her hands and backing away from him. "Oh, Mister Chris, don't make me do that! Oh, please don't makes me do that! I's don't knows what I's doing, and I's afeared I'd break the little child's neck. I's seen it happen b'fore! And if I did that, I'd just die! Oh, Lordy, I'd just die! I just can't do it 'cause I don't knows how! That's why that other little baby died that time. The midwife didn't know what she was a-doing!"

Dionne writhed from another pain. She tried so hard not to yell out, but the pain was so intense she could not help herself.

Christopher stood, ashen-faced, helpless, rubbing his mouth and trying to think. Her pitiful cries tore right through his heart.

"Christopher, Christopher, please come . . . here," Dionne murmured weakly.

He quickly complied. But upon reaching her bedside, his eyes widened in horror, for he now saw resignation and defeat etched on her face.

She clutched frantically at his hand. Her voice was weak and shallow. "Please, Christopher, listen to me. When I was on board the *Emerald Tempest* . . . and the days after . . . at times I thought I was . . . looking death in the face and . . . now, I know I am. I don't think I can hold on . . . much longer. . . . I feel my strength . . . draining from me."

"No, Dionne." He shook his head, refusing to listen, although in his heart he feared she was speaking the truth. Life without Dionne? How could he face it? Then, with a sudden awareness, he knew life without her would be impossible. "You are going to be fine!" he firmly insisted. "The baby will be fine too!"

"No, please listen. . . . There are things I have . . . to set right with you. I can't face death with this . . . on my conscience." Even in her misery she tried to smile at him. "Remember when I threatened . . . to go to Nicholas . . . on my honor I swear . . . I would have never done that." Her eyes glazed as another pain struck, but still she kept talking. "You have to . . . *aagghhh* . . . promise me something . . . Berta said the baby's heart beats strong and . . . I have a feeling mine . . . is beginning to fail. If the baby . . . is not born soon, I am going to . . . die. You have to promise . . . my baby will live. . . . If you see my death is inevitable, you . . . have to promise to . . . take my baby . . . from me. I know there are ways . . . to do it. I know it would be . . . most difficult for you, but I know . . . there are ways!"

"Dionne, please don't talk that way."

"But . . . you have to promise me."

"All right, I promise."

Remembering a promise he had made months earlier, she tried to smile through her agony. "Do I have your . . . word of honor?"

"Yes, you have my word of honor." He too recalled the other promise.

She wet her lips and gasped for breath. "You have to also promise to raise him . . . love him . . ." Seeing him about to pull from her grasp, she murmured, "No, wait, Christopher. . . ."

But Christopher could not bear to listen to another word. He tore himself from her, unaware of the silent tears slipping down his cheeks. Then, determination shone in his eyes. He quickly knelt back beside her and murmured tenderly, "Dionne, I am going to make another promise to you. You are going to be fine. I give you my word!"

Rising quickly, he said, "Berta, Grandmother, make her as comfortable as possible. I will be back as soon as I can."

"Where are you going?" Jeannine demanded.

"After Dr. Blackmon! I'm going to bring him here even if I have to put a rope around him and drag him!"

Christopher leaped from the back of the horse, quickly tethered the reins to the hitching rail, and hurried up the steps leading to the hospital.

Inside was nothing but chaotic confusion. Beds not only filled the wards but had spilled out into the corridors as well. A few patients still lay on the litters they had been carried in on. The stench of burned flesh and the pitiful cries of agony were almost overwhelming, but Christopher closed his heart to all of the sights and sounds around him. He had one purpose in mind and one purpose only, and that was to seek help for Dionne.

After questioning several people, he was finally directed to a huge ward where the most critical patients were being treated. Finally, winding his way past the beds, cots, and litters, Christopher reached the ward, thinking for a moment he had somehow missed Dr. Blackmon when he did not spot him right away. He was about to try and seek more information on the doctor's possible whereabouts when he saw the familiar figure emerge through a wide doorway.

Christopher felt his heart plummet when the doctor spoke to someone, then started back through the doorway. "Dr. Blackmon, *wait!*"

Andrew Blackmon stiffened at the sound of the voice. He slowly turned back around and waited until Christopher reached him.

For a moment, Christopher only stared at him, then with an accusing voice, he asked, "Haven't you received any of the messages my grandmother sent to you?"

"Yes, unfortunately I have."

"Then what are you still doing here?" Christopher asked, more out of frustration than from anger, even though his words had sounded sharp. "You have to come with me to Crescentview. You have to help Dionne have her baby. She's going to die if you don't."

Andrew's eyes were haunted as he made a sweeping gesture with his hand. "And what about these people? Do I leave them to die while I see to your wife?"

Christopher uttered coldly, "These people have my sympathy, Dr. Blackmon, but I have to think about my wife!"

The doctor sighed wearily and leaned against the wall for support. "Christopher, I helped bring you into this world and I would do anything I could for you and your family . . . except play God. I don't have the right to choose who is to live and who is to die. I can do my very best, and that is all. I would never be able to look myself in the mirror again if I left dying patients to go to your wife. I have six more patients to attend to here before I can even think about leaving."

Christopher wanted to grab the man by his shoulders and shake him until he got it through his thick head that Dionne was dying, that without his help she did not have a prayer of a chance. Instead, he muttered tersely, "By then I am afraid it will be too late!" Never had he felt so helpless.

"Listen to me, young man!" The doctor's face was livid, not with rage but from how inadequate he felt. "If I went to your wife, then it would be too late for at least three of my patients here, possibly four. That is not a fair trade, two lives for four!"

Christopher was not about to accept defeat, not with Dionne's life at stake. "What if I brought my wife here? Would you have time to look at her then?"

"Yes, but to move her now could be more dangerous

356

than waiting." He shrugged helplessly. "If only I knew what the complications were, I would know if there was any hope at all. But unless I examine . . ."

Christopher interrupted, "Berta told me what was wrong."

"She did?"

"Yes. She believes the baby is turned the wrong way."

The doctor's eyes narrowed thoughtfully. "Buttocks first?"

Christopher shook his head. "No, the way she explained it, the baby is headfirst, but the face is up instead of down."

The doctor stroked his whiskered chin. He spoke to himself as much as he directed the remarks to Christopher. "Uh oh, the baby is in a posterior position. The baby's head is probably lodged in the pelvis because it entered the pelvic inlet wrong. It's no wonder she's been suffering so long. While it is not impossible for her to give birth with the baby turned that way, it certainly makes it a lot more difficult. And with her in this stage of labor, I'm afraid a rough buggy ride would be too much for her." Frustrated, he slammed a fist against his other hand and shouted through gritted teeth, "But, damn it, if the mother has dilated all of the way and if the cervix has thinned out completely, a layman could . . ." A gleam suddenly appeared in his eyes, and he looked at Christopher sharply. "You can turn that baby! I know you can do it!"

It was nothing but instinct that forced Christopher to open his mouth to protest, but common sense made him quickly clamp it shut. There was no other recourse. He was Dionne's only hope.

Dr. Blackmon placed his arm on Christopher's shoulder. "Now listen closely and pay strict attention

357

to each detail, and the most important thing to do is to just remain calm. . . ."

The pain was constant now, coming in undulating waves, peaking the crests in intensity, then falling slowly into the troughs, but it was ever present, never quite ceasing. Dionne knew her hope was gone. She knew she could not fight it much longer, that she was becoming weaker with each onslaught. She could actually feel her life's strength draining from her. They knew it, too, Grand'mere and Berta. They knew she was dying. She had seen it in their eyes, and now the sounds of muffled sobs slowly drifted toward her. Or were they her own? It was so sad. She would never hold her baby in her arms, never see him smile, never see his triumphant expression when he took his first faltering step.

Oh, where was Christopher? He promised! She had to hold on until he returned. Neither Berta nor Grand'mere would have the courage to take the baby from her. She had to be strong just a little bit longer. But how could she ever find the strength?

"Grand'mere?" she muttered weakly.

"Yes, child?" Jeannine's voice caught in a sob.

"Please . . . hold my . . . hand."

"Dionne, be strong just a little longer. Christopher will soon be here with the doctor."

Dionne wet her lips with a swollen tongue. Yes, she would be strong. She had to be. Christopher was her child's only chance for life. Strength! There was a way to gain strength!

Dionne began mouthing the words, unintelligible at times, but they rang clear and loudly within her heart. Jeannine's eyes widened, then grew misty. She slowly began whispering the words along with Dionne.

"The Lord is my shepherd; I shall not want.
He maketh me to lie . . . in green pastures; he
leadeth me beside . . . still waters.
He restoreth my soul; he leadeth me . . . the
paths of righteousness for his name's sake.
Yea, though I walk through the valley of the
shadow of death . . ."

"I'll not hear that word uttered in this house again
today!" Christopher announced vehemently as he
came tearing quickly through the doorway. He placed
a small parcel wrapped in a clean white cloth on a table
and said, in a firm voice, "Berta, get me plenty of soap
and hot water. I have to wash my hands thoroughly."

Quickly kneeling by Dionne's bedside, Christopher
took her hand into his and pressed it against his lips. He
had to fight against the impulse to take her into his
arms and caress her, to tell her how much he needed
her, to tell her to please keep fighting, but there was no
time. She would have to draw her strength from him.
He spoke in a louder than normal voice in order to cut
through her fog of pain, "Dionne, listen to me. The
doctor cannot come, but he told me what to do. I have
to have your cooperation, though. Do you hear me?"

"Y—yes," she whispered weakly.

"When I tell you to do something, it's important you
follow my instructions. Do you understand?" The tone
of his voice was urgent.

"Y—yes."

"The soap and water be ready, Mister Chris," Berta
said, her huge eyes wide with fear.

While he was washing, he motioned for Berta to step
near. "The doctor gave me a small bundle. I want you
to remove the items and place them on a clean towel,
along with a washcloth, and have them ready." He
gave a long, shuddering sigh. "Just in case it is

359

necessary for me to use them. But don't uncork the liquid unless I tell you to."

Berta unfolded the cloth, looked at the items, and frowned. "What's these for?" It was a small vial of chloroform and a scalpel.

You have to promise my baby will live. If you see my death is inevitable, you have to promise to take my baby from me. I know there are ways to do it. I know it would be most difficult for you, but I know there are ways!

Only Christopher's eyes betrayed his fear as he answered, "Those are to . . . make sure Dionne's last request is granted . . . if I fail. Berta, turn Dionne around so that she is lying crossways across the bed. Grandmother, put some pillows beneath her head and please sit right up there beside her so that she can hold on to your hands. And Berta, get me a stool or a straight-backed chair, and I want you to stand right here with me. You know how her abdomen is supposed to feel more than I do, so if . . . no, damn it, not *if*, but *when* you feel the baby has been turned into the right position, let me know."

"Yes, sir! I sure will!"

Drying his hands, he stepped over beside the bed. His voice held more assurance than he felt. "Dionne, raise your knees and plant your feet firmly against the mattress, then allow your knees to drop apart."

"Oh, Christopher, I—I . . ."

"Don't argue with me," he said gently but firmly. "If we are going to get that baby born, you have to do exactly as I say." He waited a moment until she followed his instructions. "Now, let me know when you have a pain."

"It's almost . . . *aagghhh* . . . constant!"

"When you feel the need to push, let me know by

nodding your head. But don't push, that's very important."

Christopher placed his left hand on her abdomen. When he felt the womb's muscles contracting, he inserted his right hand as far as he could. With just his fingertips he felt the head high up. Christopher exerted a small amount of pressure on the head and surrounding tissue, while with his left hand he applied slight pressure on her abdomen. Then, when her abdomen relaxed from the contraction, he waited.

"Oh, be careful, Mister Chris, that ain't no chicken's neck you're wringing!"

"I'm very aware of that fact, Berta," he said calmly.

When Dionne's abdomen contracted again, he repeated the attempt to rotate the head. He repeated it time and time again. All the while he kept muttering tender words of encouragement.

Berta stood by eagerly, peering over his shoulder. "Is it gettin' there, Mister Chris? Is it gettin' there?"

"Damn it, Berta, shut up!"

Finally, Christopher triumphantly raised his eyes to meet Berta's. "I felt the head move!" Perspiration dripped from his brow, and even though he was sitting down, he could actually feel his knees tremble. But he knew he had been successful.

Huge tears of relief rolled down Berta's smiling face. "Does you want me to take it from here?"

He started to shake his head, but suddenly he felt Dionne's abdomen contract and felt the baby's head pivot perceptibly. "*Push,* sweetheart, *push!* Now relax and take a deep breath. It's almost over!" Christopher could hear the tears in his voice, but he did not care. "Now push again! Bear down and push!"

Then, suddenly, he was holding the infant in his hands. And for one brief moment, he could only stand

361

there and marvel at the miracle he beheld. He saw the strong, rapid heartbeat that showed through the translucent skin of the baby's chest. Its bowed legs kicked upwards and its arms flailed, its tiny fingers flowering out. It was a baby! A child! A real live human being!

"Clean its little mouth and nose, Mister Chris, so it can breathe," Berta urged softly.

Christopher deftly tilted the baby over, inserted a clean cloth in its mouth, and swiped. Then, tilting the baby even farther, he began patting its back. "Come on, little fellow, breathe!" he urged breathlessly. "Come on, don't get stubborn on me now!"

Then the baby started, flung his arms in the air, and let out a loud, lusty cry.

Christopher held the baby up proudly so that Dionne could see. Tears choked his voice as he said, "Look, Dionne! You have a son! A big, beautiful, healthy son!"

A wide smile swept across her face and tears of joy glistened in her eyes. "A son!" she murmured wondrously.

Berta stepped forward. "Do you wants me to take care of the navel cord?"

"Yes," he whispered raggedly. He was amazed that it took such a short length of time, marveling at the deftness with which Berta moved.

"Here, let's wrap him in this blanket so that he won't get cold," Jeannine said, smiling brightly. In the excitement she moved with ease, even forgetting the necessity of her cane.

Christopher moved to stand beside Dionne's head, holding the baby so that she could get a better view. He sensed she was too weak to hold him.

Berta ran for the door. "I'll be right back! Those folks downstairs be pacin' on eggshells!" She ran down

362

the hallway, shrieking, "It's a boy and they both be fine! Oh, thank the Lord! It's a boy and they both be fine!"

Dionne reached out a trembling hand and gently touched her child's face. "Oh, Christopher, he's beautiful. You gave me a son!" she murmured joyously.

Christopher shifted the baby in his arms and whispered, "Yes, he is beautiful, but he has to be . . . he looks exactly like his beautiful mother." He handed the baby to his grandmother so that she could clean him up. He also knew it was not over yet, that there were still things to be done. "Dionne, I am going to give you something now to make you sleep. You have to have some rest." He dabbed a small amount of the chloroform into the cloth, pressing it gently against her mouth and nose. "Now breathe deeply."

Berta came back in, still beaming. "You wants me to take over from here?"

Suddenly feeling his exhaustion, he sagged limply onto the chair by the bedside. He took Dionne's hand and pressed it against his lips. "Yes, Berta, I think you are going to have to. I doubt if my legs would have the strength to hold me."

Chapter Twenty-Four

Darkness: No pain, thank God, no pain! Soothing hands bathed her. She caught the scent of soft fragrance. A clean nightgown was slipped over her shoulders.

"Why is she shaking so?"

"It'd . . . chills. I think it . . . normal reaction, Mister Chris, 'cause she perspired . . . heavily 'fore she gave birth."

"I don't know. It worries me. I've seen men badly injured . . . like this. I wonder if there . . . a danger of pneumonia? I'm going to put . . . in my bed. There is a feather mattress on it and it is so much . . . than this cotton . . . she's sleeping on."

Strong arms held her, floating on fleecy white cloudes. And it was warm, so warm!

"Rest now, Missus Dionne, you have to sleep and grow strong for this . . . baby."

Light: Hands touched her again. A cool cloth was pressed against her brow.

"How is she doing, Doctor?"

"She has lost entirely too much blood. Be sure and keep . . . as warm as possible. Try giving her a . . . of this every six hours."

"What's it for, Doc Blackmon?"

"Mrs. Phillips needs to be kept under sedation so that her body can rest and gain strength, but I don't . . . her to fall into too deep of a drugged sleep. If she fails to respond to questions, only . . . her half the dosage the . . . time. Do you understand?"

"But that stuff scares me. What if I gives her too much?"

"Never mind, Berta. I'll sit with . . . and give her the medicine."

"Oh, thanks you, Mister Chris. That . . . will relieve my mind. I can . . . care o' everything else, though."

Darkness: Hands tenderly held hers. Lips pressed against her brow.

A silhouette of someone sitting in a rocking chair, holding a blanket, and a masculine voice crooning an old lullaby.

Light: "See your baby, Missus Dionne. Ain't he precious?"

"Come on, now, drink this juice. You have to have nourishment. Just one more . . . of broth, Dionne. Now, that's my girl. Go to sleep . . . and rest."

"She is doing much better, Christopher. Her color looks good. Decrease her medication to a half a spoonful this morning, and discontinue it completely by tonight. I'll return tomorrow. The baby is doing fine. A healthy boy."

Darkness: Pacing. Muted voices. Rocking chair creaking. Lips on her brow.

"The doctor says you going to be fine! I was so afraid. You'll never know . . . I felt when the baby was

*born. I've never felt . . . insignificant as I did when I
held . . . new life in my hands. It was . . . miracle."*

A morning light, dazzling and fresh, washed the
room. With her head elevated on white plump pillows,
Dionne awoke. She slowly opened her eyes, blinked,
then opened them again. Why, this was not her room, it
was Christopher's. What was she doing in here? Then
memories came flooding back. Memories of intense
pain, of fear, but there were also memories of her child
being held up for her to see. A tiny pink little baby with
a cap of long black hair. There were memories of
darkness, of light, and of a gray misty fog fitting in
neither world. There was a sound of a man's rich
mellow voice crooning a lullaby, and a hazy recollection of a man—Christopher?—sitting in the rocking
chair by the window cuddling a blanket in his arms—
the baby? . . . No, that was impossible. Christopher
hated her child. It must have only been a hallucination
brought about by all that terrible, agonizing pain.

Immediately, Dionne's hands moved to her stomach.
Finding it flat, she anxiously looked around the room
for the basket she had lovingly prepared for her baby.
Her eyes rested on Jeannine, who sat in the far corner
of the room, nodding peacefully.

"My baby? Where is my baby?" she murmured
weakly.

Jeannine awoke with a start, her face breaking into a
radiant smile. "Don't worry. Your son is fine and so are
you!" She helped herself to her feet with the aid of the
cane and walked toward the bedside. "You have been
asleep for three days now." She shrugged. "Well, not
actually asleep. The doctor has been keeping you under
heavy sedation so that your body would have time to
rest. You were so weak, and we were all so worried

about you."

"But . . . where is my baby? I want to see him!" Dionne pushed back the cover and tried to get out of bed, but found she did not have the strength to stand. Her head began to reel dizzily the moment her feet touched the floor.

"Now, you lie right back down, young lady! The doctor left strict orders for you to stay in bed for at least the next two weeks!" Jeannine spread the cover over Dionne. "I know you are anxious to see your son again. I guess you don't remember us bringing him in here three or four times a day so that you could see him."

She stammered in bewilderment, "I think I remember, but it seems like a dream. I'm not sure what was real and what was not." She sighed, confused. "I'm not sure. Everything is so hazy."

Jeannine patted her hand. "I imagine that is to be expected. Berta is taking care of the Little Precious in your room so that your rest would not be disturbed. That's what we all call him, Little Precious. Everyone but Christopher, that is." Jeannine laughed and mocked her grandson's deep voice, "That's not a proper name for a boy! Little Precious, humph! A boy should have a strong masculine name."

A light gleamed in Dionne's eyes as memories, much more vivid than before, came flooding back. "D—did Christopher deliver my baby, or did I just dream it?"

"He certainly did! And the finest doctor could not have done better. Even my friend, Andrew Blackmon, agreed with me, and if you had known Andrew as long as I have, you would know that he does not pass out compliments lightly. Oh, but listen to me. Here I am, a foolish old lady rattling on while you are dying to see that beautiful son of yours." She smiled sheepishly. "Besides, the doctor gave me strict instructions to talk to you for a while and make certain you were fully awake before we allowed you to hold the baby."

"Oh, I am awake," Dionne reassured her, wide-eyed.

"Then I'll tell Berta to bring him in." She knocked on the door, then opened it. "Berta, we have an anxious little mother in here who is most eager to see her son!"

Dionne could hear Berta's voice. "You tell Missus Dionne I'm giving the little precious a bath and I'll bring him to her just as soon as I finish."

"Did you hear?" Jeannine asked.

"Very clearly."

"Is there anything you want? Are you hungry? Thirsty? I'm sure you must have a hundred questions."

Dionne grinned. "Yes, to all of that! I would love to have a cup of hot coffee and something to eat! I am about to starve! But I don't think I could tolerate anything too heavy. I think I would like to have a slice of toasted bread with cheese melted on it."

Jeannine shook her head. "Toasted bread with cheese and a cup of coffee does not sound nourishing to me. Dr. Blackmon said you should eat plenty of good food to rebuild your strength, for you lost an awful lot of blood. But, since you've just awakened, I realize your stomach may not tolerate a heavy meal. So, I suppose I should indulge you, but you will have to promise to eat liver for supper."

"Liver? Ugh!"

"You can make all of the faces you want, young lady, but I had one of our beef cattle butchered yesterday especially for you. Just so you could have fresh liver and good red meat. Besides, that is what the doctor ordered." She shook her head wondrously. "I don't know whether it's just Andrew or if it is the entire medical community, but I do declare, it is amazing the giant strides in progress medicine is making nowadays. They are discovering food has a lot to do with one's health and the recovery of one who has been ill . . . and you have been extremely ill!" Jeannine went to the door, rang a bell that sat outside on a table, and waited for the cook's helper to come. After giving the girl the instructions, she came back in and sat down. She chuckled heartily. "Now that we have discussed the menu, while we are waiting for Berta to bring that son of yours in here, perhaps I can answer some of your questions."

Dionne shook her head, confused. "My memory is so hazy about the entire birth. I am not sure what really happened and what was merely a dream. Will you please just tell me what happened?"

"I certainly shall! All of the doctors in the city were called to the hospital to treat the people who were burned and injured in that terrible fire, and you developed complications that Berta did not know how to deal with. Fortunately, Christopher returned home and he managed to find Dr. Blackmon and received instructions on what to do for you." Jeannine gently touched Dionne's cheek. "I have to say, I was terribly frightened. I thought we were going to lose you there for a while. If Christopher had not . . ."

Dionne swallowed hard. She was almost afraid to ask. "W—where is Christopher?" *Please don't tell me that he has already set sail again,* she thought to herself.

Jeannine's face brightened. "He went down to the *Blue Diamond* to tell the crew about the baby! They were all anxious to know. In fact, his first mate even sent a query seeking information. He should be back before too long."

The door leading to Dionne's bedroom opened and Berta stuck her head through the opening. A grin spread from one side of her face to the other. "Looky here, Missus Dionne," she said, bustling into the room. "Look what I have for you! Now that you are awake good, maybe you can enjoys him now." She placed the baby in her arms.

Dionne's heart swelled beneath her breast. Her eyes shone with happiness and a beautiful smile swept across her face as she gazed down at her son.

"Go ahead, unwrap the blanket," Berta urged. "After I gave him his bath, I rubbed him down real good with lotion but didn't put no clothes on him. Figured you'd just undress him anyway so you could count all o' his fingers and toes."

Dionne gingerly began removing the blanket, revealing tiny little arms and legs. Tears glistened in her eyes as she marveled at his beauty. "Why . . . look! He's sucking on his fingers! And his feet! Look at his tiny little toes! And his hair! Why, it is so long I can curl it around my finger."

"Don't tell me you are going to be like Grandmother and Berta!" Christopher said teasingly. "And please don't tell me you intend to call him Little Precious, too!"

Dionne could have sworn her heart stopped beating momentarily. She slowly turned her gaze toward the door where Christopher stood, leaning against it with his arms folded together. "Why, I didn't know you were here," she said, surprised.

He chortled easily. "It's no wonder. I came in about the same time Berta brought the baby in." He walked over and peered down at the baby, trying not to show his pride as he casually remarked, "That is a mighty handsome young man you have there."

"Oh, yes, isn't he though?" Her eyes widened with astonishment as they met Christopher's. She was enthralled by what she saw, for surprisingly, they held no hatred whatsoever. She struggled to hide her confusion. She could hardly lift her voice above a whisper, "Isn't he the prettiest baby you've ever seen?"

Christopher's manner was obviously teasing as he pretended to cringe. "Oh, no, madame, not you too! With Grandmother and Berta calling him Little Precious, and with you curling his hair and calling him pretty, I shudder to think what the future will hold for him! Why, boys should be called handsome and it is girls who are pretty! I can see right now this young man will have to have a man's influence. . . ." Realizing the path his statement was taking, Christopher broke off. But he knew it had not passed by Dionne, for her eyes narrowed slightly. Clearing his throat, he shifted on his feet uneasily and said, "The crew of the *Blue Diamond* send their heartiest congratulations."

"Tell them I said thank you," Dionne replied as a faint blush stole across her cheeks. Then her eyes widened and she raised her gaze to Berta. "Oh! Is something wrong?" She placed her arm across her breasts. "I'm getting wet up here!"

Berta laughed. "A body can tell she ain't been 'round babies much. That's just your milk coming down, Missus Dionne. And it's 'bout time, too. I thinks that young fellow wants his mama's milk. . . ." She glanced guiltily at Christopher. "That is, unless . . ."

Christopher spoke up quickly. "We didn't know what you intended to do. Whether you would prefer having a wet nurse or . . ."

"I most certainly do not!" Dionne declared adamantly. "I will nurse my son myself!"

Again, Christopher shifted his weight uneasily. "Well, we didn't know how you would feel about it, and quite frankly, there was not much of a choice. . . ."

Jeannine interrupted, "What Chris is trying to say is we simply had to go ahead and get a wet nurse for the baby. While it is true we could have placed the baby at your breast and let him nurse, the doctor advised against it because he was keeping you under such heavy sedation. He was afraid your milk might carry too much of the drug and it could have harmed the child."

Dionne looked up at Christopher and something unexplainable happened to her when their eyes met again. There was something different in his eyes, a different light, a different emotion, something that had not been there before. She felt her heart increase its tempo as it began to hammer loudly against her chest.

Lowering her gaze, she murmured, "Well, I appreciate your . . . thoughtfulness, but you can . . . send her back to her home. I won't be needing her."

Jeannine spoke up hesitantly, "Child, you should not make any hasty decisions. It's very possible you may not have enough milk to satisfy the little precious. Besides"—she made a sweeping motion with her hand—"this is Josey's home now."

Dionne's face became ashen. Oh, dear God, no! She abhorred slavery, and the thought of a real live person being bought and sold on her child's behalf was terrible. She would have to let them know how she felt. Then, glancing at Berta, she decided to wait until later.

The baby wrinkled his face and let out a lusty wail. He then turned his head, opened his mouth, and began searching for something to eat.

"Why, look at him! He must be starving!" Dionne wondered just how well the wet nurse had been feeding him.

Jeannine shrugged and said to Christopher, "Dr. Blackmon discontinued the drug yesterday morning. He said it would be all right for her to nurse him this morning, if she chose to."

"You may all rest assured, I do want to!"

Berta laughed, and holding the sheet up over her, she said, "Then all you gotta do is take your breast out like that." She lowered the bodice of Dionne's gown. "And plop it in his mouth like this, then put a little bit o' cover

373

over his head for modesty's sake."

Dionne's eyes widened when the baby latched on and began to suck hungrily. "Oh!" she said softly. "I had no idea it was so simple."

The sun shone through the window, enhancing the beautiful glow of Dionne's cheeks and the radiant shine of her hair. Christopher's breath caught in his throat. She reminded him of the paintings he had seen of the Madonna and Child. His eyes softened. He felt awestruck, mesmerized at how naturally beautiful this sight was. Finally, he tore his eyes away from the loveliness and realized Berta, and his grandmother as well, had also felt the magic of the moment.

Finally, Berta raised the corner of her big white apron, dabbed at her eyes, and sniffed. "Now, if that ain't the most prettiest sight I've ever seen. Missus Dionne holding the little precious . . . feeding him!"

The spell now broken, Christopher cleared his throat. "Madame I ask you to consider this child's future and give him a proper name before that—that . . . moniker takes root!"

"Moniker?" Dionne questioned laughingly.

"Yes . . . nickname."

Berta chortled. "If you be so worried, Mister Chris, why don't you name him? After all, he is your son too!"

Dionne could feel her face redden. She slowly brought her gaze up to Christopher, wondering what his reaction would be.

He had a tight smile on his face as he responded, "I believe that is an honor his mother should have."

Not wanting Berta to say anything further, Dionne quickly said, "I chose a name for him long before he was born. His name is Jonathan Lyle."

"That is a beautiful name, Dionne," Jeannine remarked with a smile. Are those family names?"

"No," she answered slowly. "I chose the name

374

Jonathan, because I have always been a great admirer of Jonathan Swift, the man who wrote *Gulliver's Travels*. Judging from his writings, he was a man who loved to travel and seek adventures." *As does his father,* she silently mused. "And Lyle is French, meaning, "on the island." I thought that would be very suitable because . . ."

". . . that was where the child was conceived!" Christopher completed her statement. "A very good choice, madame!" He tried not to show how deeply that hurt him. "Well, I have better things to do than to stand around here all day. . . ."

"Christopher!" Dionne called sharply, tears stinging her eyes. "It so happens that Lyle is the middle name of someone I cared for deeply."

His face darkened with anger. "Madame, I don't care whom you named the child for. As far as I am concerned, you could have named him Louis as well!" The insolence in his voice was ill concealed. He glared at her with a sardonic expression before he turned and started for the door.

She gasped angrily. "Just go on about your business then! And—and take your wet nurse with you! I think you need her more than Jonathan does!"

He whirled to stare at her, quick fury rising in his eyes. He opened his mouth, but for a moment, no words would come. Finally, he replied with such intense contempt that forbade any further comment, "Madame, I don't care what you think or what you feel. And, as far as I am concerned, you can go straight to hell!"

Chapter Twenty-Five

"And how are you enjoying your first day out of bed?" Jeannine asked as she joined Dionne just outside the bedroom doors, on the upper veranda that ran the entire length of the house.

Dionne, sitting on a rocking chair with a blanket tucked around her legs, smiled. "I love it!" She deeply breathed the fresh air. "Although I will have to admit I have been wrong this past week."

"How is that, my dear?"

"I'm sure you recall how I have grumbled and complained about lying in that bed." She shook her head and chuckled. "Well, I discovered I am not as strong as I thought I was. Why, I could scarcely walk five feet without my knees trembling. There, for a moment, I actually thought I was going to fall on my face!"

"I know exactly how you feel! And, unfortunately, it seems to be a vicious cycle. A body should remain in bed because one is in a weakened condition, but it seems the longer a body stays in bed, the weaker one becomes!"

"I thoroughly agree," Dionne said as she reached over and patted Jeannine's hand. She glanced about the yard. "My, this is a beautiful day."

"Yes, it is." Jeannine settled back into the chair and

gave a pleasant sigh. "I always look forward to spring. And you will notice, as years pass by, the changing seasons seem to come faster every year. Oh, look, Dionne! Look at that robin. It is gathering twigs to build its nest!"

Dionne smiled and watched the bird as it hopped across the yard, gathering bits of grass. Then it would fly to one of the tall oaks, return, and begin the cycle all over again.

The scent of spring was in the air. Flowers were blooming in their beds, the huge oaks had already leafed out and now provided shade, the magnolia trees had bloomed, and the grass was green. Yes, it was definitely a new season, a new beginning. With everything coming back to life, it was a shame the situation was not better between her and Christopher. But, unfortunately, it had become worse during the past two weeks instead of better. She had seen him only two times since the day they had had that terrible scene. Once was when Rosalyn had come to call on her and to bring Jonathan a present, and the other time was when several of his grandmother's friends had come to visit. Other than those times, he had ignored her and Jonathan completely.

She'd had such high hopes that the tension between them would improve when the baby was born. And, now, it looked as though Christopher refused to give it a chance. Apparently all of those times he had made love to her had been nothing but lust, only a way to slake his passionate desires. She blinked back the tears that suddenly threatened. But she had known he did not love her, even when she had gone so willingly into his arms. Perhaps that was partly the problem. Perhaps her allowing him to make love to her had only intensified his belief that she was a loose woman. Perhaps to him, it had proved Celeste's accusations

378

were true. If only she had been able to deny one of the falsehoods, his heart might have softened toward her, but how could one call a dead woman a liar?

Jeannine's soft voice pulled Dionne from her reverie. "I have noticed you do not seem to be pleased with Josey. Is there any particular reason other than you wanting to nurse the child yourself?"

Dionne took a deep breath, dreading to speak her mind but realizing she might never have another opportunity. "Yes, there are two reasons." Her eyes narrowed thoughtfully as she asked, "Does Josey appear sullen to you?"

"No, not that I've noticed. Why do you ask?"

"I'm not sure. . . . It may just be my personal feelings or she may think I don't like her very much, but I have seen expressions on her face that disturb me."

Jeannine frowned, suddenly concerned. "What do you mean, her expressions disturb you?" She gripped the arms of the chair. "Are you saying you are afraid she might mistreat Jonathan?"

"Oh, no, nothing like that!" Dionne quickly reassured her. "I've watched her with him, and it is fairly obvious that she adores him. But I feel there is a sullenness about her or perhaps a resentment . . . I'm not sure." Dionne bit her bottom lips apprehensively. "I have been wondering about something. Since she was able to feed Jonathan, her own child must not be too old. But what happened to her child?" Her lips settled into a grim line. "I think it was terribly cruel of Christopher to separate them."

Jeannine was quick to say, "If this is the reason why you are not speaking to him, then you are being unfair."

Dionne heard bitterness spill over into her voice. "I haven't had a chance to *not* speak to Christopher. I've only seen him twice since that day in my room. And why did you say I am being unfair?"

The older woman never batted an eye as she stated firmly, "Because I know my grandson, and I know Chris would never willingly separate a mother and her child. But to appease you, I will ask him if he has knowledge of the child's whereabouts. Now, I believe you mentioned two reasons. You have only stated one. What is the other?"

She took a deep breath and adjusted her smile. "Grand'mere, you have to realize slavery had been abolished on Martinique . . . and it's just . . . I hate the idea of human beings placed in bondage. I hate the idea that another human being was sold and bought supposedly for the benefit of me and my child." She shuddered inwardly at the thought. "I know New Orleans and the entire South thrives on slavery . . . and you even have slaves here at Crescentview. . . ."

Jeannine slammed the tip of her cane against the floor. "Oh, but that is where you are mistaken, young lady! There are no slaves here at Crescentview . . . except for Josey, but before long she will be freed, just the same as all our servants."

"I . . . don't understand."

Jeannine's voice was calm, her gaze steady as she explained, "Regardless of what you think, all the people here in New Orleans and in the South do not believe in slavery. The Phillips family has not owned a slave in a good many years. And even though we do hold the papers on Josey, each day that she works, she is earning her freedom."

"But why should people have to earn their freedom? It just doesn't seem right to me."

"I agree, they shouldn't. And I refuse to get into a discussion with you about moral rights and wrongs and the issue of slavery. I will explain how we attend to that unpleasant side of business, and you are free to make your own decision as to whether it is right or wrong. You see, every servant in this household was purchased with Phillips money as a slave. But the moment a slave enters Crescentview, he or she then becomes a servant—a member of our household staff—and they begin earning a salary. I have determined what I believe to be a fair price for wages earned and enter it in a ledger against that person's name. Then, when that person has earned enough to pay back his original purchase price, he is given his papers, free and clear. If he has performed his duties suitably, he is then asked to stay on, and thus far, only one person has proved to be unsuitable."

"A—and Josey will be freed too?"

"Indeed she will. You see, Dionne, it is not as simple as setting a slave free. Most of these people have been born and raised on plantations. They have been told when to rise in the morning, when to go to bed at night, and what to do every hour in between. The Negroes are an intelligent race of people, but how can they know something if they've never been taught it? Even the most intelligent person will appear slow-witted if they do not know how to do something. And how does one know if he has never been taught? Here, at Crescentview, our staff is taught how to handle money and how to live in the outside world if they so choose. One of my dearest friends has argued repeatedly that we are, in fact, selling our servants back to themselves, and selling slaves is still selling slaves, regardless of how one tries to ease his conscience. Perhaps so. I do know if we lived in a different part of the country, I would hire servants and pay them a wage. So, in the long run, I see no difference."

Dionne bowed her head. "Grand'mere, I am ashamed of myself."

"Why, child?"

"Because I had no idea that was how you staffed your household. Considering all the circumstances surrounding slavery, I think you have worked out a most agreeable . . ."

Jeannine stared, wagging her finger. "Now, child, I told you at the beginning I would not enter into a discussion about this matter, and as far as I am concerned, the subject is closed . . . except that I will ask Chris if he checked into the situation concerning Josey's child. But knowing him as well as I do, I strongly doubt if he would have willingly separated a mother and child. Now, the subject is closed!"

Dionne laughed. "All right, I will not make any further comment about it to you . . . except," she added in a rush, "to say that you have put my mind at ease about Josey." She dusted her hands together. "Now, I am finished!"

Jeannine chuckled good-naturedly. "Child, you are a treasure. . . ." Her smile quickly disappeared. "If only that stubborn grandson of mine could see you through my eyes."

Dionne was caught off guard by Jeannine's sudden statement. She was sick of the battle that raged within her; the ever-prevalent desire to tell Christopher the complete story of what had happened on Martinique and the fear that he would not believe her. And now to hear his grandmother make a statement like that was a little too much for her to digest. "I only wish he would look at me and see the truth," she murmured softly.

The line of Jeannine's mouth tightened a bit. "Are you sure that is what you want?"

Confused by her question, Dionne blinked. "Of course I am. Why do you ask?"

"Perhaps he could see the truth better if he knew the truth was there to look for."

"What do you mean?" To her annoyance, she found

herself starting to feel apprehension and was even more annoyed to realize it showed in her expression.

"Now, young lady, it was not my intention to upset you. I have very good reasons for saying what I did." She paused, as if searching for the right words. "Although it appears that Chris has tried to keep his feelings about you a secret, it would take a blind man to know there is an animosity there. But—I pray to God I am not wrong—I also believe he has warm feelings about you, too. And it is obvious that you adore the man, so I firmly believe you have a good reason for not being entirely truthful with him. However, I dearly wish you would take me into your confidence. Perhaps I could even help."

Feeling terribly uneasy over the direction this conversation was taking, Dionne forced a grin. "Why, Grand'mere, I have no idea what you are talking about."

"I see right now you are not going to volunteer any information, so I am going to stick my nose into your business and ask you a point-black question." Jeannine dabbed at her brow with a handkerchief. "But, first, I want your word that you will tell me the truth no matter how painful it is."

"You make it sound so mysterious." Dionne nervously bit her bottom lip and looked away.

"Yes, I suppose *mysterious* would be an excellent way of describing my feelings, too." Jeannine's thin fingers grasped the arm of the chair. "Now, I want your word."

Dionne became increasingly apprehensive under her watchful perusal. She folded her hands together and stared down at them. "Grand'mere, why don't you first ask me what you want to know? If I feel comfortable by answering, I will; if not, then . . ."

"All right, a point-blank question, and mind you, it

is personal." She set her chin in a stubborn line and took a deep breath. "Is there any possibility that Christopher is Jonathan's father?"

Dionne yanked her head sharply about and stared with astonishment at Jeannine, then she slowly lowered her eyes. "I—I . . . don't want to . . . discuss that."

"Never mind, dear, you do not have to. Your expression fairly well said it all." She shook her head, confused. "But for the life of me, I don't know why you have kept this from my grandson. It seems to me you would want him to know the truth, that it would end so much of the animosity between the two of you. Of course, I realize it would not be that simple, especially since there is another man involved."

The pain in Dionne's heart spread like a blazing flame. Her eyes filled with tears of frustration as she pounded on the arms of the chair. "But there is no other man! There never has been any other man in my life except Christopher!"

Relief slowly swept across Jeannine's face. "You have no idea how happy that makes me feel." She began to chuckle. "Oh, I am definitely more confused than ever, but o—o—oh so relieved. Ever since Jonathan was born, questions have been gnawing at me. I felt certain Jonathan was Christopher's child, yet I knew you were not the sort of woman who would have an affair with two men at one time!" She gestured helplessly with her hands. "And if that does not sound quite right, then I am sorry. I simply don't know how to phrase it any other way." She spoke with as reasonable a voice as she could manage, "Do you want to talk about it now?"

"Oh, yes! Yes, I do!" Dionne's explanation came like a dam bursting, her words flowing like a raging torrent. She told Jeannine everything that had happened, beginning with the day she had first met Christopher in the marketplace at Fort-de-France, about Celeste, and all the reasons behind her reluctance to tell Christopher the truth.

Jeannine listened intently; her expression neither condemned nor did it accuse. When Dionne finished, she thought for a moment, then asked, "What do you intend to do now? I'm sure you realize Christopher should be told the truth. He has the right to know about Jonathan."

She nodded miserably. "I know he has that right. And . . . it makes me feel so guilty for keeping the truth from him. But my guilt is not as strong as my fear that he would not believe me."

"But I believe you," she said softly.

"Yes, you do, but you are not Christopher. You, of all people, should know how stubborn and obstinate he is." Her voice was shakier than she would have liked. "No one will ever know how many hours I have lain awake trying to figure out a way to tell him. I have thought about telling him some of the . . . intimate . . . details of that night, but he'd had so much to drink I am afraid he might not remember. And there is always the possibility that he would think Celeste had merely confided some of those details to me." Dionne took a deep, shuddering breath. "Right now, at this point in time, I believe that would make my relationship with him even worse. I honestly believe if I am forced to tell Christopher the truth without him loving me, I am afraid he never will," her voice faded to a mere whisper.

Jeannine struggled to keep an accusing note from her voice. "I doubt if you give Chris enough credit. I think he cares for you more than he will admit."

"At times, I do too. That's what makes everything so confusing." Biting her lip, Dionne looked away. "But he has to admit it to himself before he can ever admit it to me or to anyone else." Then, she brought her gaze back to Jeannine and stared at her intently, "Grand'-mere, please, I have to have your word that you will give me time to work this out my own way, that you will not tell Christopher what we discussed today."

Jeannine expelled a heavy breath of air. "Against my better judgment, I will agree . . . on one condition."

"One condition?"

"Yes, if you promise not to walk out of Christopher's life without him knowing the truth . . . without giving him time to accept the truth."

Dionne did not hesitate. "That is a fair request. I give you my word."

Jeannine started to rise. "Now that that is set-tled. . . ."

"No, wait a minute." Dionne looked at Jeannine with narrowed eyes. "How did you know? What made you suspect Jonathan belonged to Christopher?"

She chuckled. "There were several reasons. When you were first brought here, in your delirium you called Christopher's name repeatedly. Then, as I got to know you as the months passed, I knew you were a decent young woman, that you would never give your body to just any man, that you would have to have deep, deep feelings for a man before you could be intimate with him. Then, when Jonathan was born, I suppose that clinched it. You know that peculiar-shaped birthmark on Jonathan's little hip?" She chuckled smugly. "Well, Christopher's father had that same birthmark, as did Edward's grandfather and his grandfather and so on. It seems that particular birthmark surfaces in the Phillips family every other generation."

"And Christopher knows nothing about this family trait?"

"Oh, I am sure he has heard it mentioned over the years. But with him believing the baby belongs to

386

another man, I imagine he never gave it a second thought. And under the circumstances, I certainly never refreshed his memory. So," she added with a significant lifting of her brows, "if you want to reconsider your decision, there is physical proof to substantiate your claim."

Her mouth curved into an unconscious smile. "I can't tell you how relieved that makes me feel." Then, her face clouded. "But I think I would still rather wait and give Christopher a chance to fall in love with me."

Jeannine nodded uneasily and gave a disapproving sigh. "Very well, it is your decision. I will hold my tongue . . . and pray to God we don't live to regret this pact."

"So do I, Grand'mere," Dionne murmured softly as huge tears suddenly glistened in her eyes.

Chapter Twenty-Six

Celeste tapped her foot and sashayed in time to the lively music that blared from the San Francisco Saloon and Gambling Casino located across the street and three stories below her hotel room. Dancing over to the bureau and peering into the chipped, smoky mirror hanging above it, she pursed her lips and, deciding they were not red enough, dabbed her forefinger into the rouge pot and applied a generous amount of color to them. She then picked up her hairbrush and ran it through the long tresses that had already been brushed time and time again.

Then, angrily slamming the brush against the scarred bureau top, she complained aloud, "Damnation! What on earth could be keeping that man?"

Impatiently, she hurried to the door, opened it, and glanced up and down the corridor. Seeing no sign of Louis, she closed the door and ran to the window, hoping to catch sight of him as he crossed the street. He had promised to come for her hours ago, but as usual he was late again.

Folding her arms together, she sat by the window and pouted. Why did he have to be so stubborn? Why did she have to stay in this shabby hotel room all the time? What harm would it do if she went over to the San Francisco and waited until he finished with that poker game? But no! Louis had said he didn't like the way men looked at her. He said men still outnumbered women twenty to one here in San Francisco, and he would not be able to protect her and to pay attention to his cards, too. For all of the freedom she had now, she might as well be back in Martinique under her father's thumb.

Then, Celeste's thoughts grew somber. Her father was no longer there. He was no longer anywhere unless one could consider the bottom of the ocean a specific place. The poor dear never had a chance in that terrible storm. None of them did. It was a miracle she had managed to survive. If she had not made a mad dash for safety at precisely the right moment, she would have gone down with the ship with the rest of them. Celeste closed her eyes and the memory of that horror-filled night came flooding back.

Fortunately, so many of the memories remained shrouded in darkness and they would never surface in her conscious mind. But everything she could remember unfolded in her mind's eye as though it were happening all over again.

The moment Celeste reached topside, she knew she only had a few minutes, at most, of life remaining, for the ship was being torn apart by the raging tempest. Lightning crackled through the sky almost continuously, casting a strange, eerie glow on the dark swirling clouds and the raging, black-foamed sea.

Realizing she would soon be swept overboard, Celeste saw the anchor bollard, flung both arms around it, and held on for dear life. She began choking and retching from the salt water that the wind had forced through her nose and mouth and down her throat. Then, seemingly from out of nowhere, a voice called to her.

"Here, ma'am, come over here with me!" the sailor shouted over the scream of the wind and the roaring of the giant waves. "The ship is lost, we're sinking! We will have to get clear of the ship or when she goes under, the suction will pull us under too!"

"You want me to jump in the water?" She watched in horror as he nodded. "But I can't! I will drown!" Celeste could feel her hair being whipped all over her head, and her undergarments had been soaked by the wind-driven sea spray the moment she had reached the deck.

The sailor cupped one hand over his mouth so that she could hear him better, "And that's what will happen if you stay on board too! I've tied these two water casks together; they'll ride high on the waves. They won't sink! Just grab a-hold and make sure you have your hands threaded underneath the ropes and hold on with all your might. There should be a lull any second now. When it comes, help me pull the casks over to the starboard, and when the ship lists again, we'll jump on the count of three. We ain't got no other choice, lady! We either do it or we'll die. If you want to take your chances with me, fine! If not, you're on your own! I don't have time to argue with you!"

Celeste realized she had no choice and this was no time to panic. The sailor was right. The ship was sinking quickly and going with him was the only chance she had to survive. She took a deep breath and ran toward him.

Then, everything seemed to happen so quickly. One minute they were on the ship, and the next they were being tossed about in the water. To her surprise, they did not spiral down to the bottom. The casks did indeed hold them above the surface, but the waves pounded at them relentlessly. With horror, she watched as Nigel and her father plunged into the ocean less than ten feet away, but instead of bobbing to the surface as she and the sailor had done, they plunged straight down and she never saw them surface again.

Then a huge wave pushed them and the casks high on a towering peak of water and flung them a great distance from the ship. One minute she saw the ship, and the next time she was able to open her eyes it was gone, swallowed by the angry sea. She could feel her hands loosening on the ropes and she opened her mouth to scream for help, but the water forced her to clamp her lips tightly shut. Miraculously, the casks fell into a trough just as she felt her hold slipping. Now that they were momentarily in calmer water, she screamed for the sailor to help her.

The sailor released his hold on the ropes and swam after her. He grasped her by the hair of her head and began swimming back to the casks. He had just gotten her secured to the ropes when a mammoth wave broke over them, washing him away from the casks and safety.

Seeing him being pulled away by the waves and swirling currents, Celeste began paddling her feet, trying to maneuver the casks toward him so that he could grab hold, but it was to no avail. One moment he was swimming desperately toward her and the casks, and the next moment a huge wall of water swept him away and he disappeared from sight completely.

She would never know how long the storm tossed her and the casks about. It seemed to her it lasted through eternity and then some. After the one disastrous time she had lost her hold on the ropes, she was determined not to let go again. She frantically hung on, knowing her life depended on it.

Then, gradually, the wind lost part of its ferocity, and although the sea still remained angry and rough,

Celeste realized the storm had finally passed. It was then that the nightmares began as she floated, half drowned, on the water. It could have only been the wind skimming across the top of the water, but until the day she died, she would always believe the sounds she heard were the ghostly cries of everyone who had been on board the ship. Once, she even saw a ghostly specter hovering over her. At first she thought it was her father coming to help, but the face suddenly changed and became Dionne's, then Nigel's, then Nettie's, until she thought she was being driven to the brink of madness.

It was sometime the next day that she saw the lifeboat floating, right side up, toward her. At first she thought she was merely having another hallucination and tried to ignore it, fearing that the faces of all who had died would suddenly rise up from over the side and haunt her again. Then, it finally dawned on her that if the lifeboat was indeed real, it could mean her salvation.

She started paddling her feet and slowly maneuvered the casks closer to the lifeboat. But to her horror, when she finally reached the boat, she did not have enough feeling in her hands and arms to reach for the rope that was connected to the wooden hasp on the bow. Then, as the boat began to float away, she made a desperate lunge for the rope and caught it, but it was at least an hour later before she could muster the strength to drag her weary body on board. Knowing the water in the casks could mean the difference between her surviving or not, she managed to thread the bow rope through the ropes around the casks before slumping to the floor of the boat into a deep, exhausted sleep.

Upon awakening, Celeste blinked and shielded her eyes from the burning sun beating down on her and the small craft. She felt the grip of panic as she heard voices calling to her. Believing the voices belonged to those terrible hallucinations she'd had the night before, her eyes widened and she could feel her terror mounting.

"Oh, no! Please, God, not again! Please don't make me listen to them again!"

"Ahoy, boat! Ahoy, boat!" the voices shouted.

Celeste pressed her hands to her head and sobbed. "Stay away from me! Stay away from me! It isn't my fault I lived and you died!"

She squinted her eyes tightly shut and hugged the bottom of the boat. Then, when she heard grappling hooks grab the side of the boat and felt it lurch sideways, she knew the ghosts had come to claim her, too.

Then one of the voices said, astonished, "Look, mates! It be a lady in here! And she's alive!"

Celeste slowly raised her head and stared at the man gaping at her in return. He had a big hooked nose, three missing front teeth, and a dirty bandana tied around his head, but to Celeste he was the most beautiful, welcome sight she had ever seen. "W—where did . . . you come from?" she stammered.

The man pointed to a ship a short distance away. "We're from the *Lady Lea*."

He and another man assisted her into their boat while two other men hauled the water casks on board. After giving her a drink of water, they hacked holes in the bottom of the lifeboat so that it would sink and not be a hazard to other ships, then they began rowing back toward their ship.

The man talked as he rowed, "We spotted yer boat a bit ago. The storm ripped one o' our masts off so's we ain't maneuverin' too good. That's why we had to launch this here lifeboat. Could see somethin' inside, but couldn't tell if ye were dead or alive." The man paused and looked at her guardedly. "What ship were

394

ye on, ma'am?"

Celeste swallowed hard. "I—I was . . . on the *Emerald Tempest*. H—have you . . . found . . . anybody else? Any more survivors?"

The man slowly shook his head. "No, ma'am. Ye be the first, and it grieves me heart to say we've seen nothing but an occasional cask or timber, or other debris bobbing here and there in the water . . . no sign of other life. O' course, that don't mean there ain't none," he rushed to say, afraid of having a hysterical female on his hands. "Ye jest lay back and rest. We'll have you on board the *Lady Lea* 'fore ye know what's happened."

Upon reaching the ship, a harness was lowered over the side for Celeste. After she had been taken on board, ropes were lowered and the men secured the ship's boat, then it was hoisted by the davit.

The captain ordered a blanket for the woman, and after speaking privately to the sailor she had talked to in the lifeboat, he ordered the *Lady Lea* under way. He then escorted Celeste down to his quarters.

"Captain, I heard you tell your men to get under way. . . . Are you not going to search for other survivors?"

"No, ma'am," he said grimly.

"But . . ."

He stilled her protests with an upraised hand. "Rest assured, if we find anyone else, we will stop and take them on. I have even posted extra lookouts expressly for that purpose. I don't want to alarm you, but I don't want you to be thinking the captain and crew of the *Lady Lea* are heartless either. The *Lady Lea* sustained severe damages during the storm. While I am confident we will safely reach port without any further difficulties, it is impossible for us to take the time to do an active search."

"You mean . . . there is a danger this ship might sink?" Her face blanched at the thought.

"No, ma'am. We are limping, but we are still seaworthy. However, we will have to use haste to reach land." He shook his head sadly. "My mate told me which ship you were on. While I did not know them personally, the *Emerald Tempest* was a sturdy ship with a capable captain and crew. If you lost friends and family, you have my sympathy. Now, if you will excuse me, I have duties to perform. You are free to use my quarters until a cabin can be prepared for you."

After the captain left, Celeste sank onto a chair and cried. She knew it was useless to protest their abandoning the search. How could she ask men to risk their lives for people who were already dead? She had seen how quickly the *Emerald Tempest* had sunk, and anyone trapped below would remain there until the end of time. Her father and Nigel had disappeared from sight immediately, and it seemed beyond all realms of possibility that the sailor who had helped save her life had managed to survive in the merciless sea. What happened to the rest of the crew, no one would ever know. It was a miracle she had survived the terrible ordeal.

During the long days spent on the *Lady Lea*, Celeste had ample opportunity to think about her future. She grieved for her father but knew he would have wanted her to continue on with her life. Now that he was dead, she saw no reason to journey on to New Orleans and marry Christopher Phillips. She was the sole heir to Desirade and the fortune her father had amassed during his lifetime, and with her inheritance, she would be able to go to Louis and live her life with the man of her choice.

396

After the *Lady Lea* reached port five days later, Celeste had to wait three weeks before she was able to secure passage on to Martinique.

Upon her arrival, she went immediately to Louis, and after a joyful reunion, she learned he already knew about the loss of the *Emerald Tempest* and that all hands and passengers had been lost except for her. He told her that a paper had arrived in Fort-de-France from the Phillips Shipping Lines, stating that the *Emerald Tempest* had been lost at sea and that Celeste Debierne had been the only survivor. He had been surprised to see her, for the paper stated that she had been taken to New Orleans. Louis told her that, upon learning she had survived and of her whereabouts, he had immediately booked passage for New Orleans so that he could bring her home with him where she rightfully belonged.

At Louis's urgings, they went to her father's attorney and, after a lengthy discussion, decided that since Celeste and the Debiernes' housekeeper had been the only two white women on board, and since Celeste was positive Dionne had never reached topside before the ship sank, the person who had prepared the papers must have been misinformed as to where the only survivor had been taken.

Louis immediately asked her to marry him, claiming she had suffered enough and that the usual mourning period should be waived under the circumstances. He convinced her by claiming Andre's attorney was taking unfair advantage of her, and that the man was diverting part of her inheritance into his own personal account.

They were married one week later. It only took a month for Louis to decide plantation farming was not for him. He began talking about the gold fields in California, and that they would be foolish not to go there and get in on the easy pickings. Celeste, eager for excitement, soon agreed. Within three months, over half of Desirade had been sold and the rest placed under the supervision of one of Louis's trusted friends, and they set sail on the *Flying Cloud*, the first clipper ship to enter the lucrative California gold rush trade.

Celeste pulled her thoughts from the past and stamped her foot impatiently. "If it were not for my money, Louis would have never been able to purchase the San Francisco Saloon and Casino, and I think it is outrageous that I am not even allowed to enter the doors!" Suddenly, Celeste grabbed her shawl and threw it around her shoulders. She muttered under her breath, "If he thinks he can keep me locked up here in this dreary hotel room without any modern comforts, then he is wrong! I am going down there whether he likes it or not!"

She marched out the door, down the stairs, then made her way across the muddy street. Men stopped in their tracks and openly stared at her. Some even had the nerve to whistle and hoot and make bawdy remarks.

"Where are you going, honey?" one man asked, falling in step beside her.

She stopped and gave him a scathing look. "Unhand me, you—you filthy beast!"

"Oooh, filthy beast, is it?" He guffawed and grabbed himself lewdly. "Come with me to the alley and I'll show you right quick-like how filthy this beast can get!"

Much to the amusement of the man's friends, Celeste pushed against his chest with both hands and sent him sprawling backward into the mud. Seeing the angry scowl that suddenly twisted the ruffian's face, she raised her skirts just enough to avoid getting her feet tangled in them and made a mad dash for the saloon.

Rushing inside, she spotted Louis sitting at a table on the far side of the smoke-filled room. Just the sight of him made her heart start beating faster. He was so handsome, so virile. He had blond curly hair, deep blue eyes, wide shoulders, and narrow hips. He reminded her of paintings she had seen before of pagan gods.

Threading her way through the packed room, Celeste hurried toward him. Suddenly, she felt a man's hands on her shoulders and then she was spun roughly around. Her mouth opened with fear when she saw a man towering above her, the same man she had pushed into the mud.

"So, you think you can make a fool out of Big John Black and get by with it." He yanked her savagely by her hand. "Well, I'll show you who is gonna be the fool. By the time I get through with you, I'll show you. . . ." The man's eyes widened as a small dot of blood appeared on his forehead, then his body stiffened and he slowly fell forward.

Celeste yelped with terror and quickly averted her eyes when she saw that a large portion of the back of his head was missing. "Get this piece of garbage out of here!" she heard Louis say. Trembling, she raised her eyes and saw Louis holding a pistol. The people in the saloon stood aside as he hurried toward her.

"Did that bastard hurt you, love?" he asked, putting the small gun back into a holster inside his coat as he wrapped one arm protectively around her.

"No, I don't think so," she muttered, still dazed by all that had happened so quickly.

"That is precisely the reason I've told you never to come in here," he said, watching as three men carried the dead man out through the swinging doors.

Huge tears filled her eyes. "Oh, Louis, please take me back to the hotel. I had no idea . . ."

He shook his head. "I can't now, love. I've had a run of bad luck. . . ." But when he saw the expression in her eyes, he reconsidered. "To hell with the bad luck. My baby needs me." He motioned with his head to the bartender. "Harry, get one of the boys to take my place at the table. I'm going back to the hotel with my wife." He then swooped Celeste into his arms and carried her gently across the street.

Chapter Twenty-Seven

Dionne picked Jonathan up in her arms and whirled happily around the room. "Your father is coming home today!" she squealed excitedly. "After four long months, he's finally coming home!"

Christopher had left on a voyage when Jonathan was only three weeks old, and during all that time, not one word or message had been received from him. Even when the *Blue Diamond* had been carrying the many cargoes of cotton, Christopher had crossed the paths of other ships he owned and had sent word by them that he was fine and when he could be expected home. But for the past four months, not one word had been heard from him until today. A messenger had brought a note from Christopher saying the *Blue Diamond* was back in port and that he would be home sometime that afternoon.

And what would she do when Christopher returned home? She had lain awake many sleepless nights trying to decide what to do to help Christopher fall in love with her. For several months before Jonathan had been born, she had thought he was beginning to fall in love with her, but now she didn't know if it had been stirrings of love or raw passion that had driven him to her eager arms. While she thoroughly enjoyed the sensual part of their relationship, that wasn't enough. She wanted a husband, a friend, a companion, not just a lover. She wanted him to share his life with her, not just his passion. And, in order for that to happen, if he tried to make love to her again, she would have to refuse him. No matter how painful it would be, she would have to insist upon a platonic relationship. She would have to win his love before he could ever claim her passion again.

Feeling Jonathan begin to squirm in her arms, she gazed lovingly at him. "I wonder what he will think of you, little man? You've grown so, I doubt if he will even know you!" Then her eyes widened. "Oh, dear, I wonder what he will think of me?" After placing Jonathan in the middle of her bed so that he would not roll off, she hurried to the mirror and studied her appearance with a critical eye.

Her sickly pallor had been replaced by a healthy glow. Her cheeks were pink and the freckles caused by her exposure to the sun had almost faded. She smoothed her hands over her waist and stomach, and smiled when she felt not one ounce of excess fat. All the walking she had been doing since Jonathan had been born had firmed her very nicely. And except for one tiny little stretch mark close to her belly button—which hopefully only Christopher would ever see, anyway—not a soul could tell that she'd had a baby.

Dionne surveyed the mirror judiciously. She did look the same, except perhaps her hips were just a little different. Although they were the same size as before she became pregnant, they seemed fuller now, more womanly. And her breasts; those had changed too. While never giving the appearance of her bosom a second thought in the past, she knew Christopher had been fascinated by her breasts. Every time he had made love to her he had kissed, fondled, and caressed them; it was almost as if he were mesmerized by their feel.

Warm shivers of delight ran up and down her spine at just the thought of his lips pressed passionately against such an intimate part of her body. Then she shook her head, knowing that part of their relationship would have to wait. But still, what would it hurt to flirt with him just a little bit?

Dionne thrust out her chest and she could not prevent the naughty grin from spreading across her face. Who said she had to fight fair to win Christopher's love? If she had to be a little devious, then so be it. She thrust out her chest even more. If he was fascinated by her breasts before, what would the sight of them do to him now? Nursing Jonathan had made them fuller and more firm than ever. Berta had once made the remark that nursing children would eventually make a bosom sag. Maybe that was true, but it definitely had not affected her yet.

Then, her face reddened. "Stop it, Dionne. You are behaving ridiculous, like a wanton hussy!"

"Now who in this room could be a wanton hussy?" Berta asked from the doorway, a wide grin splitting her chocolate face.

Spinning around, Dionne admonished sheepishly, "Berta, you should have knocked. Why . . . you caught me talking to myself," she admitted.

"I knows it, I knows it." She grinned ever broader. "I knows you weren't tellin' the little precious that his mama was a wanton hussy. You was practicin' up to tell that to his handsome papa! But Lordy, Missus Dionne, as long as that man's been gone, I doubts if you have to tell him anythin'. More than likely he'll just bust the door down and dares anyone to disturb the two of you."

"Berta! Stop that! You are embarrassing me!" Dionne scolded. She could feel a deep blush spreading over her entire body.

"I's sorry, Missus Dionne, I won't say nothin' else 'bout it," Berta said, but from the smile on her face it was plain to see she did not mean a word of her apology. "Since Mister Chris is comin' home, I figured you would be wantin' a bath. I brought up a bucketful o' hot water, and Josey and the other girls are bringin' up some more. Josey is gonna watch the little precious while I wash your hair, and then if you like, I'll fix it for you real pretty."

"Oh, I think I would like that very much, Berta . . . and thank you," she added sincerely.

Although Dionne's sincerity had pleased her more than she would have admitted, she waved it aside. "Ain't nothin'. B'sides, if my memory serves me right, Mister Chris left here in such a powerful huff . . . it's up to us to make sure that don't happen no more. Why, I'm goin' to make you look so pretty—course I don't have to do much 'cause you're so pretty already—that man will think he's been hit over the head with a ton o' bricks!"

Dionne's happy mood instantly became somber. Four months had been a long time, and it had been longer still since Christopher had held her in his arms. What if he didn't want to hold her again? What would she do if he ignored her the same way as when he had first learned of their marriage? Her plan would not stand a chance of working if he did that. She turned large sad eyes back to the mirror and stared into their depths. Her plan had been hastily formulated; nevertheless, it was a good one. But what would she do if he did not accept her bait?

"Christopher, your grandmother said you wanted to see me," Dionne said as she stood in the doorway of his study. Just the sight of him, sitting so tall in his chair, so handsome and so masculine, made her knees tremble.

Christopher raised his eyes and stared at her hard. Even from this distance he was aware of the delicate scent of her perfume, the soft lilt of her voice, and the way her entire essence shouted of her vibrant femininity. She looked lovelier than ever before. In spite of all his intentions to ignore her completely, he could feel desire surge through his loins for her. Was there no way he could rid himself of the intoxicating spell she had cast over him?

From his silence, Dionne thought he had not heard her clearly. She made an impatient gesture. "Your grandmother said you wanted to see me. She also said it was important."

That statement was both true and false. He had asked his grandmother to relay a message and she had refused, saying he should speak to Dionne about the matter himself. But it was not merely what she had said that had made him decide to speak to Dionne, it was the way she had said it. It had almost sounded like a challenge, as though she thought he was afraid. His grandmother should have known better than that. He was afraid of no one, much less a woman.

It was a moment longer before he answered, and then his voice came strong and sure, betraying none of the discord he felt in her presence. "Come in and sit down."

She lifted a finely arched brow. "That sounds more like an order than a request."

He frowned, his eyes level under drawn brows. "I am not in a diplomatic mood today."

"No, I suppose you are not, but then, if I remember correctly, I believe you only spoke to me three times between the time Jonathan was born and when you left on that voyage.'

He shrugged and smiled benignly, as if dealing with a temperamental child. His voice was heavily loaded

405

with ridicule, "I must not have been in a diplomatic mood those three times either."

"I didn't come in here to argue with you, Christopher," she said softly, refusing to be coerced into an argument.

"I don't feel like arguing either."

"Then what do you want?"

"Actually, I didn't want anything. It was Grandmother who insisted I speak to you." He was suddenly unsure if the faint blush that stole across her cheeks was from anger or something else entirely. He pressed on, wanting to get this conversation over, "Before I left, Grandmother told me you were upset about Josey. It has taken this long to receive replies to my letters. If you are interested, you are welcome to come in and sit down and listen to what I have found out. If not"— he shrugged indifferently—"then go on about your business."

"That is hardly fair," she said as she moved toward the desk with a quiet dignity and sat down in a chair directly across from him. "Since my questions are what spurred the correspondence to begin with, I am most interested in the outcome. But I will add, since that time I spoke to your grandmother about Josey, her attitude seems to have changed. She is not nearly as sullen and she seems almost happy now."

Christopher tried to ignore the heady sensations caused by the scent of her perfume. He picked up several pieces of paper and pretended to study them. Then he placed all the letters aside except for one. "Do you want to read this, or do you want me to tell you what it says?"

"Please, just explain it if you will." It had been so long since she had been able to talk to him that she preferred to hear the deep timbre of his voice.

Christopher stated bluntly, "The letter is from

Roger F. Peabody, owner of the LaBelle plantation. Peabody cautions us to watch Josey closely because she has caused trouble in the past." Although his words had been crisp and to the point, the tightening of his lips intimated his remorse over this entire matter.

"What did he mean, *trouble?*" Fear made Dionne's stomach tighten.

Quickly realizing what must have been going through Dionne's mind, Christopher shook his head and reassured her, "From the information I received in these other letters, I seriously doubt if the trouble Peabody mentioned is anything to cause us any concern. Besides, I have asked Berta how Josey behaves with Jonathan, and she says the girl seems to adore him. But, anyway, to get on with the explanation, after receiving this letter—in which, by the way, Peabody makes it clear that he is not responsible for any problems we might have from her in the future—I went down to where they hold the slave auctions and asked around. I found out Peabody raises slaves for his cash crops instead of cotton or sugar beets."

Christopher rubbed his bruised knuckles underneath the desk. "And after a long conversation with the auction master, I also found out what the trouble was that Peabody referred to. It seems that Josey and a young buck—a young man—from a neighboring plantation fell in love, and they tried to run away. When they were found, the young man was killed during the capture. Josey was taken back to the plantation, and as soon as her baby was born—and, unfortunately, it was born dead—she was brought here to New Orleans and sold on the block." He shook his head, showing his disgust. "Most of these plantations whose major commodity is raising slaves keep the young women to replenish their stock. The way I figure it, Peabody must have decided Josey was worth the loss just to teach his other slaves a valuable lesson."

Dionne closed her eyes and shuddered. "Bless her heart. It's no wonder she looks so sullen. I would be angry too if something like that happened to me. It's a shame they can't all be set free."

"I agree, but it doesn't look like slavery will end any time soon." There was a faint tremor in his voice, as though the subject angered him.

"Unfortunately," she murmured sadly.

"There is one other thing I want to mention about Josey," he said with quiet emphasis. "Grandmother told me she explained the method we used with our servants. If you feel any reluctance whatsoever in having Josey help you with Jonathan, just say the word and we'll either find other duties for her or make other arrangements."

Dionne shrugged to hide her disconcert. Christopher was now behaving as though he really cared, but only a few minutes earlier he had acted as if he didn't even want to see her. Forcing her confused emotions into order, she said, "No, I don't think that is necessary. I have found no fault with the way she treats Jonathan. I only mentioned my concern to Grand'mere that day because Josey had such a sullen look about her." Then, Dionne lowered her gaze. "And, to be completely truthful, I was angry at you, too. I thought you had bought her without even considering her child."

"Maybe you should watch your temper more closely. It could get you into trouble," Christopher said as he shifted uncomfortably in his chair. It shamed him now, but the truth was that at the time he had bought Josey, he had never even considered the fact that she should have had a child with her. He had been too concerned about Dionne and her baby to worry about anyone else.

His eyes met hers boldly. "Now that that is all settled,

how have you and Jonathan been doing?"

Dionne's face brightened instantly. "Oh, Jonathan is doing fine. Grand'mere says he is growing like a big bad weed. And he's strong, too. Why, he is holding his head up and is already trying to scoot across the bed when I lay him on his stomach."

"And how are you doing?" he asked softly. He caressed her with his eyes.

A pink blush stole across her cheeks. "Oh, I am doing fine, too. The doctor said I am as good as new." Then she ducked her head, hoping it did not sound as though she were hinting that they could resume a marital relationship.

He nodded his head thoughtfully. "Well, that's good." Then, Christopher felt the overwhelming urge to snort with disgust. Why was he sitting here talking to Dionne when he really wanted to take her into his arms and make passionate love to her? Now that she was no longer pregnant, all of his old desire for her seemed to have burst into flames.

"And . . . Christopher, I missed you while you were gone," she murmured.

He brought his head up sharply. She had spoken the words so softly that he was not sure he had heard her correctly. "You did?"

"Yes." A different sort of expression spread slowly over Dionne's face. "And . . . Christopher, I never had the opportunity to thank you properly. . . ."

"For what?"

"For saving my life and Jonathan's, too."

"Don't give me too much credit," he said with forced gruffness. "I only did what had to be done." Regardless of what he said, he still felt an overwhelming sense of awe over the emotions he had experienced when that baby had been born. It was a feeling he would never forget no matter what happened in the future between him and Dionne.

"Maybe so, but still it was you who did it, and it is to you that we owe our gratitude." She then folded her arms together, leaned back in the chair, and chewed thoughtfully on her bottom lip. "There is something about that night that I can't seem to get out of mind . . . or perhaps it happened while I was under sedation or maybe it didn't even happen at all." She gestured helplessly. "I'm really not sure."

"What is it? Perhaps I can tell you."

She shrugged. "I realize this is probably ridiculous, but after Jonathan was born, I could have sworn I saw you sitting in the rocking chair holding him . . . and you were even singing him a lullaby."

He chortled. "You're right, it is ridiculous. It must have been the drug playing tricks on your mind." He had no idea why he did not want anyone, especially Dionne, to know how much he had enjoyed holding that baby.

"But . . . it seemed so real."

"Are you suggesting I am telling a lie?" he asked curtly.

"Why, of course not. I know you would never do anything like that!" she replied blandly.

Even though her words had agreed, the mocking tone of her voice made Christopher realize she suspected the truth. He quickly cleared his throat and looked away. Then, becoming aware that her eyes were still rested on him, he raked his fingers through his hair and stared back at her defiantly. But his defiance quickly faded. Damn it, why did she have to look at him that way? The color of her eyes was indefinable, hovering somewhere between gold and green. He saw a hypnotized man reflected in them. A man starved for the taste and touch of her. He saw a man wanting a woman—and not just any woman, either, as that humiliating episode at the whorehouse had proved. He saw *himself* reflected in her eyes and knew he wanted her!

Suddenly, unable to take her piercing gaze any longer, Christopher jumped up from his chair, stomped to the double windows, then spun quickly around. It was infuriating to see her still watching him. "What in the hell are you staring at?" he shouted.

Dionne's teeth ground together and her fingernails dug into the palms of her hands as she withheld her angry response. Then, she took a deep breath and deliberately stood slowly to her feet, all the while her mockingly intense gaze never leaving his face.

Christopher's eyes widened with rage as he realized she was intentionally taunting him. He repeated angrily, "I asked you a question. I asked you what in the hell are you staring at?"

She placed her hands akimbo, raised one brow haughtily, and laughed aloud. Then, without any hint of anger in her voice, she said, "I'm really not sure, but I believe it is a jackass!"

"What did you call me?" he asked coldly as fury raced through him.

"I said you are a jackass, a stubborn, obstinate, arrogant unyielding jackass!"

He raised his brows and drew his mouth into a mocking grimace. "My, my, this is a sudden change from the undying gratitude you expressed only a few minutes ago."

"My gratitude has nothing to do with your being so stubborn." She tossed her head and gave him a scathing look. "And if you were not so—so . . . stubborn, you would admit what I did just a short while ago."

He raised his hands palms up to indicate his confusion. "What am I supposed to admit? That I am a

411

stubborn jackass?"

Dionne walked toward him and did not stop until she could feel the heat radiating from his body. She realized the chance she was taking. If he spurned her now, her pride might never recover from the blow. Taking a deep breath, she slowly and tantalizingly wet her lips, then murmured in what she hoped to be her most sultry voice, "No, I doubt if you lived to be one hundred years old that you would ever admit to being that stubborn. But a while ago, when I told you that I missed you, you could have said that you missed me too."

Christopher gave a sharp intake of breath. He knew then he was going to kiss her and there was not a thing he could do about it. The choice had been taken away from him the moment she had entered this room. Perhaps the moment had been ordained, predestined, and he would be tempting fate if he resisted this overpowering urge. His head moved slowly down to her waiting mouth.

At first, he merely touched his lips to hers. Then, tilting her head farther back to accommodate him, he rubbed his lips against hers. His heart was pounding erratically but he did not rush. He hesitated, taking time to breathe in the flavor of her breath, to smell the clean scent of soap, water, and a brief touch of perfume. He touched her upper lip with the tip of his tongue, lightly, so very lightly he was not even sure their flesh had touched until he heard the choppy rush of air that rushed past her lips and feathered his.

When his lips met hers again, instinct took over. He had forgotten what a jolting thrill it was to kiss her. Her mouth was a sweet wet chasm he explored thoroughly. He tasted all of it because he had been so consummately hungry for it. He ran his tongue along the straight ridge of her teeth. He touched the roof of her mouth, investigated the lining of her lips, and teasingly prodded the tip of her tongue with his. And he applied the suction that intimated he would draw all of her into himself if only he could.

Dionne, with her heart slamming wickedly against her breast, sensually curled her arms around his neck and answered his questing mouth with a timid but adventurous pursuit of her own. After what seemed like a lifetime, she finally pulled from his embrace. Noting fervent desire was now etched into his masculine features, she lowered her gaze demurely, slipped a hand around her back, and crossed her fingers. Her plan had to work, it simply had to!

She murmured breathlessly, "Now that you have been welcomed home properly and I have been thoroughly greeted, your grandmother asked me to tell you to be sure and be on time for supper, that Cook is preparing all of your favorites." Turning, she started to leave.

"Wait a minute!" Christopher realized he had spoken more sharply than he had intended, and he repeated his command, but much gentler than before, "Wait a minute, Dionne."

His eyes quickly searched the tiny room for a place to make love to her. The chair? No, that would be next to impossible. The desk? No, it was too cluttered, but the papers could be swept off onto the floor. Aha, the floor! A lecherous gleam appeared in his eyes. He walked slowly toward her. As he advanced, she stepped backward until the wall loomed behind her back.

Christopher raised one arm, propped it against the wall, and rested his weight on it, while with the other hand he fingered a tendril of her hair that had come loose. He murmured huskily, "Don't be in such a rush. I believe you said that you had been thoroughly greeted. . . . Well, I certainly don't consider that one little kiss a thorough greeting." He started to lower his lips to hers again. "Let me show you what I consider to be a thorough greeting."

Ducking under his upraised arm, Dionne hurried to the door and turned the knob. Laughter was in her voice as she said, "I think you have more on your mind than a simple I'm-glad-to-be-back-home greeting—or, at least, that is how it appears to me."

"Wait a minute. Where are you going?"

"For a walk," she said innocently, lifting one keenly arched brow. "I always go for a walk before supper. Do you want to go with me?"

A smile toyed with his lips. "No, I think I had better pass. But after supper . . . maybe we can continue where we left off."

Dionne's eyes slowly swept full length over him. Then she smiled seductively. But she left without saying one further word of encouragement.

Dionne hurried up the stairs and down the hall, anxious to freshen up and change before it was time for supper to be served. Pushing open the door to her room, she came to an abrupt halt. Her mouth opened in surprise and she could actually feel her eyes protrude. Christopher was sitting in the huge wing-backed chair, holding Jonathan and counting piggies on his bare toes.

Christopher stared at her sheepishly. "I was in my bedroom . . . and he awoke . . . and neither you nor Josey were anywhere around . . . so I came in here. . . . He was crying. . . . Well, damn it, don't look at me like that! I couldn't just let him cry. Why, it could hurt him!"

Dionne struggled to keep a straight face. "Of course you couldn't let him cry." She clapped her hands together and said, "Do you want to come to Mama now, big boy?"

Familiar with the games his mother played with him, Jonathan squealed joyfully and tried to get away. He grabbed hold of Christopher's shirt near his neck and tried to crawl up his belly.

The expression on Christopher's face was one of awe. "I think he likes me! No, I know he likes me!" Awkwardly, he patted his bottom.

Dionne dared not let her expression reveal what she was thinking. She thought it was amazing that Christopher stood well over six feet tall, and that he could fit perfectly around the little finger of a baby Jonathan's size. Amazing, simply amazing.

"Do you want to hold him while I dress for dinner?"

Christopher started to nod but his head suddenly stopped in midair and his eyes widened, then he started chuckling. "No, madame, I believe your son needs his mama. Or, at least, I need him to need his mama!" He held Jonathan out away from him, revealing a huge wet spot on his shirt.

Dionne began laughing. "He just initiated you. And just think, you were fortunate. It could have been the other." She shook her head, still laughing. "I think it is amazing how a little bit of baby peepee will reduce the most masculine virile man into a bowl of quivering jelly! Here, let me take him while you go wash up and put on a clean shirt."

Later, as she was feeding Jonathan, she felt Christopher's presence behind her long before she felt his lips touch the back of her neck.

"Dionne, may I say that you have never looked lovelier," he murmured against her neck.

"Thank you, Christopher." She was relieved her face was averted from his so he could not see the confusion that creased her brow. Was she indeed lovely to him, or was he merely hungry for a woman? "I hoped you found your room in the proper order. I doubt if you were gone a week before I moved back in here."

"Oh, yes, everything is fine." He stared longingly down at the baby nuzzling at her breast. Fire began to burn in his loins. Not only was Dionne lovely, but she was the most desirable woman he had ever seen. He brushed several locks of hair from her neck and lowered his mouth to kiss her there again. But Dionne shied away.

"Please, don't," she murmured. The mere touch of his lips had sent a warming shiver through her. She could not be distracted now, she had to keep a clear mind.

"You didn't object to my kiss a while ago."

"But you were not in this sort of mood a while ago, either."

"Oh? What kind of a mood am I in?"

"You are in a making-love mood."

He chuckled. "Yes, I'll have to admit, I am."

With a moan of distress, she lowered her gaze. "Christopher, I don't want to make you angry, but I think you should know how I feel."

Christopher gazed at her with a bland half smile. "Yes, I think perhaps I should know how you feel," he said slowly as he sat down on the foot of the bed so that he could see her as she talked.

Dionne could not bring herself to look at him, for fear of losing control of her emotions. She spoke in a broken whisper, "During the time I have been here, my relationship with you has either been ecstatic or miserable. I know there was a time when we were growing very, very close, and then it abruptly changed . . . and I really don't know why. Not only did you no longer hold me in your arms, but you wouldn't even talk to me, and you avoided me, too. That hurt me deeply, and I don't want to be hurt like that again. Until things between us change, I am not willing to enter into . . . another intimate . . . relationship with you. As for my bodily feelings . . . yes, I could make love to you this very moment. . . . But the way I feel inside . . . if you rejected me again, I don't know what I would do. So, I think the best solution is for you to remain in your bed and I will remain in mine."

His expression was grim as he watched her, but his voice came low and smooth, "Is that your final word?"

"Y—yes, unless you can give me assurance that I will not be hurt again."

His expression was that of pained tolerance. "I'm sorry, Dionne, I can't do that."

Her misery was like a steel weight. "Then I guess there is nothing left to say, is there?" Her voice faded to a hushed stillness.

Christopher slowly shook his head, revealing none of his thoughts or feelings. "No, I guess not."

Christopher leaned back in his chair and patted his stomach to show the appreciation he felt for the meal. "Cook outdid herself tonight. That was delicious!"

Jeannine stated matter-of-factly, "It may surprise you to know that all the credit does not belong to Cook. Dionne prepared the green beans and the strawberry shortcake. She wanted to prepare the entire meal but Cook would not hear of it." She shook her head and laughed. "I'll declare, it sounded like a war in the kitchen there for a while."

"Yes, and you better believe it was Cook who won the battle," Dionne said, laughing. It was difficult, but it was all part of her plan to act as though nothing had happened between her and Christopher.

Christopher looked at her with a mixture of

417

amusement and surprise. "I didn't know you could cook."

Her warm gold-green eyes were full of mystery as she said, "I'm sure there are many things you do not know about me."

"Chris, have you seen Jonathan yet?" Jeannine asked.

He nodded. "Yes, I have." Then he began laughing. "In fact, I would say he made a lasting impression on me."

Dionne tried to catch Jeannine's eye. She did not push the issue about Jonathan. She wanted to proceed slowly, to take one step at a time.

Jeannine deliberately pursued the subject. "I think it was so nice that Dionne named Jonathan after Andre, don't you, Chris?" she asked sweetly as she pushed her shortcake around the saucer with her fork, wanting to prolong their time spent at the dinner table. Unbeknownst to Dionne, she had plans of her own to get them together.

The muscles in Christopher's face tightened as he set his coffee cup down a little too hard on the saucer. He scowled darkly at Dionne but answered his grandmother, "I wasn't aware that she did! I thought he was named after his . . ."

"Andre Lyle Debierne," Jeannine quickly broke in. "And, Dionne, I still think it was very thoughtful of you to remember Andre in that manner."

Christopher stared at Dionne hard. His mouth had suddenly gone dry. "Why didn't you tell me?"

"You never gave me the chance," she said softly.

Jeannine thumped the floor with her cane. "Chris, if you are through eating, come here and give me your arm. You have been on board that ship for so long you are forgetting your manners." She smiled to show that she was teasing. "Besides, you have been home for hours now and you have not pampered or petted me once. I want to go into the parlor where we can be comfortable. There are several matters I need to discuss with you. And don't forget to help Dionne to her feet. I'm sure she likes to be pampered and petted as much as I do. Now, come along, Dionne. You need to hear this, too."

Dionne tried not to let her disappointment show. She had hoped he would have wanted to go up and see Jonathan again, especially since Jeannine had so tactfully informed him that he had been named after Andre and not the man Christopher believed to be her lover. What was Jeannine doing? She acted as though she were deliberately trying to keep them from being alone.

Once they were all in the parlor, Jeannine settled back on the sofa and casually glanced around, fully noting how tense Dionne was. She sighed contentedly. "Now, isn't this so much more comfortable than that stuffy dining room?"

Christopher thought his grandmother's behavior was amusing, but he knew she definitely had something on her mind other than this nonsensical chitchat. However, he knew her well enough to realize she would take her sweet time to broach the real subject she wanted to talk about.

They chatted idly for over thirty minutes before Jeannine turned to Christopher with a gleam in her eyes.

"I had a visitor the other day, Chris."

"Oh? Who was it?"

"Our banker, Tyler Henderson."

"What did he want?"

"He wants to know what in the hell is going on with your warehouses in San Francisco? Tyler knew you were on a voyage and he spoke freely to me. He had just received a report—which, by the way, is now on your desk—that stated quite clearly revenues have dropped a drastic sixty percent in the past six months. He and I discussed it, and it is very apparent that either Nicholas is stealing you blind, or he is totally inept when it comes to business matters. I personally believe it is both reasons. Now, I want to know what you intend to do about it."

Christopher ran his fingers through his hair. "I don't know yet, Grandmother. I found the report on my desk, and it goes without saying, I wasn't too happy with what I read. But I haven't had time to decide what I am going to do about it yet." He sighed with exasperation. "Well, yes, I suppose I do know what I am going to have to do. I'm going to have to go to San Francisco and take care of the matter myself."

Dionne felt her heart lurch. She knew a voyage to San Francisco would take at least four months both ways, even with Christopher's speedy clipper ship. Then it would take him another month or two to straighten out the mess Nicholas had made. Why, he would be gone at least six months, maybe even a lot longer. By the time he returned, their two-year marriage would nearly be over—even before it had had a chance to begin.

Jeannine slammed the tip of her cane against the floor and smiled. "Good! If you go to San Francisco, then we will all accompany you!"

"You can't do that, Grandmother?" Christopher said in a low but incredulous voice.

"And why not?"

"Because San Francisco is still a wild and ruthless town. It's uncivilized and not a fit place for a woman."

"Nonsense, Rosalyn and Robert went out there—I believe, nearly four months ago—and my good friend Marcie Allen is living out there with her daughter and

420

son-in-law. From all I've read, it is quickly becoming civilized.

Christopher shook his head adamantly. "I won't hear of it, Grandmother! Why, the voyage alone is strenuous on a young person. I'm afraid your health wouldn't hold up to it."

Jeannine threw up her hands impatiently. "Good Lord, Christopher, half the city of New Orleans is being ravaged by yellow fever and you are concerned about a little ocean voyage. We need to get away from the city. Why, it is dangerous here with that fever spreading like the plague. I could get it, or little Jonathan could get it. . . ."

"Then you and the entire household will have to go to the country the way you usually do in the summer. But you are not coming with me to San Francisco, and that's final!" He kissed Jeannine on her forehead. "I hate to have cross words with you, but you have to understand going to San Francisco with me is out of the question." He kissed her forehead again. "Well, I am going to call it a day. I am tired, and to be quite frank about it, I have been looking forward to sleeping in my own bed for a change." He touched his forehead in a small salute, told them both good night, and hurried from the parlor.

Dionne turned to Jeannine with many questions, but the older woman silenced her with an upraised hand. "Now, child, I know what I am doing, and before you start asking unnecessary questions, listen to me for a minute. Have you ever been inside a captain's quarters on a ship?"

"No," Dionne answered, clearly puzzled.

"I am not sure how large Christopher's cabin is, but believe me, it is small. And as the captain's wife, you will be expected to share the small room with him. And the voyage will last at least two months." Feeling extremely pleased with herself, she chuckled. "Need I say more?"

"But—but Christopher said we couldn't go."

Jeannine walked toward the door. Upon reaching it, she turned and stated smugly, "Christopher may say that now, but mark my word, when the *Blue Diamond* sets sail for San Francisco, we will be on it!"

Chapter Twenty-Eight

"Now, young men, you be careful with my trunk," Jeannine told the strapping seamen as they carried the large container up the *Blue Diamond*'s gangplank. "And be especially careful with that black one. It contains breakable items."

Chuckling to himself, Christopher knelt and ruffled Katie's shining black coat. He still didn't know how his grandmother had managed to convince him to take them to San Francisco with him. But once he had agreed, everything had mushroomed. His grandmother swore she couldn't do without Berta, she said Dionne and Jonathan would need Josey's help, and Dionne had said she didn't want to leave Katie behind. And since he had taken Katie on several voyages with him before, he really didn't mind taking her. But he'd had no idea it took so much luggage for five additional people. Shaking his head in disbelief, he stared skeptically at all the wooden boxes, chests, and trunks that still remained on the dock, wondering where they would put it all.

He did nothing to conceal his teasing sarcasm as he gestured with a wide sweep of his hand and asked, "Grandmother, are you sure this is all the luggage or is there another carriageful coming?"

Blandly ignoring him, Jeannine looked as though

she were conducting an orchestra as she silently counted all the luggage that remained. Finally, she gave a satisfied sigh and smiled. "It tallies out correctly. All the luggage is here," she announced proudly.

Christopher turned slightly and winked at Barney, who stood beside him. "Are you sure this is all, Grandmother? If necessary, we could remove the freight from the cargo hold and put the luggage in there."

Laughing, she wagged her cane at him. "Don't get testy with me, young man. We didn't pack anything unless it was absolutely necessary." Still keeping a sharp eye on the loading procedure, she tapped one of the crewmen on his shoulder with her cane and said, "Take that chest to the galley and tell the cook that I said to be . . ."

"Grandmother," Christopher ignored Barney's amused chuckles as he quickly interrupted, "I think you would be more comfortable on board ship. Why don't I escort you to your quarters so that you can be settling in?"

"But, Chris . . ."

"Now, I won't take no for an answer. My men are very capable, and I promise they will be careful with every trunk and chest." His eyes sparkled with laughter as he placed his hand over his heart and pronounced, in a rough, raspy voice, "For every scratch or mark, I will personally give the man responsible twenty lashes with the cat-o'-nine-tails!"

She glared up at him sharply. "You are patronizing me! You know how I dislike to be treated that way!"

Christopher folded his arms and rocked back on his heels. A wide smile spread across his face. "All I can say is that you were born a woman and one to two hundred years too late. With that cane and your ability to give orders . . . why, you would have been the terror of the seven seas."

Jeannine blinked, then her eyes twinkled with merriment as she grinned sheepishly. "All right, you have made your point. If you will be so kind as to escort me on board, I promise to keep my mouth shut."

Barney stepped forward and offered her his arm. "Allow me the honors, ma'am. I'd be most pleased to escort ye on board."

Christopher glanced up at the sky and tapped his foot impatiently. Dionne, Jonathan, Berta, and Josey still had not arrived. Before Barney and his grandmother disappeared from sight, he called to her, "Didn't you say the other carriage was right behind you? Do you have any idea what could be keeping them?"

"No, I don't. All that I know is that they stopped beside a little shop. When my driver started to stop, Berta waved us on."

Christopher scowled. He wished they had all arrived together. It would have been less confusing. No, nothing was less confusing when his grandmother prepared to go on a journey, no matter how long or short it was supposed to be. When he was a child and they went to their summer house out in the country, it was always a major task to get there. And now, as his grandmother had put it that "they were going halfway around the world," she had made sure they would be prepared.

He shuddered to think what it would have been like if the entire household had come, too. The remainder of the household was staying at Crescentview, unless the yellow fever epidemic became too severe. If that happened, Andrew Blackmon had agreed to accompany the servants to the summer house and make arrangements for them to stay there until cooler weather set in. Christopher hated to impose on the doctor, but he realized it was possible that some of the poorer white people in the area could become overly zealous over the fact that coloreds had moved into the summer house without a white master. At least this way, they would all be protected.

"Cap'n Chris," Barney hailed as he rambled down the gangplank. "I thought I had ye grandmother squared away, but I turned my back and first thing I knew she be in the galley giving the cook what fer." His entire body shook with silent laughter. "I used to think ye got all yer sass and vinegar from yer father and grandfather, but now I see it be inherited from her." He shook his head as though amazed. "And to think she barely stands o'er five feet. Ah, look, Cap'n, there comes ye other carriage now."

"My God!" Christopher breathed incredulously as the carriage came to a rolling halt. "They have two more big trunks with them."

Then, Christopher and Barney looked at each other with unbelieving expressions, and together they mouthed, *"And a crate of live flowers!"*

Christopher could have sworn his grandmother must have smelled the additional luggage, for she immediately appeared on deck instructing the crewmen to bring them on board and that she would show them where they should be placed.

"I thought you said that was all of the luggage?" Christopher called to her.

"It was all of the luggage . . . on that carriage," she replied crisply.

Christopher clamped his lips together. It was a battle lost. He might as well stand back and lick his wounds, for he knew there would be additional battles ahead and he would be damned if he lost the war!

Barney, anxious to meet his captain's wife and to see their son, hurried to the carriage and offered Dionne his hand. She held onto it as she stepped from the carriage, then turned and took the baby into her arms. But as she turned to face him, he was able to see her features plainly beneath her wide-brimmed hat. The greeting smile seemed to freeze on his face as he recognized her to be the lady he had met in the marketplace, then later on the front steps of the Debierne plantation. She was not the woman his captain was supposed to have married.

"Madame Phillips?"

"Why, Barney!" She smiled pleasantly. "How nice to see you again. . . ." She shot a questioning glance at Christopher, as she realized Barney had been expecting to see Celeste.

Christopher quickly stepped forward. "I'm sure you recall meeting . . . my wife. . . . However, she wasn't my . . . wife at that time." He realized he would have to take Barney into his confidence. But he didn't mind. Barney could be trusted to hold his tongue.

Barney regained his composure instantly. Whatever there was between his captain and this lass he had married it was none of his business. "'Tis me pleasure to see ye again, ma'am. And this must be the wee one. Ah, Cap'n Chris, he be the spittin' image of ye!"

Dionne's smile faltered. Wanting to change the subject away from Jonathan's resemblance to Christopher, she quickly said, "I'm sorry we're late, but I saw those flowers for sale and decided they would be perfect . . ."

"We can't take the flowers, Dionne," Christopher said, firmly shaking his head. "They'll soon wilt from the heat and we won't be able to spare the fresh water to keep them alive."

"But . . . I wasn't planning to take them all the way to California."

"What did you intend to do? Plant them? . . ." Then

427

his curt remark was forgotten when he saw Dionne's expression. He thought for a moment she was about to cry and a desolate bleakness had appeared on her face. His voice softened. "Go ahead and explain about the flowers; I'm listening."

She wet her lips and smiled sadly. Her voice was so soft it could barely be heard. "I realize the precise location . . . where the . . . *Emerald Tempest* went down will never be known. But I thought when we reached the general area, I would throw the flowers overboard in memory . . . of all those who lost their lives. I realize it probably sounds silly but . . ."

Christopher stared at her lovely but remorseful face, and he was awed by her thoughtfulness. He cleared the lump that had suddenly formed in his throat and muttered gruffly, "It's not silly at all. Barney, will you please take my wife's flowers on board."

"Aye, aye, Cap'n." Barney easily swung the crate of flowers on his shoulder and made his way up the gangplank. He had no idea how it came to be that his captain was married to this lass. 'T'would be confusing. But after what the pretty lass had said about the flowers, for his money, the captain had gotten himself one hell of a woman!

The gangplank was finally raised and the mooring lines released from the pier. Longboats and steam-equipped tugs maneuvered the 1,783-ton *Blue Diamond* through the first lock on the Mississippi River. There, they held the ship fast until she was ready to get under way on her own power.

The first mate walked the deck, calling out orders when they needed to be issued, but the crew was experienced and the orders came few and far between. Ropes were tautly stretched. Blocks and sheaves groaned and creaked as the men, muscles rippling with strength, heaved the ropes through the pulleys as the sails made their slow, tedious journey up the towering masts. Soon, the fleecy white sails filled with the gentle breezes wafting from the river until they appeared as puffy white clouds against the azure sky. The *Blue Diamond* was off!

Dionne sat in the cabin with her head buried in her hands, listening to each sound the ship made. Each sound drove stark terror right through her heart. Each sound brought back terrifying memories of the *Emerald Tempest* getting under way from Martinique, and she could not help but remember the fatal ending of that vessel. She had dreaded this moment ever since Jeannine had mentioned going with Christopher. Knowing she would more than likely lose all hope of gaining Christopher's love if she remained behind, Dionne had agreed to accompany them. But how would she ever be able to live with this horrifying fear for the next two months? How could she do it and still keep her sanity?

A brief rap at the door caught her attention. "Yes, come in."

Jeannine opened the door. "Aren't you coming out to join us? The river is lovely." She grinned smugly. "And it was Christopher who noticed you were not on deck."

Forcing her voice to sound calm, Dionne replied, "I'm sorry, Grand'mere, but Jonathan is a little fussy. I'll remain in the cabin with him until he gets accustomed to the rocking of the ship and his new surroundings."

"Then allow me to send Josey in to watch him."

"No, I think he needs his mother right now." Just the thought of standing on that desk surrounded by water and sky made her stomach lurch with fear.

Disappointment was evident on Jeannine's face. "Well, all right, but if you later change your mind, feel free to join us."

"Yes, of course." *But I won't!* she said to herself. *I will not step my foot on that deck unless it is absolutely necessary!*

It was well past dark before the *Blue Diamond* finally reached the open sea. Christopher walked slowly toward his cabin, exhausted, but elated over how the sea breezes and the gentle popping of the sails made him feel at home. Now, after this day's work, he was ravenous. He eagerly looked forward to a tall mug of ale, a thick slice of roasted beef, a big wedge of cheddar cheese, and a large hunk of bread, then a good night's sleep.

When Christopher opened the door to his cabin, his eyes widened with surprise. He entered and slowly looked around. There was order to the chaotic confusion but how it was possible he did not know. A cradle sat near his sea chest, and two huge trunks—one standing open—had been placed in the only unused corner. Dionne sat on the bunk, calmly nursing Jonathan.

"What are you doing in here?" he asked as he tried not to allow his eyes to linger too long on her breast.

Dionne raised her brows questioningly. "Why, I'm feeding my son. Is there a reason why I should not be here?"

He raked his hand through his rumpled hair. "There are three cabins available. I thought you and Jonathan would have settled into one of them."

"Have you seen the third cabin?" she asked pointedly.

"No."

"Grand'mere insisted all the trunks be stored there so that they would be easily accessible if we needed something from them. And since the other cabins are smaller than your quarters . . . well, Grand'mere wanted a room to herself, and that left Berta and Josey to share a room." She shrugged helplessly. "So, there was nowhere else for us to go."

Christopher could feel his temper rising, but then he realized just how cozy this could be. The past few weeks at Crescentview had been miserable. He had lain awake each night, knowing Dionne was in the room next to him and wanting her so badly his body actually throbbed with pain. And now, as his eyes quickly swept the small cabin, he realized their having to be in close contact might not be so bad after all. He deliberately avoided looking at the bunk. It was a bit larger than a cot so that it would accommodate his large frame, but it was much smaller than a regular-sized bed. The smile that suddenly lit his eyes contained a sensuous flame. Indeed, Dionne's sharing his cabin for the next two months could prove to be rather interesting.

Chapter Twenty-Nine

Christopher came awake slowly. His mind was filled with the feel of Dionne warm and soft against him. Those firm, full breasts seemed to bore holes in his back. Deep in sleep, Dionne's arm was draped casually around his waist, her thighs were snuggled under his buttocks, and her silken limbs were bare against him. His manhood throbbed with desire as he thought about turning over and taking her, but certainly not by force. He could never allow himself to do that regardless of how much he wanted a woman. But he wanted to arouse her with such a gentle persuasion that she would seek his arms willingly, whether he muttered those silly words or not.

Whatever possessed him to think that sharing a cabin with Dionne on a long ocean voyage would be a sexually titillating experience? Oh, it was titillating all right, definitely titillating, but he had not been able to relieve the ache in his loins one single time.

Their first night out he had come to bed eager and anticipating, thinking that the romantic moonlight and the gentle lulling of the ship would soften Dionne's determination, but she had politely and coolly informed him she had not changed her mind. She was not about to enter into that sort of relationship with him and be hurt again.

433

Angered over her rejection, he had thought about stringing a hammock in the corner of the cabin and sleeping there, but he quickly discarded that idea. He knew she had enjoyed him as much as he enjoyed her, and if they continued to share the narrow bunk, he would soon wear down her resistance.

But they had been at sea for three weeks now, and every night had been the same thing. She would go to bed and lie rigidly on her own side of the bunk, but before the night was over, he would awake and find her cuddled close to him in her sleep. She looked so innocent and trusting, how could he make love to her under those circumstances?

Now, he felt as though he were teetering on the brink of insanity. Each waking moment was filled with thoughts of her. He couldn't get her out of his mind. And at night, his manhood and mind linked to betray him. Just a few minutes ago, if he had not awoken, his body would have commanded him to do what his conscious mind would not have accepted.

What made it all so difficult was that he knew she wanted him as badly as he wanted her, but still she stubbornly refused in her determination not to make love with him until he could offer more than just a passionate affair. That, he could not do. Not yet. Maybe not ever. Without a doubt he needed her, without a doubt he wanted her, but he was rational enough to know want and need were much different than love. He had never felt that emotion for any woman and he strongly doubted if he ever would. Women were too fickle. Why, Dionne herself was a classic example. It was just a little over a year ago that she had loved a man enough to let him give her a child without being married to him. And now she claimed to love him—or at least she thought she did. He could tell by the way she stole quick doe-eyed glances at him when she thought he wasn't looking. He wondered if she had looked at Jonathan's father the same way.

With those thoughts invading his mind, he rose from the bunk, taking care not to disturb Dionne, and slipped on his robe. The moon was bright and there was no need to light a candle. He poured himself a shot of whiskey and paced the room, now greatly disturbed. Why couldn't he put the image of Dionne and Louis Fairmount out of his mind?

Hearing Jonathan start to fret, Christopher stopped his pacing and gently patted the baby back to sleep. Unfortunately, even the baby was a sore spot with him. When he had first learned of their marriage, he had made it quite clear that he wanted no part of the child. But he'd had no idea that he would later bring Jonathan into the world, that without him the child would probably have never drawn a breath.

He did not have the audacity to believe he'd given the child life; only a far greater power could have done that. But, in a different sense of the word, he had given the child life as much as his real father had. Although Dionne did not know it, he felt a bond toward the child, a bond he could not deny. With a sharp pang of regret, Christopher realized he would give almost anything to see the little boy take his first steps, sail high on a swing, ride his first pony, and maybe even stand on the quarterdeck of his own ship—hell, if he were going to dream, he might as well dream big—or maybe even see him take the oath of office as the President of the United States. Yes, this little fellow was going to grow up to be a fine young man. And, unless he could admit to something he could not feel, he would not be around to see it happen.

Dionne struggled with her nightmare. It was late

afternoon. The sun seemed to be dropping into the sea as its magnificent dying embers painted the sky a brilliant crimson. It seemed the sea was afire. All of the crewmen of the *Blue Diamond* stood smartly at attention while one sailor played taps on his bugle and the Phillips Shipping Line banner was lowered to half mast. Christopher stood on the quarterdeck reading Ecclesiastes 3:1-8 from his grandmother's Bible. Dionne joined Jeannine at the ship's railing, and together they solemnly tossed the flowers one by one into the peaceful sea. But that was when the reality turned into the horrifying nightmare. As she started to walk away from the railing, she noticed a flower lying on the deck. Quickly retrieving it, she raised her hand to toss it overboard, along with the other flowers. At that moment, a skeleton with black eyeless sockets, wearing tattered shreds of clothing—how did she know the ghostly specter was Celeste?—grasped and held her in a death grip, then beckoned Christopher with her long, bony arms, and he walked toward her—it—mesmerized.

"Dionne, are you all right?" Christopher gently touched her shoulder.

She sat up with a start, taking deep wheezing breaths and grasping her chest with her hands as if that would prevent her heart from bursting through. Pitiful whimpering sounds came from her throat.

"Take it easy," he crooned softly, sitting down on the bunk and taking her into his arms. "You must have been having a bad dream."

Yes, yes, a dream! That's all it was, just a hideous dream. It took Dionne a few moments to come fully awake, but the nightmare had left her weak and trembling. Still breathing hard, she pulled herself from

Christopher's comforting arms and tried to assure him with a smile that she was all right.

"Do you want to talk about it?" he asked. His eyes searched her face in the flickering light, trying to reach into her thoughts.

She shook her head, her face pale and drawn. "I don't think so. Lucy—she was our cook at Desirade—always said if you told a dream before breakfast, it would come true . . . and I don't want to take the chance anything like that would happen. It was too horrible!"

He ducked his head so that she would not see his tolerant smile. It was surprising that anyone so intelligent could be so superstitious. But then, he hadn't been raised on that island as she had been.

His voice was low and comforting. "I remember when I was a small boy and whenever I had a bad dream, Grandmother always urged me to tell her about it. She said if you talked about the dream right then, you wouldn't have it anymore, that it would be out of your system for good. And she was right, because none of them ever came true."

Dionne needed no further urging. She laid her head on the comfortable nook where Christopher's arm met his shoulder. She began talking, slowly at first, then the words came rapidly as the dream became more vivid in her mind. "I've had this same dream for nights now, but I always managed to come awake before I could finish it. . . . But it always left me feeling frightened, like something was about to happen." She looked up at him. "And, Christopher, it is so strange. At the beginning, the dream is exactly like the actual memorial service that we held for the *Emerald Tempest* the other day. The playing of taps, your reading those beautiful verses from the Bible, and how Grand'mere and I tossed the flowers into the sea. Then, as I start to leave the deck, I see a flower lying there. I pick it up and walk toward the railing and toss it over with the rest. And always before I have awoken right at that precise point in my dream." She shuddered. "But not tonight." She then told him about the ghostly specter and the feeling that it was Celeste coming to claim both of them. She shuddered again, and despite her determination not to, she began to cry. "It was awful, simply awful!"

Lightly, Christopher fingered a loose tendril of hair on her cheek. His breath caught in his throat at how the moonlight shimmered on her long brown hair, making it look as though she were surrounded by an aureole.

"It was only a dream, my sweet. That's all, just a dream."

"But . . . I know it sounds ridiculous, but . . . I feel like it is a warning of some kind. Like something terrible is going to happen."

He cajoled softly, "Now, you know better than that. I've never given dreams a lot of thought, but it seems to me with us having that service the other day, the memory of the ship sinking . . . everything, it's bound to be preying on your mind."

"I suppose so, but I will be glad when this voyage is over and I feel solid land underneath my feet again." There was a spark of some indefinable emotion in her eyes as she looked at him. "Christopher, will you hold me in your arms until I go back to sleep? Please?" she added.

Even though his body felt like it was on fire with need and desire for her, he could not bring himself to deny her request. He gathered her into the fold of his arms and it was a long, long time before he was able to drift back into a restless sleep.

*   *   *

438

Christopher had warned them all that sailing through the Strait of Magellan would be wet, cold, and dangerous, but that it would be less perilous than sailing around the Horn during this time of the year. Winter was upon the Antarctic and constant storms made passage around Cape Horn extremely hazardous. But even though they had been forewarned, none of the passengers, not even using their wildest imagination, were prepared for the tempest that engulfed the *Blue Diamond*. No one, that is, except for Dionne. She had lived through such stormy seas, and before they were halfway through the Strait, she had been driven into a mindless terror.

Dionne did not know whether it was day or night as the tempest reigned supreme. The waves pounded and raged against the hull of the *Blue Diamond* until Dionne knew she was reliving a nightmare. No horizon was visible, for the sea blended into the clouds and an occasional low layer of cold foggy mist obscured even the topsails. Ice formed and caked on the portholes, and the inside of the ship became as cold as a tomb. Iron heaters were lit, but they only provided a small amount of warmth if a body stood right next to one. And the ship was crashing about so savagely such a feat was next to impossible unless one wanted to risk the danger of being thrown against the heater and being severely burned.

The farther they sailed into the Strait, the rougher and more wild the sea became. To Dionne the ship became a world unto itself, as it clawed through the crest of each wave, and then slammed down into the troughs. It seemed as though the ship were a small outpost adrift in the crashing elements of a churning, surging abyss. The seas grew wilder and the wind cruelly raked everything it could touch. Inside the ship the timbers creaked and moaned as the *Blue Diamond* tossed upon this seething mass between sea and cloud. And, at times, it seemed she would break apart under the crushing blows of the rampant sea.

Christopher came into the cabin, splayed his legs to maintain his balance, and huddled close to the stove. Even though the room was cold, it seemed almost tropical after the howling maelstrom outside. The room was dark except for the rosy glow reflecting from the heater. One quick glance about told him the bunk was empty as was the cabin, and he realized Dionne must have gone to his grandmother's cabin to ride out the passage with her. As soon as he had warmed up, he would go check how they were faring. They were not through the Strait yet but the worst was over. Navigation was always so difficult up to this point that he preferred to man the helm himself, but now Barney and the other helmsman were perfectly capable of seeing the ship through.

Christopher was just beginning to feel thawed out when he detected a strange noise. Cocking his head, he listened carefully, then to his surprise, he realized it was Jonathan crying. And was that Katie whining? But how was that possible? They were in his grandmother's cabin, weren't they? Striding quickly to the cradle, Christopher reached inside but the mattress was smooth. Then he heard the cry again and he turned his gaze to a darkened corner. Lighting a lamp, he hurried to the corner and tugged at a pile of quilts and blankets. To his surprise Dionne sat huddled next to Katie, holding a squirming Jonathan in her arms.

"Dionne! Wha—what in the world are you doing there?" He secured the lamp in the fixture on the wall and took both her and the baby in his arms.

She clutched frantically at his shirt and babbled almost incoherently, "We're in the eye, aren't we? Oh, God! The worst is yet to come! Oh, Christopher! It's just like it happened before! Your father came down to the cabins and prepared us for the storm still to come." Her eyes widened hysterically. "But . . . Christopher . . . if we end in the sea . . . it's so cold . . . Jonathan will not stand a chance of surviving! Oh, God! Please save our baby!"

Christopher firmly grasped Dionne by her shoulders. Lines creased his brow as he realized she was experiencing the horrors of that night when the *Emerald Tempest* had sunk. "Dionne, no, it's not like before. We are not in a hurricane. It really isn't even a storm. The Strait is always a rough crossing, but it isn't a storm. Why, when I came in the cabin, I could even see stars shining."

"So could I that night!" she sobbed fiercely. "But then it quickly closed around us and became worse than we ever thought possible!" Stark terror gleamed from her eyes. "Oh, Christopher, make for land! Please, it's our only chance. It isn't me so much, but Jonathan has never had a chance to live yet!"

Christopher realized he would never be able to reason with her as hysterical as she was. Words would never comfort her. She would have to see the truth for herself before she could even begin to calm down. "Here, let me take Jonathan."

"No, no, I'm his mother!" She clutched the child close to her breast, making him cry harder.

"But I am stronger than you," he reasoned gently. "I can take him to a safe place. Trust me, Dionne, trust me." Feeling her relax her grip on the baby, Christopher continued to speak in a slow, easy voice. "I am going to take him to safety, then I'm coming back after you. Do you understand?"

Something cold and fearful gripped Dionne's heart and sent a shivery spasm through her body. She clung to the end of the bunk for support, fearing her knees would give way.

"Do you understand me, Dionne?" he repeated with cool authority.

Although her eyes were glazed with terror, she nodded.

He quickly wrapped a quilt around the squalling child and started outside. But he paused by the door. Knowing the hysterical state Dionne was in, Christopher figured there was no telling what she might try to do. Not wanting to, but feeling he must for her own good, he threw the latch on the outside of the door, locking her inside. He hurried to Berta and Josey's cabin, placing the child in their care with as few explanations as possible, then he rushed back to their cabin. He noted with relief that the closer the ship came to the end of the Strait, the calmer the sea and the clearer the sky.

The moment Christopher unlatched the door, Dionne accused vehemently, "You locked me inside to drown!" She began pummeling his chest with her fists. "Where is Jonathan? Where is my baby?"

"Damn it, the ship is not about to sink and you're not going to drown!" Christopher grasped her wrists and, impervious to the cold, threw her bodily over his shoulder and marched outside. Slinging her from his shoulder, he grasped her chin in a viselike grip and forced her to look up at the western sky, where it was filled with thousands of twinkling stars.

"Now, does that look like a hurricane to you?" he bellowed. He could slowly feel the resistance drain from her body as she stared with confusion at the sky.

442

"But . . . what happened to the storm?" she asked, confused. "We should be in the eye."

Christopher wrapped his arms tightly around her, and his voice was low and smooth, "That's what I tried to explain to everyone before we started through the Strait." Feeling her shiver, he gently swooped her into his arms, carried her back inside the cabin, and placed her gently on the bunk. "The passage is always rough, but during the winter the Antarctic winds whip through the Strait with gale force, and with the passage so narrow, it churns the sea more than it normally would. There really never was a storm. It's just winter, and the seas are naturally rough."

Still disconcerted, Dionne mumbled, "Winter? It isn't winter, it is summer. But why is it so cold?"

"Not down here, sweetheart. We're almost at the bottom of the world and everything is turned upside down, seasons and all."

"And we're really going to be safe? The ship is not going to sink?" She sat up and hugged her knees with her arms.

"We're safe, and the ship is not about to sink," he stated with firm resolve.

Dionne did not know whether to laugh or to cry. Everything was so confusing. It was like a terrible nightmare that continued and continued until one did not know when the nightmare ended and reality began. Christopher held out his arms to her and she flung herself into them.

"I was so frightened," she sobbed. "It seemed as though everything was happening all over again. But this time there was Jonathan. . . ." She pulled from his embrace and stared at him fearfully. "Where is Jonathan?"

"He's in with Berta and Josey. They'll take good care

of him. But right now, I don't want you worrying about anyone or anything. I just want you to lie here and try to relax."

"Please, Christopher," she murmured softly, "please don't leave me alone."

"I have no intention of leaving you. I am half frozen to death and you are, too. There is no telling how long you huddled in that damp corner." By the tone of her voice, he realized her hysteria had ended and that she was thinking rationally again.

Her eyes widened, regret sweeping over her. "Oh, no! Then Jonathan will get sick!"

"Now, I've already told you he is fine. Berta and Josey will take good care of him."

"But . . . what if he gets hungry?"

"I thought Grandmother told me Josey nurses him once a day to keep her milk flowing—just in case something happened to yours."

"Yes, but . . ."

"Then hush. I know you are a good mother, but quit worrying about him. He will be fine!" Christopher retrieved the quilts and spread them over the bunk, then stripped off his sodden clothing. A moment later he slid shivering into bed beside her. They burrowed their heads beneath the covers so that their breath would help warm the bed.

She snuggled close to him, wincing at how cold he felt. Gratefully, he accepted her efforts, drawing her even nearer as he shook from the cold.

They lay for a long time with arms entwined before Christopher stopped shaking and Dionne could feel a warmth running through her veins instead of the icy chill that had been so prevalent.

Dionne's teeth tugged at her bottom lip as her worries began to mount. What would Christopher

444

think of her? Would he believe her to be a mindless imbecile who teetered on the brink of insanity? What sane person would have behaved as she had? She had to speak to him about her actions, but what would she say?

"C—Christopher," she began hesitantly. "I can't explain my behavior. I don't know what happened to me. I suppose I was so frightened. . . ."

"You don't have to explain anything to me. The entire thing is all my fault." His voice was laced with bitterness and remorse. "I know what you went through when the *Emerald Tempest* sank, yet when we hit the Strait of Magellan, I never stopped to think that you would associate the hurricane with the Strait's rough seas. I'm sorry I made you suffer so needlessly. If only I had explained better, it would have never happened."

"But it wasn't your fault! Now that it's over and I can think about it rationally, passing through the Strait was like setting a match to a powder keg. It was bound to happen." Her voice was shakier than she would have liked as she admitted, "I have been frightened since the first day we sailed from New Orleans. No, to be truthful, the moment I set foot on board this ship, I knew I was terrified. That's why I've been staying in the cabin so much of the time. In fact, I was afraid you would notice how much I have been staying inside and say something about it."

He raised himself on one arm and studied her quietly for a moment. There was enough light to see her, but not enough light to read her expression. He took a deep breath, deciding he might as well speak his mind now and get it over with. "How could I notice if you were on the deck or not? If you are there I see you; if you're not I still see you. I can't get you out of my mind. I have lain here beside you each night and at times it felt as though my guts were actually ripping out I wanted you so badly."

"Even feeling like that, you still willingly shared your bed with me?"

"Yes, even though I was miserable, I still wanted to be near you. But you have no idea how many times I was tempted to string a hammock across the cabin just so I could get a decent night's sleep. This has been torture for me, Dionne. And, I'll be honest with you. I cannot take it much longer!"

"Why didn't you tell me?"

"What good would it have done? You stated your feelings very bluntly back in New Orleans, and every night you have made it clear that you haven't changed your mind."

Dionne reached out one hand to gently brush away a strand of hair that caressed his cheek. She felt as if she were standing in the middle of a crossroads without knowing which way to go. One road would lead to nowhere, and the other would take her to her heart's desire. But if she chose the wrong road, there would be no turning back. Perhaps she had been wrong in refusing Christopher's lovemaking until she was confident of his love. Perhaps his need for her was enough right now. He was a strong, arrogant man and maybe, just maybe, he had to need and want something before he could ever love it. If this were not so, what did she have to lose? The happiest moments in her life had been spent in his arms. And perhaps, just perhaps, she needed a little happiness herself.

"W—what if I told you I have changed my mind again?" she asked shyly.

His eyes boldly raked her and the beginning of a smile tipped the corners of his mouth. "I'd say it was about damned time!" With that, his hands tightened in her hair and his mouth found hers with a passion she had not thought possible.

Dionne parted her lips for him eagerly as she felt the tip of his tongue begin to seek her out, then shoot deep inside her questing mouth to explore the honey-nectar within as though he had never known it before. Tenderly, gently, his tongue caressed hers, twining hesitantly at first, then swirling with a more insisting pressure when he felt her eager response to his tentative onslaught.

Christopher's hands slipped beneath the feminine nightgown to the satin-soft skin that it concealed, then with a powerful rent, he ripped the delicate fabric so that he could caress her skin without any interference. His fingers moved upon her flesh, trailing down her face and throat and soft shoulders to her breasts, where they lingered tantalizingly. Time flew by but they paid it no heed, for their world was timeless, endless as the sea and sky. Dionne's nipples flushed and hardened to taut little peaks. He lowered his head and kissed them both lightly, and to his delight, tiny droplets of milk appeared on each taut peak. With the very tip of his tongue, he tasted her and sighed heavily, wistfully, for the ambrosia was not meant for him but for another. His lips reluctantly left the engorged peaks, and he was content to gently nibble and lovingly bite the white globes surrounding the dusky nipples.

Dionne lost her hands in his shaggy mane of hair as she urged him on with tiny moans of pleasure and drew him closer against the full mounds that swelled upon her chest. His magic hands played her entire body as a master musician elicits a haunting melody from a finely crafted instrument.

He rested himself on one elbow, drawing her beneath him. His penetration was slow and sure, filling her with intense, spreading pleasure, filling her completely. Her breath caught deep within her throat, her fingers biting into his powerful arms to steady her reeling world. But it could not be done. The turbulence was inside, an ancient uncontrollable thing that thundered in her blood with an intoxicating beat.

Their loins throbbed in harmony to a primitive never-to-be-forgotten rhythm.

She moaned aloud with erotic pleasure as he took her fiercely and she locked her legs around his back to draw him even farther into herself. Down, down he plunged, faster and faster, until she arched her hips against him and dug her nails into his flesh.

"Oh, Christopher!" she gasped raggedly, then for one fleeting moment, she ceased to breathe at all.

Christopher plummeted one last time and they became fused, inseparable as they soared on lofty wings of ecstasy.

Later, much later, as Dionne gave soft mews of contentment, Christopher nuzzled kisses on the tender part of her neck right behind her ear.

"I'll give you all night to stop doing that," she murmured huskily.

"Like it?"

"Mmm hmm."

"There's only a couple more hours of night left."

She sighed with disappointment. "How do you know?"

He continued to kiss her neck, only by this time he had reached the delicate hollow of her throat. "I don't, not for sure, but I hope we have at least a couple more hours before morning."

"Why?" she teased as she boldly ran her hand down and caressed the taut muscles of his buttocks.

"Because I intend to have you again . . . and again . . . and again. And just so you will know my full intentions, I will not mention stringing that damned hammock again, nor will I walk around with a pain in my loins from wanting you."

She gave a throaty laugh. "Is that a threat?"

"No, madame, it is a promise—a promise I intend to keep. And I will begin . . . right . . . now! . . ." He gently lowered his lips to hers.

Dionne did not answer. She didn't need to. All she had to do was take him eagerly into her arms.

Chapter Thirty

Louis could feel the bile rising in his throat as he slipped inside their tent. As usual, Celeste was piled in the middle of the bed, fast asleep. Her lips were slack and open, and little snoring sounds came from both her mouth and nose. His lips curled with contempt. All she ever did was sleep, nag, and complain. The bitch! Oh, well, he shrugged indifferently as a lewd expression slid over his features. If this latest scheme of his did not pan out, he could always open a flophouse and use Celeste as his star attraction. With a little bit of opium, she would cooperate. At least he would be assured of keeping food on the table and a roof over his head—it might only be canvas, but at least it would be a roof.

He chuckled wryly to himself. Perhaps that's what he should have been doing all along instead of wearing his butt out at the poker tables. Maybe his personal gold mine lay in the little golden thatch between Celeste's legs. He stroked his chin thoughtfully. It wasn't a bad idea. If push came to shove and as a last resort, he would have no qualms about it. So what if Celeste was his wife? He could always get another if he wanted one.

Then, Louis looked around the tent and snorted with disgust. How in the hell had he managed to get himself in a predicament like this? Saddled with a wife he never wanted, and living in filth and squalor. But it was all about to change. He was going to make it change. He had been waiting too long on the money from the sale of Desirade. Waiting on the money, relying on it, when more than likely that son of a bitch had sold it, pocketed the money, and taken off for parts unknown. If he ever got out of this hellhole, he'd track that so-called friend of his down and make him wish he had never been born. Oh, there were ways to torture a man, and he would make the bastard pay dearly.

Seeing Celeste begin to stir, he stood, tossed a package on the rumpled bed where she lay, and forced excitement into his voice. "Wake up, Celeste. I have bought you a pretty present, babe!"

She came awake instantly, but it took her a few moments to focus her eyes. Then her lips twisted into a cynical grimace. "Where have you been? It's been three days and nights since I've seen you!"

Louis chuckled reprovingly. "I've been working. Now don't give me a hard time, babe. I want you to try on your present and see if it fits."

"What is it?" she asked while getting to her feet and pushing her badly tangled hair from her forehead.

"It's a pretty new dress, made especially for you!" Louis said calmly, not the least bit perturbed by the angry glare she threw at him.

"I never thought I'd live to see the day that I would turn my nose up at a new dress, but quite frankly, Louis, I would rather have a big juicy steak. I haven't had a bite to eat since yesterday." Even though she complained, Celeste eagerly began ripping open the package. "Where did you get the money? Don't tell me you actually won a hand of poker for a change?" she mumbled sarcastically.

"Oh, shut up and try on the dress!" He angrily tossed his hat onto the cluttered table and stretched out on the bed, propping his hands behind his head.

452

Celeste's eyes widened as she gaped in disbelief at the dress. It was made from black satin and trimmed with flouncy red lace, and the neck plunged all the way to the waistline. "Louis! Do you really expect me to wear this . . . thing? Why, it looks like it came directly from a whore's back!"

"Damn, is that all you can do?" he ranted angrily. "Nag and complain! That's all I ever hear out of you anymore and I am getting damned tired of it!"

"What else can you expect me to do?" Tears filled her eyes and her bottom lip protruded into a pout. "I don't like to live like this." Wrinkling her nose, she surveyed the tent with disgust. It contained an iron heater, a table cluttered with dirty tin dishes, a wooden box to store their clothing, and an old metal bed that was in dire need of a change of linens.

Bolting upright, he kicked at a pile of debris with his foot. "It wouldn't be so bad if you would get off your lazy butt and clean up around here once in a while. But hell, no! All you can do is lie in the middle of the bed like the queen of some goddamned island and expect an army of servants to come marching in and and wait on you hand and foot!"

Tossing her head with anger, Celeste placed her hands akimbo and taunted contemptuously, "Need I remind you that at one time I was almost queen of an island. . . . At least I was treated with love and respect, and I had an army of servants . . . and I didn't have to live in a hovel like this! When we first came here it was bad enough to have to live in that dreary hotel across from that noisy saloon you just had to spend all of my money and buy . . ."

Louis jumped out of bed with a flying leap and grasped Celeste roughly by her upper arms. He spoke through gritted teeth, "Just one word out of you about me losing the San Francisco, and so help me God, I'll

453

make you wish you hadn't!"

The San Francisco Saloon and Gambling Casino had been his pride and joy, but a slick double-dealing dude had moved in, and before he even realized what was happening, the dude had won the San Francisco, lock, stock, and barrel.

His blue eyes shifted, then they glinted like cold steel as he too surveyed the squalor in which they now lived. "I had a run of bad luck, babe, but it's over now." Smiling coldly, he released Celeste then and tapped his shoulder. "Lady Luck is sitting right there, and I have a feeling there is where she's going to stay for a long time," he boasted.

Celeste had heard this same story before. "What makes you say that?"

Louis pulled a thick wad of bills from his pocket, then tossed a bag of gold dust onto the bed. He said nothing about the gambling markers he had in his other pocket. "This makes me say it, babe." He grinned at the way her eyes lit up. "We are going to parlay this money into a small fortune. We'll have to start small, but at least I have a stake again. I bought the big tent that's next door to us, ordered a couple of kegs of beer, a case of whiskey, and a round felt-covered table. You and I are opening for business tonight."

"Y—you and I?"

"Yes. I figure with you wearing that dress and Lady Luck riding on my shoulder, we can't lose." Louis chuckled as he observed her confusion.

"But . . . I thought you said you did not want me around the gambling tables?"

"That was then, babe, this is now," he said without showing an ounce of remorse. "We have to play this game to win, and although Lady Luck is on my side right now, she still needs all the help she can get. With you wearing that dress and serving drinks and making

454

the men think about things other than their cards, it will be impossible for us to lose." A slow teasing grin spread swiftly across his face as he gave her a lingering appraisal. He caught Celeste by the hand and pulled her roughly to him. "Come here, woman. I've got to have some sleep, but first I need some loving." Then his lips came down hard against hers.

Excitement reigned supreme on the *Blue Diamond* as she sailed through the Golden Gate channel in the early light of dawn and cautiously made her way into San Francisco Bay. Christopher carefully maneuvered the *Blue Diamond* past the hundreds of ships that had been abandoned but still remained anchored, floating up and down listlessly as the waves slapped against their empty hulls. Many abandoned ships had sunk and their jutting masts reached into the skyline like skeletons clawing at the blue, cloudless sky.

Dionne's gaze fastened on a clipper ship leaving the harbor, which could have been the sister ship to the *Blue Diamond.* After questioning a crewman who was not busy, she learned the ship was the *Flying Cloud,* the ship that had broken all records on her maiden voyage from New York to San Francisco, taking only eighty-nine days.

The women stood out of harm's way of the crewmen performing their various duties, watching with interest all the scurrying activity on the wharf. The wharf itself was a mass of small crude buildings and sprawled along deeply rutted roads in a close haphazard jumble. Although being from New Orleans and accustomed to seeing all walks of life, they saw people of every nationality crowding the area: Irishmen, Englishmen, Frenchmen, Spaniards, Germans, Chinese, and an occasional Negro. A hubbub of voices raised in every language imaginable. It was all so exciting!

They had each repacked one trunk and these had been stacked close to where the gangplank would be placed so that they could disembark. Christopher had decided earlier to leave Barney in charge of the ship so that he could accompany the women to a hotel. From past experience, he felt it was not safe for decent women to be on the streets without the protection of a man. He also wanted to make sure they were all safely settled in before he attended to any other business.

It had been well over a year since Christopher had last been in the city and he was not sure what to expect. It had been little more than a sprawling slum then, and from what he had been able to see from the ship, it had not changed much except to grow into an even larger slum, now hosting a population of nearly twenty-five thousand inhabitants. Numerous multi-storied buildings now dotted the skyline, whereas before there had only been row upon row of tents and ramshackle, rough-timbered buildings.

Soon, they were all seated in a carriage and their trunks had been loaded onto a dray that would follow behind them. Christopher sat beside the driver, then Jeannine and Dionne holding Jonathan sat in the middle seat, and Berta and Josey sat in the rear.

After being accustomed to the sounds of the sea, of the winds filling the sails, and of the voices on board the ship, everything seemed so much louder, almost magnified. The clatter of horses' hooves and carriage wheels, the pounding of hammers as newly constructed buildings continued to rise, and the babble of all the voices in so many different languages seemed to be almost overwhelming.

Dionne's eyes were wide with wonder as they rode down the street. She had never seen anything like this before. It seemed to her that almost every other building was a saloon, and even more surprising, they were all apparently full, although the boarded walkways teemed with people from all walks of life. In her opinion, San Francisco was dreadful!

Hordes of grimy, unshaven men filled the streets; hundreds, possibly even thousands, of disillusioned men had swarmed to the golden coast where riches were so plentiful that gold could be plucked from the ground as easily as picking an apple from a tree. Unfortunately, it had been a myth. Oh, there was gold aplenty, but it required hard back-breaking work and it also required a bit of Lady Luck. Now, so many would-be miners wandered around dazed, destitute, their dreams shattered, their hopes crushed, and their money long gone. Most of the men only owned the clothing they wore on their backs. The few who had valuable possessions soon bartered them away just to survive. It was a hard and difficult time for most of San Francisco's inhabitants.

Even Jeannine was dismayed by the squalid surroundings. Leaning forward in the carriage, she tapped Christopher on his shoulder. When he turned to see what she wanted, she gestured helplessly. "Is—is it all like this?"

He patted her hand reassuringly and smiled. "It was the last time I was here, but don't worry. I have talked with other ships' captains and other people who have been here, and they told me there are now several fairly nice residential areas up in the hills." His mouth then settled into a grim line. "Of course, how long we are here will depend on what I find when I go to the warehouses. But I figure it will take at least a month or two. If I see it will take longer than that, I will check into the possibility of obtaining a house."

Dionne spoke up. "You're not going to the warehouses today, are you?"

"Yes, in fact, as soon as I get all of you settled in. I want to catch Nicholas before he gets wind that I am in town."

Jeannine glanced around at all the shanties and hovels that lined the street, and she shuddered. "If the hotel you are taking us to looks anything like . . . these buildings, I want you to instruct the driver to turn right around and carry us back to the ship. The quarters there are small and a little cramped, but at least they are clean!"

Christopher caught Dionne's eyes and winked. He pointed to a three-storied building. "Look, Grandmother, this looks like a suitable hotel for us," he said in a serious voice.

She craned her head. "Where?"

"Right there. See the name on the front? It's called Dirty Sally's." He chuckled. "Do you think she would have rooms suitable for us? Without a doubt, it would certainly be interesting."

Jeannine stared at the upper floors as they passed by. Four prostitutes clad in revealing nightgowns and wrappers hung out the windows, calling to the men on the street, urging them to come up and see them.

She gasped and immediately began banging the driver on his back with her cane, not hard enough to hurt, but hard enough to get his attention. "Driver, take us back to the ship this instant. Turn this carriage around right now!"

Christopher guffawed and instructed the driver to continue on to the Golden Gate Hotel. Then he told his grandmother that he had only been teasing.

"Well, I should hope so!" Then she began laughing. "On second thought, Dirty Sally's might have been fun. Dionne, couldn't you just see the expressions on my friends' faces if I told them we had stayed at a place like that! Why, more than likely, I would be drummed out of the sewing circle."

Dionne clamped a hand over her mouth to suppress a giggle. She could just imagine how they would react. Most of the women were so stone-faced and somber, it was almost pitiful. So many of the fine upstanding women in New Orleans had never even seen a place like Dirty Sally's, at least not that they would admit. From what she'd been able to gather from the sewing circle, the less they knew about that particular side of life, the better they liked it. Even though, Dionne figured, most of the women's husbands kept mistresses on the side and in a grand fashion.

Her eyes narrowed as she stared at the back of Christopher's neck. She wondered how many mistresses he'd had in his lifetime. Then she swore silently that as long as they were married, he would never have a reason to seek out another woman. This voyage had opened her eyes. It had been a dreadful mistake to refuse to have an intimate relationship with him. Not only had she cheated him, but she had cheated herself as well. The second half of the voyage had been sheer heaven. Delightful shivers ran all over her just thinking about all the nights they had lain in each other's arms. Even though he had never actually said the words "I love you," he made her feel loved and cherished, and there was a certain look in his eyes that had never been there before.

But she still had not told him about Jonathan. He was so worried over this business with Nicholas, and yes, even admittedly angry at himself for trusting the man with so much responsibility, that she had not wanted to place any additional burdens on him. No, she reluctantly admitted to herself, that was not entirely true. There was still a nagging fear that he would not believe her and that all the wonderful happiness they had shared recently would come to an end. But he would have to be told soon. She could not delay it much longer.

Dionne had been so lost in thought that she blinked in amazement when the carriage pulled to a rolling stop. Were they at the hotel already? Then, she blinked once more. All of the sordid little hovels and shanties had been left behind and they were now in a much nicer district. After quickly counting the windows, Dionne realized the hotel towered five stories tall, and not only that, it was extremely respectable in appearance. Although the bricks presented a false front, it was still the most elegant building that she'd seen in all of San Francisco. Potted plants stood beside the door, and the wide front veranda was spotlessly clean.

Christopher glanced at his grandmother and grinned. "Do you think this will be suitable enough, Grandmother?"

She gave him a scolding look and pursed her lips. "You knew this hotel was here all along! You scamp, you were deliberately trying to frighten us."

"Well," he admitted sheepishly, "a business associate of mine in New Orleans told me he was building this hotel, but for a while there, after all those shanties we passed, I was beginning to worry." He stepped down from the carriage and helped his grandmother down, then took Jonathan from Dionne's arms and passed him back to Berta, who was sitting in the far back seat with Josey. He then grasped Dionne by her waist, his hands gently squeezing, and lifted her to the ground. And after helping Berta and Josey too, he said, "Let's get registered and settled in. I don't know about you ladies, but I, for one, am looking forward to soaking in a hot bath."

Dionne moaned dreamily. "Yes, a hot bath. That sounds heavenly to me!" After bathing from a small wash pan for the past two months, she was also eager to sit in a tub of steaming hot water.

Christopher and his entourage entered the hotel, and after mentioning he was a good friend of the owner, he was able to obtain a suite of rooms on the lower floor so that his grandmother would not have to struggle with the stairway. In a matter of minutes, they were shown to their rooms and they began the process of settling in.

Later, Dionne reclined leisurely in the huge over-sized brass bathtub, closed her eyes, and gave a long, contented sigh. Josey had already given Jonathan his bath and had put him down in her room for a long nap, and she felt free to remain in the bathtub for hours if she so chose. Filling the sponge with water, she raised it and gently squeezed, allowing the hot water to splash in rivulets on her breasts. It felt divine.

"I am an excellent back washer," Christopher said, breaking the silence that abounded in the room.

Startled, Dionne quickly opened her eyes to see Christopher leaning indolently against the door frame, his arms folded and a naughty grin on his face.

"I didn't hear you come in."

"I know, I didn't want you to hear me. I had planned to sneak up behind you, but when I saw you were armed with that sponge, I didn't want to take the chance of startling you and getting that thing thrown in my face."

"I wouldn't do that," she replied laughingly.

Christopher closed the door and locked it, then strolled casually toward her, unfastened his shirt, and pulled it over his head. "Oh, sure I know you wouldn't. But I have always felt that a man can't be too careful." He leaned over and his lips feather-touched hers with a tantalizing kiss. He then sat on a small chair and began removing his boots.

"What are you doing?"

He stood and unbuttoned his trousers. "What does it look like I am doing?" he whispered huskily. "I am getting ready to take a bath."

Dionne's eyes widened in mock surprise. "A bath? Where?" As her gaze fastened on his manhood, she blushed.

He craned his head, staring at the bathtub she was in. "Why, right here."

"With me?"

"Uh huh, that's exactly what I had in mind."

"Will we both fit?"

He tested the water with his toe and stepped in. "Madame, I have always heard, where there is a will, there is definitely a way, and we are just about to put that old saying to the supreme test."

Dionne quickly scooted up in the tub to make room for him at the foot. Christopher sat down, oblivious to the water that sloshed over the sides, and stretched out his long legs, sliding them on either side of her hips along the walls of the tubs.

"Now, stretch your legs out and place your feet on top of my legs." He grinned after she complied with his request. "Well, how about that! We do fit!" A tingling of excitement raged through them as his fingers trailed sensually up and down her legs.

With a wicked gleam in her eyes, Dionne traced her lips with the tip of her tongue. She lifted one foot and began smoothing it over his muscular thigh, allowing it to almost reach his masculinity before sliding it back over the length of his thigh. It only took a few strokes before his masculinity began to swell.

He chuckled devilishly. "You are not playing fair."

"You should know by now I never play fair," Dionne teased. "Besides, you are the one who invited yourself to share my bath. So, you'll simply have to face the consequences."

"Do you want me to leave?" he murmured thickly. The expression on his face told Dionne he had no intention of leaving the tub.

She slowly shook her head. "Not on your life."

Water continued to slosh over the sides of the tub as Christopher raised one foot and tweaked a dusty nipple with his first two toes.

Chilly-bumps popped out all over her satiny soft shoulders and breasts as she watched his toes pay homage as his fingers and lips had done many times in the past. A naughty smirk spread across her face as she raised her foot and slowly trailed her toe down the rapidly growing shaft of his manhood.

"Madame, do you have any idea what you are doing to me?" he asked in a raspy whisper.

Dionne's desire was raging out of control too. She wet her bottom lip before she answered, "I certainly hope so." Then, she frowned, and her breath came in ragged gasps. "But we're so tangled up now . . . I'm not sure how we'll manage to do anything about it."

Christopher grasped her waist with his strong hands and pulled her toward him. "If that is what's worrying you, don't. I'm a genius. I have it all figured out."

He inched slightly down in the tub and guided her feet around his waist. He reclaimed her waist with his hands, positioned her over him, then lowered her onto his throbbing shaft.

Dionne's eyes widened. Her body trembled, her heart raced, her breath caught, and warm, delicious tremors exhilarated throughout her body. "Oooh!" she moaned softly. Her eyes were half closed, glazed with passion, her lips parted with soft, gasping breaths.

Christopher watched her eyes close and her head fall back, revealing the pulsating vein in the hollow of her throat. The muscles in his neck and arms corded and grew taut as his passion intensified. His hands guided Dionne in a slow, circular motion. Their bodies thrust with a sensual, rhythmic tempo. Over and over, he guided her body toward him, oblivious to the churning, sloshing bath water.

Rhythmically, he thrust into her, stroking the velvet softness of her, pillaging her womanhood, shattering their senses to the very depths of their souls. Christopher was a virile and lasting man, and Dionne was woman enough to step in unison, to match his vigor equally.

Their burning release came simultaneously, tumultuously, as the heady rush of ecstasy washed through them like a frothing tidal wave, lifting, rushing, soaring. Fulfillment poured forth, bathing their souls with satisfaction.

Later, as they sat over a hearty meal that Christopher had ordered earlier, there was a knock on the connecting door.

Berta called from the other side. "Is it all right if I come in?"

"Yes, Berta. Come on in," Dionne called out.

"I just wanted to come in here and get your dirty clothes. I asked at the desk where me and Josey could do some laundry and the man said to gather up what we needed to have washed and he would send for a Chinese laundryman to fetch 'em." Her eyes widened wondrously. "I'll declare, Missus Dionne, I ain't never heard of no such thing in my life. Why, imagine a man a-doing laundry!"

She walked into the bathing room to gather the clothes in there, and Dionne and Christopher grinned sheepishly to one another as they heard her exclaim loudly. "Good Lord!" Then she hurried out. "Missus

Dionne, I gotta go fetch that man at the desk. There must be a hole in that bathtub 'cause there's water all over the floor!"

Christopher stopped her. "No, wait, Berta. There's no hole in the tub."

"But there has to be. There's enough water on that floor to float your boat."

"Trust me, Berta. There's no hole in the tub," he repeated solemnly, trying to ignore Dionne's laughter as she concealed her face behind her napkin.

Berta folded her arms stubbornly. "Then do you want to tell me how come all that water got on the floor?" She noticed the satisfied gleam on Christopher's face and the rosy blush that appeared on Dionne's face when she lowered the napkin. Berta threw her hands up in the air and laughed. "Oh, Lordy, never mind. I *knows* how that water got on the floor. Don't knows how you managed it, but I *knows* how it got there!" She continued to laugh as she disappeared through the doorway.

Christopher walked around the table and took Dionne into his arms. "I hate to, my sweet, but I have to be going now. I shouldn't have stayed as long as I did, but under the circumstances, I'm certainly not sorry."

"Neither am I," she whispered tenderly.

"Don't look at me like that or I'll never get out of here," he murmured huskily. Then he took a deep breath to calm his senses. "I have to go . . . and in fact, I doubt if I'll be back tonight. I may just sleep on the ship. But I definitely want to try and catch Nicholas before he hears I am in town, before he has a chance to lose or doctor the records that contain the warehouses' inventory. I told Grandmother I would arrange for a carriage to take her out to her friend's house this afternoon, because she's real eager to see her. If you like, why don't you and Jonathan go with her and maybe even spend the night out there? I'm sure they will invite you."

"No," she said thoughtfully. "I think I'll stay here with Jonathan and relax, and just play with him. Besides, I am sort of tired."

"Well, all right," he said reluctantly. Even though they were in a nice hotel, there were too many woman-hungry men roaming around to suit him. "Be sure and stay inside, though, and keep the door locked. I'll instruct the man at the desk to send your meals to the room, but make sure he identifies himself before you open the door," he cautioned.

"We will be just fine," Dionne said as she walked with him to the door.

Christopher leaned over and kissed her gently. "I'll see you tomorrow."

"Tomorrow," she whispered after she closed the door and locked it. "Yes, if you see Nicholas tonight, I think maybe tomorrow will be the perfect time to tell you about your son."

Chapter Thirty-One

Louis wadded his best ruffled shirt into a tight ball and threw it at Celeste as hard as he could. "How in the hell do you expect me to wear this goddamn filthy rag tonight? I told you before I went to sleep a while ago that I needed a clean shirt, and what in the hell do you do? You sit on your lazy butt all goddamn day long, then expect me to wear that filthy piece of shit!"

Celeste threw the shirt back at him and spat angrily, "Don't curse at me, you . . . red-neck bastard!" She'd had enough of the ugly way he talked to her, the mean way he treated her, and enough of this squalid little hovel. But most of all, she was sick and tired of him. She had been thinking about leaving for a long time now. All she wanted to do was to go home, to try to make a new life for herself and forget that Louis Fairmount ever existed.

Louis was looking for a fight. "What did you call me?" his voice cut through gritted teeth.

"I called you a red-neck bastard! And that's all you are! Why, the way you strut around, pretending to be something you're not, makes me sick to my stomach." She tossed her head defiantly. "All those things you told me about coming from a fine Georgia family were nothing but lies!"

"Don't you dare call me a liar, you little bitch!" He

clenched his hands into tight fists.

She ignored his warning and sneered contemptuously. "But that's all you are, just a dirty rotten liar! And I've known the truth about you before you ever lost the San Francisco Saloon. There was a customer—a man—from the same county as you, who didn't take your cheating too kindly. When he found out I was your wife, he was extremely eager to tell me all about your sordid past. He told me that your grandfather was nothing but a poor Georgia sharecropper . . ."

"You better shut your damned mouth!" Louis ordered warningly, beginning to move toward her menacingly.

". . . and your mother was the town slut . . . a cheap whore! And, in my opinion, that makes you nothing but a common Georgia cracker!" She continued to taunt him. "Tell me, Louis, where did you get the name Fairmount? Did you steal that name the way you have everything else? I inherited a fortune and you've stolen it from me! You let all that money run through your hands just like water, playing the big important man, buying every broken-down beggar a drink, throwing lavish parties, gambling—did I say gambling? You can't even do that! What you call gambling is dealing out the cards, calling everybody's bets, then losing the pot to someone else. That's all you are, Louis, a loser. Nothing but a low-down lying, no-good Georgia cracker loser . . ."

Louis grabbed Celeste's dress front, roughly slung her around, and threw her on the bed, then fell on top of her. She fought, clawing and kicking, but he was too strong. He grabbed her flailing hands and arms, forcing her onto her stomach, then pinioned her against the bed with his knee.

"You listen to me, woman," he snarled, wrapping his hand in her hair and viciously yanking her head back so that she could see his face. "I won't have any goddamn bitch talking to me like that! Remember, you promised to love, honor, and obey me. I don't give a frigging damn about the love but, by God, you will honor me! You won't ever call me a bastard or a . . ."

Even though he had obviously overpowered Celeste, she was too angry and too foolish to keep her mouth shut.

She worked saliva to the front of her mouth and spat in his face. "Honor you? How can I honor a son of a whore? A lying bastard? A sorry, no-good Georgia cracker bastard!"

Louis's face blanched, then a demonic rage swept over him and his face contorted into an ugly mask. "You don't have sense enough to keep your goddamn mouth shut, do you, bitch? I think maybe you want some sense beat into you. Well, I'm just the man to do it!" Celeste had made him furious before, but never like this.

He whipped off his leather belt and quickly bound her hands together, then flipped her onto her back. All the time, Celeste was screaming and cursing at him at the top of her lungs while continuing to kick with her feet. He thrust his knee roughly into her chest, right beneath her breastbone, and applied his weight until she began to gasp for breath. Then with an open hand, he began to slap her back and forth across the face.

Louis knew how to beat a woman. He knew exactly how hard to hit without leaving bruises or doing permanent damage. "So, you don't know when to keep your mouth shut?" He continued to slap her, raining hurting, stinging blows to her face. "Is this teaching you anything, bitch?"

"Y—yes," she moaned. "Don't . . . please . . . don't hit me . . . I can't . . . breathe!"

Louis's hand froze in midair. A glimmer of sanity

469

returned as he noticed her mottled face. He lifted his knee and, chest heaving rapidly, slowly moved off her and stood over the bed. It was only then that he became aware of the throbbing hardness in his loins. Beating Celeste had highly excited him, but then, beating a woman had always excited him. Grinning evilly, he licked his lips and slowly unfastened his trousers, allowing them to fall around his feet. "Have you learned your lesson yet, bitch?"

Her voice came in gasping sobs, "Oh . . . yes, Louis. I've learned . . . my lesson. I won't ever . . . say anything . . . ever again."

"You're damn right you won't, and I'm going to make sure you treat me with the proper respect from now on!" He ripped the dress from her, relishing the way her eyes widened in horror as she saw his manhood and realized what he was about to do.

"No, Louis, don't do that . . . please don't! I'll—I'll scream!" she threatened.

He was impervious to her pleas and found her threats amusing. He laughed cruelly as he searched around for the dirty shirt, found it and stuffed as much as he could into her mouth. "Go ahead, babe, scream. Won't do you a damn bit of good now!" He yanked down her undergarments and fiercely rammed himself into her.

Celeste was dry and unwilling, and as he entered her, she thought he would surely rip her apart. She struggled for a while, then realizing her struggles only intensified his maddening lust, she forced herself to remain absolutely still.

"Come on, bitch, move!" he grunted.

But Celeste staunchly refused. She was not about to respond to his raping her, no matter how hard he beat her. Tears of pain and humiliation slipped from her eyes. Never had she felt so degraded.

"By God, since you won't move, I'll make you move!" He withdrew and, still straddling her, began to move his entire body forward. Yanking the shirt from her mouth, he grabbed two handfuls of hair. "You bite me, bitch . . . and so help me, I'll kill you!" Mercifully, Celeste fainted.

Finally, gasping raggedly he shuddered, rested a few moments, then climbed off her, cleaning himself on her ripped undergarments and fastening his trousers.

Still breathing raggedly, Louis sat on a rickety wooden chair and stared at Celeste with bitter rancor. Now she had gone and spoiled all his plans. He needed her to help make his little gambling house successful. It wasn't that he needed her so much, but he needed a sexy, voluptuous woman to keep the men's minds off their cards just in case he had to cheat the hell out of them. And Celeste was all that he had. But how long would he have her now? There was not a doubt in his mind that she would run away the first minute his back was turned. Unless . . . he could make her so scared that she would be too afraid to run. But how could he do that?

Then a caustic, evil grin spread slowly across his face. There was a solution. All he had to do was make her too frightened to run away. There would be a simple method to accomplish that, but he would have to use caution and not push her too far. A mindless idiot wouldn't do him a damn bit of good.

He ripped a sheet apart and, after removing his belt, tied first her hands, then her feet to the bed, stuffing part of the dirty shirt back into her mouth to prevent her from calling for help if she regained consciousness while he was gone. All the while, Louis kept muttering that he was going to teach her a lesson she would never forget.

Hearing her moan painfully, Louis tossed her a

smug, self-satisfied look, adjusted his clothing, and left the tent. Having a definite goal in mind, he deliberately hurried toward the most desolate, poverty-shrouded section of the tent city.

He stopped in the middle of the filthy mire and slowly looked around, searching for a man that would suit his purpose. His eyes fastened on one particular man sitting in front of a ragged tent, and a diabolical look appeared on his face. He sauntered over toward him.

"Howdy. Looks like you are down on your luck," Louis said as he pulled up a wobbly stool and sat down. He had a terrible body odor, his clothes were filthy, and his hands were crusted with dirt. The man was perfect for what he had in mind.

The man stared defiantly at Louis, took a huge bite of greasy stew, then swiped his mouth on the sleeve of his dirty shirt. "What's it to you?" he asked, chewing with his mouth open.

Louis shrugged. "Oh, nothing, I'm just looking for a man who wants to earn ten dollars. Reckon you'd be interested?"

The man froze, his mouth hanging open and the spoonful of stew stopping in midair. He ran his tongue around the inside of his mouth and swallowed. "Who do you want killed?"

"Not a soul." Then his eyes narrowed. "How long has it been since you've had a woman?" He leaned forward and explained to the man what he wanted him to do.

The man's eyes grew larger as he listened intently to what Louis had to say. A lewd grin spread across his ugly face and he tossed his plate of stew aside. "Shit, man! What are we sitting 'round here for?"

When they reached the tent, Louis told the man to be thinking about what he was about to get and to wait outside, and that he would call him in within a few minutes.

Louis raised the tent flap, walked inside, and sat down on the side of the bed. Celeste strained at her bonds, muttering and moaning, but with the shirt in her mouth her words were unintelligible.

He threaded his hands through her hair and yanked savagely thus subduing her struggles. He grinned at the terror that shone in her eyes. He spoke in a low, calm voice, "Listen to me, babe, and you had better listen good if you know what's good for you. You made me mad a while ago . . . so damned mad you're lucky I didn't throttle you. But, I've decided to give you a second chance. We're going to forget today ever happened, aren't we?" By pulling on her hair, he forced her to nod her head.

"But I have to make sure you've learned your lesson real good. I figure if I let you off too easy, sometime in the future you might forget what kind of temper I have. I figure if I let you off too easy, you might get a fool notion to try and run away from me, but you're not going to do that, are you?" He shook her head sideways.

"Well, I'm going to make sure. Seems that you have a visitor outside. I told him that you were my whore and I had caught you stealing money from me and that I needed to teach you a lesson. He's going to come in here and make you feel real good. And after he leaves, if I think you haven't learned enough, I'll go get another man and another man and another, just as many as it takes to make you smart." Louis was oblivious to the tears that spilled from her eyes.

"And I want you to think about something else, sweetheart. If tomorrow, or the next day, or two weeks, or two months, or two years from now, if you so much as think about running away from me, I'll track you down, bring you back, and line up as many men outside as it will take to screw you to death! And I'll grant you one thing, sweetheart, you'll go crazy a long time before your heart stops beating."

He sighed heavily. "Now, I'm going to call your visitor in here, and after he is through with you, you're going to get up, take a bath, put on a pretty dress, and comb your hair real pretty-like. Then we're going to go downtown and buy me a clean shirt and act like this never happened." He raised his voice, "Hey, mister, you can come in now."

The man did not have to be called twice. He rushed in, took one look at Celeste, and a hungry, lustful grin spread across his face. He quickly unfastened his trousers. "What are you gonna do, stand there and watch us?" he asked Louis.

Louis folded his arms and leered. "Since I made the lady a few promises, I think I will, just so she'll know I mean business."

The man shrugged and kicked his trousers aside. "Don't matter to me none; just make it light on yourself."

Celeste moved woodenly around the poker table, making doubly sure there was not one speck of lint or fleck of dust on the table. Everything was spotlessly clean except her. She would never feel clean again. She flinched when Louis threw open the flap and walked inside.

"D—does everything look all right?" she asked fearfully, hoping he would not notice how badly she trembled.

"Looks real good, babe, real good," he said as his eyes quickly swept the tent, noting the cleanliness of the makeshift bar and the sparkling clean glasses; how the lantern hung over the table, providing just enough light for the poker players to see their cards, but not enough light for them to be distracted by what went on on the sidelines.

He scratched his chin thoughtfully as he looked at her. "But I think we should give the men a little better view of your teats." He reached inside the revealing bodice of her black satin dress and pushed out her breasts just a little more. Stepping back, he admired his handiwork. "Yeah, that's much better."

"Hello," a voice from outside called. "Are you open for business yet?"

"Nicholas, my man! Come on in," Louis greeted him cordially. "It's a little early. The other men haven't arrived yet, but so much the better. We'll have time to have a glass of whiskey." He motioned impatiently. "Get a move on it, Celeste. Pour us a couple of glasses of whiskey."

Nicholas was the only man in San Francisco that Louis considered to be a friend. He had helped him out of a tight spot once before when he had been caught cheating in a poker game on the other side of town, and he had never forgotten it.

Nicholas Dumont pulled out a chair, sat down, and accepted the glass of whiskey the woman offered. He glanced up at her to smile his thanks, then his eyes widened and his mouth fell open in surprise. "W—what are you doing here?"

She glanced fearfully at Louis, not knowing what his reaction would be. "W—why . . . I work . . . here!"

Nicholas grasped her hand, pulled her closer into the circle of light the lantern cast, and studied her for a moment. Then he shrugged in disbelief. "For a minute there I could have sworn you were my cousin's wife.

475

You look just like her. And what's even more strange, didn't he call you Celeste?"

Still wary, she nodded.

"That's her name, too. Celeste Dionne Phillips."

Celeste dropped the bottle of whiskey she had been holding and her face turned a deadly shade of white. "Are—are you sure that is her name?"

He bobbed his head and chortled. "Lady, I'm not likely to forget it. She cost me a sizable fortune! And, I guess you could say she cost me my wife, too, because Lorraine left me after we were forced to move out here to this godforsaken place."

Louis gave a barely discernible shake of his head, warning Celeste to remain silent, then he joined Nicholas at the table. He was aware of how Celeste had tricked her housekeeper—who bore a strong resemblance to her—into switching identities with her that night of the Summer Festival. And that Celeste had once been engaged to marry a man named Christopher Phillips—one of the richest men in New Orleans. And now it seemed mighty peculiar to him that a woman who looked like his wife, a woman by the name of Celeste Dionne Phillips, had suddenly surfaced. He definitely wanted to hear more about it from Nicholas.

Trying not to appear too interested, Louis took a drink of his whiskey, then asked offhandedly, "What's your cousin's name?"

"Christopher Phillips," he replied with a sarcastic sneer.

"You say his wife cost you a sizable fortune?"

"She damned sure did!" Nicholas gave a regretful sigh. "It's a long, painful story—at least for me it's painful."

Louis snapped his fingers and motioned for Celeste to bring another bottle of whiskey. He removed the cork and refilled Nicholas's glass, then flashed a wide, friendly smile. "Tell me about it. I have all the time in the world to listen to my good friends."

Later that night, Louis lay on the bed with his hands threaded beneath his head. All sorts of thoughts were running through his mind.

There had to be some way he could turn the situation involving Nicholas's cousin, the inheritance, and the fact that the cousin married a woman using Celeste's name into his own personal gain. But how? Blackmail maybe? It stood to reason that the woman was the Debiernes' housekeeper because of her resemblance to Celeste, and the fact that the woman was a survivor from the same ship that Celeste was on. It was incredible, but both women had survived.

Was Phillips's marriage to that woman legal since the woman had used an alias? And since it was a proxy marriage and since Celeste's name had been used, could Celeste somehow claim to be his legal wife? No, that would make her have two husbands. Of course, he could always tear up their marriage license. No, blackmail was the best possibility.

However, there was another problem, a very serious one. What could he do with this startling information since Phillips lived in New Orleans? He damn sure couldn't go back there. The minute he showed his face in that town, they would hang him from the highest tree. But, damn it, there had to be something he could do. This was too good of an opportunity to cash in on easy money to allow it to slip by without doing anything about it.

"Louis, hey, Louis, are you awake?" a man's voice called in a loud whisper from outside the tent.

His hand went immediately to the pistol he kept in his boot each time he went to bed. There was too much thievery going on in this town to be caught without protection. "Yeah, I'm awake. Who's there?" he asked in a cautious voice.

"It's me, Nicholas Dumont. I need to talk to you. . . . It's important, real important."

Louis thought he had recognized the voice, but a man couldn't be too sure. "What do you need to talk to me about?"

For a moment there was nothing but silence, then Nicholas said, "I'm in trouble. I need help."

Louis poked Celeste with his elbow and whispered, "Are you awake?"

Celeste knew she should whisper too. "Yes."

"I'm going to see what he wants, but it could be a trap. The men from the poker game could have gotten together and decided I was easy pickings."

"But . . . I thought that man was your friend?"

He snorted. "Babe, out here no man has any friends. If there is trouble, cover my back."

Celeste was grateful the tent was dark, for she knew if Louis could have seen her expression, he would have killed her. *Oh, yes, Louis, I will watch your back. The first chance I get I'll stick a knife in it. I'll stick it in and twist it really slow so you will suffer. Then I'll cut your heart and feed it to the dogs!*

"Louis?" Nicholas called again. "Did you hear me?"

"Yeah, I heard you. Hold on, I have to put my trousers on first." If there was trouble, he damn sure didn't intend to be caught with his pants down. "All right, open up the flaps real wide and come on in."

"You want me to come in there?"

"Hell, yes, I'm not about to step outside and get poleaxed across the back of the head. And just in case you get any strange notions, you might be interested in knowing I have a gun on you . . . and with it dark and all, I'm not the least bit reluctant to use it."

478

Nicholas followed Louis's instructions. He stood in the entrance, twisting his hat nervously in his hands. "I'm not trying to pull anything over on you. I'm serious. I'm in trouble. I need help."

"What do you expect me to do about it?" Louis walked carefully toward him.

"Well, I don't actually expect you to do anything, but you are the only friend I have and I am in trouble." He gave a nervous laugh but it was without humor. "If I don't get help, then I am a dead man."

Louis snorted disgustedly. "Who in the hell did you kill? Whoever it was, he must have been mighty important."

"I—I didn't kill anybody." Nicholas sagged wearily onto a chair and wiped the perspiration from his brow. "You know all of that mining equipment I've been selling? Well . . . it was stolen merchandise. It came from my cousin's warehouse . . . and I just heard he's in town looking for me."

Louis's eyes narrowed thoughtfully. "Your cousin? You mean the man you were talking about earlier?"

"Yes, Christopher Phillips." Nicholas's voice caught, almost as if he were about to cry. "If he finds me, he's going to kill me. . . . As sure as I'm sitting here, he'll kill me. I have to find a place to hide, and I sure would appreciate your help. I have money! I'll be more than glad to pay!"

Suddenly grinning, Louis placed his arm on Nicholas's shoulder. Hot damn! He knew all along his luck had returned and this proved it. Now all he had to do was find a place to hide Nicholas out for a few days until he could decide what to do.

"Aw hell, Nicholas, of course I'll help you. And you don't have to pay me for lending you a hand. Why, I'm your friend, and something like this is what friends are for. I'll tell you what. I know a man who has a little shack on the outskirts of town and he owes me a favor. Let's go out there and see him before it gets daylight."

Louis moved to the foot of the bed and stood there for a moment, staring down at Celeste. "Babe, I'm going with my friend for a little while." His voice held a threat, "Do you remember the long conversation we had earlier?"

Celeste could feel bile rise in her throat. For a minute it felt as though she were about to be sick to her stomach as she realized she would have to answer him in a meek tone of voice or run the risk of making him angry. And God help her if he became angry again.

"Y—yes, Louis, I—I remember the conversation. I remember it well . . . and don't worry, I'll be right here when you get back."

"Just make sure you are, babe, make sure you are. I'd hate to have another . . . conversation with you."

Celeste lay there trembling long after he had gone. Christopher was here! Right here in San Francisco! He was the only person in the world she could turn to. He could save her. He could protect her from Louis. But how could she find him? San Francisco was an awfully large town and it would be next to impossible to locate one man. Could she take the chance of looking for him, knowing what would happen to her if she failed? If she could not find Christopher, then without a doubt Louis would find her, and he would make good his promise. Dear God, what was she to do? She was afraid to leave and afraid to stay. But she might never get another opportunity. Oh, where could Christopher be?

Then Celeste bolted upright as a thought struck her. Since Christopher was here, it was logical to assume he had sailed here on his ship! And if his ship was here, it would be in the harbor. Tears flooded her eyes. But could she muster enough courage to leave, to defy Louis? Dear God, she had to! There was always the

480

possibility he could lose his temper over some little thing, and after the degrading things he and that other man had done to her, she would put nothing past Louis Fairmount.

Swallowing her fear, Celeste quickly jumped out of bed and got dressed. Realizing she would need money, she removed the top from the hollow post of the bed and retrieved every dime from Louis's cache. Moving slowly to the flap of the tent, she peered outside, swallowed hard, then began running as fast as her legs could carry her.

Chapter Thirty-Two

The saloon was raucous with noise and laughter as the shuttered doors swung open and closed with a consistent regularity. A piano player thumped away unconcernedly in one corner of the barroom, never missing a note as he banged along, unmindful of the occasional fights that broke out among the patrons. A few painted women simpered and giggled and had no trouble in getting men to buy them a drink before they quickly disappeared with their drunken, love-starved customers up a stairway to the convenient rooms above the saloon.

Cigar smoke hung heavily in the room. Roulette wheels spun, cards shuffled, and dice rattled together. Most of the men playing those games of chance groaned and only a pitiful few shouted with joy. Some of the men stared wistfully at the huge painting of a naked lady that hung over the long oak bar. Others merely stared into their drinks, thinking about the families they had left behind in their search for riches. Two young boys who looked much older than their tender years moved along the floor on their knees with a dustpan and whisk broom, working constantly, sweeping up the small particles of gold dust that had fallen on the floor.

Christopher sat at a small table in the corner, staring

morosely at an empty whiskey bottle and a partially filled shot glass. He had come into the bar sometime during the night with full intentions of getting loose-legged, cockeyed, falling-down drunk. But after drinking a fifth of whiskey, he felt as sober as when he had first walked through the swinging doors.

He should have known better than to trust Dionne. All of these past months she had been playing him for a fool, pretending to care for him, pretending to love him, pretending to be a decent lady. Oh, but she had fooled them all—his grandmother, the servants who had been with the family for years, his friends. Barney adored her, and he would not be a bit surprised if every man in his crew was not secretly in love with her. He snorted with disgust, remembering how those rough-hewn sailors had looked upon her with respect and with awe, not because she was their captain's wife, but because they thought her to be an enchanting lady. Yes, Dionne had certainly fooled them all!

Christopher shook his head, completely puzzled. What he couldn't figure out was how she had managed to get in contact with Jonathan's father so quickly. Less than one day in San Francisco, and he had seen her in Louis Fairmount's arms.

He tightly shut his eyes and rubbed them, as if that would blot from his memory what he had seen. He had stepped inside a store to purchase some cheroots, and while he was there, he decided to look around and perhaps talk with the proprietor and hopefully learn what were the most popular items, then he planned to compare his findings with the long list of inventory that was missing from his warehouses. He had just stepped from the owner's office, a small cubicle in the rear of the store, when he noticed a man standing at the front counter, paying for a shirt and boasting in a loud voice that he was reopening his gambling house. Christopher would have known that man anywhere, his face having haunted him for well over a year now. He was Louis Fairmount.

Not stopping to wonder why he did it, he had ducked out of sight, then walked down the long aisle to the front of the store. Gazing out the store's window to watch Louis leave, he saw something that made his heart stop cold. Dionne was sitting in a carriage, and Louis Fairmount rushed out of the store and joined her. And oh, how he had joined her. That man climbed into the carriage, pushed back the veil on her hat, and from the way the back of Louis's head had moved, he had given her a long, passionate kiss. Damn her to hell!

"Bartender!" Christopher bellowed. "Where's that new bottle of whiskey I ordered?"

The first pale pink streaks of dawn were stealing across the sky when Dionne was awakened by someone pounding on the door.

Remembering how Christopher had cautioned her against admitting a stranger into the room, she hurriedly slipped on her wrapper, padded barefoot across the floor, then pressed her ear against the door and listened for any unusual noises. Hearing nothing out of the ordinary, she prudently called out, "Yes, who is there?"

"It's Hiram Johnson, ma'am. I work at the desk. Is Mr. Phillips in?"

"No, he isn't. I don't expect him back until sometime later today. Is . . . something wrong?"

The man's voice reflected his doubt. "Well, I'm not sure. There are a man and a woman out in the lobby demanding to see him. And . . . the man is rather insistent."

Dionne rolled her eyes. A man and a woman . . . That had to be Nicholas and Lorraine Dumont. And since Nicholas was responsible for Christopher's business problems here in San Francisco, there was no telling what he had on his mind. She quickly decided not to invite them in.

"Tell them Mr. Phillips is not here and that they will have to return later."

"Yes, ma'am, I will relay the message. And . . . I'm sorry to have disturbed you."

What were the Dumonts up to now? Suddenly, Dionne was frightened. What if they had really wanted to see her instead of Christopher? Just as worrisome thoughts began nagging at her, she heard loud voices coming from the corridor.

"Stop! Stop immediately! You cannot barge in and disturb our guests!"

Then, there was raucous banging against the door. "Mrs. Phillips, it be Barney here! 'Tis sorry I be to disturb ye, but I need to speak to ye or to the cap'n!"

Dionne immediately threw the door open. "What is it, Barney? What's wrong? . . ." She froze, her face blanched, her legs seeming to turn to jelly. She had to lean against the door frame for support, for standing beside Barney was Celeste.

"Celeste!" she gasped incredulously.

Very convincingly, Celeste acted surprised. "Dionne! Y—you're alive!"

"I thought . . . we all thought . . ."

Celeste pointed to Barney. "But . . . he said nothing about you. I merely asked him to . . . bring me to Christopher."

Suddenly, Dionne and Celeste were in each other's arms, laughing and crying.

Then, an incredible thought crossed Dionne's mind. She drew back and looked at Celeste. "Since you survived, too, is it . . . could it be . . . possible others did, too?"

"I don't think so . . . I don't know . . . I was about to ask you the same question."

Dionne bit on her lower lip and tears filled her eyes. "For a moment there, my hopes were raised that others had . . ." Her voice trailed off sadly.

Slumping into a nearby chair, Celeste pressed trembling hands against her forehead. She had invented what she believed would be a very convincing story, one that she could stick to even if Christopher later found out about her and Louis, or if his cousin happened to see her and recognized her.

She began speaking in a frantic voice, "Oh, Dionne, it is horrible! I don't have any memory of what has happened to me." Tears misted in her eyes, then spilled down her pale cheeks. "I . . . remember that terrible storm and the ship sinking. I—I . . . remember thinking I was about to die." She gestured helplessly. "And that's all! Everything else is a complete blank. Then early this morning, it was as if I suddenly awoke. When I came to myself, I was searching for Christopher's ship down at the wharf. And I don't even know how I got there, much less how or why I am here in San Francisco! I can't remember anything that happened to me. It's just . . . like a terrible nightmare! I keep thinking I will awake any moment, but I know I won't. It's such a terrible feeling!"

"Oh, I imagine so!" Dionne muttered compassionately.

Celeste sniffed and wiped her eyes with the back of her hands. "And you? What has happened with you?" She gestured toward Barney. "He addressed you as Mrs. Phillips. Are—are you married to Christopher now?"

"Yes, I am. We were married shortly . . . after . . .

the tragedy happened. . . ." Her voice faltered as she suddenly realized the possible significance of Celeste's return. What would Christopher do? How would he feel when he saw the woman he was once engaged to? Dionne swallowed hard, vivid recollections flashing swiftly through her mind. Recollections of what had happened between her and Celeste those last days on Martinique. Then her eyes widened as she also realized Celeste's sudden appearance could prove to be troublesome in other matters, too, especially since there were problems concerning Nicholas. If Nicholas and that vicious wife of his somehow learned about Celeste, there was no telling what they would do. And if Celeste had not changed, there was no telling what she would do, either.

Dionne knew she had to do something to keep Celeste from asking too many questions until Christopher could be informed of the situation.

She gave a nervous laugh. "Oh, dear, I am being terribly rude. I imagine you must be exhausted and hungry, and I'm sure you will want to take a bath." She began to pace the floor, rubbing her chin thoughtfully. "I'm sure I have something you will be able to wear. Barney, will you please go see Mr. Johnson at the desk and request hot water for a bath and a hearty breakfast . . . breakfast for one right now. I will eat after a while. And, Barney, there are a few matters I need to discuss with you later."

"Aye, ma'am."

Celeste shook her head. "Oh, I couldn't put you to so much trouble. . . ."

"Nonsense, it's no trouble at all. Grand'mere's room . . ."

"Grand'mere?"

"Christopher's grandmother," Dionne explained. "She is visiting old family friends and her room is empty right now. I am sure she would not mind if you used it until we can make arrangements for a room of your own." She thought it would be better to pretend as though they had always been the best of friends.

Celeste nodded, terribly relieved that Dionne had insisted she stay. "Well, a bath and breakfast do sound heavenly, and I am tired." Tired wasn't the word for how she felt. She was both mentally and physically exhausted. What Louis had done to her had almost broken her spirit, and she knew it would take her a long time to heal.

"I don't know which one the proprietor will send first, so allow me to . . ." She turned when she heard Jonathan cry. Josey stood in the doorway, holding the baby.

"Miz Phillips, I's sorry to interrupt yo' company, but dis little man be wantin' his mama." She flashed a timid smile. "I jest ain't got enough to satisfy him no more."

Celeste had paled. "You mean . . . you have a child?"

Dionne hurried to take the baby. Seeing the startled expression on Celeste's face, she could not help but lift her head with a slight arrogance. "Yes, w—we have a son, Christopher and I. His name is Jonathan Lyle." Not wanting to be drawn into a lengthy discussion about the baby right then, she added quickly, "I have to feed him now. Josey will see to your needs. Josey, this is Miss Debierne. Please take her into Madame Phillips's room and help make her comfortable. She doesn't have any extra clothing with her, so she is welcome to use whatever she needs of my clothing. Her bath and breakfast have been ordered. And . . . I would rather not be disturbed until after Jonathan has nursed."

"Yes, ma'am."

Celeste followed Josey without question into the

connecting room. She needed to be alone with her thoughts.

Dionne sat down in a chair near the window, put Jonathan to her breast and, because she expected Barney, covered herself with a light blanket for modesty's sake.

A few minutes later, he rapped on the door. "Ma'am, it be me, Barney."

"Please come on in."

He entered and stood close to the door, ill-at-ease.

Dionne came right to the point. "Barney, you heard what Celeste said. Is that how it happened?"

"Aye, it be how it happened all right. Leastways, she appeared at the wharf searchin' for the cap'n, she did."

Her eyes narrowed. "Do I detect doubt in your voice?"

"Aye, ma'am, ye do. The cap'n told me some of what happened . . . how ye came to be married to him. But somethin' smells rotten to me, it does."

"What do you mean?"

"Well," he drawled slowly, his Scottish brogue sounding more evident, "I be a suspicious mon by nature. I dona want to call the lass a liar, but me thinks it is too much of a coincidence that she suddenly regains her lost memory on the same morn that the cap'n goes after his blackguard cousin for stealin' him blind. Me knows the lass was supposed to marry the cap'n originally. Me knows ye married the cap'n using her name. And I cana help but wonder if the cousin knows this, too."

Dionne slowly nodded. "Barney, I have a suspicious nature, too. I will admit that, at first, I was thrilled to see her, but only because I thought she had died along with all the others. There are some things about her that I've never told Christopher. It is sometimes difficult to speak ill of the dead when one is not present to defend themselves. But, I will confide to you that she was a liar and a cheat. I don't know how it will come about, but I would be willing to bet that Christopher is in for some trouble. I agree with you. Something smells rotten to me, too."

"Aye!" Barney stated firmly.

Suddenly, it felt as though all the blood had quickly drained from her face as she stared with fear at Barney.

"What is it, ma'am?"

"Why . . . didn't Celeste see Christopher this morning?"

He shook his head. "I dona know what ye mean, ma'am."

"Didn't Christopher stay on board the *Blue Diamond* last night?"

"Nay."

"He was supposed to," she whispered fearfully. She swallowed hard. "Oh, Barney, do . . . you think something . . . might have happened to him?"

His lips narrowed into a thin line and his face turned a bright shade of red. "Dona worry, ma'am. I'll find the lad. I'll go to the ship and get the mon. We'll leave nary a stone unturned 'til he's found!"

After Barney left, Dionne sagged weakly against the back of the chair. Tears clouded her eyes. She had been so happy when she had learned they were coming to San Francisco. Even though the thought of sailing on a ship had terrified her, the thought of being so near Christopher for such a long length of time had made her ecstatically happy. And now, she could very possibly be face to face with the beginning of the end. Dionne gently kissed Jonathan's forehead and cried.

Chapter Thirty-Three

Thoroughly disgusted with the taste of the whiskey, Christopher slid the bottle away from him and stood to his feet. To hell with getting drunk. Dionne wasn't worth the headache it would cause.

Pushing aside the drunks, he threaded his way across the crowded barroom floor and stepped outside. He was surprised to see that it was already good daylight. Where had the night gone? Had he been inside the saloon that long? Damn Dionne, anyway, now she had cost him a night's sleep. While he had been trying to drown his misery in a bottle of whiskey, more than likely she had been in the arms of her lover. And just when everything between them was . . . Damn her to hell!

He took a deep breath and squared his shoulders, deciding the two-mile walk to the hotel was exactly what he needed to clear his head. And he definitely wanted to have all of his faculties when he saw Dionne. He wanted to be able to tell her exactly what he thought of her and he wanted to be able to remember every word he said. To hell with her. He had made it fine for thirty years without her, and he could damn sure make it another thirty years, maybe even forty. Women!

Who in the hell needed them, anyway? Certainly not him!

Dionne paced the floor, wringing her hands. She felt so helpless. Her imagination was running wild. She could see Christopher lying in some dark alley, badly injured, bleeding, calling for help, but no one could hear him because he was so weak.

Stop it, Dionne! You are being completely ridiculous! Don't allow yourself to think such morbid thoughts. Christopher is fine. There is a reasonable explanation why he did not return to the ship or to the hotel last night. He is safe. Nothing has happened to him.

She glanced at her pendant watch again. Only an hour had passed since Barney had left to search for him. But why hadn't she heard something yet? Surely Barney knew how worried she was.

Dionne's heart slammed hard against her chest when she heard footsteps, then a knock at the door. She wanted to run and throw the door open, but she was suddenly afraid, afraid someone would be standing there with bad news.

"Dionne, are you in there?" Christopher shouted.

She gave a sharp cry of relief, ran across the room, and flung open the door. She threw her arms around him, but he pushed her aside and stalked angrily into the room, quickly glancing around.

"It certainly took you long enough to answer the door! What did he do? Slip out through one of the connecting rooms?" Christopher demanded in a fierce tone, his eyes flashing blue fire at her as he stomped back and forth across the floor.

Before she could conceal it, a look of confused astonishment claimed her face. "What?"

"You heard me! Was the bastard too scared to face me?"

Dionne began shaking her head. "What on earth are you ranting about? My God, Christopher, I have been worried half out of my mind. . . ."

He scoffed. "Yeah, I'll just bet you have been worried! Worried that I would find out about you and your lover!"

"My lover?" she repeated incredulously.

"Don't play innocent with me. You know damn good and well what I am talking about and who I am referring to!" Christopher snarled in a frigid tone.

Quickly becoming angry, she glared at him. "The only thing I know is I've been half out of my mind with worry for you, afraid something terrible had happened, and now you storm in here ranting like a madman, making all sorts of wild accusations, and I still have no idea what you are talking about! But I'll tell you one thing, Christopher Phillips. I am just about to lose my temper!" She turned her head sharply toward the bed where Jonathan lay. Their loud voices had awakened him and he was beginning to fret.

Christopher laughed sarcastically. "Oh? So you're about to lose your temper? Well, let me tell you, I lost mine yesterday when I saw you with your lover! When I saw you in a carriage with Louis Fairmount. Surely you remember him? He was your lover in Martinique. And he's the father of your baby! Do you remember now? Don't you remember slipping away with him that night at the Summer Festival?" He shook his head disgustedly. "I'll say one thing for you . . . You certainly wasted no time meeting him!"

Dionne gasped at his accusations. She felt as though Christopher had ripped her heart from her breast. She said, in a choked whisper, "I swear, I have not seen Louis Fairmount. And you have to listen to me. There is something I have to tell you about Jonathan. . . ."

"Christopher!" Celeste said eagerly as she opened the connecting door. "I thought I heard your voice!" She'd heard his voice all right. She had heard him when he'd first stormed in. And since that little colored girl had finally gone back to her room, she had been able to press her ear against the connecting door and had overheard everything she had needed to hear. If things went just right, she could turn this situation so that it could be beneficial to her.

Christopher whirled at the sound of her voice and he stood, staring at her dumbfoundedly. "Celeste?"

Dionne stepped back with her arms folded, looking first at Christopher then at Celeste. She could not believe this was happening.

Completely stunned, Christopher could only shake his head as Celeste ran to him and threw her arms around his neck. He pushed her back and held her at arm's length, then finally found his voice, "I thought you were dead."

"I . . . thought I was, too. Oh, Christopher, it was awful, simply awful!" Then, with tears streaming down her face, she told him the same story she had told Dionne and Barney. Only this time, she made her voice sound so much more pitiful and heart wrenching.

"That's incredible," Christopher said, shaking his head after he had heard her story.

Celeste smiled. "I prefer to think of it as a miracle." Hearing Jonathan fuss, she walked over to the bed and wiggled one of his flailing legs. "Just like this little fellow is a miracle. And, I'll swear, Dionne, it is amazing how much he resembles Louis. Simply amazing!"

For just a moment Dionne's eyes locked and held on Celeste's. And in that moment, she saw a triumphant gleam. Before she even thought about what she was doing, Dionne raised her hand and slapped Celeste as hard as she could. "Get out of here! Get out of here, you evil witch! Get out of my life with all of your lies!"

"Dionne!" Christopher shouted as he grabbed hold of her arms and pinioned them to her sides. "Woman, have you lost your mind?"

She tried to keep from crying as she looked up at him. "Christopher, don't you see what she's doing to us? What she's done since the beginning?"

"Our problems have nothing to do with her," he muttered coldly.

She started to shout at him, then thought better of it. She took a deep breath to try and calm her temper. Then, she spoke in a deceptively calm voice, "Christopher, will you please listen to me and let me explain?"

He shook his head and glared at her contemptuously. "I don't want to hear anything you have to say."

Dionne blanched. "You mean after all we have shared together, you refuse to even listen?"

The muscles in his cheek tensed and his lips narrowed. "That's the same thing I thought when I saw you in the arms of your lover! As I said, I don't want to hear anything you have to say!"

Dionne felt all of the fight slip from her. Her shoulders sagged dejectedly. She bowed her head, and strangely, she was too hurt, too crushed to even want to cry. Finally, she raised her gaze to Celeste and muttered bitterly, "You win."

Moving quickly, she placed a carpetbag on the bed and began putting clothes into it, mostly Jonathan's things.

"What are you doing?" Christopher asked sullenly.

Dionne did not say a word. She just glared at him as she continued to pack. Then, she changed the baby and put clean clothing on him. Neither Christopher nor Celeste said anything as she went to the door carrying

Jonathan in one arm and the carpetbag in the other.

It was only then that Dionne spoke and her words were very bitter, "As far as I am concerned, the two of you deserve each other. I wish you all the misery in the world!"

Dionne was numb as she left the hotel. She had no idea where she was going or what she was going to do. Then, tears began to slip down her face as she realized she had no money, not one cent to her name. Turning blindly, she began ambling down the boarded walkway. Suddenly, rough hands grabbed her, and before she could scream, someone clamped a strange-smelling cloth over her mouth and nose, then pulled her into the alley. Just before she lost consciousness, Dionne stared up into the cruel face of Louis Fairmount.

Christopher stared into the darkness. *I wish you all the misery in the world!* He kept hearing those words, even in his sleep. She had gotten her wish. He had never been so miserable in all his life. It had been three or four days now since she had left. . . . He really didn't know how long it had been; he had lost count. How long had it been since he had slept? He didn't know that either. Each time he went to sleep she haunted his dreams. Sleep was something he would have to avoid if at all possible.

"Young man, young man! Christopher St. John Phillips, wake up right now!"

Hearing his grandmother's voice, Christopher pried his eyes open, then quickly shut them as the sunlight streamed across the bed. How many bottles of whiskey had it taken before he had been able to sleep? How long had he been asleep? He felt like it was only minutes, but the last thing he had known it had been dark outside.

"Leave me alone," he mumbled thickly.

"I will not!" She looked at the empty whiskey bottles with disgust. "Where are Dionne and Jonathan?"

"I don't want to talk about them, Grandmother."

"Well, I certainly want to talk about them! I ordered a pot of hot black coffee to be sent in from the hotel's dining room. Now you go wash your face, then march yourself right back in here and we are going to have a long, serious discussion!"

Christopher rolled over and groaned. His grandmother stood only a little over five feet tall and weighed a little over a hundred pounds, but there was something about her that would have made the bravest man in the world shake in his boots. She was the most dear and also the most stubborn woman he had ever known. He knew he would never get a moment's rest until he did as she said.

Jeannine waited until he had drunk two cups of coffee and began to feel almost human again before ever saying another word. "I want to know where Dionne and Jonathan are!"

"I have no idea where they are, Grandmother," he replied, shoveling his hand through his hair. Then his brow furrowed as he asked, "I thought you were staying at your friend's house for two weeks or so. Have I been in this condition that long?"

"It's been nearly a week," she said sharply. "And I have no idea what kind of condition you are in, or what has happened to Dionne and Jonathan . . . and I don't know what has happened to you! You are behaving abominably! Thank God, Barney somehow found me and told me there was trouble here. I returned to find that Dionne and Jonathan have disappeared, a strange woman is living in my bedroom, and you are in a despicable condition! Yes, I certainly feel safe in assuming there is trouble here!" Barney had also informed her of Celeste's miraculous return from the dead, and of his and Dionne's suspicions. She could not remember when she had been so worried!

Christopher gestured helplessly. "I don't know what has happened to me here lately, Grandmother." He glanced away miserably. "Yes, I do." He took a deep, shuddering breath. "I fell in love with the wrong woman."

"Chris," she said gently, "you have always come to me with your problems and your worries. And I believe you are long overdue. Why don't you tell me about it?"

He did. He poured out his heart to Jeannine, starting at the very beginning and ending with what happened the day Dionne left with Jonathan. After finishing, he sighed heavily, dropped his head, and added, "I guess I am a fool, Grandmother, because even after seeing Dionne in that man's arms, I can't get her out of my mind. I guess . . . seeing her in his arms opened my eyes. I . . . love her, Grandmother. Even knowing what she is, God help me, I love her. And I guess that makes me the biggest fool in the world!"

Jeannine slowly shook her head. "Chris, your grandfather was a very wise man. He always said when a man was down, don't kick him; offer him a helping hand instead. Even bearing that in mind, I am forced to agree with you. Undoubtedly, you are the biggest fool in the world!"

He jerked his head up and stared at her hard.

"Young man, it so happens that Dionne basically told me the very same story months ago. Only, I sincerely believe she told me the true version."

"Do you think I'm lying to you?"

"Oh, no, I know you are not lying to me," she answered quickly. "But I do believe you have been badly misled."

"How?"

"Did you ever stop to consider it could have been Celeste impersonating Dionne? Just think about it for a moment. You only have Celeste's word that Dionne was impersonating her. Yet, the two times you saw . . . the woman . . . with Louis, Dionne and Celeste were in the same vicinity. The night of the Summer Festival, it's my understanding that it was crowded, dark, you had been drinking, Dionne and Celeste were dressed identically, and you saw . . . a woman . . . disappearing with him. You told me yourself, the other day, Dionne was wearing a hat with a veil when you saw her with Louis . . . and this was the day before Celeste's miraculous return from the dead."

"Then why didn't Dionne ever say anything to me about it?" Christopher could feel his heart beating faster. Could it somehow be possible?

"If she had told you, would you have believed her?"

He slowly shook his head. "No, I suppose not." Then the most incredulous expression slipped over his face. "If what you say is true, then . . . Jonathan is my son!" his voice was choked.

Jeannine sighed heavily. "To my knowledge, I have never broken my word to anyone in my life, but I am about to do it now. I promised Dionne I would not tell you, but I think it has become necessary. Jonathan is your son. You may not be thoroughly convinced yet, but there is physical proof. He has a birthmark on his buttock that is common in the Phillips line. In fact, your father had an identical birthmark. And Christopher, remember, I raised you from a baby. And Jonathan looks exactly like you at this age."

"Why did she make you promise not to tell me?" Christopher could feel a hard knot forming in the pit of his stomach. He could hear Celeste's voice echoing, *Why, it's amazing how he resembles Louis!*

She smiled sadly. "Because Dionne had hoped you would fall in love with her. She wanted to know that you loved her for her, instead of just staying married to her for the benefit of your son." She frowned when Christopher suddenly stood and started across the room. "Where are you going?"

"You said Celeste was in your room. I'm going to get her. She is going to tell me the truth!"

"Wait, Christopher." Then she asked hesitantly, "Do you . . . have to hear it from her first . . . before you'll accept all of this as the truth?"

"No!" he declared sincerely. "I realize everything you've said is the truth. And I didn't mean to give you that impression. I just wanted to confront her, to make her admit all of her lies. But do you know what, Grandmother? I don't think it would matter if she's telling the truth or lying. If Dionne loves me, together we can work out any problems we might have."

Jeannine smiled broadly. "That's my old Christopher talking!"

Then he raked his hand through his hair. "I guess I ought to get my priorities straight. Celeste can wait. Dionne and Jonathan have been out there for nearly a week now." He began tugging on his boots. "I have to find them. Did Barney say where he was going when he left you here?"

She could not help smiling. "He is in the lobby, waiting on you."

Christopher headed for the door. "I won't be back until I find her, but I'll send someone to check every so often . . . just in case she comes back."

A wide relieved grin spread across Barney's face when he saw Christopher striding toward him, a determined expression on his features. He fell into step beside him. "I knew ye would come to yer senses, Cap'n."

502

"We'll talk about my senses and the lack of them later. Right now, I have to find Dionne and the baby!"

"Cap'n . . . I've been looking for her, the entire crew be searching too. Ain't seen hide nor hair of her. Yer cousin be gone too. I'm feared she has fallen into bad hands."

Christopher's eyes suddenly became cold. "If anyone has hurt her . . . so help me, I'll kill him!"

"And I'll be right behind ye, Cap'n!"

When they reached the hotel's veranda, Christopher stopped suddenly. "Barney, I have an idea. As big as San Francisco is, we could search for a month or more and still not find her, but there are a lot of men out here . . . hungry men. Let's round up the crew and get them to help spread the word. I'll offer a twenty-five thousand dollar reward for the man who finds my wife and my son."

It was late that night before Christopher received the message from his grandmother, the message that made his blood run even colder. If Dionne had been found, she would have told him. Instead, the message had been brief and to the point. The words had burned into his brain. "Christopher, return to the hotel immediately. It is urgent!"

A huge knot of fear for Dionne and Jonathan's safety had formed in the pit of his stomach and was growing larger by the minute. God would have to forgive him if anything had happened to them, because he would never be able to forgive himself. It was all his fault. He had driven her away from him. And now, it could be very possible that something terrible had happened to her. No! He couldn't allow himself to think those kind of thoughts.

Reaching the hotel, he hurried inside, and without

ever breaking stride, he marched down the corridor and threw open the door to his room. Then, he stopped dead cold, for sitting there with his grandmother was none other than Louis Fairmount!

"Mr. Phillips, I don't believe I've ever had the pleasure of meeting you. Louis Fairmount, at your service." He nodded his head slightly, then slowly lit a cigar.

Jeannine, her voice trembling, spoke up, "Christopher, he has Dionne and Jonathan." She held out Dionne's pendant watch. "He brought this as proof."

Christopher's hands clenched into fists and he took a threatening step forward.

"I wouldn't if I were you," Louis said quickly.

"Where's my wife and son?" Christopher demanded.

Louis lifted his brow. "I must say you show an incredible amount of concern for someone who has repeatedly ignored my messages."

"Messages? What messages?"

"Why, the messages I've sent, of course."

"I've received no messages!" he muttered darkly.

Louis's eyes grew hard. "Don't try to hand me that line of bullshit! I've paid good money to have messages delivered here every day! I knew they were delivered! I've stood down the corridor and watched!"

Christopher's eyes locked with his grandmother's. Both had the same thought. Celeste!

He whirled and stormed into the connecting room, returning moments later dragging a very reluctant Celeste behind him.

The moment she saw Louis, her face blanched with terror. She jerked from Christopher's grasp and began backing away.

Louis began chuckling, his laughter sounding evil. "So, this is where you disappeared to. I should have known." His eyes settled on Christopher. "I find this terribly amusing. I have your wife, and you have mine."

"Don't listen to him, Christopher! He's lying! I swear he's lying!"

Christopher abruptly grabbed her. "I don't think so!" Then he shoved her into Louis's arms. "All right, there is your wife; now I want mine!"

Celeste screamed and tried to wrench from the strong arms that had suddenly wrapped around her.

"Stop struggling, my dear! I have business with your old sweetheart . . . or maybe he's your new sweetheart. Then, I have a promise to keep to you!" He laughed cruelly, knowing his taunt would terrify her.

Then everything happened so quickly.

Louis's taunt pushed Celeste to desperation, to a point somewhere beyond the brink of madness. Finding strength she did not know she possessed, she tore herself from his grasp, and spying a pair of scissors lying on the bureau top, she grabbed them.

"I'll be the one who keeps the promise . . . you Georgia cracker bastard!" she screamed, running toward him with the scissors raised.

Louis stepped out of her way in the nick of time. He grabbed her arm and twisted, and when he did, the scissors plunged deeply into Celeste's chest.

Christopher rushed forward with his fists swinging. He smashed two rocking punches to Louis's jaw, and before the scoundrel could recover, Christopher stabbed a hard left to his mouth, then hooked a powerful right to his body. Louis staggered, but before he could fall, Christopher smashed a left fist into his mouth again, sending him flying across the room. The sound of Louis's head hitting the edge of the table echoed throughout the room. Christopher hurried forward, bent over Louis, then slowly raised his head and muttered, "My God, he's . . . dead!"

Jeannine knelt beside Celeste. "Can you help her,

Chris?" she asked fearfully.

He rushed to her side, but before he could do anything, she raised her hand as if trying to reach out for him. She murmured softly, "I'm . . . so . . . sorry." Then she died.

Jeannine raised her eyes to meet Christopher's. "You said . . . he was dead?"

"Yes, but I didn't hit him that hard. . . . He cracked his head on the edge of that table."

"God forgive me, I'm not sorry he's dead, but he . . . oh, my God, Christopher, he claimed that Dionne and Jonathan were in a place . . . and no one would ever be able to find it!"

Christopher stared at her, horror filling his eyes. He thought of all the places where they could be; all the tents, houses, rooms, the hundreds of abandoned ships in the harbor, the worked-out and abandoned mine shafts. The possibilities were unlimited.

"I don't know how, but I'll find them!" Of that, there was no doubt in his mind. But if Dionne were tied up somewhere, would he be able to find them in time?

It was late the next afternoon and still there was no sign of Dionne and Jonathan. Hundreds of men eager to earn the huge reward Christopher offered had joined in on the search, but still nothing turned up.

Christopher looked terrible, haggard, and gaunt. He had not eaten or slept. Barney had become so worried about him that he had refused to leave his side.

Hoping for some kind of news, they went back to the hotel, a predetermined meeting place just in case one of the men had gotten lucky. And all that it boiled down to now was luck.

Finding no new developments, Barney was finally able to convince Christopher he had to take a few

506

minutes to rest.

Christopher said raggedly, "There has to be something we're missing . . . something we're overlooking. Talk to me, Barney. Let's talk it out and maybe we can think of something new to try."

Barney was just as worried and just as scared as Christopher. "Well, Cap'n," he forced false optimism into his voice, "we have the crew, and several other crews of other ships, searching through the derelicts in the harbor. The mon have thoroughly combed through the north side of the city. Thirty mon are searching through the abandoned mine shafts. I dona know what else we can do," he added, feeling the sheer weight of hopelessness wash over him for the first time.

Christopher felt it, too. He raised his eyes to meet Barney's, wondering if his first mate realized he was crying. He wiped his hand over his face and realized there was a wetness there, too. "There has to be something we're missing . . . something we're not doing!"

Then Christopher craned his head, listening intently.

"What is it, Cap'n?"

"Do you hear something?"

Barney listened. "Just be a dog barking."

Both men turned to each other and said excitedly, at the same time, *"Katie!"*

That dog adored Dionne, and if she was on dry land, Katie might be able to find her!

Christopher tore into the other room where Jeannine was waiting. "Grandmother! Get me something Dionne wore! Get me something of Jonathan's, too! Katie might be able to find them!"

For a moment she looked hopeful, then her face fell in disappointment. "All of the clothing has been washed." Then she exclaimed, "But there are still some trunks on the ship!"

Christopher had already disappeared out the doorway. Katie was at the ship too. And suddenly that seemed to be their only hope, but it was more than what they'd had a few moments before.

Deciding the best starting place would be Louis's tent, they went there immediately after getting Katie and the clothing.

Christopher knelt down in front of the dog and roughed her fur. "All right, Katie girl, so much depends on you." He then pressed one of Dionne's dresses to her nose, then one of the little gowns that Jonathan had worn. "Go find her, girl, go find Dionne! Fetch!"

Katie sniffed the clothes and wagged her tail furiously. She started leaping and barking. Christopher barely managed to grasp the end of her leash as she took off in a run, baying each time her front paws hit the ground. Barney chased after them.

Less than twenty minutes later, Katie pulled loose from her leash and raced toward a tumbled-down shack. She jumped up on the door and began howling. Christopher was right behind her, and Barney was a few feet behind him.

Not even taking time to open the door, Christopher merely kicked it down, and the first thing he saw was Dionne sitting tied to a chair with a gag in her mouth. He rushed inside. Nicholas stepped up behind him with a gun, but Barney, bringing up the rear, backhanded Nicholas and sent him sprawling against the wall, knocking him unconscious. He headed immediately for Jonathan who was crying, while Christopher untied Dionne.

When he plucked the gag from Dionne's mouth, she began crying softly. "I . . . I thought no one would . . . ever come!"

508

"Hush, my love," he murmured, his throat so tightly constricted he could barely speak. How she must have suffered. "I'm here now."

As soon as he had her untied, he took her into his arms. "Are you hurt? Did they hurt you?" he repeated anxiously, all the while pressing kisses across her brow, on top of her head, any place he could reach and still hold her in his arms.

She was crying so hard her words were barely discernible, "If you are . . . asking if they . . . raped me . . . no . . . but I've been tied . . . there for days and nights . . . and I thought no one would ever come. . . . N—Nicholas said if . . . he didn't . . . hear something soon . . . he was going to kill us." Then she pulled away and looked at Christopher accusingly. "Why are . . . you here?"

He swallowed hard. "Anything you want to say to me, anything you want to call me, I deserve. But it's nothing I haven't said to myself already." He cupped his hands caressingly around her lovely but tearstained face. "You ask me why I am here." Tears choked his voice and filled his eyes. "I've been searching for my wife and for my son. I discovered life had no meaning without them. I love you, Dionne. And if you can't find it in your heart to forgive me for being such a fool . . . I'll just have to . . ."

Tears began to stream down her face. "D—did you say you loved me?" she asked wondrously. Suddenly, all the pain he had ever caused her slipped away.

"Yes, I love you . . . I've always loved you . . . ever since that first day when Barney ran over you in that marketplace. I was just too big of a fool to admit it! And, my love, I know Jonathan is my son, too. I love you, I love you, I love you!"

She wound her arms around his neck. "Oh, my darling, you don't know how long I've waited to hear you say those words!"

"And I'll say them every day of my life . . . if you'll just forgive me."

Dionne gazed up at him and smiled. "Oh, my darling, of course I will. I love you so much!"

With one arm, Christopher took Jonathan from Barney, wrapping the other arm around his beautiful wife. He looked down into her eyes and murmured wondrously, "Come, my love, let's go home."

As they stepped outside, stars suddenly shone through the fading crimson sky.

FIERY ROMANCE
From Zebra Books

SATIN SECRET (2116, $3.95)
by Emma Merritt
After young Marta Carolina had been attacked by pirates, ship-wrecked, and beset by Indians, she was convinced the New World brought nothing but tragedy . . . until William Dare rescued her. The rugged American made her feel warm, protected, secure— and hungry for a fulfillment she could not name!

CAPTIVE SURRENDER (1986, $3.95)
by Michalann Perry
Gentle Fawn should have been celebrating her newfound joy as a bride, but when both her husband and father were killed in battle, the young Indian maiden vowed revenge. She charged into the fray—yet once she caught sight of the piercing blue gaze of her enemy, she knew that she could never kill him. The handsome white man stirred a longing deep within her soul . . . and a passion she'd never experienced before.

PASSION'S JOY (2205, $3.95)
by Jennifer Horsman
Dressed as a young boy, stunning Joy Claret refused to think what would happen were she to get caught at what she was really doing: leading slaves to liberty on the Underground Railroad. Then the roughly masculine Ram Barrington stood in her path and the blue-eyed girl couldn't help but panic. Before she could fight him, she was locked in an embrace that could end only with her surrender to PASSION'S JOY.

TEXAS TRIUMPH (2009, $3.95)
by Victoria Thompson
Nothing is more important to the determined Rachel McKinsey than the Circle M—and if it meant marrying her foreman to scare off rustlers, she would do it. Yet the gorgeous rancher felt a secret thrill that the towering Cole Elliot was to be her man—and despite her plan that they be business partners, all she truly desired was a glorious consummation of their vows.

PASSION'S PARADISE (1618, $3.75)
by Sonya T. Pelton
When she is kidnapped by the cruel, captivating Captain Ty, fair-haired Angel Sherwood fears not for her life, but for her honor! Yet she can't help but be warmed by his manly touch, and secretly longs for PASSION'S PARADISE.

Available wherever paperbacks are sold, or order direct from the Publisher. Send cover price plus 50¢ per copy for mailing and handling to Zebra Books, Dept. 2402, 475 Park Avenue South, New York, N.Y. 10016. Residents of New York, New Jersey and Pennsylvania must include sales tax. DO NOT SEND CASH.

ZEBRA HAS THE SUPERSTARS
OF PASSIONATE ROMANCE!

CRIMSON OBSESSION   (2272, $3.95)
by Deana James

Cassandra MacDaermond was determined to make the handsome gambling hall owner Edward Sandron pay for the fortune he had stolen from her father. But she never counted on being struck speechless by his seductive gaze. And soon Cassandra was sneaking into Sandron's room, more intent on sharing his rapture than causing his ruin!

TEXAS CAPTIVE   (2251, $3.95)
by Wanda Owen

Ever since two outlaws had killed her ma, Talleha had been suspicious of all men. But one glimpse of virile Victor Maurier standing by the lake in the Texas Blacklands and the half-Indian princess was helpless before the sensual tide that swept her in its wake!

TEXAS STAR   (2088, $3.95)
by Deana James

Star Garner was a wanted woman—and Chris Gillard was determined to collect the generous bounty being offered for her capture. But when the beautiful outlaw made love to him as if her life depended on it, Gillard's firm resolve melted away, replaced with a raging obsession for his fiery TEXAS STAR.

MOONLIT SPLENDOR   (2008, $3.95)
by Wanda Owen

When the handsome stranger emerged from the shadows and pulled Charmaine Lamoureux into his strong embrace, she sighed with pleasure at his seductive caresses. Tomorrow she would be wed against her will—so tonight she would take whatever exhilarating happiness she could!

Available wherever paperbacks are sold, or order direct from the Publisher. Send cover price plus 50¢ per copy for mailing and handling to Zebra Books, Dept. 2402, 475 Park Avenue South, New York, N.Y. 10016. Residents of New York, New Jersey and Pennsylvania must include sales tax. DO NOT SEND CASH.